First published in Great Britain 1993 by

Pittenhope Publishing, 72 Marmion Drive, Glenrothes, Fife.

ISBN 0 9519704 2 9

Printed and bound in Great Britain

To Jim, who lit the flame
To May Marshall and
Pauline Thomson
who kept it alight

For Laurie, June,
Lisa, Scott and Lauren.

This is the second novel in a Trilogy of Celtic Queens
by the same author

Honey in the Mead
The Flame Within
The Harps are Hushed

The Flame Within won the Constable Trophy in 1989

Dorothy Macnab Ramsay was born in Rothesay, Isle of Bute, and lived for thirty years in Glasgow. Married with a son she now lives in Fife where she discovered the Picts. She had always believed she was descended from the Scots who came to Dal Riata from Ireland around 500 AD. Now she proudly claims that the name 'Mac N' Ab' means that she is descended from the Pictish clerics who were called Abs.

CHAPTER ONE

The first yell struck her like a blow to the heart. It set the air shivering with warning. Its echoes quivered through the leaves on the beeches that bordered the stream.

Tansen cringed under the weight of her fear. Her new wool robe slid from her hands into the elderberry dyeing bath. Her body curled in on itself, waiting.

Silence, as though the whole world held its breath. Only Suen the potter, far away at the homestead, deafened by his treadle, pounded his wheel, on and on, like a breathless heartbeat.

It had not happened! Nothing could spoil this happy day! For the sun shone on the land of the Pretani on the east coast of Alba. It sparkled on the waves of the North Sea. It lit the green eyes and bright hair of the girl who was coming up to her fifteenth harvest. And she was going to the Queen's Court as soon as this harvest was in. Catching up her robe she shook out the purple droplets and dropped it into the salt bath.

The second cry broke her world apart. The scream spiralled up, up, upwards till it tore at the gateway to the sky. Oh, Bride, save us all, what was happening?

Nearby the bushes opened and the kin-children tumbled out, holding their hands over their mouths to still their whimpers of fear. All they had been doing was splashing to send the fish down-stream to the nets. That was all! They did it often! No one had ever screamed at them like that before.

Tansen scooped up a couple of bairns and ran with them towards the earth-house. Nain, pigtails flying, herded them down inside, her face turned over her shoulder towards Tansen.

"What's wrong?" she cried, her mouth working, her eyes wild.

Tansen pushed the bairns at her and began to run down to the curve of the stream. How could she know? Golden-haired giants swooping up-river from the sea? But Baran, spearing fish in the shallows, would have seen the Angles and sounded the warning horn.

She parted the undergrowth. Baran lay sprawled across the flow-path, his spear trailing in the water. His dead eyes stared at her. Tansen stared back, feeling all the energy flowing out of her limbs and leaving her numb.

The sight of his entrails, bursting from his stomach, sent her hands flying to press on her mouth, so as not to scream, so as not to be sick. Oh, Mother of the Gods, it must be the Scots! They were small! They were the ones who used dirks and ripped upwards! They must have crept through the glens from Dal Riata in the west!

Her head jerked up. Then why had the herd-boy not seen them and beaten his wolf-bell? Crouching low, she ran through the barley-field. Her hard bare heels crushed the stalks underfoot. Throwing back her head she sent the ululating cry of warning before her.

In the water-meadow there was no one to hear. Cynon's ears were closed for ever. Only his eyes were open, baby-blue eyes that asked, Why, why, why?

Tears spilled, blinding her, as she blundered away, following in the tracks of his vanished herd.

Beyond the birchwood, the churning of undergrowth. She slowed her headlong rush, gliding from trunk to trunk, moving towards the noise. Then she saw them. Not the small dark Scots but big helmeted men, hewing down her kinsmen with their axes. Her thoughts whirled, bouncing off one another. The Sea-Danes! Hosting up the coast! For a fresh rump steak or a wench to use and exchange for a cask of ale!

Malorc leapt onto a tree-stump. Her hands flew to her breast to keep her heart from bursting. Her brother swung his wood-axe, once, twice, as if he was chopping the undergrowth. She knew he was doomed before the Danish axe bit his neck. His bright blood spurted. A thin wail rose in her throat. Again she cupped her hands over her mouth. There was nothing she could do! Nothing! Except cry Bride's curse on them!

Then over the stench of spilled blood, came the smell of burning thatch. She turned to make for the homestead.

A shin-bone, hard as iron, swept her feet from under her. She thudded to the ground and was up and running again before she had caught her breath. He was swifter and stronger and brought her crashing down among the ripening corn.

At once she became an animal, using her claws, fighting him, uttering small gasping cries. His foul breath scoured her face. She opened her mouth against his steaming flesh and pressed her teeth into it. As he recoiled she bunched her knees. Her body surged and arced as she thrust against him. He rolled away easily but came at her again, pulling at his bulging trews.

Her eyes fastened on his swollen purple organ. This time her feet found their mark. He fell on his side, drawing in his breath through his teeth in a high-pitched whine, his hand groping, his eyes wide with the ecstacy of his pain.

The burning wind carried the sound of screams and yells. Her feet drove against the slope. Her elbows punched the air. By instinct she dropped to peer over the brow of the hill. Flames plumed upwards from the circle of homesteads. Fish-spears and gutting knives rose and fell. And in the centre a silver streaming pennant that was the hair of Grannie Bea, the Clan Mother fighting for her Clan.

Tansen came scrambling down in the shelter of the berry bushes and plunged her arm into the nearest smoking thatch. Her fingers closed round the handle of the long thin blade that Baran had sharpened only two nights before.

On the grass a girl writhed and screamed steadily to the thrust of the man who straddled her. Tansen burst out of the doorway at his back. A low growl erupted from her throat. She thrust with her knife, first the point, then the middle, then up to the hilt, twisting deep, deep inside him. He would plant no more Danish seed in her kin! His limbs collapsed, his pale flaccid penis flopped. But Maga had died in a tangle of hair and a puddle of blood.

Pushing with her foot, pulling her blade out, she turned and faced another. His face and body filled her whole vision. The lust in his eyes started a frenzied excitement invading her groin. It was easy, skin him like a hare, gut him like a fish! One part of her mind watched his hands. The other part was filled with a blinding will to survive.

Her knife in both hands crashed down at his neck with all the force of her fury. The impact jangled through her bones. She yelled with triumph as he crumpled, his head lolling. Another shadow loomed into the space where he had been. The killing fever surged again in her groin.

This one was tall, his eyes glowing like burning coals. He chewed on a chicken leg that angled from his mouth. Her blade jarred on metal rings under the sacking that bound his chest. He swiped the weapon out of her grip and punched her to the ground with his fist. Winded, she lay, gulping air into her lungs.

Laughing, he urinated into the milk-pot. Calmly he spat out the bone and began to kick her legs apart.

This forcing open of her body to his invasion brought a frenzy of madness. Survive! Survive! She had to survive! She rolled from under his falling body and her hands found the corn-grinder under a clutter of broken pots. Rising she brought it crashing down on his skull. Once more he reared up. She beat at his head again and again in an orgy of destruction. Gobbets of blood and brain flew in the air. She only knew she had to survive!

A voice roared in her ears. The grinding stone was smashed out of her grasp. A cruel hand yanked at her hair, arcing her head back. Grannie Bea's face swam into focus, her mouth opening and shutting.

"Hush, child, breathe, deeply, deeply. Breathe in the peace of the All-Mother."

When Grannie Bea spoke in her Wise Woman's voice you obeyed, even while you screamed inside your head.

Tansen laughed wildly. She had killed three of them! Three of the filthy swine! There must be more! Where was the knife? Bands of iron held her fast. Then came the familiar aroma of bread-baking from arms still floury to the elbow. A trembling began in her limbs and spread uncontrollably. Grannie Bea drew her inside a house, strangely quiet.

"It's over, it's all over."

The cracked voice crooned in her ear. Another spasm of shivering. How had she done it? Three men! Where had she found the strength? They had wanted to use her alive or they would not have been so careless.

A crackle of burning twigs and her eyes flew upwards. A glow in the thatch reddened and faded and reddened again. Fascinated she watched the tiny flames burst into life. Filling her lungs with the drifting smoke, she welcomed the smarting in her throat. She sank to her knees. Let the smoke dull her pain. Let the flames eat at the horror in her heart. Why should she be left alive? She wanted to go with her kin! Away from this horror! Escape from the grief and the keening that would follow.

A firm grasp on her tunic lifted her and spun her sideways out of the door. There she came face to face with the full devastation. A waste-land of death where this morning there had been the fullness of life. Bodies, spread and humped, gilded by a circle of flaming thatches. Tansen retched herself to her knees. She began scooping up handfuls of earth and throwing them over her head.

The slap of icy water shocked her. She looked up into the face of Deva, the Clan Mother from the homestead up-river. Another wave from the water-bucket swept over her. She sat perfectly still, watching the water drip from her hair. Shadowy figures were dowsing the thatches, clearing the broken kegs and barrels, laying out the bodies. And slowly Tansen felt all the shattered pieces of herself begin to come together again.

Blood, brains and vomit stained her tunic. She gagged again. Warily she took the path to the washing-pond, slinking, like a hunted animal. Her lovely purple robe hung from the salt-bath, torn to shreds to bind some Spear-Dane's wound. Oh, joy, how the salt must have stung!

She fell into the pond, rolling over and over, tearing at the rags that covered her, scrubbing at her skin, knowing she would never be clean again. Then Grannie Bea was with her, scooping up handfuls of water and washing her arms as naturally as she did every morning. Tansen wondered, dull-eyed, how she could be so calm.

When Grannie Bea waded out and took the path up-stream, Tansen followed, walking towards the sinking sun. There was the red of blood in the sunset, the grey of a man's brains, the gold of her sister's tumbled hair. She keened softly for her kin as they passed the burning barley-fields and the silent birchwood. No more would they live and love in the soft hollow of the All-Mother's breasts. No more would they bring forth a child to be thrown up to catch Dagda's breath from the Sun. No more for them would the seasons turn from the sowing to the harvest.

A cluster of buildings took shape against the twilight sky. The kin-children were there at a hearth. The babies, used to suckling at any breast, were content. Nain and the older ones girned softly to themselves under their covers.

Tansen lay down with them, drawing the sleeping Fionna into the curve of her body. Against her closed eyelids, red knives rose and fell, fire ebbed and flowed, limbs twitched and fell limp. And time stood still.

CHAPTER TWO

Tansen opened her eyes to a faint glow from the embers. It outlined Grannie Bea sitting, erect and still, in the hearth-chair, her palms open on her knees.

She felt the tug at the corners of her mind and the prickle in her veins that told of a Presence. She moved to sit cross-legged beside Grannie Bea, waiting. For now there was no one else left to hear the commands of the Wise Ones and remember.

And while she waited, Tansen keened again, pulling her long copper hair over her face, rocking to and fro, using the same bleak sequence of notes over and over, dulling her senses, easing her pain. For Suen, for Maga, for Cynon, for Baran. And the rest.

And she keened for Grannie Bea whose wealth had been counted in healthy sons and daughters. And a host of grandchildren. And these fields and meadows and woodlands and a stretch of the river all bearing her name. For she held them in trust for the All-Mother, for as long as she had descendants to work them. And she had had plenty of these. And others who came to join with them because Grannie Bea was a Healer and Seer and well-loved.

Gradually Tansen became aware of movement. A mouse darted across her toes. A young cockerel tried a strangled crow from the midden. A hand began to crank the well-handle.

She swept back the curtain of her hair. The pearly light of dawn reached through the doorway and fell on Grannie Bea's face. It was waxen as though the spirit had gone from her body. With a lurching stab of fear Tansen saw her as she was. Not as the Wise Woman, not as the Clan Matriarch, but as an old woman who had seen her children die and her immortality perish.

She had to warm the blood of the old one, waken her from her long communion with the Great Ones. Tansen sprang up and fed the fire with dry twigs.

"It's morning, Grannie Bea, wake up!"

She chafed the gnarled fingers between her palms. willing her to come back. Who would command in the storm and the flood? Who would call forth the healing power when the crippling sickness came?

Grannie Bea's fingers curled. Her words slurred together as she came out of her trance.

"Since the time of the great Kings, Bridei and Brude, this land has known peace and plenty. We thought the Splendid Ones would let it last for ever."

Her eyes opened, green eyes clouded with age. Relieved Tansen knelt at her knee, looking up.

"What did the Wise Oncs say?" she cried.

Glassy unseeing eyes stared ahead.

"In my dream I made a goblet with my hands," Grannie Bea whispered. "I carried the blood of my kin to the King where he sat at his High Table, his sword between his feet."

Tansen shook her impatiently.

"But did they tell us what to do now?"

"I smeared my head with the ash of my thatch and showed myself to the Queen," the toneless voice continued.

Tansen rose at that, clenching her fists and crying out, unable to bear this reciting of dreams.

"Is this all the Wise Ones can offer? To call on our Royal Kin? To plead with Garnard the Fat? To grovel before Pertan? To humble ourselves before a Council of Elders?"

The harsh strident tones brought Grannie Bea swinging back into the real world.

"Pah! That gaggle of elderly geese. Grazing on past glories. Long ago, a new warrior King should have been married onto that Princess What's-her-name."

Firelight glowed on her grand-daughter, lighting up wide distressed eyes and the mane of copper hair.

And the woman, Beatha, felt old and drained beside the girl's vigorous youth. She coughed and spat in the fire, holding her chest.

"It's the smoke. It's left arrow-barbs in my lungs."

Instantly Tansen was at her side with water from the pitcher. The thought of a future without Grannie Bea terrified her.

"Drink this. I'll make you up a potion after breakfast!"

Grannie Bea took the cup and drank, grateful for its coolness, grateful for a moment to gather her thoughts. Her eyes lingered lovingly on the fine planes of the girl's face. Her heart twisted with pain, knowing that she must send the girl on a journey. And she would see her and touch her no more. Tansen jumped up again, restlessly.

"How are we going to avenge our dead kin?" she cried.

Grannie Bea's eyes snapped green fire as a flame erupted in the hearth. "Ach, when will you learn, girl? Vengeance spawns more vengeance!"

Tansen twisted away to the other side of the fire. The flames that sprang up between them fuelled the bitterness in her heart.

"Someone's got to go after them! To rape their women! Steal their silver! Set fire to their fields!"

Tansen wrung her hands. Her loose hair swung as she prowled fiercely around the earthen floor.

"You want to go killing and maiming in Bernicia? Innocent bairns? What good would that do?"

Beatha had choked back the words of comfort she had meant to say. Let the child stay with the terrible anger that consumed her. It would fortify her in the task ahead.

Tansen scrubbed at her eyes, trying to blot out the images in her mind and the despair in her heart.

"Why didn't you foresee it, Grannie Bea?" she cried out, her voice breaking. "Why didn't the gods warn you?"

"All these years of teaching. And it's gone like chaff in the wind." Grannie Bea stretched her hands to the fire. "You wanted the Wise Ones to warn us at Pitcarlie so that the raiders would go to Pitmuies instead, is that it?"

Tansen wished with all her heart it had been like that and hunched her shoulders in shame at her thought.

"We've got to do something." Thoughts were tumbling around in her mind. "At least we can ask our Royal Kin for help to start afresh."

"What? You and me and a parcel of bairns? Save your breath, lass. The bairns and I will do fine staying here with Deva at Pitmuies."

"Until the next raid!" Tansen's frantic fingers plucked at a frayed end on her tunic.

Grannie Bea took in a long slow breath. Her voice when it came was deep and compelling.

"Listen. Last night I saw a sign."

A surge of impatience took Tansen to the doorway. Who needed signs and portents when her spirit was crying out for action?

"The All-Mother came with a quiver of arrows at her side. And I was the bow that she chose from the rack."

Tansen snorted. Visions shrouded in mystical words would grow no grain for starving bairns.

"She fitted an arrow and flexed my body. And I was strong and supple. And arrows flew, each one a son or a daughter."

Outside salt pig crackled over a fire. The smell sent juices flowing in Tansen's mouth.

"You were the last arrow left in her quiver," went on Grannie Bea.

Tansen wrenched her mind back from thoughts of crisp bacon in a roll of bread.

"And when the Mother took you and fitted you, you shone like gold. She sent you winging southwards. And as the sun caught you, you flamed like a golden torch."

It took a moment for the words to sink in to Tansen's mind

"South? To the Capital?"

Grannie Bea nodded, still musing.

"And even further."

Tansen was not listening. She was remembering her dreams of yesterday. Shredded now, fluttering in the wind like her lovely purple robe.

"How can I leave now?" Her voice broke on a sob.

"You'll go as my messenger. To tell King Garnard that we need protection for our homesteads."

"It won't do any good! You know that!"

The children were stirring, pushing at one another, uttering small yelps like a litter of puppies.

"I can't leave you and the bairns unprotected."

Grannie Bea's heart failed her. A squalling brood, waking each morning, their energy renewed. It tired her even to think about it. But there was no going back, only forward.

"No one's ever alone." Grannie Bea rose, lifting her long hair, twisting it and skewering it on top of her head with a bone pin from her tunic. "You'll leave today."

Oh, Bride, Tansen thought, why now, with grief as my jewels and death as my cloak? She had hoped to ride through the Gate of the Capital in the glory of her maidenhood, not as a beggar. The Spear-Danes had ruined that hope.

She dressed in a fresh tunic and trousers that looked suspiciously like those that had belonged to the dead herdboy. Yet a thrill of anticipation coursed through her limbs. She had never been to Court. In all her fourteen years there had been no victory to celebrate, no new King to be elected, no Royal Marriage to witness. But now, to meet new people, to see carefree faces again. To put the horror aside for a little until she could cope with it.

As she stood, wrapping bread and pork in a rhubarb leaf she lifted her head and saw the sun rise. It shone with superb indifference on the dead homestead down-river, the burnt harvest and the crushed birchwood. On the motherless bairns who scampered and yelled and tumbled with the dogs. Its fierce white light stabbed into her being, filling her with a white-hot hatred of the Spear-Danes and the rulers of the Land of the Pretani who had stood aside and let them come. A resolve grew like a bubble inside her as she braided and bound her hair. She must waken the folk at Court to the danger from the south. Why else had she been allowed to survive?

A surly garron that nobody wanted rolled a doleful eye back at her as she mounted. A shabby cloak the colour of deadwood swirled round her shoulders and rested on his back. Gone was her dream of an embroidered cloak and an amythyst brooch and a slender-footed mare. May the Shining Ones curse that indolent Court and all who wallowed in it!

"We're a sorry-looking pair but we're stuck with one another," Tansen told the garron, digging her heels into his ribs to stop his bad-tempered frisking. Grannie Bea's hand on the bridle quietened his capers.

"You'll tell them that we need more strongholds on the coast! Filled with scouts who keep their ale-pots empty in their saddle-bags!"

"I'll tell them more than that!" Tansen gritted her teeth.

"And let Pertan know you need the Initiation! You've fourteen Samhains behind you. It's time your maidenhood was opened. Rather have it done with pleasure by a healthy man at Court and not by foreign filth!"

Grannie Bea cut the leather girdle at her waist and thrust it out. Hanging from it Tansen saw the little silver-backed mirror she had always known would come to her. It was decorated on the back with the Trumpet Spirals that proclaimed Grannie Bea's Royal Blood. And that same Blood flowed hot and heady through her own veins. She shook her head vigorously.

"Keep it till I come back!"

Grannie Bea must not give up her girdle as though she was giving up life itself. The Fateful Ones might watch and take note.

"The keys might buy you a meal." Grannie Bea's voice was gruff. The silver keys belonged to chests that were looted or burned and gone for ever. Her arms circled Tansen's waist as she tied on the girdle. She felt the warm living blood coursing through the strong young body. And she was sorely tempted to ask the Great Ones to send someone else. The lass had been tested enough. Yet who else could carry the Torch of Caterin, but a daughter of Caterin, the greatest Queen the Pretani had ever known.

"Be sure to stop and ask the Ancestral Ones to protect you."

Grannie Bea fixed her gaze on the yellow flower of Bride springing at the base of the tethering post. Tansen could see that she was troubled.

"I'll be fine, Gran. The Guardians are with me. Don't worry."

"There's weakness and sterility at Dalgynch. But there's something else. Some dark force." Grannie Bea's voice held a hint of awe. "It sucks power from the All-Mother to use for its own ends."

The old woman's eyes locked with Tansen's. Suddenly the day was overcast. A bairn, seeing Grannie Bea pull her shawl over her head, tiptoed past. Nain, bringing her a cough-potion, paused when she saw how still they were.

"I'm sorry, lass. I should send my last arrow forth with gladness, not with a warning ringing in her ears."

Suddenly there were a thousand questions to ask. Tansen wanted to throw her arms around Grannie Bea again to comfort her. But Grannie Bea whacked the rump of the beast and side-stepped stiffly from his flashing hoof.

"I'll be back soon!" Tansen cried.

Her cloak swirled and the dust flew. She had hardly time to wave round the circle to the women and bairns clustered in the doorways.

Before she rounded the curve of the hill she reined in and looked back, flinging up her arm in farewell. But Grannie Bea was holding on to the tethering post, her back bent in the arc of a bow. Then the garron leant back almost on his haunches and shot forward like an arrow in flight.

CHAPTER THREE

With the sun on her left Tansen bore south. Sensing the urgency in her hands and knees, the garron stretched his legs and found he enjoyed it. The corners of Tansen's mouth twitched. Hey, she felt like Mannan, the Messenger One, riding on Enbarr of the Flowing Mane across the wide, wide sky.

And so they were nearly past the Ancestor Stone at the crossroads before she remembered to ask for protection. And she slowed a little for her mind was filling with memories.

The first time her mother had taken her to honour their Ancestor Stone, Tansen had tripped and spilt the libation wine. Her mother had finished the incantation with a chuckle in her voice.

"I should have known better than to give the bowl to a six-year-old bairn with a trailing tunic."

She had still been laughing softly as she went to gather the reins of the mare.

Tansen had stared aghast at the red wine dripping off her bare feet into the soil of the All-Mother.

"Oh, Water-Kelpie," she had mourned sorrowfully. "And I had such a big favour to ask of you."

High above her head reared the symbols of her ancestry. The crescent of the Moon Maiden crossed by the broken arrow, the sign that was incised on every stone since King Bridei's time.

The lines in the ancient teaching tongue of the Druad had whispered through her mind then.

"And Bridei united the clans of Alba,
From the wide-mouthed Fiorth to the Isles of the Orcades,
And the clans broke their arrows and swore by the Maiden,
That they would war no more."

But stories of battles bored her. War was a stupid game played by men and boys. She liked men that used their skills in sporting and hunting. And playing with bairns.

Underneath the Moon's crescent was the symbol of an arc. Some said it was the arc of the sky where the Splendid Ones had their home. Others that it was the rainbow, sign of peace and harmony in nature. But Grannie Bea said it was a golden torc that proclaimed the Royal Blood of their kin. Far removed cousins, her mother would warn her, because the Queen had the great black Royal Bull as her sign.

On a level with her head was her clan's Water-Kelpie with his long curving snout. She had put her arms round the stone and rubbed her cheek at the placc where his long whip sprang from his head. He was a bright blue colour, by far the cuddliest of the mystical beasts that the Druad walkcd with in their dreams.

"But Queen Pertan doesn't have the royal green eyes like me," she whispered urgently in the Kelpie's ear. "You'll make me Queen some day, won't you? And give me a handsome warrior King to marry."

Suddenly she had drawn back, filled with dismay. She wasn't being nearly humble enough. She had squeezed her eyes shut, trying hard to feel humble, while she repeated her petition. But how could she feel 'humble' when she didn't know what 'humble' meant? Was it the opposite of being a Queen?

When the bairns acted out the bard-tales of Heroes and Queens, Tansen made sure she played the Queen by pulling a few plaits. Dressed in her mother's best linen tunic, she had ordered the others to braid flower chains in her hair. And wind strings of coloured pebbles round her neck.

But even Queens must placate the Powerful Ones and plead for their good will. And that bright childhood morning Tansen had tried a new plea.

"I'll give you my first pair of silver earrings when I get them. If you make me Queen."

No, that wasn't right. She was never going to earn her silver until she worked harder at the weeding and didn't stop to follow the squeaking of newborn stoats to their nest in the wall. And to wonder where the swallows went when they gathered and flew south. And why each bird had a different bird-call. Nobody else found these things exciting. The adults were all too busy sowing or reaping or baking to answer her questions.

The Kelpie had smiled at her as though he could read her mind. She had suspected he did.

"Then you must know about that empty hole in my chest," she'd said then.

That described exactly the great longing that came to her sometimes. It was many times worse than being hungry. It came to her in the scent of honey in the clover, in the sweetness of the breeze in the Blooming Season, and rose quivering from the pink-tinged landscape at sunset. And she would ache for something that lay just beyond her chubby fists, something that called to her, something that brought her spirit leaping in answer into her throat.

When she tried to put the feeling into words the other bairns looked at her out of the corners of blank eyes and went back to their games. So she had told her secret to no one since.

Yet if the Blue Kelpie made her Queen, the hole in her chest would go away. She knew it would. Just then the crystals in his stone head had grazed her cheek and she had jumped up and stuck out her tongue at him.

"Whether you help me or not, I will be Queen some day!" she had told him. And marched towards her mother, one eye turned skyward, hoping to impress the Gracious Ones with her determination. And had caught her foot in a root and ended with her face and her pride in the heather.

"What nonsense has Granny Bea been putting in your head?" her mother had called from the back of the mare.

"At least she listens to me. Nobody else does," Tansen had gulped, rubbing a grazed elbow.

"Oh, nonsense! Let's go home and see if your father's arrived."

Forgetting everything else Tansen had run to be lifted up in front of her. It was the Growing Season, in the lull before the harvest, when her tall dashing father would come swaggering down from the Caledon mountains with some of his men. And her mother would leave the work of the homestead to her sisters and go off riding with him, singing in her clear high voice.

The small Tansen had not yet noticed that her little brothers and sisters had all been born within nine cycles of the Maiden after the visits of her father. They appeared with astonishing regularity around the Festival of Bride when the lambs were born and there was fresh milk in the pitcher.

"I know we're from Queen Caterin's stock, but you'll never see the Queenship, child. There are too many Princesses between you and that office," her mother had said then.

Tansen was abashed that her plea to the Kelpie had been overheard. She didn't want adults spoiling her dream with their laughter. She only knew that Queens loved brave young men and their beauty was spun into bard-songs. Her lip had jutted out stubbornly.

"Grannie Bea knows everything. And she's a Wise Woman."

"Grannie Bea's also very old. She gets her visions mixed up."

Then Tansen had remembered a desperate need to see if her father had brought the horn meat-dagger he'd promised her. She had pressed her knees on Stardust's neck to make her go faster.

Tansen had called the mare Stardust because when she was a foal she would come galloping across the field in the dawn, her mane flecked with dew. Tansen would bury her face in it and pretend she could smell the dust of the stars.

"Grannie Bea says I'll go to Court on a white horse in a shining yellow cloak," she had announced proudly to her mother.

"And so you shall, my love. For your Initiation."

That mysterious Ceremony fascinated Tansen. Soon after her woman's blood showed she would be initiated into the pleasures of love by an older man. She knew love-making was fun because she sometimes followed her cousin, Nain, and her lad from up the coast when they met at Festival-times. She didn't know exactly what they did when they were wrapped close together under a cloak. But she knew it was good by Nain's moans of pleasure and the look of rapture on her face when she came back to sit round the hearth.

"Why do I have to go to the Court for my Initiation when Nain can choose her own lad?"

Tansen had twisted her head to look up at her mother then and her breath had caught in her throat because she looked so beautiful. Her skin was like fresh cream rose-tinted in the light of the dawn. She had unbound her hair and it streamed in the wind like a red-gold pennant. Tansen had wished she could loosen the thick braid that lay down her back. But maybe not. By nightfall it would be a tangle of burrs and thorns.

"Daughters of Caterin must be initiated at Court," her mother had said.

Green eyes that every true Daughter of Caterin inherited had twinkled down at Tansen.

Nain's mother had been a travelling woman who had arrived, given birth and gone, leaving her baby, all within seven nights. Tansen decided to remind Nain of that the next time she tried to order her around.

"You'd better start embroidering your Court cloak as soon as the Cold Season starts."

Tansen had made a face. Sewing meant having to sit in one place. Still there was a lot going to happen before the first snow winds blew from the north-east. After her father left there would be the field-harvest when the sickles would flash and the bairns would glean and winnow. This time she'd not play 'Hideaway' among the stooks. Young Queens had to walk with dignity. Recently she'd been practising.

Yet maybe she should forget about being royal during the Fruit-harvest. Queens didn't climb trees and spit pips at their brothers from mouths all red and sticky with berry juice.

Still she supposed the cloak would have to be made. Suen the potter would help the dull moments to pass. She loved when he took down his lyre and struck it with the stubby fingers that all good lyre players had. He was the man who lived at their hearth in between times while her mother waited for the return of the father of her children. Suen had made a cup with

Tansen's own special sign on it. She'd liked that. It made her feel important.

That lovely lazy faraway day they had taken a wide detour round the tree where the lads were scooping out honey, bees, grubs, combs and all into pots and Cynon had stopped licking his sticky fingers to wave.

And then her thoughts leapt to the Festival of Lugnasad when she would have to stand still again while Grannie Bea intoned the incantations and performed the Harvest rituals. Maybe this time she'd be chosen to be Corn-Maiden. If not she would daydream about Luga, the Long-Armed One, the comely young champion, with a face as bright and glorious as his father, Dagda, the Sun.

And then would come Samhain, the Festival that was always the best. It lasted nights and nights. There were competitions for dancing and singing and storytelling. And for running and leaping and hitting the target. Baran would make her a new set of arrows that would fly straighter than anyone else's. Big patient plodding Baran. Yet the girls liked him.

Samhain! The end of the Old Year and the start of the long winter sleep of the All-Mother before Dagda awoke her to mate with him so that the fruits of her body would spring forth again. Then would come the feasting, the glorious feasting.

It was her healthy appetite that brought Tansen's senses roaring back into the present. Dismounting she let the garron crop at the lush grass on the bank of a stream while she ate her salt pork and thought how strange it was that she could remember every detail of that precious day with her mother, every carefree thought that had fluttered through her mind. She had not been aware then how precious the memory of that day was to become.

CHAPTER FOUR

Tansen lay back and closed her eyes, listening to the cropping of the garron in the noonday hush while the birds rested.

Life at the Pitcarlie homestead had been full of goodness and promise. As the seasons passed, her mother had borne four more bonny bairns at lambing-tide and Tansen had blossomed into womanhood. She'd had to gather fresh moss for her bed and wash her blanket and fleece in the river so that her first blood would be restored to the Earth Mother. She had thought the good times would go on for ever and ever. They had all thought that.

Of course they knew they had enemies. They knew about the Scots on the other side of the Caledon mountains. Nain used to tell bairns with the wander-lust that the wee dark Scottie-men would break off their legs and crunch them like chicken-bones. But they all knew that the Scots who had come to Alba from Eirean would never venture this far east. So the boys played out the bard-songs about King Bridei, stamping his foot on the borders and daring them to come any further. And the wee ones made cheeky Scottie faces and were chased back to their islands and glens behind the midden.

And who who didn't know about the golden-haired giants? Fear of their ringed prows was ingrained in every child born near the coast or beside a river. Fear so dreadful that the bairns shuddered in their sleep at the clang of an axe on wood. No one wanted to put on a pot for a helmet and play at being a Spear-Dane.

Then a new memory came winging to Tansen, one she didn't want to remember. She ought to be surging onwards towards Dalgynch. Instead she rose and leant against a silver birch, remembering with pain how in the heat of the summer her father was late in coming. Each day her mother had climbed to the top of the hill where an ancient fortress was crumbling away with disuse. Everyone could see her outlined against the sky, standing on the tumble of stones, shading her eyes, her skirt blowing round her legs, waiting.

One day Tansen saw her jump and wave her arms. But it was only a lone rider who skirted the mountain.

"Oengus, the great Chieftain of the Caledonie is dead," he told them. "He'll not come again."

Her mother's face had hardly changed. Only her eyes had grown bleak reflecting the ice that had come out of season to lay bare the landscape of her life.

"How did it happen? Was it Scottie scum?" Grannie Bea had held out a beaker of ale to him.

He had taken his time about quaffing it as they all waited, each feeling the weight of his or her own loss.

"That's the shame of it," he burst out at last. "The Scots could not surprise him in his own mountains. We were rounding up a head of cattle they'd lifted from us the night before. It was a rolling stone that made his horse stumble. They both tumbled down the mountain scree and into the loch." He turned his back to them and added bleakly, "We didn't even have a body to take to the Burial Island."

Tansen had grieved then that she would never see her father's white teeth gleaming in his red beard again or hear his booming laugh echo down the glen. Yet her heart swelled with pride to discover that he had been a great Chieftain of the famous Caledonie clan.

Quietly her mother had disappeared into her hut, pulling her hair down over her face. Tansen had listened to the high keening, the same three notes over and over. She had moved to comfort her but Suen put his hand out to stop her and went in himself. He had a kindly face in spite of the sword-cut that drew his mouth up at the side in a permanent smile. Suen had been more of a father to Tansen ever since the day he had come limping into Pitcarlie with a bloody bandage on his thigh and had set up his potter's shed.

After a little Tansen had peered round the doorway. He was kneeling beside her mother, his arms round her body, rocking with her to the rhythm of her sorrow.

"Leave them be, girl!"

It had been Grannie Bea who had spoken, her broad waist slung with pouches.

"Come! We need the leaves of the trefoil. Now tell me where to find it and the spell I must say and what I'll use it for."

Ever since Tansen had been able to count her age on two hands, Grannie Bea had been taking her out every day. They gathered the roots and stems and leaves and flowers that the Mother provided for healing. Tansen always went gladly. She didn't want to be a bairn-minder like Nain. Now she was relieved to have something to do that would help her to forget that the Scottie of their childish games had become real and deadly.

At the borders of the water-meadow Tansen had snipped a few leaves off each plant with her finger-nail against her thumb.

"Spirits of the marsh trefoil, I need to make an infusion to soothe the headache of Macha," she had explained to the in-dwelling spirits.

She had been tempted to pull the flower-heads to make an orange dye for her newly-woven tunic but the scolding of a passing oyster-catcher warned her to leave them until the bees had had their fill.

Then Tansen recalled the blackbird still in his youthful brown feathers, his spirit calling to her for help although his russet breast quivered with fright. Without a thought she had taken him lovingly in her cupped hands and breathed on him.

"Who taught you to do that, child?" Grannie Bea had been watching, her green eyes luminous in the brown leather of her skin.

"No one. I'm just loving him well again."

Grannie Bea had placed her own hands over Tansen's and they had gazed at the bright eye of the bird. Power trembled from her grandmother's hands through her own.

"Have you the gift of Sight as well, child?"

As Tansen had glanced up at Granny Bea she had glimpsed a gentle misty face behind her in the darkness of the trees before it receded and vanished.

"The Guiding Ones, you mean?" Tansen had shrugged. "Only the woman that was helping us to heal the bird."

Grannie Bea had hissed through her teeth.

Then Tansen had opened her hands and the bird had flown straight into a tree. He wouldn't need to join the flock of mending wings and legs that lived on her doorstep and came to her hands daily for crumbs. And for something else that flowed from her to them and healed them faster.

"Do you see pictures in your mind?" Grannie Bea had persisted as they set off for home.

"Oh yes, every time Suen tells a good story." Tansen answered wickedly.

She had been bored then and unwilling to tell any more. Grannie Bea was always asking questions. They both knew she was different from the other bairns. She was glad she was different. But she wanted to be a Queen, not a Wise Woman.

She had begun to pick buttercups and marigolds to wind into a chain for her head.

"Stop pretending!" Grannie Bea had snapped. "You can't ignore the gifts of the gods. A gift like yours is like a garment you must grow to fill."

"I don't need these gifts to become Queen."

She had waited to see if Grannie Bea would rise to the bait and tell her more about her future. But the old woman had become strangely silent recently about what she saw in her meditations.

Tansen had shrugged. Folk with the Sight saw ghosts and foretold gloom and doom. She was content to know only the Gentle Ones who gave healing and guidance and love.

That Cold Season Tansen had finished her cloak for the journey to Court. The stitches were crooked but the colours were brilliant and she had liked it. She had held it to her breast and pictured herself riding into Dalgynch between rows of dazzled courtiers before she had folded it away in lavender in the clothes-chest.

At the Festivals the young men had begun to court her but she had kept herself aloof, dreaming now of a lover who looked like her father with reckless eyes and long waving hair.

Besides if she was going to be Queen to a foreign King she had to be a virgin. It was true that Malorc from Pitrouvie sometimes caught her eye and his touch in the dance made her tremble. But they both knew they could only smile and be friends for cousin-lovers were taboo.

Then despite all Suen's loving care and Grannie Bea's syrups of coltsfoot, her mother had fallen ill with the coughing sickness and Tansen had wakened one morning to find Suen weeping over her lifeless body.

Tansen had missed her terribly, even though sometimes she could feel her presence like a nudge at the back of her neck, a prickling as if a hand caressed her hair. Yet while she had wept for the missing of her, she had pictured her riding off with her Caledon Chieftain into the sunset with a wave and a promise to come back when Tansen's time came to pass over.

After that she grew bored with Suen's stories and began to listen to the travelling craft-folk who shared their stew and told about the ferocious Sea-Danes who hosted out from the North Humber Land. The elders would growl in their throats at the mention of this alien race who came from across the sea to raid, to settle and to rule.

Her uncle Baran had always roared his disbelief.

"Why should we fear sailors from Angel-Land?" he would cry. "Don't forget, the folk down south invited them in to protect their coast from our raiding ships."

And he would chuckle and pass the ale pitcher.

But the Sea-Danes both fascinated and frightened Tansen. She knew that long ago the two kingdoms, Bernicia and Deira had been united under King Aethelfrith of Bernicia. Edwin, the Deiran Heir, had marched north and killed him. Since then Edwin's power had spread from one sea to another, and northwards until he was facing the Pretani across the Forth. At that time the new young warrior King Garnard had gathered an army.

"And that was the last time Garnard showed us his mettle," Drest had grumbled one night. Grannie Bea's brother had come from his farm for a child-naming. "At the time we thought it was the Powerful Ones who saved us. Now, they say, it was because Edwin turned to the teachings of the White Christ."

Grannie Bea had gone on rocking the new bairn as she spoke.

"Since then Garnard's done nothing but grow fat and breed. He won't go easily. He's landless since Cadwallon devastated his portion in Gwynedd. He'll want to hang onto his rich living here. It's time we had a new King."

"Time we had a Get-Together to prod the Council into action," agreed Drest. "The eldest Princess must be a woman now."

Suddenly Tansen had realised what was going to happen. The People's Council would cast around for worthy foreign warriors. There would be a coming and going of the Clan Brothers to the Capital until the best man for the job was elected. Marriage to the eldest Princess would make him King and the Princess Reatta would become Queen. The thought of it hit her like a blow between the ribs.

"Another foreign King!" she cried out. "I'll bet there's only a trickle of Royal Blood left in Reatta's veins by now."

She knew she had said something important by the needle-sharp glances that came her way. Feeling more confident she continued.

"Every Samhain you select the best cattle for breeding before you slaughter the rest, don't you? With all these imported fathers and grandfathers, I think I've more right to become Queen than Reatta. At least, I'm a full-blooded Pretani."

"In a way she's right," said Baran thoughtfully. "Too many of our Kings have come from the south and want to live here in comfort and ease. It's time we had some rumbustious fighting blood from among the chieftains of the north."

Like my father, Tansen thought. Now that was a thought to cherish. Why shouldn't a Chieftain of the Caledonie become the new King?

"I think it's high time I went to Dalgynch for my Initiation," she announced boldly.

"You're day-dreaming again," said her aunt. "You'll have to grow older and wiser first, girl."

Reatta's no older and wiser than me, Tansen had grumbled later into her bed fleece. And lay tumbling all sorts of plans over in her mind.

Tansen swallowed a sob and mounted the reluctant garron. How could she have known, that long-ago night, that other forces were at work to change the destinies of those dear folk around the hearth-fire?

She dragged the garron's head round and turned him towards Dalgynch.

CHAPTER FIVE

"The Sea-Danes are raiding!" Tansen sent that warning cry towards every homestead she passed.

On the summits of the hills, the great fortresses had gaping holes and crumbling walls where eyes and arrows should have been. She could not believe it! Her anger came blazing back. And she tended the flame, fuelling it with fury into a roaring fire that would make the Court seethe and bubble like a cauldron until it overflowed into action.

No more grief in the night, she promised herself. But by this journey, she would make a praise-song out of the slaughter of her kin!

For a while every movement of a cow on a shieling and every boar rooting in the undergrowth brought her heart leaping into her mouth.

Not until she had forded the Tay, high up at the sandbanks, could she feel safe from raiders and free to gallop southward into Fif, where the King's scouts would be her shield.

"Hey-up there!"

She reined in on the crest of a ridge. On the skyline were the paps of the Lomonds, the same shapes that had been drawn in the dust for her by the folk at Dun Nichen where she had spent the night. The Capital must lie beyond.

Now that she was almost there a surge of conflicting emotions made her pause. She longed to see Dalgynch and meet new people. But how would they receive a stranger dressed in a dead boy's rags?

Yet she was Royal! Their scorn could not touch her. Not when Grannie Bea had entrusted her with a message and the Guiding Ones were with her. Let folk think what they liked!

They said that from Dalgynch you could see beacons from the snow-capped mountains in the north to the Pettaland hills across the Forth. She screwed up her eyes, trying to pierce the distant haze and caught only a flash, maybe the glint of a spear on the palisade.

In the distance a solitary rider had stopped between two clumps of trees, facing her where she was outlined against the sky. A prickle at the back of her neck told that her Guiding Ones were there. For a heartbeat she had a sense of looking down a long dark corridor. That two minds were meeting in some loop of time. Yet no sense of warning came, no foreboding. Only a feeling of pleasureable anticipation spreading through her body. A periwinkle blue feather curling round his iron head-piece, fluttered as the man turned his horse and trotted south.

Suddenly the sparkle of a river in the valley tempted her. She might not enter Dalgynch in style but at least she would be clean.

At a spot where the river curved, a willow tree leaned over a gathering of flat stones. Cynon's tunic was sticking to her skin. Peeling it off she pounded at it with a stone in the water and laid it out to dry. Naked she waded in and began to cleave her way upstream, feeling the water ripple over her breasts and between her thighs. Turning over she floated with the current listening to the glad song of the river as it passed her ears.

With a pang of guilt she remembered the flying greeting she had sent to the Ancestor Stone as she sped past. Now she wished she had taken time to make the libation.

"As your feet are deep in the Earth, As your head is high in the Sky, As you stand bold against the winds of change, So the clan of the Teazalie will last till the end of time."

She sent out the unlocking spell that would release the power of the Ancestral Ones and bring it flowing through the Life-Stream towards her. For she needed that power, now that she was within sight of the Capital. It was one thing to speak brave words in a homestead that nestled in the hill-side. It was another to remember that you were a young untried woman, not yet mated, going alone into the Halls where policies and decisions were made. For a moment her heart failed her.

Then she filled her mind with the proud emblems of her ancestry, the silver crescent of the Moon Maiden and the Blue Kelpie who calmed the raging waters with the whip that sprang from his head. Would the Ancestral Ones who lived within the Stone understand her need for speed and overlook her omission?

The bounce of a wave filled her mouth with clean-tasting water. Pushing all thought aside, she dived. For she was the daughter of the Water-Kelpie. The sun-dappled stones at the bottom stirred as she swooped past and upwards again in a rush of bubbles. Golden droplets arced in the air as she lashed her hair out of her eyes.

And it came to her with a sort of ecstacy that she might have missed this joyful day. She might have been lying beside her dead sister waiting for the stones of her cairn to be laid above her and for the spell that would release her spirit. Instead she was special! She had been chosen by the Life-Giving Ones. In sheer delight she rolled and dived and splashed again.

The snort of a horse, hastily muffled, sounded nearby. She brushed the water from her eyes and saw them, two rows of horsemen, lining both banks. Terror gripped her. Her limbs leapt into flight. Head low she pounded at the water, speeding upstream.

They followed, laughing and shouting at one another across the river.

Then one, bolder than the rest, sent his mount splashing into the water to follow her. She could hear the slither of hooves on pebbles as he gained on her.

In a panic she dived. Her hand found a stone that fitted it. Her aim was swift and sure. Years of practice at lobbing stones at wolves came to her aid. The stones followed one after the other till he retreated laughing, protecting his head with an upraised arm.

This time she felt for a stone with a cutting edge and waited. As soon as he lowered his arm she sent it skimming at his head. It caught him on the brow and she saw him flinch. At once, the laughter stopped. As the other riders closed in around him she took the chance to swim to an inlet upriver. But as she waded ashore more riders broke out of the undergrowth, forming a semi-circle round her. She was trapped. She panicked and screamed at them.

"Filthy scum!"

A narrow space appeared in the circle and she ran blindly towards it, shrieking at them. Two riders moved sideways to plug the gap.

"Let me go! Let me go!"

In desperation she pummelled at the thighs of the riders. It was then she saw the stirrups. Now she knew these men were foreign to this land where only knees and thighs guided horses.

The horses shied away from her and another gap appeared. In a moment she was through and leaping for a massive tree-trunk. She arced her back against it, lifting her head, baring her teeth, ready to attack. She knew if they made one move towards her that dreaded killing anger would well up from her groin and surge with a sort of hunger through her limbs. Dear Bride, not that again!

Instead they began to back-track their animals until one rider stood before her. Blood trickled from a deep cut on his forehead.

"I'm sorry if we frightened you." He spoke her tongue with a harshness that grated. "We thought you were inviting us to chase you."

How she hated him then! Hunting was a game to him! And she had been his prey!

"Don't come near me, foreigner!" She spat out the words, threatening him with another stone.

The young man's face sobered. He was bemused by the turmoil of emotions that rose in him. At first he had been merely bewildered by her fierce outburst. Now he found himself gazing, enraptured by her wild beauty. A feeling of suffocation rose in his chest and he swallowed hard. He had never seen such a magnificent body, so tall and shapely, so finely tuned, so in harmony with her surroundings. He had an overwhelming urge to sweep this glorious untamed creature into his arms before she escaped into the woodland. He glanced impatiently at the men who watched, holding in their fidgeting mounts.

His retinue shifted uneasily, wanting to leave quickly to find some other sport that would bring back the carefree laughter.

"We didn't mean to scare you!"

As if realising how inadequate his words were he flushed with embarrassment. He guessed he looked foolish but he could only stare at her glistening body in a kind of wonder.

Tansen thanked Bride there was no lust in his gaze. She did not believe for an instant that he was as innocent as he sounded. Yet her fear of being seized and ravished had gone. Now she just wanted to be left alone.

"Just go away! Let me be!"

As if he was going to take a formal farewell, the young man took off his hunting cap. His hair fell to his shoulders, gleaming like gold so fine it could have been spun by a spider. There was a shine about him that was not wholly caused by the western sun at his back. His leather riding clothes and boots had a glossy sheen. Gems shimmered in his long riding cloak.

These were no ragged raiders but well-set-up young men in rich clothes on sleek mounts with bright trappings. Yet they wore no insignia that she could recognise. So they spelled danger. The stone in her hand flew. The young man woke from his spell. This time he fielded it deftly.

His awkwardness dropped away with the stone and he smiled at her.

"We thought you were a young otter at play."

His boyish face was lit from within by a confidence that the world was his plaything and the gods were good.

"And you put me through that ... terror...for a game?" Drips fell from her swinging hair as she shook her head incredulously. Even yet she could not believe that these men could be so insensitive.

The riders stirred and began to make their way up-river. Sweet daughter of Dagda, she was not going to let them off so lightly. She would never forgive them for the anguish they had caused her.

"Shame! Shame! Shame!" She ran wildly along the water's edge, shouting at their backs.

"Listen, you foreign louts! My home was burned! My sister raped! My kin-folk murdered! And you expect me to play games? Play games!" Her voice cracked on a high note.

The fair skin of the young man had turned a fiery red now.

"I'm sorry. We didn't know! Or we wouldn't have teased you!"

His lame excuses roused her fury further.

"I fought for my life! With a fish-knife! Against scum like you!" She was sobbing with anger now and beating at their thighs, horses, saddles. "And they laughed! Like you! They laughed as they fired our grain and herded off our cattle! Murderers! Scavengers! Beasts like you! And they laughed! Oh, leave me alone, you're nothing but animals!"

With tears blinding her she began to blunder downstream.

"Are you looking for these!"

The young man held up her pathetic bundle of rags. Ashamed she ran to rip them from his hand. He held them high.

"You can't wear these!"

Suddenly it was as though all the fight had gone out of her. Her eyes filled with tears. Her shoulders drooped. She looked fragile now and very vulnerable. He had an urgent need to clothe her, to hold her, to protect her from the eyes of his men. A surge of pity caught at his throat, crackling in his voice.

"Here, take this!"

He snapped apart the strange foreign clasps at his shoulders. His cloak swung in a wide arc. Despite its rich embroidery it fell about her body in soft warm folds. Her courage came bounding back. For a breathless moment she longed to sway this way and that to see the jewels catch the light. But his eyes were watching her with a strange intentness that made her wary.

CHAPTER SIX

"Where were you making for?" the young man asked.

"The Capital!" Tansen snapped. "Where else! All roads lead there!"

"I'll take you. I must make up to you for scaring you." He dismounted in one quick movement and saw her recoil. "You're not still afraid, are you?"

"I'm not afraid! Of you or any man! Kill me if you dare! But you'll carry the burden of my death for ever!"

He was beginning to understand the depth of her fear. His brow creased with concern as he held out the hand of friendship.

"I know I'll carry the shame of this day for ever. Unless you allow me to be your protector!"

Although she did not take her eyes from his, she was aware that his retinue had disappeared silently into the trees.

"Your cloak will do instead." She whipped Grannie Bea's girdle from his hand and tied it round her bare waist, under the cloak, so that her dagger was at hand. .

"Your flea-ridden mount took off when we arrived!"

The cloak swung as she turned to face him.

"See what you've done! Now I'll have to walk to Dalgynch!"

"You can ride with me." He gave a strange little bow. "Please!"

The last word softened her heart more than she liked.

"Who are you anyway?" she demanded.

"A Prince at the Royal Court!"

Not with that accent where the words ended with a husky gurgle at the back of his throat. Now that she had grown used to it she found it exciting.

"You'll have to do better than that!" He found he was enjoying himself now. He laughed and pushed back his hair, wincing as his wound stung.

"I'm a hostage then," he chuckled. "Does that please you better?"

She studied him. That made sense! By his regal bearing and large retinue he might well be important. She could do with some support at Court. His boyish face was open and honest, his blue eyes warm and friendly. She began to believe that he might make a welcome ally. She clasped his outstretched hand in return. And felt her skin burn at the contact. By the tremor in his clasp he had felt it too. He kept her hand in his.

"I don't have to ask who you are. You're a seal-maiden."

Solemnly, as if it might have been possible, she shook her head.

"A pagan."

His eyes widened.

"A pagan?"

"A country-girl." He was definitely a foreigner if he didn't understand the meaning of that everyday word.

"Never! You rose from that stream like a waterfall. As though the river goddess had just given birth to you."

Her involuntary chuckle surprised them both.

"That's the first time I've seen you smile. It's as warm and welcoming as a ray of sunlight. Your lips are like two petals from a wild rose waiting to fall. But your eyes have the green of the sea where the cockle-white sand shines through. Your beauty takes my breath away." His voice faded in wonder.

She shrugged.

"Whoever you are you've picked up a fine Celtic way of gentling a woman with words."

"I'm more of a Celt than anything else by upbringing." He hesitated. "I don't bother with words much. But all at once it's important to tell you how I feel."

"Honeyed words won't melt my heart." Already she had a feeling that he was wooing her and she found she wanted to hear more.

"But even Celtic words are poor things. I'd need to be a bard to tell you how magnificent you looked, breaking through the foam, your body gleaming." He caught both her hands against his chest in his fervour. "I believe I fell in love with you then."

"Tell that to the birds!"

But she laughed softly as she said it. Every woman knew from birth that love came to men such as he with surprising swiftness and left when the first sweet gladness had gone. But it was ecstatic while it lasted.

Yet his eyes had lost their gaiety. They were appealing to her, confusing her with their directness. And while his words stirred her senses, his fingers teased the tender skin of her arms.

He wanted to tell her how she had reminded him of an otter at bay with fierce courage in every sleek line of her. How he had not been able to draw his eyes away. How no otter ever had such a rich red mane of hair.

He began to stretch out a hand to touch her hair that was beginning to dry and curl. Tansen twisted out of his reach, leaving him to caress it with his eyes. Suddenly he threw back his head and laughed. It was a laugh of sheer delight. And she knew that this time he was playing a different kind of game with her.

"I'm a fool to talk of seals and otters. You're all woman, lovely, earthy, exciting. And very desirable."

The terrible fear that had invaded her earlier had left her tingling with an awareness of being alive. She looked at him anew and saw how comely he was. She tried to look away but his eyes held her. She had not been fooling herself. His eyes really were filled with wonder. It was a new sensation for her to be admired as though she was someone special. Sure, she had romped with the young men back home. But they knew better than to touch Grannie Bea's favourite grand-daughter who might be a Wise Woman in her own right some day.

"I know what it's like to be alone," he said suddenly. "To be far from home and kin."

The husky voice grated no longer but played delightfully on her senses. She felt her heart soften towards him. Her legs seemed to have softened too.

"We could comfort one another. I need you to love me, seal-maiden."

She felt her own needs stirring. The need to affirm that she was alive after all the fear and death and destruction she had endured in the past few days. The need to know that the world was not such an ugly place after all. The need to love and to be loved.

"We were made to be together. Don't you feel it?"

It was a mere whisper. With the blaze of the sun behind him, it was as though Bride had sent One of the Splendid Ones to make love to her. The moment was strange and sweet and unreal.

Yet the hands that held his cap were trembling. Why should he tremble? He must have made love often. Something stirred in her senses telling her that he needed more than just a mere mating. There was some magical bond, delicate as a spider's web, weaving them together.

With her finger she touched the swell of his lower lip and wondered how it would taste. Tilting her chin, she offered him her mouth. Instead, he clasped her in both arms and held her close as though he would never let her go. And she could feel desire in every line of his body.

"Let me be the one to fill the emptiness in your heart," he whispered, against her hair.

Here in his arms she felt as though she had found someone who understood her pain, someone who could share it.

Uplifted by a sudden surge of love she swirled out of his arms and dropped cloak and girdle at her feet. As she held out both hands to him, his eyes smouldered. Urgently he began to throw off his clothes.

First she saw the curve of his back and the muscles sliding under the sun-bronzed skin. Then she saw his need in the stiffness of his organ. Something halfway between a sob and a laugh caught in her throat as she caught his hand and swept him towards the river.

They plunged in headfirst and rose together shaking the drops from their hair and laughing aloud. As they splashed and sported she felt more alive then ever before, tingling with the awareness of skin that brushed against hers, of firm hands that held her, of hair that dripped rainbow pearls. Suddenly she was weeping that the night-land of terror was over and the days ahead held wonder and promise.

He swept her from the river and laid her on a bank of wild-flowers. He kissed the tears from her cheeks and lapped the rivulets of water from her skin with his tongue. Then when she was almost wild with longing, his body arced and fused with hers.

It was terrible and it was beautiful. They surged together knowing nothing but the wild joyous passion of it. And it went on and on. Until she went beyond knowing into ecstacy. Slowly, sweetly, her body filled with a glorious contentment and she lay back.

"My dearest dear!" he whispered. His eyes searched her face looking for a sign that she was fulfilled. He must have been satisfied for he drew back smiling.

It was then he saw the blood of her maidenhood on her thighs. He touched his finger to it and savoured it on his tongue. He took his own silken shift to the river and wiped her legs clean, gently, with a kind of reverence. Gran's calf-skin girdle he fastened round her waist. Then he wrapped her in his cloak, soft as velvet, and as bright red as the blood of her maidenhood.

When he had mounted, she ignored his helping hand and sprang up behind him, feeling that she could conquer the world. Her flesh glowed. The sun smiled, the trees danced, the birds carolled just for her.

In a burst of exultation she threw back the heavy mane of her hair. Her dream had come true. After all, she was going to enter the Capital in gold-embroidered finery and on the back of a prancing horse. And more, with a handsome nobleman, bound to her by love, as she was bound to him.

The sight of the towers and gateways of the Capital cleared her love-hazed mind. At last she was here where she had longed to be. Yet she felt no elation. At first she thought it was her new-found love that had changed her. Then the memory of blackened homes and bloodied bodies came plunging back to displace the lazy aftermath of love-making.

In a sudden blast of knowing she realised that the raid had changed her for ever. She felt older and wiser. Aware of a deeper purpose to life. Aware too of that empty yearning space she had once revealed to the Kelpie.

During this glorious afternoon she had thought that she had found a lover to fill that aching hole. But it was still there, gnawing at her, as the skyline of the Capital grew nearer. For as the painted roofs rose overhead and the sentries strutted on the palisade she knew that this was grim reality.

Never again would she dream of playing the role of a Queen. It had been a childish fantasy. Once she had thought that the Queen merely carried the Royal Blood and displayed both her charms and the wealth of the land to foreign visitors. That was all Queen Pertan had ever done. Coming now as a supplicant she understood that the Queenship held a deeper significance. That the Queen must also carry the burden of her people's woes.

The great gilded Gateway loomed above her but she was no longer a part of this splendid scene. She was a pagan, a stranger in an alien place, an arrow sent by Grannie Bea and the gods. She withdrew into the core of her being where she nursed her anger, her grief and her purpose.

CHAPTER SEVEN

At the Gateway to the Capital, the Officer of the Guard slanted his spear across their path. His eyes were on Tansen. Now, the cloak, the horse, even the man behind her were less important than the news she had to deliver.

"Tansen of the Taezalie, daughter of Leona, daughter of ... " she paused, searching her memory for Grannie Bea's given name. "Daughter of Beatha, daughter of Eden, third daughter of Queen Caterin. I bring news to my kinswoman, Queen Pertan."

The Officer lowered his spear in salute. His hooded gaze said that, although her mode of entry was unusual, her lineage was impeccable.

Within the Citadel a periwinkle blue plume swirled and was gone. She had seen that blue feather earlier. In another life, it seemed. Before she had met her Golden One. Before she had become a woman.

"So you're not a water-nymph after all," said the young man as they arrived at the stables. "I'm desolate. I was going to hide you in my quarters and keep you all to myself. Ah, well! Where to now, Princess?"

The title sounded sweet in her ears. Yet sweeter still was the advantage her Royal Blood would allow her. She could count on the chance to speak her mind.

Her bare legs flashed as he lifted her down. The groom holding the bridle chuckled. She threw him a withering glance and set her head proudly.

"Take me to the Queen!"

At first, she strode confidently at her lover's side. Then the tall houses that lined the passages began to oppress her. They crowded together, pushing and shoving, elbowing to look down their long pillared noses at her. She felt trapped. Even the sky was almost blotted out, far, far above the roof ridges. She searched for a glimpse of the horizon and when she could not see it the ground seemed to tilt beneath her feet and she stumbled.

"Steady on!" The man at her side clutched her elbow.

Her shake of the head hardly cleared her confusion. For now they were in a market-place. The air was filled with exotic smells of unfamiliar spices, new-tanned hides and new-baked pies. Hoods and lutes, threads and beads, scissors and mirrors jostled to dazzle her eyes. The cries of vendors were cut across by the clash, clash of a cymbal in the indifferent paws of an acrobat's monkey. And there were eyes, everywhere, curious and sly, taking her measure.

Three women with generous bosoms, chatting round the fish-wife's creel, turned their heads to stare. Pale ringed hands smoothed rich linen over well-fed stomachs. Tansen choked down a surge of panic. She had nothing in common with these plump matrons, safe and secure behind their walls and palisades.

A bevy of young girls, plucking over ribbons and laces and slippers from a pedlar's pack, looked up and leaned against one another, giggling. Tansen's lips pressed together, tight and bitter. What did they know of fire and rape and the fear that knotted the belly?

A servant, leering round the pitcher on his shoulder, gave a swooping whistle as her cloak flapped.

At that they came out into a great open Courtyard and she stopped, awe-struck. Four tall lime-washed buildings lined the square. She had heard about the famous door-pillars in pale sycamore wood that seemed to have captured the sunlight in its grain. Planted solidly in the Mother Earth they leapt towards the sky taking with them the sculptures that epitomised the dreams and ambitions of the Pretani and carrying them upwards to the ears of the Great Ones.

An imposing figure stood in one doorway, looking down his long thin nose at the lesser mortals scurrying about their business in the Courtyard. Even the breeze did not dare to tug at his flowing white robes.

"The Law-giver," said the young man. The Adviser's indifferent gaze passed over Tansen as he turned back into the Hall.

"One of Grannie Bea's gaggle of geese," thought Tansen. Would such a man listen to a mere pagan from the corn-stooks? She must force him to listen. Somehow.

Then she saw it! In the centre of the square, dominating everything from its wooden platform, a huge bronze bell gleaming in the sunlight. She drew in a breath of sheer delight. This was the famous Bell of Queen Caterin! At the hearth Grannie Bea had told stories of Caterin's courage, stories that had left fiery trails of stars shimmering in the darkness of Tansen's sleepy mind.

"Did Caterin's knees ever tremble like mine?" she thought. And at once raised her chin, trying to hold herself as straight and true as Grannie Bea's golden arrow.

This was the real Court, no childhood fantasy. The Advisers who ruled the land were men of great learning and wisdom. How could she face them and tell them they were falling down on the job? But Queen Pertan had the right and the power to do so.

"Which way to the Palace?"

The young man touched her arm to guide her north. At the sight of the King-House, the words of a bard-song flowed through her mind.

"Hall upon hall we built,

Riding the Citadel,
Roof-trees of oak we raised,
Walls harled with quartz.
So Bridei's King-Hall,
Rose as our tribute.
Red as blood in the sunset,
White as snow in the rain.
Great is his Palace,
Yet greater his glory.
As the Palace shall stand,
So his fame shall not fade."

History! It was all here! She was in a place where the poems came alive. She glanced incredulously at the folk passing by. Did they not feel it, this awe, this sense of time stretching back to those days of glory? She laid her palm on the quartz, feeling the rough vitality of stone, fired in the volcanic bosom of the Mother, cooled and hardened in the swell of the sea, white with a crystalline purity, veined with green and pink. She touched the marks where the masons had chiselled it into shape, proud to give their workmanship to honour a great King who kept their borders secure and their pits of land safe.

The two Guards at the doorway came smartly to attention. They lowered their spears in salute to the young noble. Not by a flicker of an eyelash did they betray their surprise at the bare-foot pagan in the rich cloak who was his companion.

He led her through Halls linked by passages. Applewood braziers burning in corners, beeswax lamps and candles in niches lit their way and scented the air. Polished chairs with shaped legs lined the walls. Barring their way were huge tables set with silver bowls. Tansen's eyes widened when she saw that some bowls had strange exotic blooms floating in them.

Her new lover smiled and slowed his pace to let her look. No, she would not let him see that she was impressed. Her bare feet hurried on over floor-boards that had defied polishing after a century of nailed boots had scored them.

A young Guard peered round a curtain, waved at her guide and disappeared. From another doorway came the clacking of shuttles and she saw the backs of women bending over the looms.

At last a Guard stepped forward and stopped them before a rich purple curtain, heavy with embroidery.

Harp music and the soft comfortable chatter of women came from inside.

In a sudden fit of shyness she turned to her lover to ask him to come with her. But he made a smiling gesture of farewell and left. At least there had been a promise in his eyes, if not on his lips.

She swallowed hard. But as she recited her credentials to the Guard, her voice grew stronger. Still the spear slanted across her path and the Guard's took in her bare feet and seemed to pierce through the enveloping cloak.

"And I claim the rights of kinship and hospitality," she ended proudly.

"Wait here," he grated and went beyond the curtain.

But it was not the Pretani way to wait to be invited into the Royal presence. The Queen, above all else, was a servant of her people. And Tansen's sense of guilt at having dallied at the river filled her with impatience. Throwing aside the curtain she entered the room.

The room was largest Tansen had ever seen and bathed in light from wide south-facing windows. At her entry stifled gasps came from a dozen women sewing at a large table. A young harpist near a brazier stopped on a jarring note. Two women playing a board game froze and their eyes flew to a woman who sat near a window, her head newly raised from a low tapestry frame, her needle poised. As the Guard turned Tansen dived under his outflung arm and the needle dropped.

"Queen Pertan! I come to you with a call for help! Pitcarlie's been raided! We've been wiped out! Only Grannie Bea and the bairns are left alive!"

There was a silence, as though her kinswoman had never heard of Pitcarlie, of raids by the Sea-Danes, of death by the swinging axe.

Tansen's voice broke as she told of torn flesh, the screams of the dying and the stench of smoke. When she stopped for breath the air crackled with the echo of her words. She stretched out her arms in appeal and looked into pale blank eyes. Brown hair banded in braids encircled a pale face. The brown robe was subtly embroidered. This could not be Pertan, this plain dowdy woman. One glance at the Guard with his hand ready on his sword told her that it was.

"Pitcarlie? Grannie Bea?" The Queen inclined her head towards the Guard. Tansen clasped her hands fervently as he recited her lineage. The Queen nodded.

"You poor child. How terrible. So near to our own Citadel, too. But why do you come to me?" she said to Tansen in a voice as calm and empty of feeling as a stagnant pool.

A moan escaped Tansen. She fell to her knees, seeking for comfort, hugging the Queen's knees in her anguish. And she wept, stung by memories of the soft caring arms of her dead mother.

"You are our kinswoman, the Mother of our Clan."

Gold thread and crystals scraped at her cheeks as the Queen's knees twitched to safety under the tapestry frame.

"But how can I help you?"

Tansen swallowed her impatience. How could she expect a well-protected Queen to understand the dangers that pagans faced in the countryside?

"But it should never have happened, Queen Pertan! I passed a host of unmanned forts on my way here. The army should be billeted there in force to protect us from sea-raiders!"

She captured one of the Queen's hands. It was ice-cold and withdrew swiftly to lie on Pertan's heart. Each time she moved she fell into another pose of studied elegance.

"Of course. But the King sees to all of that. Now calm yourself, child. You and Beatha must come to live here."

Tansen drew in a deep breath of frustration and with it the scent of meadowsweet that hovered round the Queen. It caught her throat and stopped the angry scream that threatened to erupt.

"Grannie Bea would never come here! You know that!"

A feeling of suffocation sent her springing to her feet and striding to the window. The air that filtered through the slats carried the faint tang of smiddy fires, smoking fat and sweating humanity. Familiar but stifling when they were not mingled with the sweet smells of earth and sea.

"I remember now," said the Queen. "Beatha. She chose to live close to the All-Mother. Very commendable of her, I'm sure. Then she must take her chance. But an old woman and a few bairns can't till the land."

"Oh, don't worry about them!" Tansen cried bitterly. "They'll find food and shelter well enough. No one starves in the homesteads around Pitcarlie. That wasn't what I came for!" "Oh, my dear, I know."

Amazed, suddenly hopeful, Tansen turned. The Queen had recovered her needle. It went in and out steadily as though she needed to cover a gaping hole in the Citadel wall by nightfall.

"I intended to send for you, my dear. It's time I found a place for you at Court."

Tansen felt her face growing hot. She had been so sure that the Queen would rise at once to take her to the King and his Council. She tried again.

"Don't you understand? The Clan Mothers need action!" Her fists were bunched in an agony of frustration.

The Guard moved swiftly in front of the Queen. The needle had frozen in mid-air again.

Tansen threw back her hair impatiently and scanned the faces intently watching this little scene. Their arching eyebrows and pursing lips gave her scant sympathy. In a corner three girls on stools, their hands stilled over a tumbled mass of coloured wools, followed Tansen with wondering eyes.

"I didn't come here to learn dainty manners!" Tansen exploded. "Can't you see? Unless the King acts quickly the Angles will grow more confident, the raids will get worse. I've been sent to warn the King and the Council!"

"You?"

"Grannie Bea sent me! You're the Chief Clan Mother! You must support me!"

The light eyes stared incredulously at her as though she had ordered the Queen to muck out a byre. The women burst into tinkling laughter and hid their mouths behind their hands.

Tansen's eyes searched the room wildly for inspiration to shake the apathy of the Queen.

The sun shining through the window-slats laid slanting shadows across tapestries that hung on every wall. The hangings billowed in the breeze giving them an illusion of movement. Ladies danced to pipes, they threw golden balls to one another and fed white doves, they rode to the hunt with silver trumpets sounding at their backs.

It seemed to Tansen then as though the very occupants of this room had been caught in a mesh of time, waiting to be stitched into a hanging picture. One last time, she thought, holding out her hands, smiling with all the sweetness she could muster.

"You're our Queen! Those who are suffering are your kin."

Oh, Bride, help me, she thought as she spoke. Where's the vitality that comes down through the Royal Blood? Where are the passions that fill a Celtic breast? Where is the zest for life, for poetry and colour and music, for loving and sharing and caring? Has it all been channelled into tapestries to decorate a wall?

"Oh no, you're wrong," said the Queen. "My kin live in Kent."

Rage boiled up inside Tansen. She had been right! The Royal Line had become weakened, diluted with foreign blood. Pertan's father, the last King, had been a Prince from Kent. There, they said, manners and passions alike were restrained and he had brought this refinement here to this Court. Where it had turned into complacency. Even Pertan's Pretani mother had been half-foreign. A new surge of pride thrilled through her at the thought of her own father, that great Caledonie Chieftain. Why couldn't Grannie Bea have sent her to her father's kin for help?

'Because the power lies at Dalgynch!'

The answer punched into her mind with a force that startled her. The powerful feeling that Grannie Bea was somehow here, watching, renewing her determination.

But it was another Queen that was needed now. A woman like Caterin who had braved the Courts of her enemies at Tara and Dun Add and the battlefields of Cul Drebene and Catreath. The blood of Caterin simmered in her veins. She would have to find a way to reach the King and Council for herself.

Then the stillness in the room vibrated to a low voice with a faint growl in it.

"Who is this woman?"

CHAPTER EIGHT

It was a lazy voice, indolent, assured, yet it came across with an intensity that sent a joyous hope surging through Tansen's heart.

"And why is she wearing that cloak?"

The woman stood framed in the doorway. Dark brown hair coiled like a cloud about a head that angled from a long white neck. Her face was shadowed by the doorposts. Yet Tansen felt a strange impact on her senses as though some suppressed passion emanated from her. This had to be the eldest Princess, Reatta. Surely this daughter of Caterin would sympathise with her. Perhaps together they could spur the Court into action?

No one had answered the Princess. It was as though the occupants of the room held their breath, waiting. A cloud must have passed over the sun. Or was it a shiver of fear that trembled through the room? Eagerly, Tansen stepped forward hoping to make a friend and ally.

Instead the Princess sent the door curtain swishing at her back. Moving swiftly past Tansen on the silent feet of a hunting cat, she went to her mother's side and stood, fingers interlaced, head turning back at a graceful angle to look at Tansen. The light from the window caught the coils of her hair and flooded them with red as dark as rubies.

Oh, Bride, Tansen thought dismally, she's just like her mother, trying to impress her audience. Yet it was not admiration she was seeking. Reatta's posing did not arise from vanity but from some mysterious purpose of her own.

The two women took measure of one another. Reatta's small neat features might be pleasant if she smiled. But they paled into insignificance as her eyes met Tansen's. Eyes as black as jet under well-marked pointed brows probed Tansen's defences. Then the disturbing gaze moved and fixed again on the cloak. Her next words drove all lucid thought from Tansen's mind.

"I do believe she's wearing Ean's cloak!"

The Queen made a slight movement of protest and recoiled as Reatta shot her a sharp glance.

"She must have stolen it! What would Ean have to do with the likes of her?"

Ean? Tansen stared, transfixed. Ean, short for Eanfrith! Eanfrith, the Prince of Bernicia, sent as an infant to the Pretani Court! Her golden lover was one of the hated Sea-Danes!

Her stomach lurched. It couldn't be true! She wanted to run from the jet eyes, to hide somewhere to be quietly sick. She bit her lip, struggling to keep calm, to hide her hurt and her shame. This woman must never know how much this news had devastated her! For Tansen began to sense that Reatta would enjoy using that knowledge to humiliate her.

Contempt burned behind the ink-gall eyes. With a swift movement that took Tansen by surprise Reatta snatched the hem of the cloak to thrust the embroidered pattern before the Queen. Tansen's bare thighs gleamed in the sunlight. Reatta's eyes opened wide and then narrowed on Tansen's face.

"And she's naked underneath!"

Smothered laughter sounded and was hushed. Tansen's humiliation erupted into a blinding anger. These two women cared nothing for the vital role they had inherited. They primped and posed and played their petty games. While her sister Maga with all her youthful promise lay twisted and dead. She twitched the cloak from the disdainful fingers and strode towards the Queen.

"Yes, I'm naked! The grand-daughter of Beatha of Pitcarlie stands before you in nothing but a borrowed cloak! Because our coast-line's wide open to raiders! How dare you sit there sewing pretty pictures when your people cry out for help?"

Reatta glared at the Queen, daring her to reply.

Queen Pertan turned a shoulder towards Tansen and snipped off a thread with silver scissors as precisely as if she would cut off all threats to her cosy world. She would hear only what she wanted to hear and ignore the rest, even this impertinence from a young kinswoman.

Clearly Reatta was the stronger character of the two. Her play-acting was for the benefit of the sniggering women. She held centre stage now and at last addressed Tansen directly.

"Answer me! How do you come to be wearing Ean's cloak?" Reatta's sleek arrogance brought Tansen's anger thundering in her veins.

"Ask him yourself!"

"Oh, I will." White pinpoints flashed in Reatta's eyes before they turned black and opaque again. "You see he belongs to me, Pagan."

Tansen gasped. So he had only been playing with her after all!

Reatta's small precise mouth tightened in a swift three-cornered smile, savouring her slight triumph. But the eyes remained black and hard.

A tide of utter desolation swept through Tansen. He had loved her and comforted her when she most needed it. She had given him her first love. Gladly. And it had been good. Now this wonderful feeling was swept away in a tide of revulsion. It had been a shock to discover he was an enemy. Now it was a greater shock to find that he was accepted here. And that she was the alien in her own land.

Reatta's eyes began to kindle as though some secret flame burned behind them. It took an effort of will for Tansen to tear her eyes away from the smouldering gaze.

"You're welcome to your Angle," Tansen said through tight white lips. "I've no further use for him."

Only by a twitch of an eyebrow could she tell that her dart had found its mark. It would rankle if Reatta had to take the pagan's leavings.

Oblivious to the emotions surging through the room, the Queen suddenly came to life.

"Now that you're here you will share in the education of the Princesses. That's until I decide upon your future. Verna!"

Somewhere at Tansen's back a servant moved softly.

"You'll serve the Princess Tansen. Tell the Steward to prepare a room and a place at the Banquet."

"Princess is it?" Sarcasm threaded through Reatta's voice. "One of our pagan cousins sent to have the soil cleaned out of her finger-nails?"

Tansen smiled into the black eyes on a level with her own.

"But one with the green eyes of Caterin," she taunted. And was rewarded by the wave of hatred that surged across the room at her.

In spite of her pain and humiliation, Tansen laughed, full-throated, in Reatta's face, before turning to the Queen.

"And what do I wear? The homespun grey of the poor relation?"

"Verna, find some of my daughters' dresses. And let me look her over before the Banquet. There are important guests tonight."

"And Verna!" Reatta's fingers snapped. "Have that cloak thoroughly cleaned and returned to the Prince."

"Oh no!" Tansen shot back. "I'm keeping it. As a momento!"

Reatta's eyes narrowed. Slowly, lazily, her lips curled at the corners. And the smile said that her enmity would be undying, that she would have patience, bide her time, and that one day she would have her revenge.

"Give her a good scrubbing, Verna." The cool voice followed Tansen to the door. "And if you give the pagan any of my gowns, I'll have you horse-whipped."

CHAPTER NINE

A room to herself! A wooden bed with legs on it! A table set with ivory brushes and combs and silver-topped bottles! And two hand-mirrors! Tansen held one up and looked at herself. Angry green eyes stared back at her. Her full red lips had set in a bitter line emphasising the lift of her determined chin. Her skin was tanned by the sun instead of snow-white and translucent like that of the Court ladies.

So this was the simple-minded pagan who had let an Angle bewitch her with his boyish good looks! While his men, laughing and jeering in the bushes, waited till their leader had satisfied his lust! Oh Moon Maiden, what a stupid fool she had been! Foreign horsemen! She should have guessed!

But not innocent now. Not any more! She would gouge that memory from her mind ruthlessly. For she had set herself to fight the lethargy at Court. The safety and protection of the homestead circle had been shattered. This room was her home now. She had no other. The Sea-Danes had seen to that!

She scanned the unfamiliar room. Who could sleep on top of a bed with legs? She would roll off in the middle of the night! Tansen swept the eiderdown mattress and fine wool blankets to the floor.

The servant brushed through the door-curtain and laid an armful of robes and shifts on a chest.

"Are there no plain dresses?" Impatiently Tansen threw aside the embroidered linens and silks. A glowing buttercup yellow caught her eye. "Fine! The King ought to notice me in this."

She waved away Verna's attempts to help and began dressing.

"It's all right. I don't need a servant."

Verna gave a quick nervous glance at the door and Tansen knew at once that she was afraid. And probably ill-treated. Tansen laid her hands gently on Verna's anxious shoulders and looked into her poor pock-marked face. She was old enough to be Tansen's mother. Her pale sad eyes showed that she had known sorrow yet it seemed to have burned through her, leaving her empty.

"But, Verna, by the tears of the Merciful Ones, I do need a friend."

With lowered eyes, Verna twisted her thin frame away from Tansen's kindly touch.

"You don't trust me. Well, I don't blame you. I can't find it in my heart to trust anyone in this place either. But I'll win you as a friend, Verna, sooner or later."

Without speaking Verna brought forward an oaken box banded in silver. She opened it to reveal rows of silver chains and earrings, strings of agates, pearls, carnelians, and garnets. Tansen shook her head.

"Oh no! I'm forced to wear their cast-off clothes but I won't wear their old jewellery."

The purple amethyst in a silver brooch that her father had given her was ornament enough. Oh, father! What did Chief Oengus think now of a daughter who had made love with an Angle from Daneland? With the blood of his kinsmen fresh on her hands she had guided him inside her body with gladness. Sick with shame she sank on a stool and buried her face in her hands.

A comb gliding through her hair, brought memories rushing back. How Ean had lifted the weight of her damp tresses in both hands to kiss the arc of her neck. And the searing heat of his mouth as it trailed kisses across her skin. And how she must forget him! Forget that he was her first love! Forget he had brought her to know ecstacy! Her fists bunched in her lap in an excess of agony.

Yet here he was not an enemy. Reatta must have known him all her life. But none of them had seen the murderous swing of a Danish axe! Eanfrith carried the tainted blood of the golden-haired giants in his veins. In spite of his comely face, underneath he was as coarse and crooked as the rest of them. Viciousness was bred in their bones as hatred of them was bred in hers.

Let Reatta have him then! Reatta with her elfin beauty and dainty figure. Forget the desolate days and cold-hearted nights that loomed ahead. There would be other men. Red-blooded Chieftains like her father. Strangers that wore periwinkle blue plumes.

The tears she had been holding back for so long flowed unchecked over her cheeks. Gentle hands caressed her temples until her weeping became calmer. "Kinship, friendship, love," she said, her voice breaking. "I never spoke these words before. The bonds were there under the surface of our living. I thought it would be the same here. yet when the Queen used the words they were like pretty bubbles in the air, that float and burst."

She had had three nasty sharp shocks before that truth had sunk in. Her love for Eanfrith had turned to revulsion. The bond of kinship meant nothing to Pertan. Friendship with Reatta was impossible. An instant enmity had flared between them. Was Reatta jealous because Tansen had been with Eanfrith? Or was Tansen's Royal Ancestry, shining through her green eyes, a greater threat?

One thing she would gamble on. Reatta may look like a wanton sprite but this Princess must be as virginal as the fresh green of her robe. For she had to marry a foreigner who prized chastity in their women above all else. Whereas Tansen was free to love where she chose. Tansen's derisive chuckle caught on a sob.

Verna's fingers, braiding her hair, were flying as fast as Tansen's racing thoughts.

"What's Reatta really like?"

The answer came in a whisper above Tansen's ear.

"She plots."

Tansen caught the warning. Verna was afraid to speak of Reatta in case she was overheard. Yet Verna had managed to convey the fact that Reatta was malicious and ambitious. There had been an element of fear among those in the Queen's room, too. So, Reatta was dangerous. Not just to Tansen and those around her. But when she became Queen, the land and the fiercely proud pagans who worked it would also be in peril. Tansen clasped her hands tightly. She must find out what lay behind those black compelling eyes. The scorn Tansen felt for these two Royal women spilled over into a fierce determination.

She looked again at her reflection. The young carefree girl snug in the safety of the hearth-circle was gone.

Faint bluish shadows tinged the skin under her eyes. There was a sharper edge to the curve of her cheek. Two days! Had it only been two days?

Rising she strode round the room, her hands on her temples, crying, "Oh why does it hurt so much? Why does it hurt so much?"

She cradled her grief to her breast, for the loss of her kin and the false lover who had betrayed her. Blindly she stumbled to the window and searched the sky.

"Why did it happen? Why me?" A wild anger possessed her and she beat at the walls with her clenched fists. Sobbing she leaned her head on the cool stone wall.

She was alone now. A woman who must make her own decisions. Come what may she would battle on. There was nothing else to do, was there?

he cast about in her mind for some way to shock these powerful people in Dalgynch out of their self-absorption. Something that Grannie Bea would hear about and approve. Something dramatic that would arouse the Court and live in their memories. Something that would take the bitter taste of defeat from her tongue.

CHAPTER TEN

"Verna," Tansen's swift turn took Verna by surprise. "Take me to the King."

Verna drew back, her mouth opening in a gasp of horror.

"I can't do that, Princess! You've to wait for a summons."

"Oh, rubbish! The Pretani King must listen to his people. That's the Law."

"Not in these times, Princess."

"Then I'll find his quarters by myself!"

At that moment the Bell in the Courtyard boomed out with a deep mellow note. A look of relief spread over Verna's face.

"It's too late, Princess! That's Caterin's Bell."

"I heard it. What's happening?"

"It's the signal to gather in the Banqueting Hall."

"What!" Tansen stared at her in disbelief. "But that Bell was only to be used in time of danger! She erected it after the Boar Clan tried to take over the Capital!"

Now Tansen knew exactly what she must do. Her fiery Celtic nature exploded into action. Lifting her skirts she sped along the corridor. Her anger sent her storming past the room where the Queen waited, leaping down the stairs and out into the Courtyard. She slipped through the crowd making their way past the Bell, bronzed now by the low-lying sun. Fitting her feet in the spirals of the wooden platform she climbed swiftly.

At the top a huge mallet hung from a peg. Swinging it high above her head she brought it round in an arc to crash against the Bell. Her head almost burst with the reverberations she had let loose.

Below in the Courtyard the throng stilled and a sea of faces turned upwards. Tanned faces of warriors and sea-lords, framed by lime-stiffened hair. Pale thin faces of officials, heads balding and wispy. White-skinned faces of women, hair hidden under jewels. Grinning faces of servants.

"Oh, Bride, I've really done it now!" she whispered.

Shrill, questioning, gruff and scornful, the voices and laughter rose from below. She swung again and sent another resounding call shivering on the air. And as it died away her bitterness exploded into words.

"Did you hear it, you fine folk? Did you hear the warning of noble Caterin's Bell?"

The echoes of her own voice startled her. Then the faces below drew her eyes like water under a bridge. She swept her gaze over them, drawing their attention, her mind filled with condemnation.

"Then hear me! Two days past, raiders fell on my homestead. We had no bell to sound the warning! Angles from the south came! And they slaughtered the sons and daughters of Pitcarlie."

Her voice came harshly, strident with anger and determination.

"The bairns of Pitcarlie are keening this night for their mothers! Weeping over desolate hearths! Will you hear them, Clan Brothers, as you feast in your Hall? Will you hear them, Clan Mothers, as you chatter and laugh, surrounded by your well-armed Guards?"

They reeled under the accusation in her voice. Like fish caught in Baran's net they twisted and turned below her, with cold eyes and gaping mouths. Their hands fluttered like pale fins, smoothing hair, patting gems.

"I ring Caterin's Bell as she meant it to be rung! As a warning! The raiders are coming! The raiders from the sea! The Sea-Danes!"

A figure came from the Palace entrance. The massive silver chain encircling his equally massive waist proclaimed him King. When he was younger and leaner he must have had a fine proud bearing. Now his rich attire strained over flabby unused muscles. Here was the source of the lethargy that had fallen on the Capital. This fat lump of lard! Tansen directed all her venom at him, knowing that only high-sounding words would catch his attention.

"King Garnard, I accuse you! You have ignored the plight of the pagans, unprotected on the coast. You dally while raiders jump yelling from longboats. More and still more. Till one day they'll be hurling themselves at your gates. And will you ring the Bell then? And what will it signify? More feasting?"

The King stared aloft for an instant before jerking a nonchalant hand at a Guard. His utter rejection of her brought her frustration to fever-pitch. Years of listening to bards brought words rolling from her lips.

"The Angles are coming! You can be sure! Caterin raised this Bell to be a clarion call! How dare you use it as a supper-gong?"

The heads below quivered and reared and turned like waves at the meeting-place of two currents in a river. At the King's back the Queen had emerged, a withered brown rose in the centre of a posy of Princesses. Helmeted Guards began to make their way towards her, cleaving the crowd like ships through the billows. She took a deep breath to still her rising panic. Her eyes streaked again towards the King.

"I call upon King and Council to restore the ancient rights of the pagan Clan Mothers! The right of protection! The right to elect a new King! I ring Caterin's Bell as a challenge to you, Garnard, King of the Pretani, to you,

Pertan, Chief of the Clan Mothers, and to you, Council of Elders, Brothers of the Clan Mothers!"

The wooden tower shivered as a Guard set his foot on the lowest rung and began to climb. She swung the mallet. And again the Bell answered, peeling out over the palisade and drawing Tansen's gaze with it.

For an instant she saw the swathe of sea beyond. From her high vantage point it felt as though the world was only waiting for her to come and conquer it. If she stretched her arms she could soar outwards and upwards like an eagle. And some day, she promised herself, she would.

Words spilled into her mind. She was full of confidence now and a sort of euphoria.

"And I warn you further, Council and Courtiers alike!" Her voice had taken on a deeper note. "Unless you act now, the Clan Mothers will rise against you. They'll pour from their homesteads with carving knives and sickles! Just as the women of Pitcarlie did two days back! And died under Danish axes! This is the word I bring from Beatha of Pitcarlie!"

A shimmer of sound seemed to ring through the Bell and sigh with joy through Tansen's spirit. And she knew it was the voice of the Caterin, praising her, urging her on. She threw up her arms to the sky, knowing full well she was going to shock her audience to the core.

"Oh, Caterin, make them understand!" she cried aloud. "Oh, Bride, open their eyes! Oh, Dagda, open their minds!"

A great groan went up from the crowd. It was taboo to speak the names of the Splendid Ones. Except in the most dire torment. Tansen shook her raised fists at them, supremely confident that Bride and the Compassionate Ones would understand her anguish and her need.

A helmet appeared over the parapet. In a moment he was towering over her, leaning to grip her arm, blowing through a tight thin-lipped mouth-hole.

"Give her twenty lashes and send her home!" the King bellowed. A gasp of horror rose to Tansen's ears. Twenty lashes from the iron spiked rope was certain death.

"Don't dare touch me!" she hissed at the Guard, ready to swing the mallet at his head. "That mountain of fat won't be King for much longer!"

His cruel eyes narrowed.

"Stop!" The voice seemed to resound from the sky. It echoed from building to building like a chord struck on a deep-toned harp.

CHAPTER ELEVEN

The Guard turned grunting and Tansen saw the man who had spoken. Standing at a corner of the Square was the tallest man she had ever seen. Long silver hair rippling as sweetly as any woman's, mingling with a beard that flowed like a waterfall over his chest. A noble jutting nose pointed towards the King. Around him, like petals round a calyx, blossomed the orange robes of student Drui.

"Hark!" Again he spoke and the Bronze Bell echoed him. "This is a daughter of Beatha. She is a Princess of the Blood Royal."

It was Marten, clothed in the majesty and magic of his office, the great Arch-Drui, greater even than the King. And he must have heard everything. Tansen's breath came in shallow gasps. Her hands flew to her throat, half in awe, half in relief.

The Guard cringed as though Drui fire had seared his body. Garnard's face took on a purple tinge. His fingers plucked at the gold tassel on his collar as he struggled with his loss of pride. Then he turned in fury on the Captain of the Guard.

"Why was I not told when this woman arrived?" he blustered. "I'll have someone's head for this!"

The Captain's face reddened as he spoke in the King's ear. Tansen longed to hear what he said. That she had come naked and unfit for the King's presence? Or that they had under-estimated her importance? Or that the Queen had not bothered to inform him? Garnard, irritated, hoisted his fur-trimmed collar on his shoulders. Ungraciously he snapped his fingers.

"Make a place for the woman at my Table."

As he turned to Pertan Tansen saw him shoot a question at her. She could almost read his lips.

"Who is this woman they call Beatha?" The Queen smiled blandly, not altogether displeased at his public humiliation. The crowd parted leaving a passage-way and the Royal Family moved in slow measured procession towards the Banqueting Hall.

If she had hoped to climb down with dignity, the breeze had other ideas and gave the young Drui waiting below an enjoyable eyeful of firm bare legs and maybe more.

"I suppose Verna did the best she could with that haystack of hair." The Princess Reatta paused in passing, tossing a sleek head braided with pink Tay pearls and tiny gold balls that tinkled.

"May the Gracious Ones send her the gift of kindliness before she becomes Queen," hissed the Drui under his breath.

Again the crowd parted, leaving a pathway straight to the waiting Arch-Drui. Inquisitive eyes, gloating faces, nudging elbows, here and there a look of pity, the folk melted away as Tansen went to meet Marten.

Close to, he was immensely tall. His blue eyes pierced deeply into hers until she felt that her whole spirit was laid bare before him. She humbled herself before him, bending to touch the hem of his robe. A surge of power crackled at her finger-tips.

"You have come at last, my daughter. Welcome."

Despite the kindliness that mellowed his stern voice she stayed down-bent.

"Once I knew you were on your way I came from my grove to greet you."

So Grannie Bea had sent her mind spinning over the landscape to Dunino. Or had he seen her riding the garron in the flames or in the fall of the bones? Then he could have seen the raiders creeping inland to Pitcarlie. She straightened and the awful question that she should not ask came spilling out.

"Why did you let it happen? Why did you not forewarn Grannie Bea?"

The orange robes trembled and hissed around her at such impertinence. The Arch-Drui stamped his staff on the ground to silence them.

"Beatha was right. You have a lot to learn. And as the corn grows tall in the sun so your growing-time has come."

It could be Grannie Bea speaking. And she asked again, full of resentment.

"Where were the Guardian Ones when we needed help?"

Marten placed a hand on each of her shoulders so that she was impaled by his gaze. She gazed back, burning with anguish and bitterness.

"Each one of us chooses the path we must take and the lesson we need to learn before we come to this earthly plane. So do not blame the Gods for the hardships that come your way."

"We didn't choose to be in the path of the raiders," she cried. She was being deliberately stubborn, needing to hurt as she herself was hurting.

"If all experience was benign how could we learn? How could our eternal spirits grow and expand? It is how you overcome your hardships, how you bear your suffering that matters in the end."

"How can you overcome a hardship if you're dead? What sort of lesson was it for Maga, to die of rape? She was only a child."

The blaze of his eyes and the sudden fierce grip of his hands frightened her. Until she sensed that the man in him had flared with an anger and compapssion that matched her own. And when he spoke again she listened, knowing that he spoke from a caring heart.

"Maga's test is over for now. She is resting with her mother. You are the one left with the burden of grieving."

Her lip trembled and her eyes glazed with tears but she threw up her head and would not let them flow. Her shoulders throbbed with the power that flowed from his hands. It was a healing power that billowed through him, straight from the Great Ones. And suddenly the Great Ones were not remote and implacable. For they were sending power through human hands whose touch was tender and compassionate. And she gave a little sigh as her spirit calmed and her mind quietened.

Now he laid a friendly hand on her neck and guided her towards the Banqueting Hall. And she no longer felt like a stranger.

"Oh, Arch-Drui," she said. "Why have things come to such a pass in our land? What can a girl like me do to make the Court understand? Only you with your influence can rouse them to action."

He measured three steps before he answered.

"Oh, I have the power, child. Be sure of that." The white eyebrows met sternly above his eyes. "And I didn't need a yellow-hammer pecking at the Bell to tell me that the Clan Mothers are sharpening their knives."

Suddenly Tansen felt foolish. She was a rough-mannered pagan, after all. This was not a village hearth where impassioned words could win an argument. This was the Court. Everyone knew that Courts were a cauldron of plots and subterfuges. All she had done was to shame the King before his Court. How could she have thought that showing up the King's weakness would solve anything?

She had forgotten that the Arch-Drui could read thoughts.

"You are right. It was not wise to force me into a confrontation with the King in front of the people." Marten's voice had become harder. "He's uneasy enough. His own lands in Merioneth, have been devastated by King Cadwallon. They are barren of grain and fowl. The people are starving. If he is forced to abdicate no other ruler will accept his blunted sword."

"He'll find somewhere to place his fat bottom. He's been a King. They stick together. It's the pagans who are left to suffer? Why don't the Guardians tell us what to do?"

"They do, if they are asked. If you sit in silence you can hear the still small voice within you. But often you do not like the answer. Or you think it is your imagination. And remember, everyone has free-will. That is the Natural Law. The Guardians may advise from their wider knowledge but people will always choose their own paths to follow."

She thought she understood. He was telling her that folk make their own decisions and must live with the results. A spark of rebellion flared inside her and died. He was right. Every human being needed freedom to choose. It would be unnatural if it was any other way.

"You are but a child yet, daughter of Beatha," said Marten. "Go and make your choices freely. Take your rightful place in the Hall. You have fulfilled your promise to Beatha. But have no doubt, some day when you are ready the Gods will call upon you to follow your destiny. And even then, you will have the right to choose."

She grasped at his words and wanted to ask more. But it was as though a veil had fallen across his face and she knew she was forbidden to question him. Then suddenly, the white beard parted and lips that were both sensitive and firm, broke into a smile.

"No harm will come to you in this Court. From now on you are under my protection."

With a finger he tilted her chin to scan her face and she thought she glimpsed a twinkle in his eye.

"Beatha always was a survivor. So are you, my child."

Whenever Grannie Bea had spoken of Marten her mouth had always curled in a secret smile. Now Tansen wondered. Had they had been close in the past? Did they have private memories to share.

At a side-door to the Hall the Druad withdrew and went for their own simple repast.

Her despair and guilt had lightened. She had a powerful friend in Marten. Now she could face these strangers in the Hall. And she would study them till she knew their strengths and weaknesses and could turn them to her own use. She would listen and learn, how to persuade, how to manipulate, how to gain power. For her choice had been made for her by Marten, whether he intended it or not. 'This woman is a Princess of the Royal Blood' he had announced before the whole Court. She felt young and vital again, eager for life. And very, very hungry.

CHAPTER TWELVE

A mist of yellow light enveloped her as she paused on the threshold of the Banqueting Hall. Light from lamps hung from metal branches suspended from a roof-tree so high it was hidden by a haze of smoke from the hearth-fire. Rays of light stung her eyes, shafting off swords aslant on walls and awash with rubies and amethysts, glancing off gilded shields enamelled in reds and greens and blues, shooting off golden bows and arrows alight with pearls and garnets. Men, arguing, back-thumping, elbowed to their places. Women streamed in like bees homing in on a flower-meadow.

A woman, sighting Tansen, stifled a squawk of surprised laughter. The King glanced up and glowered, jowls as heavy as those of a hunting-hound quivered. He snorted and a hush like an indrawn breath fell on the Hall.

Here was that insolent pagan chit at last. Tripping in with her head in the air. In a cast-off robe of the Queen's too. A shade too tight, wasn't it? And somebody should have tamed that tempestuous hair! Look at the arrogant jut of her chin! And the jaunty way she swept towards the Royal Dias. Was she going to harangue the King again? And how had she squirmed her way under the protective cloak of Marten? Still light-headed from his last trance, you could only suppose.

A bench scraped as someone stood on it for a better view of the rage that mottled the King's face. A sly chuckle erupted from a shadowy corner at the blaze of venom that flashed in Reatta's eyes.

So Reatta's nose was out of joint. There was a promise of an enjoyable clash of tempers here. But the dark one would win. The Princess wouldn't see a pagan in her way. And she had all sorts of unhealthy tricks up her brocaded sleeve. Mind you, there had been something brave about the way the pagan strode up the length of the hearth-fire. And her words had had a touch of the bard about them. Here and there an eye winked, an elbow nudged.

Tansen caught the glint of a yellow sapphire as the King's fingers drummed in irritation on the High Table. Her gaze narrowed in contempt on the Advisers, fat and sleek and prosperous in their linen and calfskin and fur tippets. At the gold torques on their upper arms, badges of office, intended to bind them by oath to carry out the wishes of the People.

There was no seat for her at the High Board. She snapped her fingers. An upturned barrel was swiftly rolled in beside the smallest Princess who sniffed and tilted her nose. Tansen arranged her skirts and sat. She had already learned that she would have to compete for attention. She had no jewels or fine clothes. But she had courage and wit.

"Now what happens?" she asked brightly and turned a wide smile on the world at large.

A trumpet sounded.

"Dale, son of Maddern, son of Neithon, Prince of the Britons of Strathclyde," sang the announcement.

A tall long-limbed youth strode forward to stand at the far end of the table. Dark hair, wet and freshly combed capped his head as smooth as polished oak. A clean-cut scar, not yet healed, ran from his temple to his wide square jaw, that jutted as if expecting a blow. He held his lean body awkwardly, with an anxious intensity. Yet the wide pleasing face held an expression of honest goodwill. And the strange yellow eyes, that he fixed on Gartnait glowed like lanterns. He held his head-piece as if afraid to set it down in case it vanished. And from its crown curled a periwinkle blue plume.

It was shock at seeing the plume again that trembled through her body, Tansen decided, not the man. Although he seemed ill-at-ease in this courtly company, there was an indefinable aura of young kingship surrounding him.

"I bring greetings from my father, King of Strathclyde, to Garnard, Overlord of Alba," he barked in a rough soldier's voice and jerked a bow.

It seemed to Tansen that the King was barely listening. A full serving platter had been placed before him. For a moment he hovered over it, savouring the aroma, eager to choose the finest portions of fowl to put on his guest's plate. Then he paused, fingers poised, and glanced slyly down the table.

"Yet didn't I hear that your father was no longer King of Strathclyde? When Morfael was thrown out of Traprain by Edwin, he and that rabble of Lothian kings went west. And didn't they combine forces for once to oust your father from his Capital? Now, I believe, they're stabbing one another in the back as merrily as before on your Dun Barton rock. All that just when you were growing into your first coat of mail, too."

The Prince's open forthright face did not change but his yellow eyes muddied to a sludge brown.

"It's true I'm landless. And that's why I'm here. To offer my sword and service to the Pretani." And he clamped his mouth shut as though it might betray a certain vulnerability in the youthful swell of his lower lip.

The King sucked gravy from his fingers.

"So you want to help me chase Dal Riatans from our border, do you?"

"I'd rather clear the Lothians of Edwin's Earls. Then I might regain my Kingship in Strathclyde."

"But your father Maddern is dead, isn't he? And you bring no trained band of men with you?"

"I offer my skills as a warrior. Test me and I'll prove my worth."

Absently the King wiped saliva from his chin with his hand, looking with obvious disfavour at the simple peasant face and awkward stance of the lad.

"Ah well," he said vaguely. "Here's some fine breast of grouse for you, Dale of Strathclyde. You look as though you could do with some fattening."

Tansen tucked her skirts under her bottom before her thighs became corrugated and wondered how Maddern had been killed and where his bodyguard were now and where Dale had been trained. And why the King had not asked him these questions.

She decided that the King was afraid to probe too deeply. For this fine British Prince looked a likely candidate for the Kingship. He might be dispossessed and have no army at his back, yet his roots were deep in the soil of Alba. And lucky Reatta. Despite his immaturity, those eyes would shine warmth into any woman's heart, she was sure. Yet what ambitions lurked behind the shining simplicity of his expression.

The ritual of hospitality was not over yet. The King cocked his head down to the place of honour beside Tansen at the other end of the table. A young chieftain, lean and weather-beaten, hair as bright as a sliced carrot, came with a long swinging step to stand at her side.

"Liath, High Chief of the Caledonie, son of ..." sang the Herald.

"Hold your peace, man! They all know my antecedents. Let the King get to his supper." One sprouting red eyebrow slewed upwards and a blue eye challenged the King.

A sudden hush in the Hall. Above the royal neck-ring, a roll of fat bulged. The King wheezed and gasped and bellowed. A pot-boy ducked from an explosion of froth and gravy. The King clapped his hands. Thanks be, he was laughing. The talk flowed again as the honour-platter was handed down the table.

"So you're the lass from Pitcarlie." Liath's long plaid-covered limbs folded in on themselves as he hunched over his platter. "By the Great Wings of the Golden Eagle, you rang a fine clarion on Caterin's Bell!"

His eyes slid in appreciation to where her robe deepened and swelled at her breasts and nipped her waist.

"It'll take more than you or me to kick Garnard's fat haunches into action." White teeth snapped a chunk of meat off his dagger point. "There's not a man in this Court worth a docken. Yet watch them. They're looking down their nostrils at the pair of us like cows with a pain in the belly."

Tansen liked his boldness.

"You live in Caledon. Did you know my father, Oengus?"

"Hey! My sister's husband's brother! King Gussie of the Fiery Thatch." Strong wiry eyebrows danced across his weather-beaten brow. "A grand man, that! His mouth would have filled with praises at the sight of his daughter this night."

The ruddy skin of his cheeks crinkled.

"Aye, you're Gussie's lass all right with that wild, wonderful hair and your face alight with that same eager look of his." Liath's grin was blatantly sensual. "If you've the same hot quick blood romping through your veins, only Liath of Caledon can set it alight."

Tansen grinned back. At his fine words her spirits brightened. Once she had dreamed of riding off with a man like this into his mountains with the liquid light flowing over their mantle of snow.

He leant nearer, his warm breath fanning her cheek.

"Come back with me to my mountain fastness. Where the vigour of men flourishes, the glory of forests is unspoiled and the mountains are fair from crest to ground." His eyes gleamed with a certain malicious merriment. "Where we play naked with a curly stick and a hole in the ground for a goal and the head of a Scot for a ball."

"Where the rough wind spreads my hair across the heather, and I dip my fingers in a snow-chilled stream and a mad ardour comes upon me to race horses." And her eyes sparkled with the fun of trading phrases she had heard her father recite. "Go with you and live on the border with the Dal Riatans? Not me!"

Liath laughed down at her. And every man in the Hall envied him.

"Border, you say? There's no border nowadays." His horny fist crashed on the table. "It took a man like Bridei to plant his heels on the tops of the mountains and shout, 'This far and no further, you Scottie scavengers'."

His grin challenged her. His voice became soft and seductive.

"You and I could make the mountains ring with joy this cuckoo-tide, daughter of King Gussie."

As course followed course and quip followed quip she was sorely tempted. He was like a thin sword blade that rang with vibrancy. When their plates had been removed he laid his hand on top of hers.

"What do you say? Will you sail down Loch Linnhe with me in a bracken-filled boat and set fire to Dun Ollie?"

"When I hear that you've given over sweet promises for sweeter action, I'd like that fine," she said. "Folk would rather follow you than Garnard.

You could make us strong again. Then I'd ride with you to the home of the Angles and play hurley with their heads."

His long limbs unfolded as he rose and looked solemnly down on her.

"Their hair's too long for a hurley ball." He shook his head sadly and left.

Smiling she watched him go. He would never seriously think of fighting Angles when he had his own private feud with the Scots to keep going.

Turning she found herself eyeing an unusual pattern on the hem of a purple tunic.

"What flame burns in your heart, then?" she asked, lightly, raising her eyes to meet Dale's gaze. And was sorry she had teased. For the innocuous facade was rent for an instant to reveal the vulnerability of a boy who believed passionately and deeply in the rules he lived by.

Then he was a man again. Their eyes met and held in a sort of secret intimacy and for a long moment she felt bathed in warmth.

"The flame of freedom!" he barked.

The stiff-necked phrase hung between them in the air, insubstantial, and fraught with too many different interpretations.

"Freedom's too big a word in every sense," she said quietly. "It touches too many fearful places in my heart."

Her answer seemed to fill Dale with something akin to embarrassment for his chin jutted more fiercely and took on a red glow.

He held out his horn to be refilled. Then he smiled, a long slow smile that was as wide and square as his jaw. And he took hold of the word and faced it squarely.

"But freedom's something you hold dear," he said. "I heard your warcry from the Bell-Tower." His approval kindled a glow in Tansen.

"I'm a daughter of Caterin." To those who knew their history, that explained it all.

"This land needs another Caterin." That name on his lips gave her a sense of common belief and purpose which was strange because he was a Briton.

"As your father-land needs a strong King."

She sounded as pompous as he did. But a strange blankness was gripping her mind. And those compelling eyes were reaching down into her spirit where some well-spring of emotion had begun to bubble gently.

"But this is my mother-land. And it's still free."

Before she could ask him what he meant he bowed stiffly from the waist and stalked off towards the King. Her mind kicked back into action. If his mother had been a Pretani he would have announced her name and clan and claimed kinship. He was talking in riddles. Maybe he really was as stupid as he looked.

Throughout the Hall speculation about the jumped-up royal chit had palled with the advent of these two well-set-up young men. Were they candidates for the Kingship? The redhead had a pawky wit but would his sword be as sharp. And the Briton with the incredible eyes? A bit raw round the edges, perhaps. But not too fond of his food. Funny how they'd both had a word with the pagan. But not loud enough for straining ears to catch a tasty bit of gossip.

Tansen watched Dale speak to the King. Those mild looks must be deceptive. She could sense a quality of tough-minded ambition in him. That could spell security to a Kingdom. And strength to a woman. Yet why was he alone without a retinue and still claiming to be a Prince? She smiled grimly. Those disturbing eyes were dangerous. The strange feelings they had aroused in her were a warning not to trust him.

The small Princess beside Tansen dipped her fingers in a bowl of water and called for a cloth. So that was what the bowl was for. She was nothing but a country cousin after all. And a giddy light-headed one at that. Casting sheep's eyes at every good-looking gallant that came her way. A silly young girl perched on a barrel trying to look royal. And indifferent. And wishing she had a cushion.

Harebell-blue eyes sparkled at her from a table near the hearth. Suddenly there was no one else in the Hall but Ean. Her limbs turned to jelly and flooded with delight.

His mouth teased a sliver of venison from the bone. Those lips had rained sweet kisses on all the soft places of her body. She squirmed to quell the surge of desire.

Long ago her mother had sung a lullaby about a maiden who lived in a tower hidden among ivy and roses. How every day she watched a golden huntsman on a cream-white mare, sporting with his gos-hawk. How the maiden had lured the hawk with rain-washed meat, sending her back with a string of pearls tied to her jesses. How the young man had come riding and carried the maiden off.

And she had gone to sleep dreaming that some day she would know the love of a golden huntsman and lie in the soft hollows in the twilight with him. Except that her golden huntsman had been born an Angle.

Another swift glance. Oh Moon Maiden, send her strength. He was blatantly wooing her with his eyes over the rim of his drinking-horn. Why this pull at her heart when she knew that Angles were roaring giants, scarred and uncouth, vicious and cruel? Yet here was Ean, not much older than herself and not much taller, so comely and courtly and with every thought openly expressed in his vivid face.

The tip of his tongue slid round his lips. She remembered how that mouth tasted, like herb-flavoured wine. Her need grew and swelled inside her until she could hardly bear it.

When the King sat back, belching, throwing a bone to the Queen's lapdog, it was the signal for the cup-bearers to run harder and the bards to strike up.

A man began weaving his way towards her and he was neither young nor gallant. He was big and muscled and came steadily, his mean tight mouth pursed, his rugged face alight with a sort of joy.

He lurched against the edge of the table and leaned over her, blocking out the light, breathing ale fumes at her.

"Who d'you think you are? You think you c'n go scot free after insulting the King. But you'll pay for it. You an' that mucken Drui." The Guard on the Bell Tower, off-duty now, with enough ale in him to dowse his fear of Marten's magic. At least someone was loyal to Garnard.

He lifted a beaker of red wine and flung it full in her face. Shocked she dabbed her stinging eyes and cleared them in time to see Eanfrith pull the man round by his shoulder and smash a massive blow into his stomach. And another to his face. The Guard shook him off like a fly and lumbered towards him head down. Eanfrith was nimble, athletic and sober. His blows were fast but light and the man rode them easily and came back with ham-fists and knees that rocked Eanfrith back sagging against a pillar. Only now that it was turning ugly did the grinning King lift a finger. And when the drunken Guard had been hauled away, she found that Ean had disappeared also.

Tansen sat still, staring down at the deepening stains on the Queen's yellow robe and a curious feeling grew inside her. Eanfrith, the Angle, had been the only one to rush to defend her. She could have had a good go at the Guard herself. Elbows and knees in tender places. But Ean, half the weight of the man, had waded in, expecting to end bloodied and beaten on the floor. That had a sweet gallantry about it.

Someone slipped into Liath's seat and her senses were filled with an awareness of Eanfrith.

CHAPTER THIRTEEN

Tansen turned a composed face to meet the harebell-blue eyes.

"So you're a Spear-Dane! A bloodthirsty savage!" she accused him.

Even yet she wanted to wound him with words, to wipe the glitter of innocent youth from his face. For being an Angle. For being comely.

"And you're a Picti. A paint-daubed barbarian!" he countered amused. "It depends which side you're on."

"If I'd known I'd have crawled to the Citadel on my bare knees."

"If I'd known you were going to miscall my Host-King from the Bell Tower I'd have let you." Ean's laugh sobered at the fury in her eyes.

"Your people slaughtered my kin!"

"Come now. I've lived here all my life. I'm more Celt than Angle, believe me."

A lean-shanked running-hound with a garnet-studded collar pleaded his master's cause with big brown eyes and a wet tongue on her hand. She pushed him aside and whisked her hand away from Eanfrith's grasp.

"Oh, fair scented flower of the blushing fruit, unless I get a gentle word you'll be my destruction."

The flippant bardic words rasped against the background of her sorrow. He was worse than Liath. For he meant it.

"And what happens if Reatta takes a fancy to you? And wants you for the next King? You'll hang me on the wall among your cloaks to use when the wind changes?"

Ean brushed her words aside lightly.

"A Kingship? Mind you, I'd be tempted. What else can I do? Banished here, I've no rank, no land. I can only give my allegiance at the Court where I was raised."

"So if you've to choose between the Kingship and me, I might as well retire and grow silverweed."

"Don't worry. I'm not the great leader the Council want! I couldn't lead in the field. No experience. And less knowledge of strategy. They'll choose the lamp-eyed Briton, if anyone."

Yet there was a wistfulness in his voice that disturbed her.

"What if there's a bright hope in Reatta's mind? What if there's Danish gold in the pouches of the Council?"

Ean shook his curly-crested head and whispered.

"Oh, maid of the splendid white-flanked body, come with me. Let my arm make a pillow for your head." The harebell eyes had grown hot and bright.

"Fine Celtic phrases can't hide the Danish twist in your tongue."

A boy with a tuneful pipe sent a spray of notes falling around them.

"Edwin killed my kin, too, remember." He smoothed her clasped hands with his long pale fingers. "Let's fill the empty spaces in our hearts with love."

Twisting away her field-roughened hands she hid them within her wide sleeves.

Her eyes skimmed restlessly over the wasteland of empty unknown faces across the Hall. Women leaning back, at ease, laughing with their men, wiping jellied fruit and cream from their lips with napkins. And, still as a crouching cat, her jewels rippling like a lustrous pelt, Reatta watched them, her cloak of pheasants' feathers and quills thrown back to show off a lining of swansdown. A single white-hot flash of enmity sparked between them. And Tansen was a pagan no longer but a Daughter of Caterin. And she would not let Reatta have him.

"I know a wood," whispered Ean. "And a gate in the palisade with a sentry who'll look the other way."

She felt herself being torn in two. He was an Angle, a bitter enemy of her people. Yet her yearning to love and be loved, to be enfolded in warmth, was overpowering. The thought of the cold empty room in the Palace chilled her. What did anything matter but this living passion that Ean offered? And the dusky night coming softly down outside.

On a bank starred with flowers their heightened passions sought and found fulfilment. Ean lay back, spent and released, to watch the pale face of the Moon come and go among the swaying branches.

"Greetings to you, Gem of the night." Eanfrith stretched in the aftermath of pure rapture.

"Beauty of the skies, Mother of the stars." Tansen continued the poem, drowsy with love-making, revelling in the knowledge that he loved her. Yet she also had her way to make in the world. She had vowed to listen and learn and go forward. She needed to plan how to reach a position of power to help the Clan Mothers. So she needed to know where she stood with this man, Eanfrith. Rousing herself she sat up and hugged her knees.

"Ean, what about North Humber Land? Edwin's heirs have all been sickly. What happens when he dies?"

A cloud floated over the moon but it was nothing to the shadow that fell across Ean's face.

"I've two older brothers in Dal Riata. They'd claim the Kingship."

"Why aren't they here with you?"

"It's a long story. It goes back to the time when my father was King of Bernicia. He thought it made sense to unite Bernicia and Deira against our neighbours who wanted to push us back across the Danish Sea."

"And who could blame them," Tansen cried. She pushed back her sleeves and settled her elbows on her knees ready for a good argument. For the gulf that separated them yawned wide and black. He came from a different breed of people. An ambitious people who came to claim ownership of the land and the pagans who worked it. "You see, your people are barbarians after all. They lay claim to the body of the Earth Mother! That's sacrilege! The Mother can't belong to anyone but herself."

"Angles don't make a god of the land." Ean sounded annoyed at her interruption of his tale. "It's there to be farmed and that's what they do. So why shouldn't it belong to them?"

"Ah, but it's the other way round. Folk belong to the land. You can't buy or sell it or expect to leave it to your sons. For it's only borrowed and held in trust for those who follow."

"Does it matter?" He sounded sulky.

"Of course it does! It's the law of Nature. We've never fought and killed to extend our clan boundaries."

Ean, lost in his memories, did not hear her. The silence lengthened and she began to relax against him again. He was not to blame for the habits of his countrymen.

"So what happened?" she asked.

"Later Edwin of Deira came north with a Kentish army and slew my father." He hunched into his jacket.

"But you escaped?"

He pulled a blade of grass and chewed on it.

"My brothers were spirited out of Edwin's way in bundles of dirty washing and taken to be fostered with an uncle in Dal Riata."

It struck her as the height of folly to hide two golden-haired giants among the small dark men of Dal Riata.

"I was a baby. My mother fled in a company of travelling stonemasons. When she saw Edwin's warriors on the horizon, she thrust me at a woman and rode eastwards to draw them after her." His voice grew husky. "Edwin tortured her. But she told him nothing before she died."

She recalled, years ago, dozing while a fuddled bard sang this epic tale. Now, in spite of herself she was caught up in the drama.

"Edwin must know where you are by now."

"At first he sent spies out. But he was the legitimate heir on the Deiran side and a skilled warrior. My people accepted him. So once he felt secure he let us be."

Her sympathy, born of her own grief, flowed towards him and she folded him in her arms. For a moment he rested his forehead trustingly on her shoulder like a child.

"The Picti had a bad reputation on our stretch of coast. I don't know if my mother knew it but she'd given me to a Danish woman married to a Pretani." "Maybe she hoped you'd come storming back one day in command of a Pretani fleet."

He gave a wry chuckle.

"I know she wanted to separate us to make it harder for Edwin to kill off the whole Bernician dynasty at once. Ragnie reared me with her own son until I was old enough to train as a warrior and then she brought me to King Garnard."

Suddenly their mutual losses had bridged the gulf between them. Swiftly Eanfrith took her in his arms, dispelling the chill of the night air and her sense of foreboding at one and the same time.

She gazed at him, wide-eyed, seeing the young noble in a padded white and gold jacket, silken breeches and soft riding boots. And herself, a pagan in a wine-spotted cast-off robe. She leant back on her arms and smiled. Clothes. That would be Verna's first task tomorrow. To have some new ones made. And how they would both enjoy it!

She sprang up and ran back through the trees touching each trunk gaily like a child. By the time she came onto the pathway she had left her dark thoughts behind. The future might be hidden. But her love for Ean was bright and shining and right here for the taking.

Later in the bare little room Verna was re-arranging the bedding on top of the bed. It would be strange to sleep on planks of wood, knowing there was another room underneath instead of the hard-packed soil of the Mother. And stranger still to be imprisoned on all sides by walls and passages. And tapestries. Dusty faded hunting scenes hung on each wall. She pulled aside the shutters to let the breeze scour them. Outside roof after roof went marching towards the palisade.

And she fell into a reverie, wondering how she could rest without kinfolk, breathing and warm nearby and a bairn crying out in sleep? How could she walk without the feel of the Earth Mother alive and tingling in the soles of her feet? How could she live without the cawing of rooks in the high trees and the sigh of the wind in the thatch? A harsh medley of sound, the rhythmic pound of boots on cobbles, a hoarse command, the clang of weapons brought her out of her dream. The Palace Guard was changing.

There was no point in pining to be back in Pitcarlie with everything as it had been. She had left the life of a pagan behind when she had set out for the Court.

"Where do you sleep, Verna?"

The servant nodded towards a pallet near the door.

Tansen began unlacing her bodice.

"I've never slept by myself. Come and cuddle in beside me."

Slowly and carefully Verna smoothed the pillows.

"And we won't tell the Queen." Tansen knew she had guessed aright. Verna was afraid of being punished. When the servant turned, her eyes were no longer blank. There was still pain there but it was overlaid with a sheen of gladness.

Verna tucked the covers around them with the tender touch of a mother. Half-asleep Tansen reached down into the core of her being to feel her own mother's presence. But there was no one, only Verna breathing steadily beside her.

Then she was fighting her way out of a black wooden coffin. She'd been buried alive! She gasped and struggled, suffocating, moaning into empty air where there should have been the crackle of hearth-fire, the lowing of unmilked cattle, the waking scuffles of children. And at the slither of a sandalled foot she reached for a dagger that wasn't there.

CHAPTER FOURTEEN

"Hush, child!"

The wooden coffin became the unfamiliar room in the Citadel. Slowly she remembered that Pitcarlie was no more. The blackness was her own bitter grief. Verna's arms comforted her. Then it was other arms she remembered. Strong and tanned and male.

Glowing through the horror, dispelling the darkness, came the image of Ean, filling her mind and body with happiness. The blithe and bonny man sent by Bride to bring her joy. She rose from her bed and met the day as if there was no tomorrow.

Adults under twenty were required by law to keep fit by daily exercise. Princesses were no exception.

The citizens gave only a cursory glance as a groom led his bevy of mounted Princesses through the Gate, holding the two youngest on a leading rein.

At first Tansen rode proudly. Some childish fancy prompted her to show off that the pagan had been accepted into the Royal Family despite her outburst from the Bell. But she could not resist throwing a challenge to Reatta.

"Race you to the sportsground!"

Tansen dug her heels into the sides of her straw-coloured mare. Reatta ignored her, pulling down a veil to protect her white skin from the sun.

At the training ground Tansen watched the wing-browed Briton throw spears that arced and fell like a sun-shower. Somehow in action his bare limbs and torso fitted together smoothly and worked with consummate grace. It was a pity that his oiled skin was marred by the criss-crossed scars of old lashings. Now, what crime had he committed to be punished like that?

Beyond in the sports arena, the Caledonie whacked and hurled a leather ball with a hardwood stick, yelling at his team like a man inspired.

But Tansen was drawn to where the swordsmen feinted and slashed. For Ean was there, a joyous uninhibited Ean, using his supple wrists, his springing stride, and brilliant improvisation to create a curtain of iron round his opponent. She wondered if his skill was perhaps more elegant than deadly but watched with delight until hunger drove her back to the Citadel.

After the noon meal, the Princesses practised embroidery. No giggling and chattering filled the small stuffy room. They worked quietly, subdued by the brooding presence of Reatta.

A heap of amethysts and pearls, carnelians and garnets, glass beads and crystals twinkled from a polished wooden bowl. Tansen delved deep and watched with pleasure as a rainbow of gems cascaded from her fingers. Reatta's voice bit into the hush.

"Keep your pagan hands to yourself! These are for the next King's cloak."

The last bead rolled and fell among the floor rushes. Masking her anger Tansen ground it under her heel and picked up a basket of silken threads. These were finer than any she had ever used. And she could not wait to embroider them into a pattern. For that morning Verna had been waiting, an unusual pleasure lighting her eyes.

"Look! I've been to the weaving shed." Swathes of heather-purple, poppy-red and cornflower-blue cascaded from her arms. "Choose what you want for gowns and cloaks."

"Verna, they're lovely." Tansen fingered the wools and linens and saw how finely they had been woven.

"And this cloak, from the sewing women."

Dyed a delicate blue, the fine wool shimmered in a ray of sunlight like the gleam on the river where she had met Ean. Green for the ripples, white for the curving foam and somehow she would purloin Reatta's gold thread for droplets of water, bright in the sun. She threaded her needle and began to stitch. And remember.

Wraith-like, a young Drui, still in the orange robes of the last years of his student-ship, slipped into the room. He stood, his head almost touching the rafters, his hands clasped sedately in front, and began reciting the tale of the birth of Cruithne and Cruithna, and the creation of the Pretani race. His voice was deep and resonant yet his tone was curiously flat as though his emotions were being held in check. And his story was for the younger ones. Tansen could have told it better herself.

Idly sewing and dreaming she felt a sharp tingle of curiosity when the voice of the Drui cracked and faltered. He stared at his feet, white-knuckled, red-cheeked. Until with a sucked-in breath he gathered his practised phrases around him and continued his chant.

"And the breasts of the Earth-Mother over-flowed with the fruits of the land. And her thighs opened ... " he gulped.

Reatta bit her thread calmly, the corners of her mouth quirking.

"Oho," Tansen thought. "He lusts after Reatta and she encourages him. Why?"

"And the thighs of the All-Mother opened and Cruithne and Cruithna, the father and mother of our race, came striding forth."

Tansen let her thoughts swirl around this dark mysterious Princess.

Reatta must know the History and the Law backward by now. What did she hope to gain by teasing the man? Was she after the secret of communing with the Wise Ones? Now there was a heady thought. Or training in the use of medecines? Somehow Reatta did not strike her as a healer. Of course, there were other uses for potions. Combined with a cunning spell she could poison a rival Princess. Or bewitch a Drui.

"History sounds better in song." Tansen told him, winking at the gleeful girls. "Try it! Draw the hearts out of our bodices and float them to the skies on a tide of passion."

"That's enough, Aeran," Reatta said, stabbing her needle into her work and rising. "It's time for my private tutoring."

Aeran followed her, open-mouthed like a fish caught in her net. That was one Drui who had definitely lost his way!

But when Tansen glanced up at the angle of the sun she bundled up her own sewing and threw it on the table. Ean would be waiting with horses at the gate.

They made love gloriously, hidden in a sandy dune, to the sound of the gentle frothing of waves.

"I'm glad I was your first lover," Ean whispered later, tracing feathery patterns on her stomach.

"I thought Bride had sent One of the Splendid Ones to initiate me."

The beads of sweat on his bare shoulder tasted salt on her tongue.

He laughed, thinking she was teasing him.

"Why Bride? Why not call on Dee, or Tay or Clyde? The river Goddesses would suit the daughter of the Water Kelpie better."

"You mean Deva and Tatha and Clotha." She liked the old names for the Flowing Ones better. "Let the Citadel folk have them. For pagans like me, Bride's Festival's the best when the lambs are being born and the ewes coming into milk. And new fleeces begin to grow and there's fresh mutton in the pot."

He stroked her thighs and moved his fingers to her silky secret hair still damp with her excitement.

"Just the same, I'll enjoy living in the King-House," she went on. "I won't have to burn my fingers baking bread in the ben-room or go out in the rain to the squatting hut."

Ean's laugh resounded along the shore.

"You'll have to stop talking like a pagan now."

"Never! I'll always be a pagan at heart."

Suddenly she shivered although the late afternoon sun was warm on her skin.

"What's wrong?"

"I don't know." She stood up, fixing her skirt, filled with disquiet. "Pagans survive by tuning in to the weather signs. But I sense different signs in the Capital, hidden in knowing glances and subtle undercurrents."

She sat down again, hugging her knees under her chin, needing to talk it through with him.

"Reatta's eyes speak. In long lingering looks at the Drui. And he blushes as red as his robe." She studied a cloud on the horizon, watching it change shape. "Did you know she has a session alone with Aeran? I wonder what he's teaching her then?"

"Or what she's teaching him." Ean rolled over and wanted to kiss her again. Tansen pushed him away, busy with her thoughts.

"She wouldn't dare give her precious chastity to a mere Drui. But she's drawing Drui magic out of him, I'm sure. She's like a broody hen. But what's she hatching?"

"Reatta's like me, too lazy to bother plotting." Ean was on his feet now, searching for stones among the sand.

"And she's embroidered the Moon's crescent on the new King's cloak. Upside-down. That's bad magic for somebody."

But Ean had left her to send stones skimming along the water's surface.

Tansen lay on her back, looking deep into the cobalt blue of the sky, hearing the wind whisper in the coarse grasses and the crackle of dry seaweed under Ean's feet.

Where had Reatta inherited her deep passions? Not from her parents. Certainly not from the Queen's Kentish father who had given the Pretani folk a fine chuckle at his precise Latin and his gold-embroidered toga. Yet, for sure, one of Reatta's ancestors had had a burning ambition for power. And Tansen determined to watch her with the relentless hovering gold-irised eye of a goshawk.

And as sharp and clean as a knife-thrust it came to her. Why not make a bold bid for the Queenship herself? She held her breath, savouring the thought. It was no longer a forbidden fantasy. She was as Royal as Reatta. How should she go about it? The Clan Mothers would back her. The King was elected by the Brothers. But who chose which Princess became Queen and Chief Clan Mother? Would she have to discredit Reatta first?

"Come along, Kelpie!" called Ean.

She folded the idea into the back of her mind and found a stone that scalloped the waves till it lost itself in the deepest green of a trough.

Each day, Tansen found a new place outside the Citadel for them to make love in, She needed to celebrate her love in all the gentle and wild nooks and crannies of the Mother. And each day Ean fielded her thoughts like a ball and threw them back at her.

"Let's lie among the flowers in the water-meadow," she suggested one day. "And share our gladness with them."

"And you'll make a garland of them to embroider on a cloak!". Ean found making love under the sky wildly exciting.

"Oh, no, never!" She was horrified. "Not the flower-beings. If you make a picture of something you draw power from it. Birds and beasts are virile enough to stand the loss of power. But the essence of the flower-spirits is so fragile it's taboo to use them."

Ean was bundling up his jacket to make a pillow for her head. She let herself be drawn into his embrace.

Afterwards she lay watching the tall seeding grasses, the rosebay willow herb and cow-parsley dance and sway against the sky. And wondered how many folk were like Ean, folk who would never understand how precious were the plants who gave their essence for healing. And gave it gladly as a gift. Busy folk like Ean living in Citadels and places of power. Never knowing. Never caring. Never giving thanks where it was due.

She turned on her elbows to look towards the hills and seemed to see them bare and bitter in the sleet of the wind for evermore. And folk huddled under a wet blanketing cloud. And she knew that one day the Earth-Mother would wreak some terrible vengeance on folk who had not learned that all forms of life move forward together. And her blood flowed cold under her skin.

"Why am I so different?" she cried silently to Bride. "Why does my mind keep churning on? What am I striving towards? Why can't I live only for this day? That's the whole purpose of being here, isn't it?"

And again, that deep yearning yawned inside her, crying out for fulfilment.

Far in the distance a lone horseman idled by the edge of a wood. He seemed part of the landscape, giving and taking. And by his long stiff back she knew it was Dale. As though she was inside his mind she listened to the birdsong and turned to watch the long slow glide of the breakers, to breathe in joy and peace from the air. And he suddenly stopped beside a mountain ash clothed in its last glorious burst of colour. And laid his hand on its trunk as if to give thanks for its beauty.

Dale would understand. Yet he was young, awkward, still seeking himself, still striving for a place in the scheme of things. She wondered if he was like her, intensely curious, always asking, always wanting to learn. Or if ambition had made him a loner among men.

She turned on her back. She missed the noisy debates on politics and policies that echoed round the evening hearth at Pitcarlie. When news came of the judgments of Councils or the wars of Kings, Baran, his face black with rage, would bang his fist on the roof-tree till the spiders scuttled. Or when a Clan brother came out with a new idea and Grannie Bea would slash his argument wide open with a word as sharp as the claw of an eagle.

"What do you talk about among your friends?" she asked Ean.

He grunted, half-asleep.

"Weaponry, hawking, horses."

"Politics?"

He rose, irritated, and prowled around on restless feet.

"I leave that sort of stuff to the Council. Why can't you?"

"Because they're all men," she answered. "If I was Queen I'd put Clan Mothers in the Council."

Ean's laugh sent a prickle of annoyance across her skin.

"Embassies from foreign Courts wouldn't deal with a pack of women."

She screamed with rage at him then. And lifted her skirts and ran towards the Citadel. Tears choked her. Because she loved him and hated him. And needed him. And would surely meet him tomorrow.

CHAPTER FIFTEEN

The day they found the three Standing Stones, Tansen raced Ean seven times, moon-wise, round in a Circle. With the last remnants of breath they came together on the grass in an explosion of passion that was quick and infinitely satisfying.

"Look!" she cried afterwards. "Everywhere, rosemary, thyme, chervil." Her hand brushed across the herbs releasing tiny puffs of perfume. "Dill, marjoram, tarragon. Healing herbs! The Attecottie plant them here." And she sat up, half-hoping for a sight of the Wee Folk.

"You'd smell their burrows if they lived nearby."

"You talk as if they're animals. Yet their ancestors built great temples and tombs and planet observatories."

"Where are these marvels then? All I can see is three broken-down stones."

She spread out her hands then, palms downwards and walked the earth, eyes closed, sensing.

"But there was a circle!" she cried. "I can feel the disturbance in the earth where the pillars once stood. Here! And another here!"

"Romantic nonsense!"

She stopped beside him.

"They were wooden pillars that have rotted," she said firmly. "But in the Orcades where there was no timber they made pillars of stone and they lasted. Some day I want to go there to see them."

"So what happened to these wonderful cathedral builders?"

He was looking at her out of the corners of his eyes.

"You're an Angle," she said. "You don't know the story. How they probed the secrets of the skies until the Godly Ones became angry and drew a veil over their minds to make them forget all their learning."

He laughed.

"Then tell me this?" he asked. "How can you measure the movements of the planets with a sprinkling of humped stones?"

She didn't know how to answer him and felt devastated by her lack of knowledge. She sat up with her back to the leaning stone, screwing up her eyes and trying to recall the tales by the hearth-fire.

"It's something to do with the alignment of an outlying stone." She turned her head and saw a stone set into the hillside.

"And it was aligned to a cleft in the hills where the sun dipped at the winter solstice." And she saw the v-shaped cleft in the mountains to the south-west across the green moor, stippled with purple and yellow. "Or was it midsummer?" She shook her head in shame at her ignorance.

"Maybe one of their precious planets took a mad turn and wiped them off the face of the earth, eh?"

There was a poem about a star with a fiery tail that had plummeted down on Alba. And the Attecottie who survived were youngsters and had no knowledge of the skills of their elders. It was a sad song. She sat cross-legged, blinking like an owl. Some day she would seek out these people and learn about them.

"It's far more likely the Picti brought new diseases that wiped them out."

"They welcomed the Cruithne when they landed on these shores. And shared their food and land."

"Why didn't they defend themselves like honourable men?"

"Because they believed in the brotherhood of man."

"I'll bet your people sent them scurrying back to their bolt-holes. Or put them to the sword."

Her brow darkened. He was making fun of the history of her people. Perhaps everything, except hunting and fencing, seemed trivial to him. Perhaps one day he would even mock at their love. But she fought back a feeling of panic and summoned all her patience.

"My people learned a lot from the Attecottie. And we acknowledge it, by using their language for the ritual."

But Ean was not interested. And the day was too fine to spoil. She gave him a friendly push.

"Besides they didn't have metal for swords back in those days, silly."

"Did you bring me here for a lecture on aboriginals?" he said. "Or am I allowed to kiss you again?"

Her hands on either side of his fine-boned face, she looked solemnly at him, at the irrepressible pout of his lower lip and the soft rounded chin with the nick of a badly-ground razor.

"I brought you here because lovers who love within the Ring of Stones will have a lasting joy of one another as long as they both shall live."

Ean caught her mood and repeated the words, like a vow.

"As long as we both shall live."

With his arm he laid her down, crushing the herbs under her body till the air was filled with perfume. She lay filled with happiness, gazing up at him. It was wonderful to be so much in love. It seemed as though this perfect delight in one another must go on for ever.

Why then did the great monoliths beyond his head seem to be converging to crush them, leaning over, gloating, wavering and trembling as though they could hardly contain the power of the Ancient Ones within their gritty substance.

"Do you ever get the feeling that the world is holding its breath, waiting for something to happen?" she whispered.

"I've only one over-riding feeling at the moment," he said, munching her ear-lobe.

She bunched her fists and knees and threw him from her.

"Have you nothing else on your mind but that stick of manhood between your legs."

And she staggered as she went from him, grazing her arm on a pitted surface. And then he was at her side, trying to look in her face.

"Tansen, listen! I was only teasing!"

She marched on, ignoring him.

"I love you."

He was pleading now. Next would come the promises.

"I want to marry you."

That stopped her in her tracks.

"Why?"

He faced her, red and white coming and going in his cheeks, searching for a word to soften her anger.

"To bind us together for ever."

"Hah!" She resumed her march. "What's more binding than love. Marriage is for landowners."

"But what if you have my child. It'll be a bastard!"

"There are no bastards in our homesteads, only bairns. You call yourself more Celt than Dane! You know nothing about us! You live among your retinue in the Court like lug-worms in a bag."

"But what if ... ?"

"What if?" She stopped again. "What if I have a son? You won't be able to pass on your non-existent wealth or your non-existent land. He'll belong to me and my kin. He'll share in our wealth. And the richest clan is the one with the most bairns."

"But I'd be the father. And I'd have rights."

"Only if I decide to acknowledge you."

"But if we married I'd have rights!"

He was not interested in bairns. Except to hold her, to have power over her.

"Rights! I was a virgin. I should have had an older man to open me to pleasure. He'd have made sure that I didn't conceive."

He flushed, confused and hurt.

"I've only been with older women. They looked after themselves. I was never with a virgin."

He fell back. She strode on, head high, knowing she was hurting him more than he could bear. And yet when he made love it was with tenderness as well as passion.

She looked back and he was staring after her with his heart in his eyes. Her foot caught in a root and she hit the ground hard. And he was running and lifting her with concern. And she was in his arms and he was kissing her. Her mouth, her cheeks and her neck. And she took his face in her hands and kissed his nose lightly.

"But you did all that the Initiator would have done. And more. Besides, I know a potion that would keep me from child-bearing but I've not had time to mix it."

"Why didn't you? We don't want to make a child. Not yet."

"The choice always lies with the woman."

His face cleared.

"If you didn't use the potion you must want a child. Then we'll marry."

"I love you, Ean. If our love's strong enough it'll become a lasting pair-bond. Nothing can part us then." Yet, as she spoke, a cold fear again clutched at her heart. "Unless you leave me to go back to your own country."

"Never!"

"Even if our two countries went to war?"

"Ho, that's not likely. Since Edwin became a Christian, he's given up his bloodthirsty ways."

She kissed him into silence. Foreboding was for those who revelled in its drama. She had golden moments to cherish and she wanted none of these dark feelings.

"Tomorrow let's meet in the herb garden. These days there's a chill in the haar that comes in from the sea."

Yet she knew that the coldness was in her heart and had come from within the Circle.

There was a walled garden inside the Citadel where a Wise Woman in a bygone era had nurtured flowers for her medicines. They still grew in profusion and climbers had made secret bowers for lovers. They began to meet there when they were free.

Ean was usually there before her because the Queen kept the Princesses hard at work for long spells and Tansen did not want to make too bold a show of independence. As she made her way there she would strain her ears for often Ean perched on a low wall and played simple tunes on a be-ribboned lute.

One day, all was silent except for the tuneless whistle of a gardening boy as he scraped with his hoe on the other side of the wall. The garden was empty, except for a broken catgut, discarded on the grass. Ignoring the stone bench, she bunched up her skirts and sat crosslegged on the ground glad to be free of formality.

The honeyed scent of clover was strong in the air. A tiny glinting green beetle climbed a stalk and fell off. She inhaled a warm sense of the Mother and the security and peace that emanated from her.

Here she felt at home. The garden was protected from mischievous sprites by a rowan, its blossom long gone and its berries still green. Grannie Bea had trained a rowan tree in an arch across her lintel.

"When the nights are cold and drear and the mist hides the shades in the forest, there's aye a rantree with its arm above the door," she would say to calm the fears of the bairns who cried at the eerie wheep of a curlew.

The sound of trumpets, the hooves of many horses and the chime of harness intruded on her thoughts. Surely Ean's duty was over by now.

She leaned back to watch a buzzard wheel and mew high above, envying him his freedom. As the clouds formed and changed shape she wondered idly if Aeran was teaching Reatta his shape-changing magic in her room in the Palace.

A movement at the gateway caught her eye and her heart leapt until she saw that this man was not the spring-heeled Ean but boasted the dark winged brows of Dale, the Briton. She drew back, watching. He had none of the whippy fire of the brigand, Liath, and none of the arrogance of the trained warrior. Instead he had that calm look that farming men have, walking purposefully as though he belonged to the ground beneath his feet. He raised his large bright eyes to look over the wall and into the distance as though he, too, felt constrained by palisades. When at last his eyes lighted on Tansen they glowed like lanterns in recognition.

"Did Garnard enlist you into his Guard?" she called.

Dale shook his head, smiling that long slow vacant smile that had become a habit when questioned. He had stepped out as he often did, away from the jesting and gambling in the barracks where he had been quartered. He liked to roam alone over the countryside and sit beside a hearth for a cup of milk or a chat with veterans of earlier wars. Or to watch the ship-builders at work and ask why they did things that way and not this. Or to take over the bellows from the boy in the smithy and hear the smith talk of his work and his life between hammer-blows.

"Have you always been a mercenary? You'd fare better with a body of your father's men behind you."

Dale let the sting in her words flow past him and concentrated on the ripple of sunlight dappling the copper of her hair.

"Did you not think to step into your father's place as leader once he was killed? Or did they desert you?"

On his travels Dale had seen Tansen and Ean riding together, their faces shining with love. He had had a pang of regret that she was so taken by the boy with the curling hair who seemed to indulge every passing whim like a butterfly in the sun. Whereas this girl had strength of character behind those thoughtful eyes. He had watched that steady green gaze measure the courtiers. Had watched the way she drank like a man, lifting her cup in her square-tipped fingers. He would have liked to sit and talk with her.

Tansen's eyes narrowed. She had been spelling out her questions as though he was simple-minded. Yet she sensed a brain behind that calm clear gaze. And maybe a past that was better buried. He was strangely reticent about where he and his father went to live after Morfael took over Dun Barton. One thing for certain he was not going to tell her where he came from. Or where he had been trained. Or where he had received the sword-scars and the lashings.

"Why do you want to throw in your lot with a weak-kneed King like Garnard?"

His gentle laugh was deep and soft.

"I ask myself the same question."

"There's booty and land to be won down south."

"I'll stay in Dalgynch at present while Angles are filling the courtyard and guest-house."

"Do you mean Eanfrith and his retinue?" she asked, puzzled.

His gaze swung over an expanse of golden rod and reflected their clear translucent yellow.

"An embassy has arrived," he said, half-grudgingly. He had been enjoying this moment of nearness with her and knew he was ending it now.

"They've come from the North Humber Land. King Edwin has been killed."

The eyes he turned on Tansen then were like deep sad mountain pools.

Tansen felt a cold hand clutch her heart. These were Ean's kinsmen! Forgetting Dale she ran to find Ean, her hand clenched at her breast.

CHAPTER SIXTEEN

It was true! Angles in battle-dress with axes in their belts lounged in the courtyards. Servants ran with jugs of ale and plates of cheese. Tansen averted her eyes as she ran past them..

At the entrance to Ean's quarters swords clashed across her path. Above seamed cheeks two pairs of eyes, seaman's eyes, appraised her. Her mind misted over and she saw the blood of her kin drip from their swords. And the image was so vivid and terrible that her pent-up nerves exploded in an angry scream. Stained teeth appeared in the straw-like beards.

Then a face she knew peered round the curtain. One she had glimpsed in Ean's retinue.

"What's all the noise?" he demanded angrily. "We're in conference here!" Then a thread of grim laughter ran through his voice. "Ah, it's the water-kelpie." A crooked eyebrow acknowledged that he remembered more of her body than he could see now. She froze.

"Tell the Prince that Princess Tansen is here."

The young man did not try to hide his irritation.

"Look, Lady. You'd do well to steer clear of him from now on."

"What right have you to speak to me like that! Who are you?"

He blew impatiently through pursed lips.

"Wulf's my name. Eanfrith's milk-brother. And we're busy!"

Although he was the same age as Ean there was strength in his jaw-line and maturity in the expression on his lean face.

"Busy doing what?"

Wulf studied her, probing for her motives. She was not the kind of woman he had expected. Eanfrith's love affairs flared up quickly and passed. This girl had a quiet dignity about her that he could not help but admire. Yet the wild untamed sprite of the woods was latent in every taut line of her body and in the luminous green fire of her eyes.

"Ah well," he said shrugging. "I should send you packing. But since you're royal I'll explain first. And then send you packing."

She stiffened, knowing that the moment she had been dreading had arrived.

"King Edwin's dead and left no heirs. The Witan has called Eanfrith to the Kingship." A grin split his face. The brown eyes softened with something akin to hero-worship. "Think of it! My milk-brother, King of the North Humber Land!"

Long days and nights of loneliness stretched before Tansen.

"I must see him!" she cried.

"So you're going to make a scene after all." His lip curled. "But you always knew he was a Prince. And that his marriage would be arranged. You'll find King Garnard has plans for you, too."

Her hands flew together beneath her breasts. In her imagination she had faced the possibility squarely. But the reality bit deep.

"You mean he'll have to marry some fat Danish wench with broad hips for child-bearing." Vainly she tried to blot the thought out of her mind. "He'll refuse!"

"Oh no, he won't. And you know it. You can forget any promises he made in the heat of passion."

Her head went up defiantly.

"I'll not hold him to ransom for loving me."

"That was your pleasure, my dear." He led her outside. In his averted gaze there was no sympathy. "I'll tell him you visited."

"Don't trouble, milk-brother. You can't keep him from seeing me."

In the Banqueting Hall unseen knives quivered in the air. The King, a sweating mountain of crimson and gold, fidgeted with the tippets of fur at his collar. Uneasy blue-robed advisers wavered at his back. The chairs at the High Table lay empty. The Royal Family had been banished. Tansen stayed at the side but made sure she could be clearly seen.

Marooned as if on an island, the Danish party stood stiff and exposed while the incoming folk parted around them and flowed, soft-footed, to their places like a deep quiet river. And stood in ranks at their benches, perfumed, delicately dressed, like flowers in a garden.

Without a signal from the King, six leaders of the Embassy stepped up to fill six of the empty places at the King's Table. Their cup-bearers followed to stand behind. Their retinues grouped round nearby tables. Eanfrith with two red spots of excitement glowing on his cheek-bones strode through the throng and leapt up to stand beside the King.

"Eanfrith of Bernicia."

Noisily Garnard cleared some of the panic from his throat and spoke again.

"Mothers and Brothers of the Clans, I present to you Eanfrith, son of Aethelfrith, and now designated King of the North Humber Land."

The courtiers shrugged and raised indifferent eyebrows. What was the fat old fool waiting for? An acclamation? Let the lad's own kind do the cheering! Maybe once he'd had oil poured on his head a polite clang on a shield wouldn't come amiss. What did this have to do with good Pretani folk, wanting their dinner? Yet wanting to know why there was an army outside. And where the King's Guard was hiding. And why the King's small shifty eyes flickered nervously from roof-tree to board.

A hound with a stolen bone growled near the door. Somone kicked it outside as Garnard spoke again.

"And to ensure peace between our two peoples, a marriage has been arranged between Eanfrith and Reatta, the eldest Princess of the Royal Pretani Blood."

Out from the shadows came Reatta, ablaze with rubies and triumph. And, folded neatly in her hair, a copy of the golden circlet that Danish queens wore. A silent scream rose inside Tansen. It was like a scene in the misty world between waking and sleeping.

"No!" A groan burst from the crowd. So that was it! Garnard had sold the Kingship for a plate of stew and peace to sup it! Never! A shout of fury was bitten off as Danish small-swords appeared, drawn from short cloaks slung carelessly over shoulders! The sharp hiss of indrawn breath. Swords in the presence of the King! A handful of men grabbed meat-daggers and surged forward.

Quickly Madden, white-domed Law-giver, stepped forward. Above the confused babble he addressed the Hall.

"Put down your daggers! I assure you that no Laws have been broken." No one remembered when Madden had last spoken with such authority. He spread his hands as he spoke to the Angles. "Put away your weapons! Such a display is not fitting when you are received as honoured guests." His eyes glittered over the Hall. "Let us sit and eat!"

A sigh wafted through the Hall, as though the courtiers knew their moment of decision had been and gone on a puff of perfume and a haze of silk since this silent iron-clad force had crept up on them. Madden retired, mopping his brow with trembling hands.

Tansen's first impulse had been to cry out against the marriage. She stifled the words with her hand. Marten had shown her that was not the way.

Reatta fastened one hand on Ean's arm and sent a long slow glittering look towards Tansen. She raised the other dainty hand, palm upwards,as if to say 'You see? You had no chance, Pagan.'

Tansen ignored her. If she really exerted herself she could keep Ean from Reatta's bed for ever. Ean's eyes sent a quick message to her, pleading for understanding but promising nothing. She sent him a withering look and turned her head to hide the tears that blurred her sight. Now was not the moment to let him see how he had hurt her! Why had he not told her himself instead of letting her find out in this cruel way?

Her eyes swung to search the faces of the courtiers. Did they not understand what was happening? That by a neat stroke a new King had been imposed on them by foreign King. That an Angle would become King of the Pretani some day? That the Law of Election had been ignored?

A murmuring had begun deep in the swell of the crowd. They understood, all right. Yet it was little more than a buzzing of swarming bees making ready to change their hive and their allegiance. Tansen could only shake her head in angry disbelief. It seemed incredible that the Law was being flouted and the Court were accepting it. Was no one going to protest?

Then from the haze of the lazy hearth-fire Liath of the Carrot-Head sprang forward to confront his King.

"What shady business is going on here?" he demanded. "An Angle to marry the Princess? An Angle to follow you into the Kingship? An Angle who's also King of North Humberland?" His voice rose. His long finger stabbed into the faces of the Council. "And what did the Angles buy you off with? And you? And you? Five hides of land in Deira and a puckle of slaves to work it?"

A halloo of protest erupted from the Master of the King's Guard, a man of grizzled hair and flabby muscles. Liath stepped in front of the quivering Law Adviser and waved his pointing finger like a sword before the man's ashen face.

"This is treason! I demand my right as Chief of the Caledonie to elect my own King!"

The crowd shifted and strained to see him better. A few voices growled in agreement. Not enough.

"What shall I tell my Clan when I return to the mountains? To men and women whose forefathers sent the Romans scuttling back behind their wall! Whose grandparents fought under Bridei to stem the tide of Scots! Where's our freedom to choose a man proven in battle, respected in Council and tested in leadership?"

His bright plaid swung round as he appealed to the crowd with outstretched arms. A woman withdrew quickly, scattering pearls as she went.

"What say you now, men and women of Alba? Shall we stand idly by and let the Angles plant this boy King at our head?"

The Master of the Hunt put out a restraining hand. And yelped as Liath's fist set the boards of the High Table quivering. Dale was suddenly beside Tansen.

"Cowards! Traitors!" Liath turned to face the throng again. "Fellow-warriors! I, for one, will not accept this untried youth, so cunningly fostered within our Court. Will you?"

Suddenly two blades had crossed wickedly at Liath's throat. Hot blood suffused his face. For a long moment Tansen thought he would lash out in an explosion of rage. Instead he gave a three-cornered grin and slowly his open hands came up in a gesture of submission. Yet it was not fear that she glimpsed in his eyes, but defiance.

"Go back to your kale-yard in the mountains, Caledonie!" said the King. "You and your pack of ruffians haven't the guts to lead a rebellion."

"Guts is it? You've plenty of those, I see!"

Ignoring the lowering swords Liath's scornful eyes travelled slowly around, sliding across the rich embroidered clothing, the winking jewels. Eyes shifted under the flaying blue gaze. He gave a slight grunt at the impassive face of Dale. His look paused on Tansen and his eyebrow asked a question. He did not pause for an answer.

In the doorway he turned, laughing, and sent a challenge ringing out."Hail Caledonia! The land of the free!"

And Tansen, stirred and exalted, her own war-cry ringing in her mind, would have stepped out to follow him, until an iron hand clamped on her upflung wrist.

CHAPTER SEVENTEEN

"He's not after winning followers," Dale hissed in Tansen's ear. "He can't cope with them. And there are better ways."

No one else moved, stunned by the enormity of the Danes' demand and the King's easy capitulation. And who was going to give up a fine house in the Capital to live on a wind-scoured granite rock?

The King slumped into his chair and beckoned to the Steward. The servant who brought the platter stumbled and slopped gravy on the King's robe.

"What better ways?" Tansen asked Dale, rubbing her wrist. But Dale was gone, standing, one foot on the dias, talking to an Angle with hair like the pelt of a wildcat.

Traitor! Already, she thought, he was sounding out the Angles to see if there was a place in their company for him. He was a slippery as an eel, that one, after all.

She toyed with her food, hearing Reatta's triumphant bray above a score of half-hearted conversations.

Before the bards had got under way, the foreign nobles and Ean left the Hall. Tansen had no wish to hear the praises of the King either. Or a poem about the beauty of Reatta.

She stormed from the Citadel, straight towards the humble hut that Marten used when visiting the Citadel. Her head was filled with a hundred different reasons why this marriage should not take place.

The Drui who sat cross-legged at the door rose at her coming.

"He's expecting you."

Marten was not in the hut. A stir of cool air and a flicker of light took her out again into the mild twilight. He sat erect in the shadow of a tree, his robes irradiated with turquoise reflected from the pool at his feet, as if he was sculpted in green Iona marble. The light from a lamp flitted lightly over hair and beard, glowed on his noble burnished nose and glinted in eyes that spanned infinity.

At once she knew she was in the presence of One who was in communion with the Great Ones. She sat at his feet so that her head was lower than his and waited for him to speak. A languid sigh rustled like a dry leaf. The bench creaked as he stirred.

"There is a Marriage Ceremony to be performed within the space of two nights, the Council tell me," he chanted softly without greeting.

She hesitated. choosing her words.

"But you'll refuse, Wise One," she whispered. "Won't you?"

"The signs are there in the fall of the Bones of the Royal Bull. The omens are good. The Powerful Ones are satisfied."

She bent her head to hide both her disappointment and the stubborn set of her mouth. The Arch-Drui had been her brightest hope. Suddenly she wished she had never come to Court. She was beginning to despise them all, even Marten. Her anger blazed out. And if the Powerful Ones were listening, so be it!

"Why didn't the Council elect an Heir before this happened? Someone like Dale, the Briton. Then the Embassy could never have forced this marriage on us!"

"The Briton has no forces at his back. His time will come."

Marten's voice held the patience of eternity.

"We need someone now! Why not the Chief of the Caledonie?"

"Skirmishes are the spice on his daily venison. What can he do with his ill-assorted bunch of clansmen?" The Arch-Drui's eyes closed as though dismissing her.

What he said was true. But the image of Reatta, purring like a cat at Ean's side, spurred her on.

"And why should Reatta be Queen? She's arrogant and self-centred! She's not the Queen the Clan Mothers need. I'm a pagan like them! I'd make a better Queen for them!"

Even seated in his chair, the Arch Drui was able draw himself up to an immense height.

"You?" At the contempt in his tone she cringed inside herself. "You are only a child with a dream of greatness!"

She wanted to weep with rage and helplessness. She beat her fists on her knees. And stilled as an idea burst like a ball of flame on the horizon of her mind, flitting and dancing into her consciousness and becoming brighter and sweeter.

"You said there was to be a Marriage? Between a Daughter of Caterin and the Dane?"

The vision came strong and clear, taking her breath from her. She and Reatta were the same age. If she married Ean instead, the Angles could not control the Kingship. Reatta would be free to marry the next elected King. And as Queen of North Humber Land she would ensure that her people were saved from domination by the Angles. And she would be with the man she loved.

"I'm a Daughter of Caterin," she cried, emboldened by her elation. "I'll stand beside the Dane in the Grove at Dunino!"

The Arch-Drui fell silent for so long that she thought he had forgotten her.

Then his strong hands stretched forward and cupped the crown of her head. Power jolted down her spine with the zig-zag of a lightning flash.

"Consider it well, my child. That path is fraught with danger."

"I love the Prince," Tansen said simply. "And I can serve my people from North Humber Land."

Tansen saw him smile at the innocence of her reply. But all at once he nodded in agreement.

"If that is your wish."

Her body flooded with delight. She could hardly believe it had been so easy.

"You have a great gift of loving, my child. Like Beatha." There was sadness in Marten's deep voice but a shine of gladness in his eyes.

The lips that touched her forehead held the warmth of a kinsman.

"Trust me. You will serve your country. But not as you imagine."

Kneeling she rubbed her forehead on the hard-packed earth as a sign of humility to the All-Powerful Ones. Her mind churned with fresh possibilities opening before her. With a finger guiding her chin Marten turned her head towards the lamp. And her mind quietened.

The pear-shaped amber flame shafted its tapering reflection straight across the pool, a golden arrow-head pointing towards her where she knelt.

"A flame within a pool. The flame is vigour. The water is peace. Carry the image with you. Call on it and you open your spirit to the flow of the Universal Good."

She left his presence backward, bowing, and rose beyond the hut feeling as though she was flying among the stars in the black velvet sky. There was a strange wild excitement in her veins as she ran back to the Capital. There were so many things to do now that Marten had promised she would marry her golden lover.

She burst into her room and stopped as a robed figure rose from a bench. Verna, seeing her sparkling eyes and flushed cheeks, stepped forward to give her a moment to calm herself.

"This is the Law Adviser. He has a summons from the King."

Tansen drew herself up. She was learning how to school her emotions. No one could know about her talk with the Arch-Drui. But guilt washed her body in a tide of heat. Madden's fingers drummed on the edge of her table and the little pots of perfumes and colours danced alarmingly. He was not at ease either.

"There is a matter to be discussed," he said through dry precise lips.

Tansen followed him, suiting her steps to his dignified pace. She tried to cling to her joy as it slowly evaporated in a cold mist of apprehension. The King must have other plans for her as Wulf had predicted. It was beyond possibility that he would consent to her marriage to Ean. Even if ordered by Marten he would still fear the vengeance of the Angles. As for Reatta with the secret purring smile, she would defy even the gods to suit her whims.

Hearing voices raised in argument, Tansen held back at the doorway of the Room of State to allow the Law Adviser to announce her. The King stopped his pacing, swirled the cloak of Kingship across the back of his Chair and sat, sliding pudgy hands down his thighs onto his wide-stretched knees.

"Come here, girl, and let me look at you."

Now that there were no Angles present his blustering tone had returned. She stood her ground in the centre of the room, despising him for his cowardice. His advisers formed a plush gem-strewn half-circle around her, ruthless eyes dissecting her layer by layer.

"You're the one who beds with young Eanfrith," said the King. His eyes skimmed over her ripe breasts. His wet tongue quivered against his upper lip.

She waited, not deigning to answer. The King knew well enough that Ean was her lover.

"Would you marry him then?" he asked. Instinctively she tensed to cover her shock. Her interview with Marten had had a dream-like quality about it. She had not been able to tell if the idea had come from Marten or if it had been there in her mind all along. Now the same suggestion was coming from the King. Had Marten planted it in the King's mind? She tried to think clearly. And only knew that she could not trust Garnard. There must be a catch in it somewhere.

"How can I? I'm not the eldest princess."

"The Angles don't know that."

The crafty look on his face gave her the clue to his thinking. If Ean married Reatta it might hasten his own abdication. He had to thwart the Danes' plan to rule through Ean. Warlike defiance had never been his style. But guile would save his face. Her plan was going to work.

"You truly believe you can fool that gang of ruthless politicians?" she asked drily.

The King choked over the implied insult. The Law Adviser stepped in smoothly.

"It's the only way. You'll be saving your people from slavery. You must do it!"

She let them wait Their eyes, gloating over their secret plan, became anxious. They had thought she would jump at the chance to marry a King. And she wanted to marry him. Oh, how she wanted it!

"Oh, I can see all the advantages for you. But I'm baring my neck for a Danish axe!"

Somehow in Marten's magnetic company she had not thought of the risks. But among these men her suspicions flared.

"Now, don't you worry your pretty head." The Law Adviser made to pat her shoulder. She drew back sharply. "Let older and wiser heads work out the consequences."

"Don't patronise me! You sound like a foreigner, not a true Pretani!"

"Don't you see," he went on, his patience wearing thin, his long twitching finger-nails rasping on his padded coat. "We're stalling for time. This way we can appease the Angles and keep our Law intact."

"And have a spy in their court in North Humber Land," she snapped. "And we all know how Angles treat spies. I need my hands and my tongue."

The Master of the King's Estates brought his negotiating skills into play.

"The King will arrange safeguards for your life. A bodyguard. Threats of war."

Her laugh was strained. Garnard's threats meant nothing. Her brain whirled at the enormity of the risk she was undertaking.

"And when are they likely to discover this infamous piece of trickery, do you think?"

"Not until after they've acclaimed you as Queen. You can depend on that. They're in a hurry to leave. They must not leave their land leaderless with Cadwallon of Gwynedd on the prowl."

"And Reatta? Will she agree?" She looked straight at the King.

"That young woman will remain in her quarters until you are married." The King's temper was rising.

She withdrew her gaze from his, and found it drawn to wall shelves laden with sculpted ivory and amber, swirling shapes of coloured glassware, vases cut from solid marble, green and blue-veined and pink. It was part of the People's Treasure, gifts from embassies to the Pretani. Not donated to this self-centred King. She lifted a huge raw amethyst, raising it before her eyes as if she might read her future there in the clear purple crystals.

"Stop this nonsense, girl! You're royal and you'll obey me!"

It had all been decided beside Marten's pool. Only the details had to be thrashed out here. But now the pain began.

"You're sending me into exile."

The King snorted and beat his palms on the arms of his chair.

If she took this step would she ever see the sweep of her own landscape again? Would the chance to lead the Clan Mothers ever come again? Marten had said she would serve her country but not as she imagined. But there was Ean. A babe in arms among his scheming nobles. A lump came in her throat.

"And you'll tell no one. No one!" Garnard stressed. "I want no word of this to reach the ear of a single Angle."

Tansen let him think he had won his victory. She paused in the doorway.

"When I am Queen of North Humber Land, I shall expect daily to hear news of your abdication and the election of a young warrior King."

It was a wooden door. And she slammed it behind her with immnse satisfaction.

Later as Verna pinched out the light and came to the bed., pictures of Ean tumbled through Tansen's mind. Upright and handsome, arriving on the Drui's Rock at Dunino and the light in his eyes when he found her waiting. He wouldn't care that she had deceived him. But the King was right. If Ean caught word of it beforehand he would not be able to contain his joy. He would blurt out the secret to Wulf and Wulf, afraid for Ean's life, would stop the rites. It was better to surprise him where Marten's presence would still his fears.

Marten. How she wished these mystics would not talk in riddles. Yet the power of thought did not travel by words but by symbols that must be interpreted. Her forehead burned where he had kissed her. And he had kissed her with all the tenderness of a father.

Marten and Beatha? Was it possible that Marten had fathered a bairn in Beatha? And that that bairn had been Tansen's own mother?

CHAPTER EIGHTEEN

By the slant of the sun on the morning of the Marriage Tansen knew she had slept late. She skipped like a bairn towards the garden of the Wise Woman, tying the laces at her throat, hoping that Ean would come, wondering if he would escape Wulf.

Then there he was, hurrying along with that unmistakeable bounce as though he could not wait to go from one place to the other. Joyfully he kissed her full on the lips.

"What do you think of it all, my little Hazel-nut." He sat sideways on the bench, looking eagerly into her face. "Yesterday I was a foreigner without lands or position. Now I'm a King!"

He was utterly absorbed in himself and his good fortune, like a child with a new toy. How could she blame him for wanting the Kingship so desperately?

"And you'll come south with me? Say you will?"

She knew then that he had no inkling of the new plan and bowed her head to hide her secret smile. She hesitated before answering, feeling the need to probe the depths of his feelings for her.

"Is that what you want?" she asked.

His face grew serious. His gaze swung from the trees to the sky, anywhere but at her face.

"You know I don't want to marry Reatta. I objected but they said ... " His eyes were bright and bitter. "The Angles are holding my sisters hostage."

Ean swung off down the path beating his fists on his thighs, his brows dark. He'd never known these older sisters. Odd pieces of news had filtered through. That they were married. To Angles. He guessed the Embassy were bluffing. Yet he couldn't be sure. And in a way he wanted to believe them. It sounded more honourable to accept the Kingship to save the lives of his sisters. Oh, this was all such a mess! He turned abruptly.

"What choice do I have, Tansen? I'm the son of a King, after all! I'm due this honour."

Again Ean pounded the path. Tansen would understand. She must! She wouldn't want him to miss this golden opportunity. Still, she'd vowed never to share him with another woman. But it wouldn't be fair if she deserted him. A man should expect more from his woman. How could he face his new life without her? Somehow he had to persuade her that this marriage was a political move. Maybe if he offered to give it all up it would soften her heart.

Tansen saw his eyes narrow and grow crafty.

"If it means losing you, Tansen, I'll refuse the Kingship. I'll let my sisters take their chance."

A queer kind of pain came into her heart, knowing that he did not mean the words he spoke. She answered sharply.

"Oh no, it would raise a barrier between us for the rest of our lives."

Ean shook his head. "I'd never blame you." Yet his cheeks reddened and his tone was sulky.

"Look! I'll father a son and heir in Reatta and never lie with her again."

"But then the Pretani will want a Royal Princess," she said flatly.

He flung away from her, ruffling his hair till it stood on end.

"Oh, why did they choose me? Why not my brothers in Dal Riata?"

"Because they don't want to annexe Dal Riata. It's on the west coast."

Suddenly Wulf skidded round a rose-bush, furious.

"Your watch-dog's aptly named," Tansen said.

"Your nobles are waiting to consult you, King!" Wulf called rudely, ignoring Tansen and all pretence at protocol.

Ean could not hide the leap of excitement in his eyes. For the first time in his life he was going to be consulted on important matters of state. He spread his hands in apology and followed Wulf.

Above her head, sombre black clouds were forming with an ugly tinge of orange in them like the dull blaze of a thatch on fire. The season of storms had come. As Tansen made her way back to the King-House the gaudy banners and pennants and streamers that decorated the Citadel for the Marriage wilted in the humid air

"Rain will wash their dyes out before this day's done." Verna closed the shutter firmly and beamed on Tansen. On a chest she had laid out a green Bride's gown fragrant with meadowsweet. And beside it the ritual dyes and pigments and quills to decorate a Royal Pretani Bride on the day of her marriage. Tansen gave a whoop of surprise and hugged her.

"How did you guess? No one told you I was going to be married today. I know! You read thoughts?"

"Not me! You talked in your sleep."

Tansen lay on the couch, solemn and vaguely sad as Verna drew the swirling colourful patterns of Bride's benison on her skin. Today was no gladsome handfasting with her kin around her but an affair of state. And she was afraid, deeply afraid of the dangers this day might bring. The touch of the feathers painting her skin aroused her senses, heightening her excitement, sweeping her mind clear of all thought but Ean. And so she was smiling as Verna finished powdering her dry.

A dagger-handle struck the lintel of the door.

"Bodyguard reporting! Ready to escort the Princess Tansen to the Marriage of the Princess Reatta."

It was Dale! Stiff, erect and expressionless. Until he saw the barbaric swirling rainbow of her skin. And the lamps of his eyes glowed, first in heart-stopping admiration, then with dawning knowledge.

Tansen knew with a sinking heart that she could not trust him to keep silent. Dale's unfettered loyalty was another danger she must face.

"Quick!" cried Verna. "Hide this bottle of wine for the libation in your cloak."

. . . .

Ean rode blithely to Dunino with Wulf at his side and the Embassy, armed and velvet-cloaked behind him. This was not how it would be once he was annointed. He'd have a fine war-horse, a shining gold crown heavy on his brow, a trio of trumpeters to go before him. And gold coins in his purse to throw to folk lining the paths, cheering at the sight of him.

This pretence at a marriage would soon be over and he'd be free to sail to his homeland. His brow wrinkled. What would they expect him to do with Reatta? He'd lie with her tonight, of course. If he'd drunk enough. But they wouldn't expect him to take her with him, would they? By Odin's beard, he wished he could think things through like Tansen. She must have seen ahead. That was why she'd not yet promised to come with him. The impact of that thought shuddered through his body and stopped his horse in its tracks. He couldn't go through with this wretched ceremony and lose Tansen.

Wulf turned his mount, aghast, when Ean stopped. Gravely and with purpose the horsemen gathered, sidled close, holding Ean within the tight knot and urging his mount forward.

Ean filled his seething lungs, seeking desperately for self-control. He'd never been so terrified. These men were far more dangerous than he'd realised. Yet down south he'd be walking in the footsteps of his father and Edwin. These Kings had had power and used it.

"Make room there!" he ordered. And grinned as the Angles eased aside.

It was the fear of losing Tansen that came uppermost in his mind as he rode on. Her fresh vitality and love of life matched his own and had drawn the heart from his body. And she had something more. A wise head on her shoulders. He couldn't live without her. She was all his strength and his comfort. And he'd need both in the days to come. She knew all his needs and satisfied them. She'd know how desperate he felt. She couldn't fail him now. Once this ghastly ritual was over he would seek her out and rest in her arms again.

The clouds in the north had turned black by the time the procession arrived at Dunino. They almost missed the narrow entrance flanked by rearing banks of undergrowth but Wulf found the hidden path.

When the path opened out Ean found himself in a circular area bounded on all sides by sheer walls of rock. It was full of people, standing, sitting on fallen boulders, muffled against the rain that was sure to follow.

From the branches of one gigantic oak-tree hung weary rags, pathetic pleas for healing. On the bark, iron nails showed where healing had been given and thanks returned. An elfin face peered and whistled at him from among the dangling skulls of sacrificed animals. And was promptly ordered down to stand, staring resentfully at broad unyielding backs.

Ean pulled irritably at his horse's mouth. The place was eerie. Not a breath of wind stirred the rags. Not a bird sang to lighten the heart with its music. The throng stayed silent, watching the Angles with wary eyes. Thunder rumbled in the distance.

He had never been in the sacred grove before. Wulf's mother had never been sure what gods he should propitiate. She was an Angle who had been baptised a Christian before coming north with her Pretani husband and two sons at the breast instead of one. But at least his foster-mother had taught him his kin-language.

The clouds growled again. A wind came from nowhere, whipped through the shaggy leaves and died.

"How primitive! A Marriage in a Grotto! And it's going to rain on us," said a Bernician at his back.

"It's the Drui's weather magic. He's going to send us back with a lightning bolt in each ear."

Sniggers sounded from among his retinue as they dismounted. Ean hunched into his cape, heavy in the moist air, ignoring them, blanking from his mind the ordeal in front of him. This was the first of many political acts he must perform. But surely the most distasteful.

With an indescribable feeling of relief he saw the King and Queen seated on High Chairs carried from the Citadel. The King's Remembrancer, the Law Giver, the whole Council were there, ranged behind. Even Dale, the Briton, for some hidden purpose of his own, no doubt. But not Tansen. He was uneasy about her non-appearance.

He opened his mouth to ask after her when a white flash of lightning blanched rocks, oaks and the florid face of the King. Quivering like leaves on a tree they waited for the thunder. Instead the sharp crack of a staff on stone drew every eye upwards.

The Arch-Drui had appeared on a jutting rock of sandstone. Above on the cliff-top, in the half-light a circle of torches ringed the Grove. And the torch-bearers, still as statues, were Drui, men and women, their naked bodies painted gold upon turquoise, vermilion on ivory, amethyst on russet, scarlet on amber. Savage, primitive, brilliant and beautiful. Sweeping curves of colour that lost themselves in secret folds of skin to bloom elsewhere with renewed vigour, emblazoning the faith of the Pretani in their gods and in themselves. And at their backs, like dark outlandish birds of prey, the stolid figures of cloaked and booted Danish soldiers. The thunder rolled, nearer and more menacing.

Wulf muttered a warning at Ean to move. But Ean stood rooted to the ground, deeply impressed by the towering figure of the Arch-Drui on the rock. A headdress of leaves, skilfully intertwined, gave him added height. Trailing leaves cascaded down either side of his face, mingling with his beard, seeming to sprout out of his mouth.

Ean found himself strangely moved. This was no light commitment he was about to make. If only it had been Tansen he would meet on the rock the commitment would have been welcome.

He smiled grimly. When he was still a callow youth Reatta's mystic beauty had attracted him. Her eyes had beguiled him till he felt he was drowning in their sea-black depths, struggling, feeling his will-power eroding and he would be trapped for ever if he did not escape. If only Tansen was here, beautiful Tansen, whose presence fed and strengthened him.

Wulf prodded him towards a flight of steps cut into the Rock. He shook himself free and braced his shoulders. With each reluctant step he felt the trap closing about him. Wulf and the Angles below, Reatta and the Arch-Drui above.

The Arch-Drui's cloak billowed in the breeze. In its midnight blue depths were embroidered all the signs of his weather-magic, signs of nature's power formalised into the insignia of the tribes of the Pretani, the jagged lightning, the arc of the rainbow, the crescent of the Maiden, the discs of the rising and setting sun. What was he letting himself in for? Was the Kingship of the North Humber Land worth all this turmoil in his breast? Yes it was! Think of the power he would command, the adulation. He could be as great a King as Edwin. And more. Given the chance.

He bounded up the last few steps and came face to face with three more figures. A Drui on one side holding the everlasting flame in a golden bowl. On the other, a Drui holding the life-giving water in a crystal bowl. Between them stood a woman with a light veil over her face, a strange exotic face of many colours. And he looked deep into the glorious green eyes of Tansen.

His whole being expanded with love. He did not know why she was there. But suddenly he was on fire, his blood molten gold, his sinews rippling bronze. There was nothing he could not achieve if he had Tansen at his side.

CHAPTER NINETEEN

Wulf, watching his milk-brother, was silently asking the Great Ones to ensure that Ean carried himself bravely in front of these suave courtiers from the North Humber Land when he saw the adoration break like the sun from clouds on Ean's face. It seemed that the next bolt of lightning flashed inside his brain. That woman up there! It could only be the Water-Kelpie! This was the wrong Princess!

He pushed through the Angles and stared upwards, unable to believe his eyes. Although her face was veiled he knew without doubt by the way Ean leapt forward. This morning he'd found them talking in the garden. Ean must have known then. His hurt at Ean's deceit exploded like a dagger-wound in his chest. Never before had his milk-brother lied to him. His breath caught painfully in his throat at this bitter blow to his love for Ean.

The figures above began making the motions of the ritual. He clenched his fists. The Arch-Drui, the King, everyone must know about this exchange of brides except himself. Which idiot among them had thought up this ludicrous plan? The Water-Kelpie, of course! He grasped at the excuse. Better than believing Eanfrith had deceived him.

Smothering his hurt, he thrust through the crowd. He must save Ean from this folly. These soldiers were not fools to be easily duped. Ean was risking his career, his life! All for a fleeting love affair.

Halfway up the staircase a naked Drui arm barred his way. Over the two bowed heads the Arch-Drui's eyes bored into his. Wulf's heart beat wildly. He had taken his kinship from his Danish mother to be like Ean. Yet the blood of his Pretani father feared the power of the Arch-Drui.

Thunder growled, gathering volume. It filled the sky and resounded in Wulf's head and it was the voice of Marten. What words were used Wulf could not say. But the strength drained out of his limbs and he fell back helplessly against the rocky wall.The pair were kneeling now where a smooth basin had been hollowed out on the top of the natural platform, and were cleansing their hands in the pure water.

"Let the sowing-hand of the woman grasp the sword-hand of the man."

Rose-painted fingers, silver-tipped, held fast the hand of his milk-brother. The woman was helping Ean with his responses in Attecottie. He let his mind absorb the suspicion that it was the Arch-Drui and the woman who were using Ean in a plot against the Angles.

He twisted his head away, meaning to shout downwards to the Angles. He saw triumph glittering in their faces, craftiness in their grins, greed in their eyes. And he paused knowing real terror for the first time. It had bothered him that the nobles were all from Bernicia. Why was there not at least one Deiran to stamp the seal of his approval? He snapped his mouth shut.

"May the Shining Ones smile ..." The rest of the Drui's words were lost. Lightning like the flash of a javelin cracked open a tree on the cliff-top as though the giant axe of Thor had split it. Down came the rain, hissing in long silver rods. The cloaks of the people below billowed as the rain drove them before it out of the grotto like fallen leaves.

Those who stood on the pillar of rock were sheltered from the storm by an overhang. The Drui's powerful voice commanded that the strength of the Omnipotent Ones would flow through him into the hearts and spirits of the young couple.

With that the ritual was complete. The libations had been made. In the rush to mount and ride back to the Citadel, Wulf eased himself behind Ean to protect his back. He could see no way forward that was not ringed with peril. Despite the darkness of his mood, he was aware that Dale rode knee to knee with him as if he too sensed danger.

Back at the Citadel Wulf barged in on Ean kissing his woman in the privacy of his chamber. His anxiety and hurt overflowed.

"I hope you know what you've done, you fool?" he hissed through his teeth in Danish.

Ean's grin flashed over his shoulder and he tightened his arms round the woman's waist.

"They have their marriage! And I have my Princess," he retorted lightly in Pretani.

"You've put all our lives in danger! Wait till they discover that the eldest Princess is still free to marry another King."

The woman turned, positively glowing with triumph and desire.

"Sorry, Wulf! At a time like this, a wife's closer than a milk-brother!"

Wulf, sick with fury, could not bring himself to answer her.

"Why didn't you tell me what you planned?" he shouted at Ean.

"Because I didn't know myself. And I'm glad I didn't. Because I'd have let it slip to you and you'd have stopped it."

Some of the hurt went from Wulf but not his bitterness at the woman.

"Can't you see she's tricked you into marriage?"

"Don't talk rot, man!" Ean growled. "Go and fiddle your tune somewhere else, brother Wulf."

"The Angles won't accept a Queen with byre-muck between her toes!"

"Wulf, do I have to throw you out?"

Suddenly Ean was shaking Wulf by the throat.

"Stop it!" The woman with the painted face stood between them, thrusting them apart. Wulf recoiled from her touch and stood adjusting his tunic. From now on she would always be there between them. The thought sickened him.

"At least listen to this much before you wallow in bed! These nobles are all Bernicians. Not a Deiran among them. Doesn't that strike you as peculiar?"

"Why shouldn't my own kin be sent to bring me back?

"And they've big plans for you."

"Great! Scamper off and find out what they are, there's a good chap." Ean threw off his jacket.

Wulf swallowed the insult. He had already asked questions of the Angles and had been told to mind his own pot of stew.

"Any fool can read their minds."

Ean turned sharply at his acid tone. Quickly Wulf jumped in.

"You never thought to ask how Edwin died, did you? It was Cadwallon of Gwynedd who defeated him. Since then he's devastated the North Humber Land. The Embassy need this Pretani alliance to show they have friends in the north."

"Well, they have it, man!"

"But not the army and the treasure you would command once Garnard went. They want you with your foot planted firmly in the door of the Kingship. Now that plan's gone out of the window."

Wulf had Ean's full attention now. He rushed on hardly pausing for breath.

"If Garnard had refused the marriage alliance, at least they had a King who could marry a daughter of Cadwallon to get the best terms for peace. Now you're no use to them. When they find out they'll dump you and go off to proclaim one of your brothers as King."

The implication hit Ean between the eyes. He could lose his precious Kingship. His hands fell from Tansen. He stood perfectly still for a heartbeat. Then he pushed the threat from his mind with an angry wave of his hands.

"I don't believe it. They've nothing to gain by allying with the Scots in Dal Riata. You're letting your jealousy run away with you. Get out!"

Ean stalked stiff-legged to the window, his mind opening to the fact that the whole east coast from Deira to the Orcades could belong to a King of

North Humber Land. Maybe he should have safeguarded his position by marrying Reatta. Tansen would have understood. She always did.

Wulf left to allow Ean time to think things through, leaving the bead curtain swinging and rattling behind him. Outside he leaned against the Courtyard wall, wiping his brow to clear the hurt from his mind. He was glad Ean had not lied to him. He had just been more gullible than usual, his mind ensnared by that woman. Wulf clenched his fists, wishing they were round her throat.

For the first time he found his oath to Ean more than he could bear. He was bound to Ean and therefore to the Angles. But at times he longed to throw a blanket on a horse and set out to find his father and brothers and work with them. He ran his hands over the shaped stone of the wall and his fingers found the mason's mark, a trident, in a corner. How good it would be to chip and chisel at a stone and make something that he could look at with pride even if it was just a perfectly shaped corner-stone. He rubbed the dust off his fingers and the fantasy from his mind. From now on he would hide a dagger in each boot.

Behind Ean's rigid back Tansen held a taper to the lamp at the door ledge and lit every cruisie she could find. Unusually thoughtful, Ean turned and she swished the heavy curtain across the window, shutting out the dismal day. Then she stood in the centre of the room and dropped her robe.

Ean sucked in his breath as her wonderfully painted body took fire in the glow of the new-lit lamps. A rainbow of gem colours, vivid and glossy, flowed like syrup as she moved, tempting him until his breathing tightened the laces across his chest. His finger-tips followed the rivers of sapphire and carnelian, topaz and aquamarine, beryl and jasper, coiling, meandering, undulating to where they wreathed into her secret sappy places. He raised incredulous eyes to her face and her smile, for him alone, was more radiant than her body. And he forgot everything, caught in a mill-race of passion, and his being melted into hers.

But Tansen's mind wandered, missing the whirr of a pigeon's wing and the pound of the surf and the slow beat at the heart of the Mother. The bed heaved and squeaked alarmingly. And the enormity of what she had done came back to haunt her. Now she had to face the fury of the Angles when the deception was discovered. Wulf's words came back, stabbing her with fear. The Angles had wanted the Treasure and an army as well as power over the whole east coast. She could bring none of these with her. And now they could not even use Ean to marry Cadwallon's daughter.

She buried her face in the soft skin at Ean's neck. But the sweet sleeping smell of him gave her no comfort. Oh, what a fool she'd been!

She was surrounded by enemies now. Wulf! How he must despise her! Ean had lost a valued friend and protector. The Angles whom she had betrayed! And Reatta! Garnard and the Court who had sacrificed her for their own well-being! How could Marten protect her now?

Another memory came winging in and would not be stifled. It was while she was standing on the Rock at Dunino. The rain had come. And she had lifted her head, aware of the smell of the Mother opening her earthy pores to the life-giving rain. And she had breathed in the living essence of the Mother as she used to do at Pitcarlie. And that familiar yearning had yawned inside her, hungry and unsatisfied, an empty space that Ean could not fill. For he was a child who needed her and would give nothing back in return.

Nothing but his love, she reminded herself. And surely that was enough.

CHAPTER TWENTY

In the dusky red of a harvest night, Tansen lay half-asleep on a clover-scented haystack, as round and yielding as a woman's breast. Ean twined red poppies in her hair. And there came a trampling and turmoil around them and she sprang up shouting "Quick! The kye are in the cornfield!" She wakened abruptly.

Armed men filled Ean's room, throwing back the curtain, calling for Ean. And as the bright noon light invaded the room Tansen quickly found a veil to cover her face. But Ean's retinue ignored her, helping Ean to dress, laughing and pumping him on the back. And they went hunting, leaving the air tingling.

She ambled round the bed-chamber, opened a chest and bent to inhale the essence of Ean from the linen and wool inside. The cloak on a peg at the door was the one she had worn to enter the Citadel. She draped herself in it again, fumbling with the unfamiliar central pin of the shoulder clasps, admiring the garnets sunk in gold foil on a base plate of solid gold. She unrolled the kid-skins placed neatly on a shelf and saw the oiled precision of the weapons therein, Wulf's handiwork. And knew she did not belong in this foreign male domain.

Nor did she belong in that other room in the King-House where Verna waited for her.

The morning's downpour had given way to a bleak drizzle. In the Wise Woman's garden Tansen took shelter in a bower. The flowers had withered and fallen. Their leaves gathered the fine rain into droplets that swelled and fell and sank into the sodden earth. But here she felt at home, welcome, still in her Bride's dress, her hair flowing free. The dank smell of wet earth touched some deep primeval need within her. And she felt the pull of the Mother and knew she would never be free of her. The need to be close to her was ingrained in the deep dark throb of her blood.

In her imagination she went burrowing with the worms and grubs under the dark brown earth, fulfilling their own needs and the needs of the soil at the same time. And she looked at the idle hands in her lap as if they belonged to someone else.

Then in her memory she was walking barefoot in the wet red clay of Pitcarlie among the reek of woodsmoke and dung and a new-ploughed field and tending the needs of land and beasts.

At Pitcarlie she would have been setting up her own hearth with her own man and they would have worked together in the the age-old routine of the seasons. The cycles of the year would have given meaning to their life together. Here she was a Princess yet she was nobody. No beast, no being, no living crop depended on her. She was entrapped in a game of plot and counterplot, a game played in Courts that in later years would not even be worth a bard-song. Far less a poet's dinner.

While the land would outlast them all, long after their flurries of petty pride had blown away on the wind. And those grey muddy clouds so close above her head would sail southwards forever, trailing swathes of mist on the hilltops.

The slither of a foot on a wet leaf. No one in sight. But a feeling of someone, nearby.

She waited, listening, then shook herself. It was a pity that now she had gained a little of what she wanted she no longer felt that first fine excitement. Instead she felt entrapped in a loop of time, waiting. Waiting for the Angles to find out the truth. Waiting to see if they would accept her as Ean's Queen. Waiting to see what lay behind Reatta's dimpled smile.

It was queer that the dimples did not deepen innocently in Reatta's cheeks but tilted the corners of her mouth and pushed her lips forward. Somewhere she had seen another face like that. It had been carved in stone and had pointed ears and eyebrows and had made her shiver.

A form took shape in the darkness of a hedge. Aeron, his robes hidden by a cloak, beckoning. Curious she followed him round the back of the King-House down the dark steps of an alley-way. A glint of mail before a low door hidden in ivy and she guessed that Reatta was being kept under guard.

Who had been given the task of telling her about the substitution? Had it been Marten, austere and indifferent to her rage? Or Garnard, certain it was his idea? With a new string of pearls and a whisper of a handsome stranger to come. At least, Ean would not have to wear that ill-omened cloak. It would fall on the shoulders of some unsuspecting foreigner.

At a glimpse of Aeron's Drui robes the guard stood aside.

"Does the Arch-Drui know that Reatta uses you as her errand-boy?" asked Tansen.

Aeron hid his tortured face in his hood as Tansen passed him to enter. The dank smell that came from the darkness beyond made Tansen turn her head away in disgust. Steadying herself she took a step into a dim cavern of a room, lit only by a single flame from an oil-lamp and two high square windows.

As the curtain whispered back into place wild shapes reared and writhed around her. Stems spiralling out of pots, straining up the walls in slow sinuous ascent. Tortured leaves twisting, pleading. Silent prayers for light screamed in the air.

"There you are, Pagan, still stinking of cows' udders and mealy puddings, and thinking how you've netted a bonny King and a gold crown for your head."

The throaty whisper floated from behind a spray of long slippery leaves. It was a setting designed to invoke mystery and awe and to suggest that power burgeoned here unchallenged. It was agonising and it was pitiful. And indescribably false. And Tansen, admiring the green canopy that hung from the roof, struggled with a strong desire to laugh.

"In the name of the Green Man of Grindgold, what sort of cuckoo's nest have you built here?"

Enthroned among the plaited ropes of a vine, Reatta smiled at Tansen's remark. A cheap jibe, she thought, the only weapon the pagan has left. Until this woman had arrived, Reatta's life had been a bridle-path leading smoothly between serried ranks of flowery courtiers. Now she would uproot this weed and throw it on the dung-heap. Amusing for a day or two, even exciting, but in no way a challenge.

"You think there's been a contest between us, I expect. And that you've won. Yet you must have wondered why I allowed the Marriage to take place."

Tansen communed with a stunted willow, weeping in its bowl.

"Because you were forced into it as I was."

The faint chuckle did not stir the mild leaves.

"Oh no, you underestimate me. No one forces my hand. It was my idea from the beginning."

Braced to meet some fanciful excuse, Tansen found herself utterly astonished. First she herself, then Marten, then the King, now Reatta. So who had planted the original idea in someone's head? Her fingers caught and stilled a trembling leaf.

"Yet you told me you wanted Ean for yourself," she said softly.

"I toyed with the idea. He's a pretty boy. Gullible. And handy. One quick thrust of his knife and my father would be out of the Kingship."

"So that's the way your mind works," Tansen replied. "Why, you're uetterly ruthless! At least I've saved Ean from humiliation. And worse. Innocent he may be but he's good and wholesome and loving."

The dark smokey voice spoke again.

"I've no desire to marry a puppet who dances to the tune of the Angles. When I'm Queen, I'll pull the strings. Besides I prefer men with muscles in their thighs."

Tansen had assumed she was a virgin. She should have guessed. Reatta's body was a merely tool she would use to achieve her ends.

Suddenly Tansen began to gasp for breath. Her hand went to her throat. She was suffocating! This was not just an over-abundance of plants. And then she had it! The air was vibrating with a silent sucking power. Reatta was drawing the living strength from the plants. And giving nothing in return. She felt Reatta's hidden gaze on the nape of her neck seeking to leech energy from her also. She had diverted Tansen's mind so that she would not notice.

Now a misty blackness invaded her mind, seeking to overpower her. Tansen fought against it.using the words of old familiar spells that invoked the gods. In her panic the words meant nothing but she repeated them over and over. Slowly their amcient power began to block the invasion of the dark force.

Reatta gave a low growl of frustration and Tansen found herself thinking clearly again.

"You sensed me there on the edges, did you?" A soft laugh, like the gurgle of a blocked drain. "It was a warning. If I cared to use my powers to the full, you wouldn't be able to withstand it."

But I did withstand it, Tansen thought. And now that I've been warned it won't happen again, my girl. I wonder how many people know that you've sunk to such depths of depravity.

"What do you hope to gain, Reatta? You have everything, chests full of jewels and robes, servants. You'll be Queen in time. Your beauty is a bard's delight."

"You envy these trifles, do you, pagan? Yet all my life I've slept in swansdown and played with golden balls. They mean nothing to me."

"Your days could be filled with light. Yet you spend them in this strange half-lit room, dank and festering like the inside of a fairy hill. Why?"

"I want power." It was a mere puff of breath.

"And you'll exploit anyone to gain it."

"How clever of you to realise that. You've more wit than I expected in a pagan. Still to me you're nothing but a shabby little fireweed and I'll grind you under my foot before your seeds are blown on the wind."

Reatta was feeling exultant. Excitement brought a warm tingle flooding from her groin, firing her nipples into life against the silk of her garments. Ever since the pagan had rung the Bell and tried to gather the people to her cause, Reatta had wanted to see her cringe in defeat.

"You thought you might be Queen some day, didn't you? You were going to rouse the Clan Mothers against me, weren't you?"

Suddenly Tansen knew what she had done. Thinking only of her own desires she had betrayed the Clan Mothers and Grannie Bea. By marrying Ean she was leaving them in the hands of this perverted creature who would suck the land dry to satisfy her consuming lust. She had allowed the King to make use of her to cheat the Angles. Because of her love for Ean she had sold her people into a worse slavery than the Angles would impose. .

"Not even a sniff at the Chair of the Queen, Pagan. I made sure of that. Take your Angle and leave, before I'm tempted to destroy you."

A beady baleful eye peered from among the leaves. A raven tottered along a branch that bent under his weight. Before he could spread his wings his tether pulled him in an ungainly flurry to the ground. He shook his feathers, deposited a white heap on the floor and waddled with dignity into a corner.

A hysterical giggle rose in Tansen's throat. The gods had sent a sign. She had at least one weapon she could use against Retta, a good earthy sense of humour. She gathered all her calm and courage and prepared to gamble against this breathy disembodied voice. "Oh, come out from behind your fake greenery and stop play-acting, Reatta."

After a long moment the overhanging leaves parted and Reatta came to stand above the solitary lamp so that it lit the planes of her face with a queer opal light and left her eyes as mysterious black holes. Her robe fell away into the shadows. Yet, Tansen noticed that she was breathing harshly through white nostrils and her skin was sheened with a pale film of sweat.

"You're not fooling me with your pathetic show of power, Reatta. The performance is over and the audience has not cried for more!"

"You don't understand!" said Reatta. The curl of her lip was so slight it hardly dimpled her cheeks. "I have the power to destroy you!"

They faced one another across the lamp, their voices low and intense, their faces composed, their hands calm and crossed, only a faint milky-whiteness at the knuckles.

"You! You've nothing! Except unsatisfied lust."

"That's true. Where other women lust for men, I lust for power." Reatta breathed.

As if released by her avowal, she began to sway, undulating like a serpent, fastening her gaze on Tansen. Tansen's head began to spin again. She opened her lungs, to fill them with air and smelt only the feral scent of a cat in heat. Strands of power radiated from Reatta's head. This was how the Druad focussed the minds of their pupils on the gods. But Reatta was using it to cast a spell on her. And she had to break the enchantment. Her voice cracked slightly.

"Power? All you have are a few tricks you've gouged out of Aeron. And a skill in drama you learned from your mother."

Reatta's angry hiss had the effect of clearing Tansen's mind again. The lamp brightened on Reatta's hair. Tansen saw that it had been lime-washed to stuck out stiffly round her face. She broke into a spontaneous laugh.

"Oh, Reatta, that hair-style does nothing for your mean little features."

The air between them crackled.

"You know nothing of the powers I can conjure up. Come!" Neatly, Reatta picked up the lamp.

Tansen followed her into an inner room, glad to escape the tortured greenery. The lamplight fell on a vast hanging tapestry. Tansen recognised the shapes of the weather-signs of the Druad. But the Druad had forbidden the use of their magic signs on tapestries. This one seemed to have been worked by a child, and badly stitched at that. Then she became aware that the shapes had been deliberately distorted. She flinched back, repelled, and sucked in her breath. And by the blaze of pride in Reatta's eyes Tansen knew she had woven evil spells into the shapes.

A shiver ran across her skin from shoulder to thigh. This was a dangerous game Reatta played, re-creating the mysteries of the Druad in a new and loathsome light.

"Do you really think you can match wits with Marten? It takes twenty-one years to learn the secrets of the Druad. You're gorging yourself on half-truths without taking time to digest them."

Now Tansen knew that she also had to be ruthless, had to strip Reatta of her pretence. How?

CHAPTER TWENTY ONE

Reatta turned a slight shoulder and placed the lamp on a table where its light spilled onto leaves and stems, roots and flower-heads and seeds.

"What's this?" Tansen realised with a leap of her heart that she had Reatta at her mercy. "You bought these from a pedlar, didn't you?" She picked up a bunch of dried elder leaves. "Did he snip them on the right day and in the right way? For if not they'll carry the curse of the Elder Mother instead of her protection."

She saw Reatta's head jerk and smiled inwardly. She had guessed aright. She could not see Reatta creeping out in the dawn to take the good of the plants when their potency was at its height.

Blatantly showing her contempt she sniffed potions, pinched dried roots and ground powders with her thumb in her palm.

"You'd have learned more if you'd been born a pagan," she said."Oho! Pearlwort juice? Is that what you slip into Aeron's drink to make him pour out his secrets."

Tansen shook a bunch of roots in front of Reatta's blank face.

"Purple orchis! You've enough here to have him running naked, climbing trees, and spewing out how to commune with the All-Powerful Ones." Tansen opened her hand and the roots thudded on the table. "But only if you pull them before sunrise and with your face to the East." Reatta clutched the edge of the tabe. How dare the pagan humiliate her! In her own chamber too! Only a chosen few had ever been invited inside and they had crept away struck dumb with fear.

Long involved curses surged into Reatta's mind. She would gouge out Aeron's eyes and hang them dripping round his neck! She would pick out the feathers of that shitting raven one by one! But sweetest of all would be her revenge on this woman!

Not by a flicker of an eyelid did Reatta reveal the depths of her humiliation. But an icy serpent coiled round Tansen's heart. For she guessed she had touched the woman's core.

"So that's the dream that festers. To challenge the power of the Wise Ones."

Reatta's open artless eyes widened till the iris was a jet island in a sea of white.

"What other delights can the world offer that I've not tasted and found wanting?" For all its low husky overtones it was a dry sexless voice.

Tansen let out a pent-up sigh of sheer incredulity.

"Reatta, once upon a time you were a laughing child, pure and innocent. What made you choose this corrupt path?"

Dainty fingers fluttered at Reatta's waist and stilled. She gave a slow undulating sigh from some deep dark depths of her being. Suddenly her eyes misted and softened in a silent appeal, as though she had a sad desperate need to be saved from herself.

But when Tansen, touched by the fear she had glimpsed, put out a hand, the eyes became black empty pools again, like lonely tarns hidden between bare bleak hillsides, reflecting nothing. And Reatta spoke, a perverse smile in her voice.

"Do my powers not frighten you?" she asked.

Tansen knew if Reatta had had a moment of truth, that it had passed. "Frighten me? Hah! You've only made a fool of yourself! This is a pathetic display of powers you'll never possess. Oh, there was a certain bravado about your performance." She became more confiding. "But I'll tell you when your magic will strike fear in my heart. On the day when you stop showing it off. Because then I'll know you really do possess powers beyond mine."

Reatta's lips parted. She gave forth a tiny, shuddering scream like a thwarted child.

"Father god, Mother god, and all the host of Guardians, deliver me!" The childhood prayer flooded Tansen's mind. "Go, with my curse upon you!" Reatta whispered. "That you'll never bear a child to your pretty King!"

A blue film covered the trance-like eyes. Tansen tried to keep her voice steady.

"I'll leave you with your toys. But I'm warning you! You're tampering with forces you can't control!"

With Reatta's throaty chuckle receding behind her Tansen sped up the dark alley holding her skirts from contact with the elfin forms that seemed to be lurking, darting, sniggering in the shadowy corners.

In the Garden of the Wise Woman she stood for a moment, panting, letting the rain cleanse her face and hands. Still she felt unclean. Quickly she made all the signs to the Guardians to protect her against the Dark Force. From Reatta's table she had taken a root of rue and now she went on her left knee to say the spell and bind it into a ring for her finger to arm her spirit against Reatta's spite. The ring of rue was harsh against her skin. But it was like the spells and prayers she had been taught as a child. The words were queer and strange and meaningless. Yet to a mind that was numb with terror or grief they were a lifeline till the dark dread passed.

But then she found herself slumped on the wet grass, holding her head and rocking. Oh, what had she done? Love had ensnared her. She had been too willing to believe that Marten would solve everything, that she could forget her mission and enjoy life. She had forgotten her origins and become puffed up with pride, sitting at the High Table, wearing fine cloth, deriding Reatta. Scheming to marry her lover and become Queen of the Angles. How could she? How could she?

She had seen her kin murdered and raped. And now she was betraying them by going to live among the same hated Spear-Danes. She who had vowed to make a praise-song of the suffering of her kin.

She had rung Caterin's Bell and railed at the King and Queen and Council, sneering at them for the vanity that possessed them and coloured their decisions. And what was it but vanity that was making her leave her own kin-folk to fend for themselves while she went off with an Angle? She moaned in an agony of guilt, despising herself. She was no better than Reatta.

"Now you know the size of the task I set you!"

And warm and golden into her mind came the presence of Grannie Bea. And she answered.

"But it's too big for me. I can't do it."

And words came storming through Tansen's brain. 'Of course you can! You have a whole lifetime before you. Go forward towards the light', over and over until they faded away into nothing.

Then gentle as a sigh.

'And now I can go home.'

Tansen knew she should be glad. For Grannie Bea had passed over to join her children. But a feeling of deep loss overwhelmed her.

"Oh Grannie Bea, tell me what to do. How can I go on without you?"

'Home,' sighed the damp leaves.

No one could help her now. Grannie Bea's arrow had fallen, broken, short of the target. And the Dark Force was still there in the Citadel, working through Reatta. For when Reatta became Queen she would suck the land and the folk dry as she did with her plants.

Caterin's Bell boomed into her thoughts. Nothing had changed. It was still used as a dinner gong.

Verna had done wonders with the weaving women and held out another new robe for her to wear.

"It's time you looked like a Queen. Why don't you ask the Keeper of the Treasure for some jewels?"

"I'll go as I am - a plain pagan," said Tansen, splashing water on her face.

That night the King had a gumboil. A scarf held a hot compress to his cheek. And he had been drinking to ease the throb in his jaw. He glowered at the saddles of lamb, growled at Eanfrith and Tansen at his side and eyed the Angles with sour distaste.

Their mission accomplished the Angles were merry, loud in their eating and drinking. While the Court ate wormwood and drank gall and, falsely smiling, enquired of the Angles when they would be escorting their new King home. For a drunken Adviser had mumbled the secret of the false Marriage to his lady and the whisper had taken wings.

Later, springing on tables, yellow hair flying, the Angles bellowed bawdy songs and coarser riddles and challenged the young Pretani men to wrestle.

The swaggering and arrogance and reckless vitality, the beauty of buttered limbs and straining sinews had an earthy vigour that Tansen liked. This was nearer to what a King's court should be. Not a ritual adoration of food with a grovelling praise-song at the end.

Ean was enticing the reluctant Dale to throw off all but his leggings. And Tansen saw, above the livid stripes on his back, the mark of a slave-ring. Someone had owned him once! And might own him still! For if his sword could be bought, so too could his loyalty.

Then down by the long hearth came Reatta, pausing in her sweeping passage neither for hurling body nor grinning firedog. At once Tansen knew she should have thought about her appearance after all. For Reatta was magnificent, in a dress the colour of rich clotted cream slashed by strands of blood-red and overlaid by a blaze of gold and a sparkle of gems. A black velvet cape fell in straight folds from the nape of her neck to her heels. And at her back, tottered a protesting guard with a bleeding arm and carrying a bloody Drui robe.

Gradually the circling and somersaulting, the feinting and double-feinting stopped. Gouging heel and gripping hand fell away.

"She should have been shackled in irons!" someone growled.

Tansen knew then that she should never have humiliated Reatta. For she had come to seek her revenge, to destroy the woman who had belittled her.

Reatta halted inside the circle of tumbled bodies, swaying slightly so that light sparked from her jewelled breast. She outshone the brown Queen and the plain pagan. She looked what she was, a woman of importance, the eldest Princess. Aghast, the Angles compared the two women with their eyes.

"Take her away! She'll destroy us all!" In one swift horrified movement the crowd rose to their feet. The King stopped nursing his gumboil, threw out his hands and bellowed at his daughter. The Council came slipping, tripping, stumbling down the steps, hands flapping, to silence her.

But the Angles had all the confirmation they needed. Reatta had chosen her moment and her position well. The Angles moved, muttering, to encircle her. And she knew she was safer with them than with her own folk. For the Angles would always need the eldest Princess to gain access to the Kingship.

Reatta waited, fingers neatly laced over an emerald belt, sweetly, silently in control of the drama. And the powers Tansen had scorned so bravely were already there, burgeoning like black smoke from a greenwood fire, behind the obsidian eyes.

"Spear-Danes." The voice, resonant for one so slight, oozed condescension. "You really must oil your brains as well as your bodies. Now do you see the truth for yourselves? That you've been tricked by the deadliest hold in the world. You have yielded the first and last fall. And to a woman. That woman!"

She pointed at Tansen.

Ean sprang up from the High Table and stopped transfixed by a knife lovingly placed at the soft pulsing side of his throat.

"I am the eldest Princess! And free to marry again! Your Prince Eanfrith has married a pagan trollop! Now he can never be King of the Pretani! Unless she dies!"

Vengeance in their eyes, daggers snatched up from tables in their hands. And Dale leaping from nowhere to shield Tansen with his body

CHAPTER TWENTY TWO

"How very interesting!"

Smooth as silk, speaking perfect Pretani, an unknown voice rang through the Hall. A thunder of running boots. Pewter tumbling and clanging. Sharp short grunts of grappling men. Cries of outrage, screams.

Through the haze of heat and smoke came a small neat man, tawny as a fox from his soft-stepping toes to his pointed beard.

Tansen, her spirit bare and burning on the edge of terror, came from behind Dale's shoulder to see the Bernicians caught and held by unfamiliar soldiers. And Reatta, her brilliant breast heaving, black burning discs of eyes fixed on her prey, her cloak unfurling and beating through the air like powerful hunting wings, making for Tansen with upraised dagger.

Dale sprang, clasping Reatta's pearled wrist, whirling her round, clamping her to his body. Face to face with him, she broke into a series of short panting squeals. And stopped in mid-gasp as her eyes rippled over the glittering band of nobles, swords unsheathed, spreading out to cover every corner of the Hall.

The Master of the King's Forests flicked the dagger out of her grasp with finger and thumb. And Dale wrested her aside.

"It's Lord Beofric!"

Where the whispers came from Tansen could not tell but they grew in volume. And neatly embroidered on the short riding cloak of the fox-like man, was the Deiran insignia.

"My Lord King!" came Lord Beofric's high barking voice. "We pray pardon for intruding on your feast. We did not dare to send a herald. It was imperative to land under cover of night in silence and secrecy. For there is treason afoot."

The bandaged head of the King, rose, glowing as orange as a turnip lantern, and threw a garbled query aloft.

Taking the King's permission as granted, Lord Beofric swung to scan the Hall. The Bernician Embassy, still stripped to their waists, were now ringed with swords, their cup-bearers and retinues disarmed. Ean's retinue, too, had been caught in the rush to protect him. Wulf stood halfway up the steps, swords crossed over his breast, his eyes blazing.

Lord Beofric bowed exceedingly low, ending with a flourish, smacking, Tansen thought, of mockery.

"No harm will come to you and yours, my Lord King. As you see, we have the villains we came for." Lord Beofric chuckled smoothly. "Rebel

Bernicians who betrayed their King and dared to try to control the eastern seaboard. My lord, they cannot even control themselves. They would have turned your banquets into orgies, rutting on tables with your wenches and vomiting on tapestries!"

"No!" It was Ean crying out in anguish, seeing his Kingship slipping away. "That's a lie! You Deirans have always scorned us Bernicians! Now you're trying to discredit us!"

Two strides and there was a stocky man standing at the Deiran's dagger-side, the Bernician insignia on his tunic. Both men glanced at each other and then with interest to where Ean stood, every golden hair gleaming with sweat. But their business must be with the King whose land they had entered unlawfully. The Bernician spoke.

"Yes, these are my kinsmen, my Lord King, I grieve to say it. Fortunately but a traitorous few, with their skins full of greed and their tripes full of lust."

"My Lord King," said Beofric smoothly, "you must have thought it strange that an Embassy from North Humber Land consisted only of Bernicians, younger sons and landless at that."

And the King, struggling to unwind his scarf, stiffened, caught unawares by this unexpected news.

"Indeed," he enunciated carefully at last out of his lop-sided mouth. "But they informed us that King Edwin had been killed in battle by Cadwallon. I assumed that the brave Deirans were still pursuing the murderer."

Lord Beofric paused to let the face-saving lie die a respectable death. "My Lord, hear the sorry tale from my Bernician comrade, Earl Theobold."

Lord Beofric's act had been perfect. Every speech had been backed with strength yet held an added face-saver for the King.

But the stocky man raised eyes that were clear and honest and without guile. His voice was resolute although his new-learned Pretani stumbled and he turned once or twice to Beofric for a word.

"For seventeen years Bernicia and Deira have lived in peace under Edwin's rule. But young men lust for gold and glory and land. They saw Edwin shower these gifts on the Church and their resentment grew. When Cadwallon rose in rebellion in the west they seized their chance to betray Edwin."

A sword whistled and clanged. A hand, creeping for a dagger, was snatched back, spilling blood where there had been fingers. Smoothly Lord Beofric took up the story.

"On the eve of battle they alerted Cadwallon that our King would draw aside in prayer with his commanders. And at dawn, in a tiny chapel behind the lines, Cadwallon's men fell upon Edwin and his commanders and sons and murdered them. Our leaderless army was destroyed and scattered. Now Edwin and his heirs lie dead, betrayed by these very traitors who have feasted in your Hall."

Tansen moaned, feeling the shock and apprehension that must be sweeping through Eanfrith's body.

"Now Cadwallon's savages are cutting a wide swathe through our land, leaving behind them rape and slaughter and fire-blackened earth." Lord Theobold's voice shook with the fierceness of his anger.

The King's swollen face took on a greyish tinge. His shaking hand found his cup. A trickle of wine from the corner of his mouth dripped onto his tunic.

"Cadwallon is set on exterminating Angles," went on Earl Theobold. "This ruthless barbarian spares neither women nor children, putting them all to death most horribly and ravaging our countryside."

Lord Beofric seemed to have little emotion to spare for the country folk.

"This rabble here plotted to strike while North Humber Land was in confusion. First, to put Prince Eanfrith, in your place, my Lord King."

Garnard growled.

"Then to bring the youth south at the head of your army and to annoint him as King of North Humber Land. For, you see, he is a younger son too, a Bernician, and landless, like themselves and he would reward them with the estates of us Deirans. Or so they thought."

Garnard growled again. Tansen thought it was the safest contribution he could make. Eanfrith stared at the speaker with stricken eyes.

"I have the proof here in words written by a nobleman whose son is a member of this vicious plot. Since the father's disclosure came too late to save Edwin, he has joined his King on his last voyage."

A cry arose from one of the plotters. Beofric turned to the disgraced Bernicians and snarled softly but with venom.

"You scum! You have betrayed a great King and sent him to his death." His chest swelled. His hands spread-eagled at his thighs. "I regret that out of politeness I cannot have you massacred where you stand. I will teach you that you cannot use Deirans like pawns in a board-game."

The King sucked on his swollen lower lip. Tansen guessed that his pride was stinging worse than his mouth.

"We ask permission to hold these men in your prisons until the executions are carried out."

Earl Theobold had neatly diffused Beofric's anger and handed the King back some control of the situation.

"Where's my Commander?" The King hurried to exert his authority. "Ah, there you are! Have these prisoners removed!"

With uncommon zeal the soldiers of the King's Guard beat the bare-backed Bernicians with the flat of their swords into a shuffling procession and led them outside.

"Leave the Prince and his retinue here, you dolts!"

Ean, released, lifted his head proudly but the weight of his disappointment was more than his shoulders could bear. Tansen left the shelter of Dale's broad back. She took Ean's arm, trying desperately to comfort him, guessing that he was barely aware of her. The King rose, shifting the weight of his robes and the chain of office on his shoulders.

"Show me your credentials then, if you come in peace," he said.

One by one the nobles laid their swords and scabbards at the feet of the King. Beofric produced a roll of vellum from his sleeve with a flourish. The King's gloom deepened for only the Master of the Records, a Drui, could read and he was visiting the Drui School of Learning at Pitversie on the Tay. Beofric lifted a knowing eyebrow.

"I will read you its contents," he said blandly. "You will see at the bottom the Great Seal of the Witan of North Humber Land. 'To our esteemed friend and ally, King Garnard of the Pretani, we beg leave to announce that our beloved King Edwin, may God take him to His breast, has died along with his living heirs. Therefore we have charged the Earls Beofric and Theobold to offer the Kingship of the North Humber Land and Overlordship of the Lothians to Eanfrith, son of Aethelfrith, hostage at your Court.'"

It was happening all over again. Tansen watched Ean's face change from sick despair to joy.

The powerful arms of the Commander of the Fleet burst through the wavering white robes of the Council. Ginger beard and furious freckles stood out as he shook his fist at Beofric.

"This reeks like the bowels of a slave-galley," he roared. "You're still after a puppet-king to rule the eastern sea-board!"

Lord Beofric raised his eyes and gave him a steady glare. Quietly but with authority he took command again.

"Therefore the Witan begs that Eanfrith is released from any obligation or duty or oath which, as a Royal hostage, he may have vowed to yourself or your people."

"Humph!" said the Commander and wished he was back at sea again.

"Therefore I call upon Eanfrith, son of Aethelfrith, to show himself."

Tansen swallowed, half-laughing, half-weeping. Her spirit soared on wings of pride as Ean stepped forward, pink-cheeked, golden-haired and now hurriedly dressed in snowy-white silk. His voice came gruffly and he paused to clear his throat.

"I am Eanfrith."

"Do you accept?"

"I accept."

The Deiran Beofric and the Bernician Theobold bowed before him. And then they were all clapping one another on the shoulder. And pushing Tansen aside to greet Ean's retinue. She stood alone, forgotten, on the edge of the circle, struck with a growing horror. 'Released from all oaths and obligations'! How would these newcomers take the news of the Marriage?

But she was not alone. Dale had padded to her side, flexing his oiled muscles like a sleepy cat, his great yellow eyes watching every move in the Hall.

And she was not forgotten. Reatta's dimpled smile still held a promise. And the black pools of her eyes still held a threat. Above the urgent throbbing of her heart, Tansen heard Beofric's polished tones.

"We have a ship waiting in the estuary, ready to sail home on the tide tomorrow. With your permission, my Lord King."

And Tansen swept forward, knowing it was time to make her presence known. It was the King's Remembrancer who interrupted and spoke for her.

"Yet there has been a Marriage with our Princess. It was performed by the Arch-Drui in the presence of our gods. And it must stand."

"A Marriage?" Lord Beofric shook his head. "I'm afraid not. We've been sorely defeated by Cadwallon. We need to sue for peace with him. We intend to offer a marriage alliance with one of his daughters."

An empty hole opened in Tansen's heart and stretched long into the future.

"It will be more to your advantage to have an alliance with us." The Law Adviser stroked his beard. "Otherwise our young warriors will enjoy a day's pleasure trip down the coast while your country is in this weakened state."

Again Beofric shook his head, this time with a thinly disguised sneer.

"Our King was reared at this court. That is enough assurance of our peaceful intentions," he snapped.

The King slammed his wine-glass down so hard that it slashed his sleeve with purple liquid.

"May I remind you, Lord Beofric, that you are in a foreign court. You have violated my Hall. Your small force is no match for my Guardsmen who ring this Citadel and a thousand men who are already being summoned from their farmsteads."

Beofric smiled, knowing that there had been no time for such an order to be given.

What has put the iron in Garnard's back-bone this time, wondered Tansen. And realised that he foresaw another long search for a new Heir while he remained King.

"I demand that the daughter of the Pretani will sail with you tomorrow and be acclaimed Queen at the side of her husband."

The Deiran's head tilted. His gaze slid to where Tansen stood. Used to having his own way, he was also well versed in diplomacy. He bowed to her, his foxy eyes mocking.

"Let the marriage stand then. But may I remind you, Lord King, that our enemy, Cadwallon, is overlord of the Lothians at present. Some day you might stand face to face with him across the Forth. So it is not wise for our kingdoms to fall out over such a trifling matter."

Garnard's face had turned a sickly green. Tansen felt a bit sick herself at being considered a trifling matter.

Then the King pulled his robes and himself together with a mighty heave of his shoulders. He snapped his fingers and ordered places to be made ready and food to be brought for the Deirans. Suddenly Tansen found Dale pouring her wine and standing at her back as though he had been a cup-bearer all his life. She felt a blow as though a ball of stone had lodged in her stomach. He was there because he thought her life was in danger now that the King had forced her upon the Angles.

Afterwards it was clear that Ean and the Embassy were going to make a night of it. Let them celebrate, she thought, and left to go to her own quarters.

As she crossed the Courtyard, Dale's soft leather boots squeaked behind her. She faced him under a wall-torch.

"Why are you setting yourself up as my bodyguard?" She kept her voice low. "Is it by order of the King?"

Somewhere he had lost his stiff defensive air. His jaw widened, his eyes glowed with an innocent joy.

"I volunteered. I'm coming with you."

"Why? I remember you once made a vow to smash the Angles."

"And perhaps some day I will. My packing's done. Is yours?"

She needed someone at her back. She smiled into his eyes and left his motives unprobed. And he laid on her shoulders the light cloak she had forgotten and left her in charge of the Guards at the King-House.

Verna was hunched over the torn lace on Tansen's best nightshift. She raised a face full of a desolation that was beyond tears. The news had reached her already.

"What's the matter with you?" Tansen cried. "You're coming with me, you goose. I couldn't do without you now. Let's pack. But first let's burn this dowdy robe!"

At dawn, cloaked and ready, she opened the unguarded door to Ean's quarters and met a gale of boisterous laughter. She found his entire retinue making a pig's breakfast of binding his bleached linen sleeves and leggings with gold-embroidered ribbons. She made to leave so as not to interfere with the ritual but Ean had seen her. "Pity me, Tansen!" Ean called across to her "I've to suffer this indignity every morning for the rest of my life."

"Look at them!".He was quivering with enthusiasm to be off on this new adventure. "All full of high hopes now. They came north to be with me in exile, younger sons of Thanes of Bernicia who had no patrimonies. They took a gamble and it paid off. Now they see grants of land and ruby rings at the end of it."

At last the ribbons were criss-crossed from wrist to shoulder, ankle to thigh. With difficulty because he could not keep still, they slid his feet into cream kid-skin boots. Wulf fastened a girdle round his waist on which hung a purse of exceptional beauty.

"Look here, Tansen!" Ean took her to the window to see the lid of gold and ivory with panels of garnets and designs laid out in tiny coloured glass pieces. She thought she had never seen anything so beautiful.

"It's my birth-gift from my grandmother."

In the centre outlined in gold were swooping birds in red and blue enamel. Ean slid back the gold catch to release the pouch and gold coins rolled across the table.

"She saved them up for years. Each one made by a different mint in the south. There should be two more for the thirty-nine gifts to Freya but she died before she could buy them."

A trumpet blew in the Courtyard.

"Lord Beofric is anxious to be off! My drinking-horn, Wulf!"

The auroch's horn had her gasping at the size of it.

"You could get an army drunk with that!"

Ean held the smooth curving horn in his hand. It was encased in silver gilt with panels of interlaced animals, ending at the tip in a bird's head. For the first time, his heirlooms held significance for him.

"This horn has been in my family for generations. The young bloods used to hunt the auroch to prove their courage. What a pity they hunted them out of existence." His doleful sigh was for the loss of an exhilerating out of existence." His doleful sigh was for the loss of an exhilerating pastime and not for the extinction of a noble species. "Fasten it to my saddle, Wulf!"

Once outside the chamber Wulf became extremely wary. Only the King and a few Guards waited in the Courtyard. The King was glumly aware that two boils were going to be lanced that day, and was unable to decide which would bring most relief. He presented Tansen with an enormous silver hanging bowl.

Verna was unimpressed by the enamelled insignia of the seven clans who sprang from the seven sons of Cruithne, and despaired of finding room for it on the luggage wagon.

Tansen stood high on the wagon-step, looking for the Arch-Drui. She had almost persuaded herself that he and she were kin but he had not come to give her one word of farewell, one crumb of comfort that she was doing the bidding of the gods.

But Dale was there mounted, scanning the brightening sky. And by sidestepping the over-excited antics of the retinue he was subtly proclaiming - 'I serve no Danish prince, so neither be jealous, nor stand in my way'.

Tansen plumped up the downy cushions and sat, assuring herself that from now on her duty lay in curbing the ambitions of the Angles. In truth she was leaving one den of intrigue to make her home in another.

Swinging from the wattle palisade were grisly stumps of dripping flesh. And stuck on spears, the heads of the young men who had wrestled and quaffed wine last night.

They had no sooner left the Capital than a man's finger pointed upwards. The soldiers cried out eagerly. An eagle floated effortlessly before them as if leading the way. Well removed from its habitat among the high corries it was the happiest of auguries as they set their faces south. Only when the travellers turned south-west towards the Firth of the River Fiorth did it wheel away to the north.

Tansen watched the hills of the Lothians draw near with interest. First, rising from a plain the solid hump of Berwick Law with a beacon fort on top. And to the west a rising cliff, cut off as if sliced by an axe, that was called the Seat of Artur, son of Aedan, who had left a wealth of legend behind him.

The Firth was quiet. Once a great thoroughfare, the Pretani had deserted it and based their fleet in the Firths of Moray and Tay. Because of the unpredictable Kings that ruled across the water, few ferries plied between the banks, still called the Queen's ferries, though which famous Celtic Queen had used them, no one could remember.

Out from the shore, lay a magnificent vessel lined with shining bronze shields. Proudly from the prow rose a gilded bird's head. From tall poles gay bunting fluttered like wings. The ship pulled at its anchor, as if eager to fly home.

A horn blew and left its notes hanging in the air. Their party had been sighted. The Master came to stand in the prow, a tall muscular fellow in sea-stained leathers with curling yellow hair and beard. Sailors erupted from between the shields and leapt into small boats that shot towards the shore. In the shallows the men leapt out and splashed ashore to welcome Ean.

Ean sat astride his horse, proud and erect, all white and gold and full of youthful promise. The sailors drew him from his horse and carried him shoulder-high, tossing him about from one group to another in their delight. Ean roared with them, loving it. Strong sinewy arms cradled him and set him in a boat. Those who lost the race to row him, swam.

CHAPTER TWENTY THREE

"Bernicians or Deirans?" Tansen asked Wulf, eyeing the sailors.

"Both," he replied shortly. "New King, new promise of gifts. We're all one these days." And went on directing the transfer of the baggage and despatching the horses back to the Capital.

Give me a grain of corn for every Angle who thinks otherwise and I'd reap a fine harvest, thought Tansen. It was clear that Wulf was determined to be wholly Angle.

The great open vessel had a narrow deck running round the gunwales. Amidships the sailors had erected a wooden cabin with a high pitched roof decorated with branches and flags. By the time Tansen was handed over the side Ean was reclining in expansive mood on a couch strewn with white fox pelts. He threw his arms wide to Tansen. "Isn't this glorious?"

Lord Beofric came hurrying along on pointed feet, twitching his fine wide sleeves out of contact with the sweaty bodies of sailors. Tansen nipped smartly before him to take the place at Ean's side, spreading her skirts wide. Beofric paused, drew breath to complain, thought better of it and joined the thanes watching the forty rowers squirm into their places. Earl Theobold, on a coil of rope, half-hidden by baggage, carles and retainers, winked at Tansen. Dale, sitting, legs astride a barrel, thoughtfully studied a new-spliced rope.

The helmsman from his platform in the stern called out the first line of his chant. The rowers responded with the next line and a mighty heave on the oar.. Back and forth went the song, the rowers slowly picking up the rhythm and increasing the speed until they were all pulling as one.

Tansen watched the estuary widen and the last of the small islands float past, and drew in a deep breath of sheer delight.

The Master gave a thundering stamp of his bare foot on the deck. The worksong stopped in mid-flow. The oars flew straight up. The carles amidships took their places at the mast. At a resounding clap of hands from the Master, they leapt into action, hauling at ropes, sending Theobold scrambling to his feet and the idle thanes tumbling. The huge sail rose upwards almost from nowhere, billowing out to show the scarlet longship blazoned on it. The helmsman threw his helm hard over and the mainsail caught the breeze from the north-east. With a sigh like a contented woman, the ship leaned on the wind and flew along, her wake creaming behind her.

The Isles of Maie and Bass thrust from the water like sentinels on either side of the entrance to the estuary. Well out from the hidden rocks round the Bass, the Master turned the ship towards the south.

Tansen, watching the shore-line slide past, thought of the pagans, the Votadini, her kin, clinging tenaciously to the Pentaland Hills, while rulers and emperors and kings came and withdrew or were slain and grew vague in folk's memories. Like Cunedda, the Lion, who took his Gododdin folk to Gwynedd to fight the Irish, remembered by the Pretani only because his blood ran in the veins of the great Bridei.

For the pagans toiled while countless forgotten kings divided the Lothians among quarrelsome sons bent on murdering their brothers and cousins and uncles for a taste of power. Maybe it was better for these pagans to be under Cadwallon's protection rather than under the sway of Angles. For Cadwallon was descended from Cunedda and a native Briton. And she sprang to her feet and left Ean, running to the side of the ship to thrust the forbidden thought from her mind.

"I'm going to watch from the Master's platform."

It was Dale who caught her as she staggered, holding her arm until she learned how to bend her knees to the heave of the deck. Together they watched the great sail billowing and cracking in the breeze, heard the slap of waves on timber and counted the splashes of diving cormorants.

"That's Bernicia, over there, in the mist," said Dale, twisting Tansen's salt-sprayed hair from his cheek. "Deira's further south."

"Why do they distrust one another so much? They're all kin, squeezed out of Daneland by Jutes and Saesons."

Dale leaned back, his wide eyes straying from sail to sky to sea and back.

"Ah, but the Deirans were the younger sons of nobles. They came first and took the best land. The natives didn't care who protected their fields and farms. They had to pay tithes just the same. So the Deirans prospered and travelled and forged ties with kingdoms in the south."

"And they settled in York and built a great city," Tansen remembered, watching a gannet, its pale beak gleaming, beat on slow sweeping wings across the bow.

"The next boatloads were sons of farmers. They had to push north to find land to settle on." Dale leaned his foot on a bundle that had started to roll. "But the land in Bernicia was harsher to farm, hadn't been properly tilled for centuries. They needed all their skills to feed themselves and overcome rebellious natives. They'd no time to travel and study like the Deirans. And they were hemmed in by that quarrelsome rabble, the Votadini. Even yet the Deirans taunt Bernicians about their origins."

"Will they be loyal to Ean then?"

"Yes, while he's the only golden boy on the horizon." Dale's wide brow was serene.

"So Ean's really a pagan like myself?" Tansen thumped the gunwale, laughing.

"But not likely to joke about it," warned Dale. "Guard your words or some day you'll be brought up in a fishing net, head down."

His eyes skimmed between the helmsman and the Master, striding towards them across the planks.

"The Bernicians might have been rough farmers once," went on Dale. "They've shorter tempers and they're quicker to loosen their swords. But for all that they're the better folk of the two, more blunt and honest. I could work with them."

"Is that what you're doing now?"

Dale rubbed his hands and looked directly at Tansen for the first time. "I smell rain and a storm brewing. Come back to the shelter."

The wind was changing direction, straining at the sail. The high wispy clouds had lowered and become darker, their dense grey reflected in the choppy sea. Hand in hand they ran to shelter.

"Squall to leeward!" bellowed the Master.

Thanes spun on their rumps as ropes uncoiled beneath them. And leapt for the canopy, high-stepping over rolling barrels and loose tackle.

Under the canopy the carles had just handed out bread and cheese and ale. The sailors lashed down loose articles and stood by their ropes. Behind the ship, a sinister black shadow rolled towards them with white crests beneath it where the wind was churning up the sea. Tansen felt a quiver of excitement start in her stomach.

The first sharp gust of wind made the whole ship creak as it took the strain and set up a whine in the shrouds. Then came a heavier blow as though a clenched fist had struck it. Beofric slid past on one hip, vaguely green, elegant fingers curled round his beaker. Ean imprisoned her with his arms.

"Don't be afraid!" he called above the scream of wood as his couch careered sideways.

She gripped his wrists and freed herself and clung to the poles that held the cabin firm. For the sea was calling and her spirit was answering. And there was no room in her heart for the fear she had thought would strike her.

At that the main force of the squall hit the vessel and it heeled over in a massive cant. With arms outstretched, hands wedged firmly, she stood between the poles. A hissing curtain of rain soaked her to the skin. The wind lifted her wet hair and lashed it round her face. And she laughed in the teeth of the gale, loving its fury, her body swaying with the heaving of the ship.

CHAPTER TWENTY FOUR

The helmsman threw his helm over. Slowly he swung the nose of the ship back round to face upwind. Sailors unclewed the sheets and clung, waiting. The Master's arm went up. Strained arms twitched and held, twitched and held. Bit by bit, they eased the sail round a little at a time, the hemp snaking across the deck, until the sail was end-on to the wind. And slowly the ship came upright.

The next gust slammed at them from a different direction. The sailors eased the sail round again, men at their backs checking the smooth ebb and flow of the coils. A sodden rope whirled free and slammed a man against the gunwale. Two sailors dragged him screaming down a hatch. Tansen worked a hand loose to find it caught in Theobold's grip.

"Don't go to help! Your servant's there. Sick as a dog. A few broken ribs will keep her mind off herself."

The Master's two arms slashed down and the sail was made fast. Tansen looked deep into an abyss of green water as the bow plunged downwards. Then the wave broke over the ship and she was inside the swirling mass, fighting for breath. Till her head surfaced and she saw the bow come free, swinging upwards from the bottom of the trough and beginning to climb. The ship hung on the crest for a heartbeat, tilted and plummeted down into another frothing green chasm.

When they surfaced again, she laughed, looking round at the faces at her back, shining with spray and sweat. A stray leaf from a garland was caught in Beofric's dripping beard. Wulf and Ean, grim-faced, shared the contents of a flask. And she laughed again. Courtiers, soft as boiled eggs! But now she knew why their forefathers had married their boats. This was exhilerating stuff, a challenge worth meeting.

Again the squall striking and the ship trying to wheel away under the blast. Again the Master and helmsman balancing tiller and sail, protecting their vessel from strain. The helmsman, a giant of a man, grinning with glee and the joy of battle. The Master, too, lending his weight to the helm, white teeth flashing, talking to his ship, coaxing her to right herself. The sailors dancing like wild men over the rowing benches, from one sail-rope to another, slipping, sliding, their laughter blown away on the wind. Only the serfs, chained to oars of solid beechwood, heaved and strained and did not laugh. And a man that looked like Dale high in the shrouds, cutting a snarled rope.

Now she knew why they were called Sea-Danes. The sea was their enemy, the wind was the howl of its challenge, an invitation to battle every time they sailed. This creaking lurching ship was a kicking battle-chariot in which they rode the wind and waves, knowing by instinct when to lean and lighten, when to pull and heave. And she felt herself part of the desperate fight between the tiny humans on the frail craft and the mighty elemental forces of nature.

Some day they might lose the battle. They would be swallowed by the monster they sported with. But not this day. Always the next time.

Another massive wave flowered over the deck. Tansen saw the leap of the water and took a huge breath and was engulfed. And felt a massive blow like a fist between her shoulder-blades that tore her hands from the poles. Water whirled her away, sucked her to its heart and slammed her on the deck. Her fingers and toes fought for a hold as the sea drained away, gurgling and defeated, into the scuppers. The next wave carried her high over the gunwale. Till something caught at her skirt and held hard till she thudded onto her back and two arms gripped her. And she knew it was Ean with a rope round his waist who had saved her and raised a radiant face.

But it was Dale, dogged and sodden, taking the strain of the rope. And she hated him then.

"By the nine glory-twigs of Odin!" Ean cried, white and shaken. "I thought I'd lost you."

Tansen lay on her back, her legs dangling over the rowing deck, and coughed up sea-water.

"What were you thinking of, throwing yourself out into the gale? You nearly drowned."

"Someone pushed me!" she cried and went into another spasm of coughing.

"Nonsense! It was a rope that broke loose! I saw it." Lord Beofric spoke sharply, pale and glistening with sweat. "At my back?" she spluttered. "I was inside the cabin!"

Ean loosened her sodden cloak, gathered her tight against his body and swung his dry cloak round them both. For the space of a sigh she was comforted. Then.

"Someone pushed me!" she repeated stubbornly in his ear.

"Away with you! You're far too headstrong. The sea's a monster. You'd better learn to respect it and fear it." "I am afraid," she told him. "But not of the sea. It's the men on this ship that terrify me. Lord Beofric most of all."

Ean's hand pushed her face into his shoulder.

"Don't say that!"

She pushed against him.

"Why not? It's true!"

"Because someone might hear you. And it's not true."

He didn't want to believe her. Yet it had been a fist that had launched her out into the storm. Who had taken the god-given chance to get rid of her? Any one of these nobles that had hovered at her back. Garnard could never have proved that it had not been an accident. And Ean would have been free to marry a daughter of Cadwallon.

She stayed close to Ean, warmed by his body, rubbing at her hair, until the wild heaving of the ship began to steady. There was still the heart-stopping plunge down to the depths that seemed to go on for ever. Still the hesitant lift and the straining to climb out again. Yet there was a certain rhythm to the surge now.

"The squall's passing over."

The mainspar had stopped its wild swinging and was made secure. The helmsman began to gentle the ship onto her new course as tenderly as a big man handles a baby. Seamen with blistered palms knotted ropes and cleared the litter from the deck. The sail, tattered and in ribbons, flapped above their heads.

"Well, that livened up a boring journey." The Master pushed his head in, his wet hair and beard curling madly. "Any injuries?"

"Curse you, man! Why didn't you lower the sail?" demanded Lord Beofric, hiding his sweat-sheened face in an orgy of brushing down his sea-stained tunic. "Did you want to drown us?"

"Finn's teeth, to think your father was called the Giant of the great North Way. You've been striding the billows in his wake today." The Master winked at Ean.

Beofric pretended not to hear.

"We'll lie up for the night in the nearest harbour. I refuse to land in this sorry state."

So it was next morning before they rounded the tip of the Low Farren Islands where the ebbing tide would soon leave a causeway to the mainland.

"Our forefathers were besieged there once by Urien of Rheged," said Wulf, narrowing his eyes thoughtfully.

"But we overcame them and won it back, didn't we?" Ean's eyes roamed over the strip of shoreline like a beggar at a feast. "And we'll do the same with Cadwallon."

Tansen dropped her eyes. It would take a braver man than Ean to win back Edwin's power. She looked for Dale who had risked his life to save her. When she could not find him she felt a sense of safety. He must feel sure that no sly hand or whipping rope would endanger her today.

Across the water they saw a flat strip of coast-line broken by a rearing crag crowned by a fortress. The look-out on the mast sent a blast from his horn across the water.

"So that's Bamburgh," whispered Ean. "That bone of contention between Bernica and Deira. But, no more, my hearties, no more!"

The deep and mellow note of a horn answered across the water. Tansen shaded her eyes with two hands. The mighty curved horn hung at the top of a tall watchtower, dwarfing the coastguard who pushed it out with all his strength to blow again.

"Down-sail." The look-out straddled the cross-piece as it came down, waving his horn and leaping off nimbly before the huge mangled sail collapsed into the well.

Small boats, dangerously full and rocking, a whole flotilla of them, pushed out from the shore, filled with shouting, waving people. Ean's eyes were filled with stars.

"Oars out." Each oar slid slowly out with perfect precision and was held steady, poised above the water. Tansen waited for the chant. Instead.

"Hold ha - a - a - rd!" The helmsman leapt from his platform, landed on the nearest oar and was off, running, hopping, dancing lightly from one oar to the next. To dive off into the water at the end and come up, shaking his shaggy pelt and roaring.

Trumpets blew, fists thumped on boards, feet thundered on the deck and there was a man ready on the other side. He leapt over, slipping, flying, waving, tripping. Cheering and yelling. And another and another. One side after the other. Madcap figures, skimming, skipping along on the slender oars, showing off all the skills they had used in the storm. Ribald jeers as an oar wavered or a foot skidded and a body dived twisting into the waves. And Dale, enjoying himself for once, arms balancing his thin trunk, fitting his insteps round the curving shafts, great joyful eyes fixed on the oar ahead. "My turn!" Ean would have sprung forward but Lord Beofric clamped a hand on his wrist.

"For Thor's sake, keep your dignity!"

"A clever rider's as good as any seaman!"

"And the first oarsman that envies your silken tunic will nubble his oar," hissed Beofric.

Under cover of the swirl of his cloak Wulf clamped a hand on Ean's other arm.

"Take a hold on yourself! Fine sight you'd be with sodden embroideries and seaweed between your toes. Who'll cheer you then, man? Stand up on the Master's platform and show yourself all bonny and blithe!"

Muttering Ean shrugged himself free and climbed the ladder. But his sulky frown cleared like the sun coming out as he faced the fierce delight of the crowd.

"From now on, he'll be doing the Dance of the Oars between Bernician swords and Deiran daggers."

The disembodied voice dulled the bright day for Tansen. A sob caught in her throat as she watched him wave his sword, his hair like a bright sea-freshened plume. So noble and so beautiful. So young and innocent.

"They say his father looked like that in the beginning."

Wulf had come to stand beside her, speaking quietly so that only she could hear. She could hardly believe that this was the same man for here he was openly joining with her in gladness, as though together they had gifted the blue sea and green land to Ean for a playground.

"Yet Aethelfrith had a strength in him that could weld two kingdoms together and keep them united," she whispered back.

Wulf stirred uneasily, scuffing with his toe at a salt-encrusted rope as the woman voiced his unspoken thought. More and more he was realising that their joint understanding of Ean could create a bond between them.

"How can I protect that boy from these powerful thanes and nobles?" he asked.

"By making sure that one of us is always there to shield him," she said laying her hand on his arm.

Wulf saw his own love for Ean mirrored in her eyes and felt the friendship she offered him in her trusting hand. He had misjudged her! Like himself she knew Ean's weaknesses and loved him still. He could not ask for a better ally in the days that lay ahead. Yet by her very presence she spelled disaster to Ean.

He threw off the trusting hand and leapt to enfold Ean in a long purple cloak that would lend dignity to his slender figure. Leaving Tansen wondering if it had been Wulf's jealous hand that had sent her hurtling into the sea?

Dale drew his shirt over his head and a trio of dolphins twisting in an incredibly yellow sea appeared on his chest.

"Somehow, they're not quite you," she said.

Dale ran wet hands through his hair.

"It was either dolphins or a ram's head with rainbow horns and glaring eyes." He dried his hands on his cape and tied it firmly over the picture on his chest.

"Where did you learn your seamanship?"

"On a longship trading out of Dublin." And he slid down a pole to the baggage hold.

"Wait, I want to thank you for saving my life."

Saffron eyes gleamed from the shadows.

"I was in the right place at the right time. Anyone would have done it."

But Ean hadn't done it. It was such a little sigh she gave then.

She knelt to speaak softly.

"Did you see who pushed me? Was it Beofric?"

He heaved one of her own chests up beside her.

"A dainty wee man, that. And deadly."

"Theobold?"

"Does his duty. I don't think it includes murdering young women."

"It had to be one of the nobles behind me."

Dale spent a long moment squinting into the Royal Pretani cauldron. It had been his duty to rescue her. But there had been a moment when she had almost slipped from his grasp and he had thought his heart would burst. Afterwards he had spent most of the night on the high bow-platform until he could face her calmly again.

"Impossible to see in that storm. We'll never know."

He hooked out a flattened herring and smiled that wide calm smile at her. "Until the next attempt," she said bitterly. She could not trust even Dale although he had saved her, for he was playing some deep dark game of his own. "Bretwealda, Bretwealda!"

The shouting brought Tansen back from the black hole of despair she was contemplating. The sparkle on the water, the joyful faces called to her youth and courage. There was a life to be lived here and she had chosen it.

At one with the crowd she raised her head and saw the figure of Ean as an ideal, his beauty and innocence derived from the gods. And wished it was not so. For beauty and innocence were no safeguard against the realities of a Kingship.

"Bretwealda!"

Black heads as well as yellow heads bobbed in the boats and the water. Dale leaned on the gunwale beside her.

"Natives and Angles together?" she asked.

"Edwin deliberately allowed the herds of the natives to expand and their barns to overflow. Folk with full bellies don't rebel."

"Can Ean fill their barns and bellies again?"

Dale left the words hanging in the air between them.

Tansen looked beyond the shore to the land, longing to feel the earth solid and secure under her feet again. And she pressed her hands together, desperately wishing she was setting up her own home, cosy round the hearth with a friendly field-mouse lurking in the corner.

"Breatwalda!"

"Oars up!"

The oars shot upright in a long ordered row, pointing to the sky.

Bright-edged ropes slung from land to vessel tightened and pulled them ashore.

The grinding of the bow on the shelving shingle beach was the signal. The horn blew and the trumpets called.

"Bretwealda! Bretwealda!"

"Not Bretwealda!" cried Ean. And in the shocked silence the waves rushed and hissed. His arms encompassed the fair heads of Danes and the dark heads of natives. "Not the Ruler of Britain! Not yet! But some day!" He punched the air. A tumult of flying woollen caps and waving kerchiefs. "Today it's enough that I come to defend your fields and store-rooms. Enough that I come to bring peace. Enough that I bring an alliance with the Royal Bull of the Pretani."

No one cared that he had not promised the defeat of Cadwallon. They would have cheered anything on that auspicious day.

Tansen smoothed her hair and flounced out her best green cloak to show off the gold border. Now he would present her to the people. As her shoe hit the first step of the ladder to the Master's platform, Ean vaulted over the side. As his foot touched the shore, he bent and grasped a handful of sand, rubbing it on his forehead as a token of his homecoming. And the people loved it and went wild, standing on upturned fishing cobles to see him better. A thane with a big shapeless nose ran to kiss his hand.

"Welcome, King of the Bright Danes. Honour me and my lady by taking the Cup at my Mead Hall."

They carried him shoulder high to a great charcoal-brown stallion. And Dale, seeing Tansen kilt up her skirts in a fury, had her over the side, down the gang-plank and running for the last remaining horse.

CHAPTER TWENTY FIVE

At the entrance to the Hall, amid a flurry of horn-blaring and trumpet-blowing, three heralds competed to announce the arrival of the King.

The Thane's Lady swanned from the Mead Hall, in a blue mantle over a white ankle length tunic with a white silk square covering her head. And sapphire eyes flashing a message to the new King that her lord and master left an empty space in her bed too often.

Tansen sucked in her breath and marched forward on flat determined feet. "And the Princess Tansen, Consort to King Eanfrith!" she announced boldly, caring nothing for the Lady's pout of surprise and beating down the glare of the nobles with defiance.

The High Table held a nice variety of decorated green drinking-glasses.

"Very pretty." Tansen smiled sweetly to the Lady and took her place at Ean's side. She glanced with the sharpness of a silver dagger at the noble who eased in at her other side.

"Earl Theobold," she greeted him, her senses raw and tingling. "I'd have brought my own fanfare if I'd known the Danish heralds were so short of breath."

Theobold inclined his head and nodded, acknowledging her rights. But when the guest-plate was laid before her, Tansen forgot her dignity, threw back her cloak and ate hungrily of the roasted meats and fowls. Only once her knife stopped half-way to her mouth as she caught Theobold hiding a grin behind his hand.

The eyes in his craggy face seemed kindly enough. Brown haired, brown bearded, brown-skinned, he reminded her of the forthright peasant breed she knew and trusted. But she would not trust any noble until she knew who had hurled her into the scuppers.

Scarcely had they finished before Beofric, the only noble who had managed to obtain a clean shirt, was on his feet, suavely explaining that the King had to reach Gefrin before nightfall.

For this journey Tansen demanded a decent horse and rode alongside Ean, sharing the thrill of his first sight of the countryside. At every ford and crossroads people had gathered for a glimpse of the new King. Earl Theobold's pleasant brown face appeared at Ean's dagger-side to point out landmarks. But it was Tansen who asked the questions.

"No, no. The wall that Emperor Hadrian built is south a bit, a good day's ride from here."

"Yes, it was good King Edwin who put these brass drinking-bowls at every spring."

"And who do the peasants and travellers drink to?" Tansen asked. "Edwin's new-fangled saints or the ancient spirit of the well?"

Lord Beofric was trying to insinuate himself between Tansen and Ean. When she would not yield, the smooth mask slipped for a second and his lips curled in a silent snarl. And the fear that was always with Tansen now shivered restlessly in its nightmare.

She looked round for the dolphins. And was caught in the limpid golden gaze of the Briton.

"And what's Cadwallon doing while we're riding north?" she asked. "Sticking a pin in a map to decide which stronghold to rule you from?"

"He'll need a long map," said Beofric wryly. "Stretching from the Forth to the Thames. And all the glue in the world won't hold it together for long."

"He's only following in the footsteps of his grandfather, Rhun."

"But too late, my dear." Beofric smiled blandly, his eyes half-closed against the sun. "We've been accepted here for generations. His Welsh rabble and Penda's Mercians are aliens here. And hungry armies are never welcome."

A massive fortified hill reared before them from a plain ringed with hills.

"That's Bryneich." It was Theobold now, asserting himself. "The ancient British kings ruled from there and the people have always looked to the rock for protection so naturally we made it our Capital. That's where the name Bernicia comes from."

And the British rulers hot-footed it north, leaving the farmers and craftsmen whose descendents were now pouring from hearth and field to stare curiously at the new ruler who would feast on their tithes and whose name would be sung by the bards.

"We're not expected to live on that draughty perch, are we?" Ean was asking.

"No, the wind tears holes in tapestries up there. We found a mellower spot. Yeavering Bell it was called. Edwin rebuilt it and named it Gefrin."

"Yeavering Bell." Tansen whispered to herself. The name fired her imagination.

She could see it now in the plain, the Royal Centre, sheltered by the circle of hills, protected by a ditch and a bank with a high palisade on top.

The surrounding land was split into portions by stakes but the wattle houses crept close to the palisade for safety.

Mounted thanes, all red-gold cloth and emeralds, fastened hurriedly over working tunics, came from within to carry the King's banner before him into the Centre.

Inside, timber houses tumbled over one another. Just asking for a fire, thought Tansen and sighed for rugged grey stone and white quartz and a feeling of permanence.

One building towered over the rest, its gilded roof catching the low rays of the western sun. Its door pillars of local light-coloured stone were sculpted with birds and animals and scrolls and swirls that had a familiar look about them.

A solid central pillar of gold-bedecked crimson turned out on closer inspection to be a prelate of the White Christ, his egg-shaped head sunk into a ruff of ermine. And at his side, all in white like a pillar of salt, her linen head-cloth held by a thin gold circlet stood Edwin's Queen, Ethelberga.

"Welcome to the Mead-Hall of Edwin." She proffered the Hall Goblet to Ean in pale frail hands.

The formal phrase was a mere whisper.

"Tut!" The prelate bloomed like a red rose. The pale flower at his side wilted. The prelate raised a narrow hand.

"Until there is a promise of baptism into the True Faith, there will be no Cup of welcome."

Lord Beofric, taking the three steps in a stride, sketched a bow to the Queen and faced the prelate.

"Move aside, Bishop Paulinus. It's roasted veal I smell coming from the spits inside, not incense."

The nobles, surly after their long ride, stretched and grumbled.

"A heathen King shall not defile the Hall of Edwin." Long tapering fingers grasped the air in front of Ean's face.

Then over Ean's shoulder Paulinus saw Tansen and it seemed that his ermine collar had come alive to take its revenge and choke him.

"The servants of God will not eat at table with an avowed pagan until she is purified from worship of the devil."

"Then," said Tansen stepping forward, "the servants of God must eat elsewhere. For our stomachs are drowning out your protests with their rumbling."

Surprisingly, it was Ean who took matters into his own hands. He took the Goblet from the nerveless fingers and quaffed it. With a hand on the door-post he cried to the nobles.

"Welcome to the Mead Hall of King Eanfrith the Golden." He glanced up at the antlers branching from the walls.

"I name this Mead Hall, 'Heriot the Hart'."

And handed the Goblet to Tansen.

A bowl of washing water would have been more acceptable, thought Tansen, and passed it on.

Inside it was obvious that no one had thought to send ahead news of a Queen. Tansen felt her temper rising.

Earl Theobold raised an arm swiftly. A trumpet flashed in the lamplight and sang out a fanfare. And Theobold roared out her entitlement.

"The Princess Tansen of the Royal Court of Pretani and wife to King Eanfrith of the North Humber Land."

"It would be a pleasant change, not to be an afterthought," said Tansen, deftly laying her cloak across his upraised arm and brushing past him. To find Ean in the High Chair hemmed in on either side by the pillars of salt and crimson gold. So the Bishop had decided on a change of tactics. Point taken, thought Tansen and stepped without pausing to the honour-place at the far end. The Queen bowed her head over joined hands while the Bishop twitched his skirts back from contamination as she passed.

Ean flung his arm up in surprise as she seated herself at the honour-place. His gesture was taken by the house-carles as the signal to start the meal. So grinning broadly, he chose the finest pieces of veal for her plate as though it was a game she was playing out for his delight. Instead of a tragic ballad whose every new cadence filled her with nameless dread. Copying the Queen, Tansen placed her knife and spoon on a line with her beaker. Thought better of it and laid them the Pretani way on either side of her plain wooden platter.

"Would you believe," came Earl Theobold's voice in her ear, "that when Ethelberga arrived from Kent she was a bundle of fun called Princess Tata?"

Earl Theobold, assured of his place at the High Table, had taken time to wash himself clean of dust and leather-stains.

"Nor do I believe it's chance that you're always at my elbow."

Tansen was studiously scraping her veal free of a dressing of mushrooms in butter, wine and cream that had somehow arrived on her plate on its way down the table from Ean.

"She was heart-breakingly lovely. Running, eyes sparkling, laughing, to meet Edwin, her belly always swelling like some fruitful harvest goddess."

Tansen studied the noble face, white transparent skin tight over the fine bones of cheek and jaw.

"Her father was King of Kent. In the first flush of his conversion he refused their marriage because Edwin wasn't a Christian. So she promised her father to convert Edwin. Why don't you try the sauce. It's rather tasty."

"And handy for a servant with a gold coin in his pouch to slip in a few drops of poison." Tansen met his startled eyes squarely.

Theobold took a long sip of wine to regain his composure. What fool had said she was an ignorant goose-girl?

"So the bride's father sent Paulinus with her to help with her task. You see that silver mirror hanging from her girdle. Pope Boniface sent it as a gift to remind her of her duty. Look at her now and you'll see what it's cost her."

The gleam of lamps lit a face resigned to an existance empty of faith and unlit by hope. As though, now that she walked no longer with her love, she walked no longer with her god.

"And where once she supped with Edwin and her sons, now her elbows touch those of strangers," Tansen mused gravely.

"And only Paulinus for a cold sort of comfort." Theobold's loaded knife stabbed in the direction of the prelate. "I blame him for the state she's in now. He kept her fasting and praying until she lost her health and her sons had a habit of dying in their baptismal robes. Eanfled and two sickly infants are all she has left."

A girl of Tansen's own age, ghostly thin, sat shuddering at the food on her plate.

"The sorrows that folk bring on themselves are the hardest to bear. The Queen must have known that fasting would kill her bairns."

"She believed she was sacrificing herself just as her Blessed Lord sacrificed himself on the Cross."

"She's like the virgins in the bad old days, who sacrificed themselves for the honour of it. Until the Drui stopped the cult because it was becoming unhealthy."

"Something like that." Theobold gave a fleeting smile. Sacrifices abounded in his religious background too.

"I thought these barbarian practices had gone for ever. What will she do now? Go back to Kent?" Then another thought struck her. "Or do they hope to convert Ean?"

Theobold leaned back, resting his chin on his coarse-woven tunic. His lack of ornament contrasted with the embroidered Dierans.

"And how would Eanfrith react to that?" he said.

Tansen found she did not know the answer. Ean was easily swayed. The hawk-nosed prelate was talking with animation to Ean while they ate their heron baked with plums. She shrugged.

"He won't convert Ean while I'm around. All the more reason for keeping me alive and whole." She cleaned her knife on a napkin, tested its edge and spoke without looking up. "And what stance do you take in this tug-of-war?"

Theobold belched discreetly and loosed his jerkin. He would not give a broken lace for that son of Aethelfrith in the High Chair. But this girl, now she was a rare one! The solemn green eyes demanded an answer. And it would have to be an honest one.

"I do my duty and pray to whatever gods are in favour at the time. What's the difference in a name?"

"Maybe none at all," said Tansen. "The trouble starts when mankind makes rules and regulations and claim they come from their particular god."

Why, he asked himself, had this able young woman chosen to wet-nurse a weakling like Eanfrith? The nobles wanted the boy because he would work well on a leading rein. But this filly was a leader, not a follower. She had a wise head and a pouch-full of courage. And a fierce independence that came from her Pretani background. Pity she would have to go if Cadwallon made noises about marriage alliances.

Tansen's gaze lingered on her dish of heron stewed in plums. Ean had not chosen those pieces. Verna would have to visit the kitchens later and pretend to have an enormous appetite. Unless Verna was expendable too. Dale was eating with hearty enjoyment among the retinue. She supposed it was too much to expect him to taste her food as well. Reluctantly she waved the heron away and resorted to argument to appease her hunger and draw Theobold out.

"The Men of Rome have made laws and if you question them you're a heretic. Every word in the Drui ritual must be perfect or the gods will be angered. Maybe the humble monks from Columba's Isle have the right way of it. Each one in his cell communing with the Guiding Ones and finding his own truth to suit the level of his spiritual development."

Caught for a moment by the depth of her own thought, she paused, smiled apologetically at Theobold, grasped her cup in both hands and drank it off.

Thinks and drinks like a man, thought Theobold. No, he was being condescending. She was all-woman with a deep sexuality that stirred his middle-aged loins.

Tansen held her wooden beaker out to Dale. She had seen him draw mead specially from a fresh cask.

"At least there's no ostentation about her table-furnishings."

"The silver-ware was made into chalices for the Church."

"What a pity," Tansen said wickedly. "Some one should tell the Bishop that the rich cannot enter Heaven."

Lord Theobold's teeth flashed in his iron-grey beard.

"And he will reply that the treasure is to beautify the Church and glorify God."

But Tansen was staring into the sweet honey-coloured mead, seeing floating specks. They could be unfiltered wax. Or grains of poison. She set the beaker aside.

Oh, Bride, what am I doing here, she thought. Among wealthy landowners and starving serfs, rich Churchmen and beggars, and toiling pagans harried by armies and spat upon by nobles. Why had she left her familiar landscape? Where animals and plants and man and woman were brothers and sisters sharing the land and knowing their place in nature and the vast scheme of things.

"What attracts Ethelburga to this New Faith?" she asked.

"Well, you see, our Valhalla's only for warriors. The Christians offer a Heaven that's open to women and to men who are not warriors. And to slaves."

He emptied his beaker and rose to his feet to address the comapny.

"Before we're all legless let us present the King with his Accoutrements. Clear the High Table and bring them forward."

Under cover of rising laughter and scraping benches Queen Ethelburga and her women quietly effaced themselves. Theobold extended his arm to Tansen. She sat tight in her place of honour.

"Is there a law against women staying? If there is, I'll see that it's amended."

Theobold's mouth snapped shut and his goodwill evaporated. He selected a silver-gilt war-corselet from among the bright armour held by the house-carles. He laid it on the table before Eanfrith.

"May you be bold in array, may your pleasure be lordly."

Now Lord Beofric held high a sword in a gold filigree scabbard. Bernician and Deiran taking it in turns so that no one could claim precedence. Like two pigeons, pecking in order.

"May you be noble in equipment, may you vanquish mightily."

Now that was a shade beyond Ean at the moment, Tansen thought. And a vain hope for North Humber Land.

A golden helmet with dazzling cheek-pieces.

"May your face strike fear into the hearts of your enemies, may your voice be joyful."

Bishop Paulinus eased the damp ermine from his neck, his eyes following the glitter of gold.

"Oh, nobly born man, may your praises reach to where the sea laps at the home of the winds."

"Here in this Hall, each Earl is true to the other, loyal to our Lord, ready to acclaim him."

And that last line added a real comic touch as far as Tansen was concerned.

"Loyalty? From both sides?" she enquired grimly as Theobold finished his task and planted his solid body on the bench.

A light-haired bard had taken up the song of the Hero Beowulf and the bloodthirsty saga of Hengist. Nobody was listening.

"Believe it," said Theobold. "Forget those brutish youths who thought your land was ripe for the picking. We need a King quickly to sue for peace with Cadwallon. Eanfrith will be acclaimed at first light tomorrow, King of a united North Humber Land."

The house-carles were on the move again with jugs. Faces grew ruddier, voices grew raucous. Ean was matching the young nobles cup for cup.

"And shall I be acclaimed as his Queen?"

"Not tomorrow. Later."

Tansen leaned forward to force him to meet her eyes.

"I was told that you Bernicians at least were honest in your dealings. Why don't you say it out? None of you want me as Queen."

He scratched his head and did not look one whit abashed.

"So that's why you married the lad. For the Queenship. And why not, a lively lass like you. I'd like you fine as Queen. But there's a time and a tide for all things. And the tide's ebbing fast on our shores."

"And the Deirans?"

He spread his hands on the table and did not answer. And Tansen knew he would not lift a finger in her defence if the Dierans decided to drop her quietly in a bog. She found Wulf with her eyes.

"I want to rest now. Which room will the King and I sleep in?" Wulf's mouth opened to protest and shut, twisting wryly.

"I'll find out," he said.

A minstrel let his notes trickle and fall and lifted his voice.

"He has come in the ring-prowed ship across the whale-road.

"The guardians of the coast welcomed him on the broad sea-cape.

"We saw the banner that was borne before him."

Tansen made little stabs in the board with her dagger. The shouting and staggering reminded her of the storm. And the blow that had sent her swirling helpless into the waves. And here she was again, rudderless, sail-less, friendless. The dolphins had disappeared, beneath the table or below the waves. What was he, servant or bodyguard, this man with the eyes of a new-born fawn and the slow wide smile of a happy tippler?

The minstrel was tucked in a roof-tree. A man leapt on the table beneath him, urging him on, clapping to his beat.

"He has come to the Mead-dwelling that stood profitless without him,

"It has fallen to the King's own minstrel to proclaim joy in the Hall,

"Let song and music mingle before the King."

And Tansen felt like a bird singing in the darkness. If a bird had faith that the dawn would surely come for him, so could she. Against all the odds she had won and married Ean. After tomorrow Ean would be their lawful King. Then nothing would keep her from the Queenship. And in that position she could thwart their ambitions to dominate the Pretani. She gripped her knife and stabbed it once, twice, three times hard into the coarse-grained wood.

Men were jostling, singing, challenging, brawling. The minstrel stood on the plank and raised his voice.

"Let there be laughter of heroes, cheerful sounds, winsome words,

"Let the prince of the Spear-Danes receive the Hall-Goblet.

"Good fortune be his and glory in battle."

There might have been more but Ean stood up. He threw a ring through the air to the expectant poet who caught it with a flourish. A mighty cheer rose. Ean had given his first praise-gift.

"Where does he get the praise-gifts from?" Tansen asked.

"He's a wealthy man now." Theobold looked surprised at the question. "He owns all the land round Gefrin. And its produce. Don't tell me you didn't know."

Then Ean held up the Hall-Goblet, staggered, and drank, spilling half of it in two brown rivers down his tunic. The men cheered.

"I have come at your call to be King of the North-Danes.

"I see before me valiant thanes and staunch men.

"You all know my lineage."

His voice petered out into a dazed muttering. His glazed eyes opened wide on the refilled Goblet and his voice rang out again.

"I come to inherit my father's rank.

"To use the ring-hoard as I choose.

"To decree tha feasts shall never fail."

It was what they wanted to hear. They slapped one another on the back.

"To rule over the people, the treasure, the fortress.

"To accomplish deeds of heroism before I spend my last day in the Mead-Hall,

"To fulfill my promise to the East Danes in the Gift-Hall decked with treasure."

As Ean's voice died away a thane jumped on the board and began a parody of a poet's song, pleading blatantly for a gift, miming a tantrum when it did not come, dancing down the table kicking plates and cups before him as he went, falling off untidily at the end.

A lyre began to pass round from man to man and each one sang a riddle. If the others could answer it they dowsed the rhymster with ale.

"Come on," hissed Wulf in Tansen's ear. "Time all good Princesses were in bed."

Tansen tied her knife very loosely on her girdle and followed him.

"Hey Wulf!" Ean, tottered over. "Man, you always need to relieve yourself when the harp goes round!"

"We should take him with us," Tansen whispered.

"And shame him in front of his courtiers?"

Wulf showed her into an unheated chamber and lit a small candle.

"Don't wait up for him. Neither he nor his manhood will stand erect tonight." He left abruptly.

Tansen sat in an ornamented chair looking about her at the rich hangings and the finely woven mats on the floor and wondered what she was doing in this foreign citadel where her life was in constant danger. And her man was either swimming in a fog of mulled wine or being sick.

A rustle at the door had her in the centre of the floor, dagger upraised.

"That's the last of our bundles," said Verna. And pursed her lips to hide their trembling as she cut the ropes and unpacked their belongings.

The bed was a white sea of coolness and calm after the heat and noise in the Hall. But each time she fell asleep the dolphins were there, their yellow red-rimmed eyes winking and whirling inside her head. Like the flecks of wax that had danced in the mead.

CHAPTER TWENTY SIX

Tansen rolled out of bed and went, flying, falling, crawling, stumbling into the side-room, glimpsing Verna peering owlishly over a bed-cover, and made for the washing bowl. And drank and drank till Verna's firm hands were holding her bursting head together and she was being copiously sick.

Somewhere a candle burst into life and she was wading through shadows that leapt to engulf and destroy her. Finding a tapestry with her fingers she gripped and held it while the pain spiralled. She was dimly aware of the tapestry tearing, falling upon her. And being lifted and craving water and feeling it pouring salty down her throat. And climbing out of a quicksand that sucked at her body. And being sick, so sick that she wanted to die. And Verna tickling the back of her throat with a feather till she was helplessly sick again. And she was blind and deaf and swimming in a sea of pain and being dragged down, choking. Till she could fight no more and sank into dark oblivion.

And was roused again sharply, dragged upright by her hair. And walking again till she fell and prayed to Bride to end it. And Theobold, his friendly smile widening to euphoric glee. And Beofric, foxy and sly, gloating. And Dale with wicked rainbow horns, and eyes like suns offering her mead in a cup where maggots swam. And a host of merry nobles, their laughter echoing in the cavern of her head. And she beat at their faces and was up again, dragging one heavy leg after the other.

Only Verna saw the rays of the newly-risen sun strike through the slats. Only Verna knew how many candles had burned low and gone out. And knew that whether the poison had worked its way out or not, the girl was at the end of her resources and must rest. And washed the yellow stretched skin and the nail-marks in her palms and the bruises where she had hammered on the wall. And laid her in her bed.

The door opened with a crack. Tansen, flinching from a spearhead of light, saw two feet in rags of leather oozing blood, come through the door. And Ean unconscious, shoulder high. And black thunderclouds in her head. And pain, creeping up on her till her body was racked with it again.

"Get out of his bed, you Picti slut!"

And her body heaving as they bounced Ean on the bed.

"Drink yourselves silly elsewhere." Verna, in a blistering rage, scooped up her mistress and deposited her on a stool in the next room.

"Ean? Is he dead?" She was drowning in weakness.

"Him! He was jumping over bare swords half the night." Verna's voice was pure vinegar. "Now he's come to play with his ceremonial baubles."

Tansen heard the splash of water and Ean spluttering. Then his voice, slightly blurred.

"Thor's thundering balls, this hilt has gold knobs on it. A man can't fit his hand round it. It's a waste of a good blade!"

"Ach, it's only for show! We've a deadlier one for you. One with the victory-rune on its killing edge."

Verna was tidying the mess, bringing fresh water. Then she was flapping the folds out of Tansen's clothes, pulling at her night-robe. Tansen's skin felt chill and clammy with sweat.

"Leave me alone."

"You're getting dressed and going to that Acclamation."

"Oh, no, no, no! I can't!" Wailing like a child.

"You have to! You'll march in the Procession and hold your head high and look like their Queen."

Tansen drove herself towards the doorway. More hallucinations! A second sun had risen in the room beyond, floating above the heads of the men, more brilliant, more magnificent than the real sun. She closed her eyes and looked again. It was still there, a golden face, its fierce beauty catching fire from a piercing shaft from the window.

"What's this? My helmet? Is this supposed to frighten my enemies? By the Axe of the Thunder-God, they're more likely to die laughing!"

The face swam into her vision. Bronze eyebrows, inlaid with silver, edged with garnets and ending in a tiny boar's head. A close-trimmed moustache under a bronze nose-piece. Warriors battling across the cheek-pieces.

"No, take it away," she cried. "It's inhuman!"

No one heard her. Ean had stuck it on, waggling his hands like sprouting ears.

"My brains are rattling about in here like peas in a pail!"

His men took it off to pad it with leather.

By the time Verna had washed and dressed Tansen, the other room was empty. Pain and nausea hovered, waiting to pounce, but she could stand. And one thought was clear. Someone had poisoned her. To keep her from appearing at the Acclamation. Yet the Pagan Princess would be there for all the people to see.

Outside in the yard, she gulped in the clean morning air. Ean sat on his war-horse in shining armour with the brilliance of the sun behind him. Now with the living eyes behind it the golden mask was awe-inspiring. Bronze medallions lay on chains on his mount's sleek skin. The oiled feet danced impatiently setting gold bells tinkling on the braided mane.

For a precious moment Tansen thought the eyes in the rose-gilt mask looked straight at her.

Then the Royal Standard took up its position, gilded peacock feathers in wrought-iron. Ean moved off, twelve men of his retinue packed closely at his back. Followed by Theobold and Beofric and the members of the Witan. Before they had all got into the swing of the march the Royal Standard faltered. Ean's horse slithered to a stop on the frosty cobbles. And Tansen, weak with fright, climbed on a wall to see.

A shimmering host of butterflies, barred Ean's way. She squeezed her eyes shut, gulped and opened them.

It was the Bishop Paulinus, gorgeous in red and white, blue and gold, holding aloft a massive Cross of Gold and backed by a bevy of clerics. Her command of the language was just enough to follow the words.

"Eanfrith, son of Aethelfrith! By the great Cross of Edwin, I call upon you to accept Christian baptism before your Acclamation!"

A clatter of hooves and Earl Theobold, ox-like shoulders hunched, cut across between the King and the Prelate.

"Get out of the King's way, man!" he called roughly. "Let us get on with our business!"

"Eanfrith! I call upon you to be anointed at my hands as a Christian King in a Christian land."

Lord Beofric, his horse sidling daintily, was more polished.

"According to my memory, King Edwin took fully eleven years before making up his mind. I claim the same period of private meditation for the new King."

Paulinus's voice boomed out with the full authority of the Church resonating behind it.

"King Edwin was baptised in the waters at York and in the Church of St. Peter the Apostle. You should remember that Easter Day, Lord Beofric. You accepted baptism with him."

"Indeed I was there at Jorvic," said Lord Beofric smoothly. "And I remember that you promised Edwin great earthly rewards after his cleansing."

"And he received them! All the territories of the North and West were brought under his sway by the blessing of Almighty God."

"Only because he raised larger armies in a shorter space of time than his enemies!" Theobold's horse struck impatient sparks from the cobbles. "Make way there!"

Paulinus ignoring him, addressed Eanfrith again.

"With the Light of the Gospel behind you, you will enjoy greater power than any King of the Angles before you."

"Yet Edwin had only six short years to enjoy his bounty from the King of Heaven." Lord Beofric spoke out with more passion than Tansen expected. "Then Cadwallon, also baptised a Christian, destroyed him. Is it Cadwallon's turn for six years of glory?"

"He's reaping his rewards by ravaging our country, sparing neither woman nor child!" Theobold's cry was full of fury. "He shouts from the hill-tops that he means to exterminate us. Now we're forced to sue for peace with this 'Christian' barbarian. Away with your promises and let's get on with acclaiming our King in our own way!"

He set his horse at a gallop at the Prelate. Paulinus defied him until he was in danger of being trampled and side-stepped smartly up the steps to the door of his Church. The line of priests broke in a multi-coloured panic.

"Lead on, Standard-bearer!"

Tansen, only half-understanding the exchanges, had slipped down behind the wall to be sick again.

"Protect my man, Gentle Ones!" She gave a half-gasp, half-groan. A savage King to be placated. A powerful Prelate to be outwitted. And a viper's nest of nobles whose servants had bungled the amount of poison needed to ease an unwanted Queen out of the way. She made Bride's sign under her cloak, wiped her mouth with a handkerchief dipped in scented water and looked round for a mount.

"Only the King and his Witan ride today." Dale's moonface rose over the wall. "Ealdormen, sherriffs, riff-raff and unwanted pagans walk. Come out from behind that wall or we'll miss the whole scintillating spectacle."

"You with your mead from a fresh-opened cask and a phial hidden in your sleeve!" she accused him. And was promptly sick again.

"An Heir on the way already? Beofric will be delighted to foster him."

And Dale grasped her arm and slotted her neatly in near the end of the procession.

"Breathe deeply and walk like a Queen," he said quietly."Or folk will be asking who's the green-faced woman in the cloud of lavender. I wondered why that cask disappeared smartly."

"Fine bodyguard Garnard chose for me!"

"Correction. I volunteered."

"Seems like you need a few lessons!"

"Seems like a good time to draw the fire on myself."

His eyes gazed serenely to where Paulinus, on the steps of his Church, was lecturing the procession. By the time they reached him he was in full spate.

"Everlasting doom! Heathens! Idol-worshippers!" Spittle sprayed over the crowd. His eyes fastened greedily on Tansen.

"The pagan harlot herself! Foul apostate Picti!"

It was the slap in the face Tansen needed to recover herself.She stopped. The crowd jammed against her back like logs in a stream.

"Picti! Picti!"

The crowd circled her, leaving her stranded as though she had struck a leper bell. Snarling men with hot, hate-filled eyes.

"Spawn of a filthy Picti raider!"

The insults were plain from their tone.

"Go back into your stinking Picti bog!"

Women crossing themselves, hissing curses. One spat with deadly accuracy.

Tansen scrubbed the spittle from her cheek with her cloak, her eyes sea-green and stormy. Paulinus folded his arms over the great jewelled Cross and gazed with satisfaction at the scene he had stirred up. Her forehead stung, cut by a flying stone. Feeling in her pouch for a cloth to stem the blood, she found that her hands were trembling.

"Make way! Move!" Dale's cloaked arm shielded her and his sword made V-signs in the air as he forced a pathway. Bareheaded, dressed in dark brown, he looked like a monk himself. His great mild eyes gathered the crowd.

"You're the ones that queued to be baptised like lambs skipping through the cleansing trough." His voice was mellow, not accusing. "But I hear that pickling few of you turn up to hear Paulinus preach. Now that's awkward of you."

His eyes, roaming over the crowd, were filled with sorrow. But his jaw widened and they found themselves smiling back at him.

"No wonder he disguises himself as a singer. And sings a bawdy song or two in the market-place. It's the only way he can gather a crowd to listen to his sermons, eh?"

Chuckles in the crowd that swelled into a gale of laughter as the well-known story was passed back. If the Earls could spurn the cleric, ordinary folk could have a laugh at his expense too.

A fowler, round and ruddy-cheeked, with a hawk's head on the brooch at his neck leapt to Dale's side.

"Remember his famous miracle in the Mead Hall."

"God sent the fire!" shouted a woman. "Paulinus alone hadn't a blister on him."

"Is that what your man told you?" The fowler grinned wickedly. "Well, here's the truth of it. All the perfumes and peacock's feathers were in the upper room. But the real drinkers were downstairs, juggling with brands pulled from the hearth."

"I knew it!" The woman scowled.

"Aye, we'd had a few jars. Too far gone to notice that one fire-brand had lodged snugly in a corner. Until the whole burning ceiling caved in on us and the big shots came tumbling down, arse over top-knot. Except for Paulinus. He'd been sitting at the end of the table. And there he was, astride a beam. And he'd wit enough to swear his God had stage-managed the whole thing."

Paulinus disappeared in a swirl of red and gold indignation.

"Forget Paulinus!" Dale slid his sword away. "There's a new King to be acclaimed!"

The thought of the spectacle they were missing proved too much for the crowd. They looked at the height of the sun and surged onwards.

"I waded with the crowd into the river." The King's Hunter, long-boned and lanky, beckoned to his wife and they fell into step beside Tansen. "I thought I'd find out what comes after this life. But I've gone back to the old ways. That way I know what signs to make and what prayers to say without having to think about it."

The fowler followed, his idle chatter helping Tansen to forget her fear and pain as she placed one foot carefully in front of the other.

"Paulinus took all the credit for converting Edwin. But it was Coifi, Edwin's own High Priest, who clinched it."

The fowler began to whine, playing back to the semi-circle of folk that had built up around Tansen subtly protecting her.

"My Lord King, no man's been more zealous in the work of the old gods than I. Yet you heap gifts on everyone but me. If these old gods of mine had been any good, I'd have had all these riches instead."

Tansen found she could laugh a little.

"And that converted Edwin?" asked Dale.

"Most folk thought he'd gone mad."

Suddenly their laughter was throbbing through Tansen's head. She staggered. The Fowler's wife steadied her with an arm round her waist.

"It's a child, is it? Are you going to throw up?"

Tansen, hearing the trumpets welcoming Ean into the arena, shook her head and stepped out again.

CHAPTER TWENTY SEVEN

The amphitheatre swarmed with folk. Row after row, filled with men, women and children, lining the steps, clinging, pushing, jostling, squeezing into corners, climbing onto projecting spars.

The arena was a vast desert of sand broken by a dais, so small it held only the King's High Chair. Dale had sent serfs ahead to keep a front row bench free for them with Verna somewhere behind. Tansen threw off her cloak and bore down on her nausea with a will of iron.

A great cheer spiralled upwards taking with it a flock of pigeons who had been strutting unnoticed in the sun. Ean had entered.

From the distance he looked like a tiny toy soldier as he came and sat on the dais. The Witan splayed out like purposeful ants into a circle. The cheers settled into the drone of a million bees about to swarm. But when Theobold and Beofric began the words of the ritual, their voices resounded around the arena and silence fell.

Tansen feasted her eyes on her splendid lover while the meaningless words advanced and retreated in the air. Then she grew bored and her eyes wandered. The enormity of the place stunned her.

"I thought Danish Kings had a Moot Hill for meetings where folk could debate with their King."

Dale leaned towards her, his eyes never moving from the dais.

"Moot Hills and debates went out of fashion. Eanfrith's father built this arena."

"So everyone can hear the King. But the dissenting voice from the top tier is carried away by the wind?"

"Exactly."

"My people wouldn't stand for it."

"No? You'd to ring a bell to catch Garnard's ear! Now, stop asking questions."

Tansen swallowed hard. By talking she was trying to distract her attention from her swimming head and her queasy stomach. By this time the sun had appeared above the rampart of seats and it was hot in the arena. Then Dale's amazed voice pierced the fog in her head.

"Look at that!"

It was an enormous whet-stone carried upright by four straining men.

Tansen barely looked. She was distinctly annoyed with Dale. Each new experience seemed to fill him with pleasure. And her own brush with death had affected him not at all. So had he slipped poison in her mead or not?

“The King is the Smith, the Forger, the Giver, the Whetstone on which his warriors sharpen their swords,” droned Beofric.

Now, she thought, if Dale had volunteered to be her bodyguard was Garnard paying him? Unlikely. So who was paying him? And why? He couldn’t be receiving much. Most of his gear seemed to have been plundered from men fatter than himself. Like that ridiculous dolphin tunic that sprouted out from his leather jacket at neck and sleeves and waist.

Mercifully a cloud came and blotted out the heat from the sun. Tansen’s head had cleared but she still felt sick. And sick at heart too, thinking that the burden they were placing on Ean’s shoulders was as heavy as that great ugly whetstone.

A grotesque stone face stared outwards from the head of the Stone.

“May you have the strength of Thor the Mighty.”

As the men endeavoured to turn the stone it tilted. Tansen’s stomach heaved as they struggled to balance it. Another stony mask came into view.

“May you have the wisdom of Odin’s runes.”

Again it turned and another face appeared with corn sprouting from its hideous mouth.

“May the blood of Frey enrich your soil.”

The last mask had the face of a woman.

“May your seed bring forth sons from the daughters of Freya.”

Tansen gulped and swallowed. If Ean had planted a seed in her it had been washed away by the ravages of the poison. She gritted her teeth and set herself to endure till the end.

Suddenly the sun blazed out again. It picked out a tiny bronze stag right at the top of the Whetstone and sent its shadow streaking across the yellow sand of the arena. And spreading its monstrous branching antlers straight to Ean’s feet and upwards, black on white and gold, until the wicked points lay as if pinned to his breast.

A thousand throats rasped with an indrawn gasp of fear.

“By the nine glory-twigs of Woden, it’s an omen!” someone was muttering.

Slowly the shadow reached out to engulf her too. She tried to push it away. Heard her own voice cry out. Then she was staring at the sky. And wondering where she was.

Verna, scarlet-faced, her hair flying, looked as though she had fought with the Furies to reach her.

“I knew I was either going to faint or throw up,” Tansen said weakly.

“I’m glad you chose the least messy.” Verna was loosening the laces at her throat.

The memory of that ill-omened stag came racing back. Tansen pushed herself up on her elbows to see. Earl Theobold, his back rigid with determination, was marching across the black shadow in the sand, spurning it with his feet. Dale, his attention still fixed grimly on the arena, leaned sideways to help her up to her seat.

"A trick of the sunlight," he said blandly. "Pull yourself together."

Imprinted on Tansen's closed eyelids was the image of those enormous antlers pointing at Ean's heart. Yet when she looked again at the Whetstone, it was such a puny little stag to have made such a great black menacing shadow.

Verna edged herself onto the bench beside her.

"Here is the gleaming sword, Hrunting by name," Theobold intoned. "Choicest of weapons, trusty and splendid."

Suddenly Tansen was terribly afraid. For the first time in her life she sensed an emptiness in the air. She had no feeling of the presence of the Invisible Ones. As if they had never graced this airless arena, leaving it first to Coifi, the last High Priest, and then to Paulinus the Prelate.

"I must get out of here! It's an ill-omened place!"

"Shush!"

"Dagda curse you, you're an insensitive beast!" But it was Dagda's golden disc that was shining mercilessly down on her aching head.

"Royal Helmet, decked with treasure, circled with diadems, wrought in white heat, to guard a King's head."

Unseen horns sang their eager King-song.

She rose, looking round wildly for a way out. She must not disgrace Ean by being sick in the sand at his Acclamation.

"It's nearly over," said Dale placidly. "We'll slip out now before the crowd starts moving."

Outside the air was clearer. Tansen slid wilting onto the wall of a well. Verna brought cups of herb tea flavoured with honey from a stall. Tansen drew back from it sharply.

"So it wasn't only the heat," said Dale seeing her reaction. "Pregnancy or poison?"

"Both, or either."

"Surely you know, woman."

"Right now I don't care!" Tansen snapped. "But you! You were watching my drinks."

Dale stared at her with a rare anger and drank off her tea.

"I didn't poison your cup."

"Then who did?"

He shrugged as if it was of no account.

"Back to your chamber to rest, my girl," Verna interrupted

"I'll wait here for the King."

"To whisper in his ear that you suspect two hundred of his nobles?" Dale said. "Go on home. He'll be judging chariot races and riding displays and axe-throwing contests for the rest of the day."

Tansen stared at him, her eyes dark with outrage. But he was right. She must rest so that she could face the nobles in the Banqueting Hall that night.

Dale watched as she pushed herself to her feet. He nodded as her back straightened and she forced her leaden feet forward. And he gave a savage blow to the wooden handle of the well that sent the bucket clanging from side to side down into the echoing depths below.

When the pains gripped, Tansen clenched her fists. Against her closed eyelids she still saw the image of that fearful stag with the wicked points.

"That poison's still working in you," sighed Verna.

In her room Tansen went on walking, staggering from tapestry to chair to chest to bed, drinking whatever Verna forced on her and bringing it up with fearful accuracy. Until she fell exhausted near the brazier. And lay feeling the spasms dwindling and sank into a lurid, nightmare-filled sleep.

Verna listened till the throaty breathing eased and went to a small bundle not yet unpacked. She drew out a box and a gannet's wing feather. She moistened the point on her tongue and, throwing back Tansen's stained garments, set to work.

Long after, Tansen woke, feeling the quill riding her skin and the tingle of the feather.

"Why are you painting me?" she asked.

"You, a Pretani. And you need to ask that. Louder than words, deadlier than blows, this will show your contempt for folk who spit and throw stones and poison cups. Besides it will hide your poor pale face." And she blew on her work and appraised it. "Turn over. Careful! That scroll isn't dry yet."

Tansen turned and lay, her cheek on her painted arm, feeling a welcome peace invade her body.

"Would Theobold do it?" asked Verna. "He was sitting with you."

"If he was persuaded it was his duty he'd do it. But he'd have a sneaking twinge of guilt. It could have been anyone, servant or noble. Even Dale."

"Next time it might be a dagger."

"No. Always something that can be passed off as an accident. Garnard could still turn nasty." Her throat felt raw.

"That's why you must show yourself tonight. But eat and drink nothing. I'll cook something later." Verna laid down her quill and clasped her dye-stained fingers. "What are we going to do? You can't go on like this."

Tansen lurched to her feet and held up the mirror.

"Ean will sort them out now he's King."

Verna gathered the dyes, hiding her sceptical face.

"Can he?"

"Of course he can. Verna, I look magnificent! Tonight even Paulinus will pale into insignificance."

Lapis-lazuli serpents spiralling up her arms flaring into malachite trumpet-heads on her shoulders. Intertwined sea-horses, turquoise and sand-yellow, rippling across the skin of her face. Birds in coral and amber, with malachite claws and coral beaks, flaming across her breast.

In the Mead Hall Ean, smelling of sweat and leather, told her she looked gorgeous. And Tansen played the part of a Danish Lady ablaze in a riot of Pretani symbols. It was a pity that Bishop Paulinus and Edwin's Queen had elected to eat privately.

"Did you see that Whetstone?" Ean bubbled over with sheer enjoyment. "I thought they were going to drop it in my lap. I'd have landed on my backside in the sand with the weight of it."

It was a sumptuous feast. Fresh poached salmon, pink and garnished. Pork and lobster balls drenched in cream and wine. Haunches of meat cut dripping off the spit. Whole hard-boiled eggs stuffed with cream cheese and herbs and built into pyramids on platters. Honey scones flavoured with a syrup of apples and cherries. Black berries becalmed in a sea of thick cream. And Tansen laughed a lot to cover the hunger growling in her stomach.

"No more praise-songs!" cried Ean when the bards began to tune up. "No more promises! You all know by now that none who serve me shall find me wanting in gifts."

"Riddles, then! Riddles!"

"I know a new one!"

The man who sprang onto a bench screwed his face into a leer.

"There came a lusty bachelor. He went where he knew her to be, standing in a corner. He lifted his garment and thrust his stiff tool under her girdle where she stood."

The clapping and stamping of feet grew louder.

"Both of them shook as he wrought his will, faster and faster."

His eyes winked, his hips rotated.

"Under her girdle something began to grow. Something good that men desire and buy with money. Who was she?"

"A butter churn!" They roared and pelted him with beakers and bread.

It was a man's joke and cheapened her love for Ean. Yet it kindled a heat in her moist secret places. She draped herself over the arm of his Chair.

"Come to bed, love," she whispered and bit his ear-lobe.

"It's early yet!" cried Ean. "Another riddle!" He threw his arm round her and nuzzled her neck, heightening her desire.

Wulf's face loomed at Ean's other side.

"Sire! There's a herald come from Gwynedd," he said quietly.

"Tell him to come back tomorrow!" cried Ean.

Tansen rose, sensing from Wulf's face that Ean's rejoicing was going to be short-lived.

"Gwynedd?" Lord Beofric's foxy ears almost stood up from his head. "Let's hear him!"

The herald was black-browed and stolid British Cymry. He stood before Ean like an immovable rock.

"Greetings from Cadwallon, ap Catfan, King of Gwynedd, High King of Mid Britain."

There was an instant hush, filled with the hiss and crackle of the last of the ox-fat dripping into the fire.

"King Eanfrith of Angleland. The High King Cadwallon summons you to appear at his stronghold at Lleyn to swear allegiance to him as your Overlord."

"Overlord, is it?" roared Theobold, starting forward, reaching out a great paw to grasp a bunch of the messenger's clothing.

Lord Beofric's voice cut in swiftly.

"There's more?"

"King Eanfrith must appear before seven nights have passed."

"Curse him! We've only just set our new King on his High Chair this very day!"

"Should he fail to appear, the High King Cadwallon will set Eanfrith's hands and head on a stake on the Wall of Hadrian as he did with Edwin."

"Carry your own hands on stakes back to your master!" Theobold's flashing dagger went spinning into a corner. Someone nearby had reacted quickly.

"Steady, my lord!" said Beofric, his own voice quivering with barely-suppressed emotion. "Tell your master our King and his embassy will be at Lleyn within seven nights."

The herald turned. Angles at every table and bench blocked his passage to the doorway.

"Let him go!" commanded Beofric. "The first man who harms him will be the next messenger to Cadwallon to meet the same fate!"

Ean rose unsteadily, holding on to the table.

"Odin rot the man! The next seven days were to be for rejoicing!"

"It was a calculated insult," agreed Beofric. "The man timed his arrival nicely."

Then Theobold struck the board a mighty blow. He raised his fists to the roof and shook them.

"Curse that barbarian Cadwallon!" he cried. His great voice was rough with frustration and rage. "How have we let ourselves become so weak and defenceless? We thought we'd finished him off years ago when we threw him into the Eirean sea! Instead he came rampaging back with a pack of Irish mercenaries ravenous for plunder and the blood of Edwin." His harangue stopped on an indrawn breath that was almost a sob.

Tansen, half-hidden behind Ean, stroked the back of the wooden eagle that perched on the Chair.

"It was these fancy Irish bards that turned Cadwallon into a Cymry folk-hero." Lord Beofric padded along by the hearth-fire on the soft feet of a caged fox. His eyes blazed red, stilling the muttering of the men around him. "Now he's fished a sword out of a dungheap and given it a heathenish name and calls himself the new Arthur. The one name with a ring of magic in it that would rally the Cymry kings to him like hens round a cockerel." He threw his arms wide. "How can we fight against a dream in the hearts of a people?"

Tansen smiled wryly, liking the sound of a leader with a magic sword and a dream of a new Cymry Britain.

Men's voices rose, arguing with one another.

"They'll run like cattle, these Irish. They won't face up to us!"

"And we've a new Warrior-Hero to lead us!"

"But not enough men or arms! We need time for houses and barns to be rebuilt, crops to be sown, food gathered for the winter."

"Time to use all that treasure in the Church to buy axes from the Low Country, spears from Daneland."

"The Pretani fleet! Have Garnard strike at Cadwallon's back in the west!"

"Garnard's fleet?" A tumble of Anglian oaths. "A wasp-sting, no more!"

Long ago Tansen had thrown away the idea of using the Garnard alliance as a weapon. They feared neither his wrath nor wanted his goodwill.

"We must play it softly and sweetly for now." Lord Beofric swept the air with his hand and the angry buzz of voices quietened. "The marriage alliance! We still have that card up our sleeves."

"With one of Cadwallon's daughters, as we'd planned."

"A Cymry Queen in North Humber Land and a parcel of dark-haired Welsh heirs. Now how would Cadwallon's Welsh chiefs like that?"

"It would take the edge off his threats."

Tansen leaned her cheek in her hand and listened. She would need all the information she could get just to save her skin. Her quick mind was already leaping ahead through all the aspects of the situation. And she was learning fast how Angles thought. No different from any other defeated race, she guessed. For not only must she save herself. But she must aim for a position of power when the dust settled.

"I'd even let Paulinus sanctify the marriage if it would give us time to win new allies and recruits."

"Penda was the only ally worth having. Now he's snug in Cadwallon's pouch."

"Think a minute. Why is Cadwallon demanding allegiance and peace? Why has he given us this respite? Because he needs time, too! That's why!"

The nobles talked across her, hardly aware of the girl, her face luminous in the golden lamplight, her head slightly bent, listening, knowing their arguments made sense.

Abruptly Theobold summed it up.

"A marriage alliance to give us time. Then we strike back. And we make his devastation of our land seem like child's play."

Beofric leaned over the High Table, thrusting his face at Ean.

"My Lord, we must start tomorrow. It will take all of seven nights to reach Lleyn."

"I'm King now. I decide." But Ean's mouth was slack, his eyes heavy-lidded. "I'll have my full term of rejoicing. Cadwallon can wait."

"Sire." It was Beofric at his wiliest. "Your passage to Lleyn will be a most royal and majestic procession. All along the way your loyal subjects will flock to greet you."

Smiling, Ean preened the feathered gold of his hair with his hand.

"Just you wag your head at everything Cadwallon says," growled Theobold. "For come the spring we'll muster and cross the Pennines and smash him. Only this time, we'll not let him escape to Eirean to rise again."

And Tansen spoke loudly but coolly.

"And what happens to me when you all come trooping back with a daughter of Cadwallon? Will you strike off my head into a bucket? Or hide me away in a nunnery?

CHAPTER TWENTY EIGHT

Ean stared at Tansen and shook his head to clear it.

"I won't have my celebrations cut short! I won't marry anyone else! Not anyone!"

Ean's fist crashing on the table made no impact on the stony faces of the earls. He paused as if he sensed he was pointing an arrow at her breast. Lord Beofric spread his fingers under Ean's elbow.

"This way, Sire. We'll talk in private."

Wulf's arm barred Tansen's way as she tried to follow them into the anteroom. But at the entry a tapestry eddied and showed her a guard-niche where she could hide before the servants lit the lamps.

The anteroom was where wars were planned and letters written.

Ean, still carrying his cup, hoisted himself onto a desk laid out ready for a scribe. Maps were pinned on the wall behind his head.

"I made a commitment to the Lady. I'll hear no more talk of marriage alliances."

"And that shower of fine promises that poured from your lips today meant nothing?" Theobold placed his hands on broad hips.

"You forget yourself, my Lord King." Beofric took a quill from a silver box and began to sharpen it thoughtfully with a little ceremonial knife. "You made a new commitment today. To a land and a people."

"Aye, by the rune of my mother's name! You're committed to the nobles who protect it and to the poor who've had enough of war with nothing but sorrow to show for it. As our King you must accept Cadwallon's terms whatever they are."

"So that you can muster an army next year! And the next again!" Ean rose and walked stiff-legged to face his nobles from the other side of the desk. "Don't talk to me of commitments. You care nothing for fatherless bairns and plundered corn-fields. Not so long as your army is fed. I made two commitments and I'll keep them both. The Lady becomes Queen. Or I get rid of the lot of you and form a new Witan!" Pale and grim-lipped he looked round his thanes.

A sudden angry movement and the quill in Beofric's hand flew. It feathered Ean's cheek and stuck quivering in the map behind his head. Ean went white.

"My Lord! The Witan had three choices for King." With slow deliberate fingers Beofric laid the ceremonial knife in the tray of sand in front of Ean. "You, Sire, have two."

Ean stared unwinking at the wicked blade and its garnet studded handle.

"You may vacate the Kingship you have so lately acquired and leave it free for one of your brothers."

Aghast, Ean raised boyish blue eyes, full of anguish.

"Or?"

And Tansen came from her hiding-place, wholly composed, stepping softly among the nobles until she reached the desk.

"Or you cover your head with your robe and wait until a dove comes cooing that your mistress has had an unfortunate accident with a toy quill-knife."

She lifted the knife from the sand and snipped the laces of her Danish over-mantle. And as she swung it aside the mosaic of Pretani symbols on her long arching neck, her proud shoulders and arms, her long graceful legs sprang forth in all their radiance to meet the light of the flaring lamps..

"Shameless! Picti slut!" The words hissed like a wakening sword. And brought a burnished deepening of the colours that laced her skin.

"Before you do business with natives, my Lords, it's wise to refer to their history."

In the glimmering light her eyes were fathomless, mysterious.

"Once there lived a King in the Lothians, kin to my people, called Cunedda. And he was a thorn in the flesh of Vortigern. But then so were the Irish."

She stilled the rustle of impatience by a swift movement of her own that took her into the centre of a cluster of lamps. The light caught the ripple of barbaric colour. Theobold gave a strangled cough.

"So Vortigern lured Cunedda with his troublesome clan to the fine lands of Gwynedd. And set him up there as a bulwark against the Irish. Later King Arthur recognised Vortigern's wisdom and gave Cunedda power and wealth."

Letting the tale hang there for a breathless moment, she took a swirling dancing step, smiling into eyes that tried desperately to take in each part of her glorious body.

"Since then every King of Gwynedd has claimed descent from Cunedda. And half the Kings of the Pretani too. So you see. You already have what you need. A Queen who is first cousin to Cadwallon."

In the silence that followed she sensed the minds of the nobles working like yeast fermenting in the dark. Her winning smile deepened the ornamental arrows that dappled her face. And boldly she launched her last bolt towards its mark.

"The Cymry daughters of Lleyn might have broad hips for child-bearing. But I'm already bearing a child. A son who is blood-kin to Cadwallon. A son who will be named Kenneth after his noble grand-sire, Cunedda."

Holding the dagger between finger and thumb she let it fall to embed its point in the soft sand.

"Tansen!" Ean ran to clasp her but she had more to say before she was engulfed in his excited embrace.

"If you want an ambassador to Cadwallon, I'm more fitted than any of you to deal with him. I understand how he thinks."

Suspicious eyes narrowed, grim mouths tightened. She went on.

"How can you be sure Cadwallon's playing for time? That your heads and hands won't decorated the Wall of Hadrian beside Edwin's? But with a pregnant Queen in your midst he'll think twice before attacking you."

"And where will your loyalties lie, kinswoman of Cadwallon?" Beofric's fingers slowly followed the lines of his moustache to the point at his chin.

"Where my best interests are served. Where else? You see, when Cadwallon finds you've spurned his kinswoman he'll ally with Garnard. You'll be encircled. And the only escape will be by sea. Back to the land of your forefathers."

Theobold gave a great rumble of a laugh as if acknowledging her astuteness. Beofric sent him a sharp glance and drew the nobles aside. Only then did she turn to be enfolded in Ean's embrace.

No one but Bride knew how much of a gamble she had taken. No one now remembered the whys and wherefores of the Cunedda story but all the Kings of Gwynedd had used it when it was to their advantage. Why shouldn't she? And it was the best she could do for herself and Ean. As for Garnard making a war-like gesture. If the Angles had not been so vulnerable themselves they would have dismissed it. Yet Garnard allied to Cadwallon and Penda of Mercia was a different matter.

Judging by Wulf's face he was cursing the moment when his attention and his arm had slipped to let her enter.

Surprisingly Dale was there, looking utterly foolish, as he leaned his head to catch the nobles' talk. Suddenly he smiled and nodded straight at Tansen. Her stomach swooped up into her throat with fear. Beofric with a set face did his best to stamp towards the door.

"So be it!" said Theobold.

And Ean, putting both feet right in it, flashed a triumphant smile at his nobles.

"That's settled then. Now I'll take my Queen to bed," he crowed.

He ran with her like a bairn to his chamber, yelling, whooping with relief whirling round serfs till they dropped their baskets and held their ears.

Then belt and girdle, slippers and shoes, trousers and tunic fell unheeded. And together they blended into a wild dance of rippling muscles and undulating colours painted on golden skin. They filled the night with the noise of their laughter. She swayed her hips and jangled her earrings at him. Tonight had to be special, like that first wonderful day beside the Leven. Once again she had survived.

For both it was a dance of praise for Life, for Love, for one another. For Tansen it was a web woven with a deeper meaning for it was the night of Samhain when the old year ended, when the fairy mounds opened and the little people streamed forth. And those that knew stayed within the bounds of their homesteads for if they were caught outside the rowan circle they would never be seen again. And although the Angles knew it not she was keeping her own Dane safe within the bounds of her love. So she celebrated Samhain in her own way in the Dance.

Ean's body was aflame with love for her. So much honour had been heaped on his head and only now he realised how much he hungered for her love-making, how she gave his body all he desired. And more. For had she not lifted the weight of an impossible choice from his shoulders.

He laid her on the couch, his breath catching in his throat at the blaze of love in her vivid face. His arm found the niche in the wall that he sought. And he laid amber beads round her neck till they flowed like rivers over the mounds of her breasts. And pearls that lay stranded in the ebb and flow of her breathing.

"Gems cannot match your beauty, precious mother of my child." He slid a gold ring on her finger. "The runes on this ring say, 'A woman is a weaver of peace'."

And they laughed again for who could be at peace when passions ran high and the blood flowed sweetly.

He poured wine from a flagon into a fluted gold goblet and offered it to her.

"For my one and only Queen," he said. "Now you have a royal bowl to drink from."

She dropped her eyes to the cup and there, as if swimming in the wine was a tiny silver salmon, symbol of everlasting love. As she drank, full and deep to dull the last spasms of pain that were still clutching at her, the fish flashed, swinging this way and that on its silver stem.

She hid her pain and fear and her guilt at the lie she had told and rejoiced with him. And wondered how it would be if his bairn was really growing inside her and wished for it to become true this night.

When Ean had fallen asleep, having plundered her bright blooming body, taking the honey and leaving his pollen, she lay drowsily content. And saw before her that dark path between the breasts of the All-Mother where no man's foot had ever trod, where only woman faced the moment of breaking asunder. And slept peacefully in the knowledge that this was how the All-Mother had decreed that the race should continue.

Next morning, the Samhain fogs held sway over the land. Moisture dripped from the very air. Yet they dare not wait for a gale to sweep the mists away.

When Tansen arrived in the Courtyard, ready for travelling, Ean was inspecting the Royal House-Carles, newly sworn in that morning. Dale nodded serenely from the outskirts of the retinue. She hardly recognised him with the dark stubble of a growing beard on his chin. The Steward brought the Hall-Goblet and Ean held it high, mouthing the phrases that flowed readily from his lips nowadays.

"On my return there shall be peace. Treasure shall be common. Men shall greet one another across the gannet's bath. Ring-prowed ships shall bear love-tokens across the meeting of the tides."

During the seven-night journey Tansen flaunted the fact that she was Pretani-born. She rode in leggings, aware that no Danish woman would dare. At Edwin's holy wells her incantations to Bride, were loud and long. Her Pretani hunting songs kept time to the hoof-beats. Never for one moment did she let the Angles forget that she was Pretani and Pagan. And the wide sweep of the land and the broad sky from horizon to horizon could not contain her joy in the countryside.

After spending so much time within Citadels, it was good to be wakened in the first light of day by the crowing of a cock, boasting to the dawn, that he had escaped Cadwallon's pot.

But as they drew nearer to the Gwynedd border, the smell of smoke hung heavy in the damp air. Grisly shrunken fruits hung from stark trees. And their path led between the sad sorry stumps of walls, blackened thatches and scattered rags. The horses shied from the acrid smell of burning flesh in the air that seeping mists had not yet deadened. And sleek scuttling rats and black gorged crows, watched and waited.

Yet everywhere people rose from battered walls, from charred skeletons of roof-trees to greet the new King who would save them from Cadwallon and his Irish plunderers. Men left their oxen-yokes tilting in the black mud of their strip. And limped to wave a crutch or a stump of an arm. Women left their soggy bonfires of rotten stakes and dead wood and raised faces streaked with soot that hardly hid the scars. Old folk hobbled from canvas shelters, huddled against ruined walls and lifted children to see the King. Bairns with burns that flowered pink against the ingrained dirt. With limbs that ended in unsightly knobs. With an empty eye-hole or ear-hole, fringed with frilly flesh. And Ean scattered gold coins from his purse and called them his loyal subjects.

A lame fowler, spreading his nets, straightened and shouted, "I'll have a young hawk tamed for you by spring, Sir King!"

A hunter carrying a deer-net on a boar-spear opened it up so that Ean could choose the best hare for his soup. It broke Tansen's heart when the villagers gave the last of their meat to the King, swearing with crossed fingers that the rest of it was salted for winter. For meat in that area was more precious than the gold Ean dispensed with such ease.

And wherever they stopped the King was welcomed into the best house, recently wattled and often only half thatched. And when she could dispel the ugly images from her mind, she slept surrounded by Ean's retinue with the rest of the men camped in a circle outside. She learned to play tafl with the children, trying to reach a corner-castle with her King before he was captured. Often she would borrow a rough-hewn lyre and sing Pretani love-songs, charming the men round the fire with the soft lilt of her voice.

On the last day within their borders as they rounded a copse they saw thatches still smoking. And their horses ground chicken feathers and broken pots into the dust with their hooves. Stained humps lay beside the loom, the oven, and the trough, leaking black puddles that had almost dried into the earth. And a pink-fleshed bairn, pitted with gaping holes, spilled from a shawl. Two servants were left with spades and orders to bury the bodies and make their own way home, for the party would not return that way.

And Tansen wept on Ean's breast but did not tell him of the terrible fear that was in her heart.

CHAPTER TWENTY NINE

Lleyn WAS a rough soldier's garrison. There was no flutter of colour, no smell of baking, no clatter of looms that betrayed the presence of women. Only mud-grey walls, dung and sweat, and the clang and rasp and buzz and clash of an army preparing its weapons.

The Chief Guard who met them on the uphill roadway gave them no honour. He jerked his thumb for them to enter a bare soldiers' hall where spears and shields and a bodyguard of interested Irishmen leaned at all angles against the walls. Flames licked along a line of pink and blue and white charcoal in a long brazier. Beyond the black mountain of a man stood, side-on, beside a table loaded with food.

The Angles spread out in a semi-circle behind their King. Tansen stayed in the background, cloaked and hooded in dark wool and deep shadows. Suddenly the air came alive with sound. It started as a hiss, searing and sibilant, and grew into a snarl of savage rage. And Tansen was barely aware of two glowing eyes before a powerful body hurled itself against the bars of a cage, with a force that reverberated round the room. And the laughter of the man rumbled after it.

Cadwallon's head turned a fraction, small eyes swiveling to watch their reaction, moist red lips drawn back as his teeth tore at the rib of beef that was sending the hungry animal into a frenzy. The musky odour of mountain cat came at Tansen across the hot coals.

On splayed heavy feet, Cadwallon came forward, chucking the bare rib to a hound and wiping his fingers on the greasy tunic that fitted his massive body like a hide. And she saw for the first time the face of the savage who speared babies and chopped off childish hands for pleasure.

It was a formidable face, dark and secretive. He threw himself sprawling into a high-backed seat pulling open the laces at his neck to reveal a pelt as sleek as a well-fed rat and as black as the hair that came to a point low on his forehead.

The mean blue-black eyes that were set too close to a large fleshy nose measured the Angles one by one and fastened upon Ean. His expression was cold, flat and merciless.

"Come!"

He spoke in his own tongue, his voice holding as much savagery as the snarl of the mountain cat.

"Kneel!" He pointed at the floor with a new rib of beef.

The one word stopped Ean in his tracks. Leather creaked and boots stamped into the stale straw as Ean's retinue came to terms with their humiliation. The veins on Theobald's turkey red neck swelled.

Then Ean dropped to one knee amid the mud and dirt, his shoulders bent as though the whole burden of his people rested there.

"Swear!"

The cat crouched, snarling softly at the flames in the brazier.

"I, Eanfrith, King of the North Humber Land, swear ... " His voice faltered and faded. Tansen's grip on the folds of her cloak tightened, knowing that, in his inexperience, he had no idea of the correct words to use. The cat padded softly and restlessly round its cage.

Cadwallon, indolent to the point of laziness, threw the bone. It struck the bars of the cage and fell. And the cat raised his black head and roared, exposing its glinting red throat and curving fangs, gleaming white and polished like whalebone.

"... that the land which you hold is held on behalf of the mighty Cadwallon. That your duty in war and peace is to Cadwallon, your High King."

Cadwallon tapped a broken dirty finger-nail on the arm of his seat. Ean cleared his throat.

"I swear."

Cadwallon's eyes slewed to the shadows where Tansen hid and his great chin lifted. She could almost hear the word 'hostage' in the air. But the slight kneeling figure drew his fascinated gaze back again. He smiled a thin gloating smile.

"So, you're the spineless coxcomb the Danes have pitted against me."

Suddenly he roared out in a voice choking with triumph.

"Did they not tell you, I've sworn to exterminate all Angles? To send you tumbling back into the Danish Sea."

The pig-eyes were on fire now with the depth of his loathing.

Silence. A throbbing hush that beat like the wing of a bird in Tansen's breast. She could hear the angry breathing of the men around her as Cadwallon taunted them.

"Who invited you here to settle in our land? Vortigern, it was! Not the Kings of West Britain! Never!"

He was trying to bait Eanfrith, knowing he was young and inexperienced, trying to measure how weak or how hot-blooded he might be. Ean swallowed, desperately aware that he should make some show of protestation.

"I come to sue for peace for the sake of the farmers." He stumbled over the unfamiliar tongue.

"So that you'll have time to raise another army behind my back?"

Cadwallon did not wait for an answer but sprang up, moving surpisingly lightly on his large spreading feet. He strode from side to side of the Hall, his men jerking swiftly out of his path.

"Ah, if only Arthur had lived into old age he'd have sent your forebears scuttling home, axes dangling between their legs. Now there was a great King, wouldn't you say? Eh?"

He came around the brazier to them, glaring, shoulders hunched.

The Angles stared back in frozen silence. Beofric's finger-nail tapped on the hilt of his sword, on and on, like water dripping from a river-dam with a hole in it, waiting to burst forth.

"You ignorant foreign scum know more about the failures of Beowulf than the victories of Arthur. A Briton, he was! Like me! The last Roman Emperor, they called him. Till he cast aside his Roman upbringing and called himself the first King of Britain! He took a handful of piddling little kingdoms and moulded them together inside his strong grasp."

And Cadwallon's mighty fist swept up a roll of bread and shook it high above his head.

Tansen knew the temper of the Angles could not be kept in check for much longer. Apart from Beofric and Theobold the thanes knew few British words and these were to do with farming and taxes, not with dreams or ideals. But they could make informed guesses.

"Arthur banished the barbarian, the war-monger and the power-hungry. He brought law and order, truth and peace to the land. It was a golden age, that time, under Arthur." He stopped, his fists clenched, his eyes brilliant, fanatical, seeing his vision evolving, pictured large on the bare planks of the opposite wall.

"And he gave his life to keep Britain for the British."

Tansen gripped her hands together and began to wonder what she was doing here on the side of the enemies of Arthur.

"And the breasts of the mothers give forth tears for their sons to suck. For that Arthur had no heir to keep his Empire together! And when he went, his Empire broke up into footling little estates all at one another's throats. A hundred .. useless .. scattered ... kingdoms." Grimly he loosened his fist and slowly let the crumbs of the bread-roll drop at Ean's feet.

"They forgot the lesson that Arthur had tried to beat into their meagre brains. That strength comes through unity."

Tansen shut her eyes and his dream came to life behind her eyelids. An army of pagans, the Britons who called themselves Celts and the Celts who called themselves Britons, united and victorious against the usurping Angles.

"But there was one who remembered. A youth, conceived like Arthur out of the secret love of a great King for the daughter of another. A princess whose destiny it was to die bearing the new Saviour of Britain. A man who would spring forth from the land of the Dragon."

Tansen saw the march of men and women setting their course towards the distant glow of a high beacon, the goal of freeing Britain from the Angles.

"The golden age of Arthur will come again. The barbarian, the war-monger, the power-hungry will be swept from the land."

Tansen was with him in her Celtic heart, among his people, cheering him as a hero.

"Arthur left his mantle for this youth to lift and wear when his time came." The voice came low and reverent to Tansen's ears.

"Who will unite the Kingdoms of the British again? Who will combine all the petty little kingdoms from the Thames to the Forth."

She opened her eyes and saw him, uncouth and coarse, his expression set hard and his eyes terrible.

The Angles were coiled like springs, and their swords had not been taken from them. Was Cadwallon hoping that someone would make a hasty move, to give him an excuse for a massacre?

"Who but the man who holds these lands now in the palm of his hand? Who but myself! Take a good look, you Sea-Danes! Behold the new Arthur!"

But Tansen saw lumps of gristle on trees and charred bodies of children in the devastasted south of North Humber Land. And beyond that she saw the bloody flesh of her kin on the sweet soil of Pitcarlie and heard the screams of her dying sister. And hated them all, Briton and Angle, alike.

Cadwallon crushed his open palm into a fist and slammed it into Ean's shoulder with all his strength. Ean staggered under the blow, and stilled, not knowing what was expected of him.

"I came to negotiate ... "

"And what do you have to negotiate with?" sneered Cadwallon. Swiftly he caught Ean's arm, twisted it round his back and hissed into his ear. "You came to hear my terms."

At that Tansen came forth from behind the thanes, straight towards Cadwallon, a pulse beating in her throat. The ink-black eyes narrowed as she emerged. She hardly knew what she was going to do. Only that it would be something that no one else in this Hall could do. Some gesture that only a woman, and a bold one, could hope to succeed with.

CHAPTER THIRTY

Cadwallon's eyes widened wickedly at Tansen. He let Ean's wrist drop and thrust out an arm to halt the rush of bodyguards. Grease glinted on his spreading lips.

Tansen, stopped a mere sword's-length away from him and showed her weaponless hands.

"I greet you, cousin," she cried, bold and defiant as any Caltic warrior Queen.

Reaching up she plucked the beef-rib from his fingers and tossed it away. Amid a stupified silence she tied the laces at his throat, patting smooth the wrinkles at the neck of his tunic. And breathed in the wild musky odour of his pelt.The enormous chest expanded, as if drawing in fuel for an explosion of wrath at this familiarity. Tansen's mind sent a desperate message to the Angles to cool their tempers. And to trust her, for Bride's sake! Two of Cadwallon's spearsmen growled behind her back.

Swiftly she swept his heavy cloak from his High Chair and held it up, challenging him with rock-steady eyes.

"Let the mantle of Arthur fit the shoulders of the new hero."

The powerful head tilted and the red fleshy lips curved as he watched her fasten it on him with the great round brooch.

"Let the light of Arthur's sun rise again in the sky!"

Carelessly hooked on a knob of his Chair was the headband of his Kingship, copied from the bardsongs that described Arthur dressed in his majesty. She planted the jewelled circle of gold firmly on the black springy hair. Tilting her head, she gave him the full benefit of her most radiant smile.

"Let the light of Arthur's power blaze again across the land!"

She raised her fist in the age-old gesture of unity and slammed it into his shoulder as he had done to Ean. And held her breath, afraid she had gone too far. But if she had knelt, he would have spurned her with his foot. Instead she had treated him as an equal, equal in birth, equal in purpose. And she had given him what he most desired. A full quota of admiration. His black beard did not hide the grin of satisfaction that snaked round his moist lips.

"The Pretani woman, by all that's wonderful!" He roared his delight to the roof-tree. His spies must have been busy. He knew about her.

His arms went wide to pull her into his embrace but she stepped back and threw off her mantle. Verna and she had wakened early that morning and retired into the undergrowth. Cadwallon's eyes lit first on her riding trousers, gartered to show the shapely swell of thigh and calf. And then flew upwards to the painted symbols that leapt and rippled across her arms and breast and shoulders, glowing with barbaric brilliance.

"A Celtic Queen for a Danish King. By the open thighs of Branwen! You'll heat his cold sea-blood for him!"

But if the name of the goddess was on his lips, his eyes were intent on the body that swayed tantalisingly before him.

"Send for mead, my King!" she cried, slipping from the hand that curled round her buttock. "A toast to the new Arthur!"

Ean's face had gone white and queer. Beofric sneered openly at the vulgarity of the scene. Theobold bunched his fists and stared with disbelief and contempt. Tansen pleaded with the Great Ones to bring them to understand that she was merely a woman fighting for the life of her man.

"Set the boards for the feast!" Cadwallon snapped a finger and thumb at the servants.

And Tansen had to forget the disdain of thanes who thought she was a traitor and the pale green sheen of sweat on the cheek of Ean. For Cadwallon was sweeping her with his arm to the other side of the brazier where the cage of the jet-black cat stood. And her heart stuttered and stammered as she fought to capture his groping hands.

Cadwallon's whole life had been spent in dominating others. Men obeyed him, women submitted. Few tried to flatter him. None succeeded. Yet this lass had not flinched nor cringed. She had met his look with candid eyes that held a fine promise of Celtic mischief. By God, she had taken him by surprise. That simple gesture of dressing him in Kingship, the way she had accepted his role as a second Arthur as though it was the most natural thing in the world, now that had sent a quiver through his gut. God's blood, she was a rare one! He banged his fist on the cage and watched her as the enraged cat slashed at the bars, its unfurled claws only inches from her face. And she did not shrink.

"What are you doing, a wildcat like yourself, saddled with a babyfaced brat of an Angle?"

"Why do you think the Pretani King married me to the Angle Eanfrith?" she whispered.

He looked down, admiring the heave of her breasts and a low growl started in his throat.

"You're a spy! A damned spy in their Court!" He too had lowered his voice.

"You can see that he's no great warrior. And he was raised in our Pretani court. He thinks like us. He's as much a Cymry in his own land as I am. He's no threat to your plans."

She had used the word 'Cymry' with its true meaning of 'foreigner'. But she had heard that Cadwallon was now using it to describe the Britons of the east, his own people. A light dawned in Cadwallon's eye.

"No threat to .. our .. plans." His hand pressing on her breast tightened on the word 'our'. His voice had thickened. For he had plans. Plans to sink himself in the white flesh under those breeches when she spread herself under him later. My, but she was a ripe and luscious wench. And randy, too, needing a real man, not a boy. Still he would curb himself awhile. She was no trash to sport with on a bed of straw. She was as royal as he was.

"Yet I hear that the Angles refused to acclaim you as Queen." He moved his bulk closer and enjoyed the arousal between his legs at the womanly smell of her. "Now as Queen you could be my eyes and ears in that nest of vipers! Think of it! Together we could work to bring about the downfall of these bastards."

It was not a question and Tansen gave him no answer except a brilliant smile that she hoped would promise enough. With a new and surprising courtesy he took her hand and led her to the High Table.

Cadwallon, used to dealing with cut-throats and traitors was finding he had little defense against this lively and eloquent young face. Something about the way she held herself made him respond with polite gestures that he scorned in others. He would show these Angles a thing or two. Show that bewildered boy-King that Cadwallon was no coarse barbarian. He could be as charming as any courtier. When he chose. Ean, seated with his Embassy, looked through the flames towards Tansen with eyes full of questions. She could give him nothing more than a little nod that was an appeal to him to trust her.

His thanes certainly did not. Beofric swallowed his meat as though it was sawdust. By now Cadwallon's barbed insults and threats had been translated to them. And here was the Picti woman, looking like she had gone over to the enemy. Only Theobold was uncomfortably aware that she had saved him from a hasty and ill-considered action that might have cost them their lives. And he wondered what lay behind the innocent green eyes that tilted towards Cadwallon so appealingly.

Tansen forced herself to eat, trying to still the revulsion that shivered across her painted skin each time he leaned over her and his meaty breath seared her cheek.

"Maes Cogwy!" Cadwallon called to his bard as he threw aside his plate at last. "Do you know the place, Pretani woman? It's a pleasant little plain not far from here."

And the place where he and his forefathers habitually chose to meet the armies who rose against him.

"I saw the field of Maes Cogwy," the bard sang out.

"Armies and the cry of men pressed hard,
Cadwallon brought them aid.
Till I am in my oaken coffin,
I shall sing praises
Of Cadwallon in his glory."

He slewed round in his chair, grinning arrogantly at Tansen, his fingers scratching at his groin.

"Seven hundred was the army in his court,
Great was the fortune, the glory in battle,
Cadwallon won who led the attack.
My heart was aflame like a firebrand,
The heir of great Arthur, our strong fortress,
Our Cadwallon, the full-famed lord." And Tansen felt fear building up in her again and bit hard on her bread to stop her mouth from trembling.

Then the bard began to sing the songs of Taleisin's making, who was the bard of Maelgwyn and Rhun, past Kings of Gwynedd, close kin to the Pretani Queen Caterin and the songs were all about war with the Angles. And the words and tunes from the past lilted in her heart.

Cadwallon knew he was stirring her by the hot blood that came and went in her face. But past glories, however fine, were nothing to the sweet victory he hoped to savour that night. He held up his palm and the bard squeaked into silence. Cadwallon squinted across the brazier to the Angles and gestured for them to rise.

"And now for my terms!" As the thanes rose to their feet, taut and wary, he muted his great voice almost to a whisper so that they had to lean nearer to hear

"Except for thirty thanes in the King's retinue, you'll disband your entire army."

"What army?" came a low growl from Theobold.

Cadwallon's sharp ears caught the gist. His eyes skewered Theobold to the floor.

"The one you intend to build up to come back at me! I didn't annihilate it altogether. Instead you'll transfer them to work on the land to feed my peace-keeping force. I've assigned a serjeant to each of your regions to assess the tribute once he's seen your harvest in."

The heads of the thanes bent to hide the chagrin in their eyes. What harvest? They had known the terms would be harsh. But, Odin's teeth, they vowed, come next season and they would be doing the same and worse to this coarse clodhopper!

"Now, let's consider your navy! You had twelve forty-benchers and eight thirty-benchers at my last count. Is that not so?"

Beofric sucked in his breath sharply. Cadwallon let out a wheezy chuckle. "A good agent is worth a battalion of archers," He paused, letting the wait lie heavily on their shoulders. "Half of these ships will sail round to my west coast to keep the Irish sea quiet. The other half will remain in the east under Banhed here."

The ruddy cheeks of the new commander bulged as his neighbour thumped his back at the promotion.

Cadwallon cupped his hands comfortably round his rough pottery ale-mug and leant forward. His tongue wet his lips.

Theobold's throat had gone dry. He took a gulp of ale.

"Now, we'll consider the gold."

Theobold choked. Cadwallon waited till the spluttering stopped.

"Arthur had a sword he plucked from a rock. I'll pluck my treasure from the land of the Angles. I hear that Edwin had a great Cross of Gold. I fancy it would shine grandly before me as I go into battle." He winked round at Tansen. "And I'll have my pick of the gifts Edwin gave to the Bishop Paulinus."

A loud groan was forced from the throat of Beofric. Tansen guessed he had other plans for that gold.

"These gifts were given to the Church."

"It may surprise you but we have Churches here too. They could do with a few golden chalices."

Cadwallon rose, grinning.

"As for the Kingship."

He placed his hands on the shoulders of a young man whose arrogance was the image of his own. Tansen held her breath.

"Now Bryarch here has earned a ripe Kingship. Under my guidance, of course." Tansen closed her eyes so as not to see Ean's face. She had failed after all in her bid to get them out of this dung-heap of a place safely. Cadwallon was going to put a sub-king in Ean's place. And surely Ean would be put to death.

"Ach well, Bryarch," Cadwallon's eyes slid back to Tansen. "Maybe I'll put off your promotion for a while yet."

Tansen's eyes flew open on Ean's face and she saw her own relief mirrored there.

"But on one condition. Hear me well, you Angles. That the Pretani woman is publicly acclaimed as Queen."

At last she had a real champion! And she wanted to scream at him not to be a fool. She could have made it on her own. Now she would be branded as his spy and her life would be in even more danger. She clenched her fists as he came and stood solid and sinister behind her chair.

"Show the Angles to their quarters. You and I, Picti, we'll talk for a while. Your company pleases me."

She had not eaten much but she felt sickness rise in her throat. She could not go on flattering him and evading his embraces. She had to find some excuse to win her way out and follow the Angles. Exhaustion dragged at her eyelids and limbs. Her paints were beginning to run with the sweat from her body, rivulets of ruby, carnelian, cobalt and emerald merging to mud-brown in the folds of her body.

The nobles, filing through the doorway, saw her raise her head on her vivid gleaming neck. And cursed the day they had brought her with them, to sell them out and wallow in the stinking bed of that lustful tom-cat.

"The Angles will carry out your orders," Tansen assured Cadwallon.

Swiftly she rose.

"But that last one will stick in their gullets. They're looking for another Queen with a better alliance tucked under her girdle."

The hot smell of him filled her nostrils and throat as he spread his legs, cutting off her escape.

"I'll flay them alive, one by one, if they spurn you!" His throaty whisper feathered her ear. The bulge of his stomach pressed her against the table.

Her mind shrieked scurrilous epithets at him.

"Already they've decided I'm a traitor and a spy," she hissed.

Her back was arched backwards until she feared it would snap.

"If I stay here with you tonight I'll be an adulteress as well."

His organ hardened and reared between them.

"And what two kindred spirits ever minded about that? We're birds of a feather, us two."

"But it's enough of an excuse for them to dispose of me altogether."

Cadwallon's eyes narrowed. He had drunk just enough to titillate his senses, not enough to dull them.

"That wouldn't suit our little arrangement, would it?" she said, giving him a teasing smile.

My, she was a luscious piece. Those huge green eyes were spiced with sensuality. And crafty with it.

"Then you'd never have a taste of what I have to offer."

Aye, she might grace his table as well as his bed some day if he could get rid of the boy wonder and the fat drab that gave him none but unappetising daughters.

"And we would never share our dream, you and I."

Maybe she was worth waiting for, this one. His hands kneaded her inviting breasts. Then he might have more than Arthur ever had. A Queen that shared his dream, that rode to battle with him, her hair streaming like a pennant. He allowed his mind to savour the image for a second. His eyes glazed. He ground his groin against her hips with a convulsive movement before he tore himself away

"Aye, then, give me time, my bonny Picti." His ponderous weight eased from her body. "Give me the winter to train more men and sharpen more spears. Then I'll come striding over the Pennines to bed you."

She ran from him, laughing, and whirled at the door to make him a grand curtsey as she had seen the thane's wives do. Outside she scurried round a wall and paused while dry sobs tore at her throat. Fiercely she scrubbed her hands over her arms, her breasts, her thighs and stood, letting the biting cold in the air cleanse his smells from her body. She heard the crackle of frost under the feet of the guards. And looked up to where the stars hung. And her spirit sailed upwards and exulted for she knew she had reached for a star and won.

Cadwallon's steward came from the small-hall where he had left the Angles. And she ran, shivering for she had left her cloak behind, and knew that she had to gather her strength and her wits for another gruelling test.

Raised voices met her and stopped as if sliced by a knife as she appeared. The menace in the air raised the tiny hairs on her skin. Swiftly, Wulf stepped between her and the semi-circle of grim nobles and wound his cloak round her bare shoulders.

"What in a month of moons were you whispering about with that disgusting brute?" demanded Ean.

"How to put a bell on his wildcat," she said loudly pulling out the nearest tapestry and scanning the wall behind it.

"What sweet little arrangement did you come to with that scurvy lecher?"

Her head had disappeared behind another wall-hanging.

"That bells only suit jesters." She pushed at a knot-hole with her finger but found it solid. "Or Angles with crossed eyes who can't see an inch in front of their noses."

"I warn you!" hissed Beofric.

She came out from behind another tapestry to find his sword at her breast.

"And creep up behind honest folk when they should be searching for spy-holes!" she yelled, angrily.

Beofric's eyes flickered.

"We'll not take back Cadwallon's spy in our midst."

"Don't be such fools!" she hissed. "If I hadn't flattered him, you'd have gone back with your King's head in a sack at your stirrup!"

The nobles had fallen back but their hands still hung loose beside their hilts.

"What is it with you Angles? Is that all you're good at - boasting in your ale-cups and kneeling when your empty words come back to choke you?"

"And winkling spies out of corners like snails out of shells," Beofric barked.

"Think, man! Cadwallon was game to squash you between finger and thumb. What good did your puffed-up pride and dangling swords do at his banquet? I used the only weapons we had."

She let the last wall-hanging swing back into place. Either Cadwallon was a fool or he had a spy-hole somewhere else. She lowered her voice to an urgent whisper.

"Of course he asked me to spy for him. But it's too late to revive the legend of Arthur," she told them. "Danes, Angles, Saesons, you've been settled in this land for generations. I don't like it. But I'm all for peace between us, not war."

She threw down Wulf's cloak in a corner. She looked in vain for washing water and decided against it.

"I want to be Eanfrith's Queen. I deserve it. I gave you good value tonight whether you've the wit to realise it or not." She rolled up her over-mantle into a pillow. "And I warn you, I sleep lightly!"

With Ean and Wulf on either side of her and her back against the wall, she would be safe for the time being.

Slowly her eyes wandered round the group. Someone was missing. Dale. Dale, the Briton! She went over his history in her mind. He and his father must have sought allies to win back their kingdom. Now she thought she knew the answer to a number of questions. Who was his paymaster? Why he had appeared out of the blue at the Pretani Court a few nights before the Bernicians. Why he had volunteered to come south. He was spying for Cadwallon in the hope of gaining an army to regain his kingdom. Yet why the lash-scars and the livid weal of the slave-ring?

She let her hair sweep cool and slow across her face. And what new plot was Cadwallon pouring into Dale's ears now in the dead of the night?

CHAPTER THIRTY ONE

At dawn, the Angles, eager to be gone, threaded their way through ramparts where no gate was directly in front of the other. Fine and handy if an attack was expected from outside. But not if there was every chance of an ambush from behind.

And there he stood, astride an earthbank, Cadwallon, black and menacing against the slatey dawn, flourishing his great sword.

"Remember, Cadwallon is coming, Cousin Picti!"

His bellow thundered down the passageways echoing off the ramparts. And his sword stilled on Ean's figure, pointing, leached, leaden and full of purpose.

Tansen's cry of horror was drowned in the clatter of hooves. She lost her unfamiliar stirrups and let her terror-stricken mount take her flying out beyond the last gate. Out in the freedom of the open countryside she mastered her own fears and that of her mount and came round in a wide circle, laughing, to face the grim eyes of the Angles.

"Don't heed him! I'm no cousin to that bairn-slayer! If the need is there the Royal Pretani can claim kinship to every jumped-up Lord in Britain. It comes from being fathered by foreign Kings." She swung out her arm towards Ean. "Come, Ean, my lad, we're free of him, that great lump of lard with the pelt of a bear on him!" As Ean spurred his horse and joined her she twisted in her saddle and cried to the Angles. "And we never did find out the fancy name he's given that grand sword of his."

The rumble of relieved laughter started in Theobold's throat and followed her as she set her mount steaming across the plain with Ean in hot pursuit. Slowly and reluctantly the Angles were coming to the conclusion their lives had been saved by a slip of a girl with a painted skin. Yet she was a wily one, worth watching.

When the troop closed up behind her, Tansen realised that Dale was not with them. So be it. He had used her to reach Cadwallon. Then let him kiss the sword of the bairn-slayer and swear by his mother's bright head. She had no need of him. She was her own bodyguard.

They took a different route back to bring them through Jorvik, annexed by Eanfrith's father, Aethelfrith. Now it was the seat of the Holy Roman Church in North Humber Land and they called it York. Its position on the river had made it prosperous and, despite a few half-hearted attacks by Cadwallon, there were wealthy landowners and traders here who must kneel to the new King. And bring gifts.

Now even Beofric and Theobold threw off their gloom. Ean and the nobles waved at long-legged lasses in the bleaching-fields, and Tansen's smile brought nods from sweating smiths leaning on hammers and whistles from lads mending fences.

Tansen told herself there was nothing more to fear. She had the support of two Kings now. She had earned the trust of the Angles. She was going back to make a home for Ean and any bairns that might come. And the name of the Citadel at Yeavering Bell was a song that pealed joyfully in her heart.

Cadwallon had made sure there was little meat for the winter-kill. And the Blodmonath was almost past. But word had gone before about the peace treaty and each village brought its first meagre sacrifice so that the King, the saviour of his people, could crumble salt over it.

Churls came to kneel before him. Would the god-given King himself place the bannock under the plough before they cut the first winter furrow? And Ean would dismount and speak the spell, proudly and boldly.

"Erce, Erce, Mother of Earth
May Freya grant thee,
Fields growing and springing
Fruitful and strength-giving.

"And remember that I gave you peace to sow and reap instead of calling you to cut furrows through the enemy and reap a harvest of heads."

"Let Thor's axe rest!" the people would cry.

Once, Tansen felt a claw-like grasp on her foot. Three wrinkled grandmothers stood there. One of them, her eyes whitened with age, spoke.

"Remember the Clan Mothers, Picti, when they make you Queen."

"I will! I'm a pagan like you!" was all she had time to cry before they were riding again.

The old women had given her a sense of belonging. Though the Angles might rule, the folk that mattered were those who worked the land. They were all kin, those who tended the Mother. And this was one promise she would fulfill. Once she was Queen.

It was a glorious thing to be riding carefree at Ean's side, although the early days of lovely lingering love-making were gone. Even home at Yeavering Bell their passion would be tempered by the need to think grandly in terms of war and peace, craft and guile, and the demands of a kingdom.

Yet those first few nights when the early twilight came upon them and they stopped for the night Ean did not seek to be alone with her but spent his time round the fires on the village greens, drinking and boasting and gaming. His talk was all of pride and glory and treasure, of tales of war and warriors and how he would return one day to shatter Cadwallon's power. The young men would light more torches. And there would be boxing and wrestling, cudgeling and fencing, duels and sparring, and sometimes brawls and scuffles and scrapping.

But one night, surprisingly, he leaned his head back and looked at her and caressed with his finger the line of her cheek and the fall of her hair, gilded by the fire.

When he took her hand she sprang up readily drawing a shawl round her shoulders against the cold damp air. He led her outside the circle, The fire behind them glowed on pale startled faces of herd-boys with slings and horns at their belts, tempted from the hills for a glimpse of the King. They raised a ragged embarrassed cheer and ran.

"They cheer me now. But some day they'll tell one another that a new King should have met Cadwallon head on in battle." Ean's teeth dug into his bottom lip. "My first act as King! And the gods decreed I should grovel before a lecherous brute of a man!"

A torch tilted in its iron basket and flared on the wattle walls of the houses, blank like shuttered faces. And the silence became a breathing thing of soft whimpers, sudden snorts and the low throbbing moans of a woman drowning in love.

"The women will remember that you gave them one more season with their men."

Then they were in the moonless darkness beyond the torch, slipping a little on wet grass and dying leaves, following the snicker and stamp of the tethered horses until they found a refuge, private and dark, among the warm flanks. And Ean leaned his forehead on the sleek arched neck of his stallion.

"None of my training at Garnard's Court prepared me for Kingship. We were playing ourselves. Now I've a fight on my hands just to survive."

Life on the land was a good training in survival. But Tansen did not say it. Instead she parted his damp curling hair to kiss the soft vulnerable nape of his neck.

"From now on I'll accept every challenge, use every defeat. Until I become a great warrior at the peak of my power."

"Why not be known as the King who abolished wars?"

The stallion tossed his head, and his warm breath reached out to them.

"You don't understand!" Ean spoke quietly, absently smoothing the tumbled mane. "Unless I die with honour I won't feast in the Great Mead-Hall in Valhalla."

At that she was filled with fury that already he was caught up in the savage spiral that drove the Angles to slash and cleave and thrust and stab their way towards more land and more power and more treasure. For some dream of rollicking for ever in the Otherworld.

"Don't, Ean!" she cried. "Don't force yourself into that sort of slavery. Just to junket with a crucified god and his glass-eyed cronies."

"What else is there to do!"

"There's no meaning to life if that's at the end of it! My people haven't a god of war! They don't aim for a drinking hall like Valhalla." It sounded smug although she had not meant it that way.

"Perhaps that's why you found it so hard to spur them into action!" he snapped. "And what else remains in the bard-songs but a hero's honour?"

She laid her head on his breast and held him close, filled with a queer kind of pity. And from some deep well within her the fateful words came.

"You'll be honoured as a King, whether you've earned it or not."

"What madness is this you're talking? Honour has to be won. More so for a King. He has to surpass every man in his retinue for skill and daring."

Her breath caught in her throat for there was a sort of despair underlying in his curt words.

"I make a vow, here and now, that I will not let sword nor spear nor sinew nor muscle rest until my fame as a warrior is praised the length and breadth of the land. Whether I carry your approval or not!"

She turned her face away, refusing to be drawn into his inner conflict. Yet a queer compulsion was burgeoning inside her to forget herself and her ideas, to live only for him and to give him happiness. For in a few days when they reached Yeavering Bell they might never be close in this way again. And some day soon Cadwallon might come striding over the Pennines, his wax-white sword raised against Ean.

So she brushed her eyes with her hand and began to talk of Yeavering Bell.

"What kind of house shall we live in?" she asked him.

"What do we need a house for? I need to travel around my kingdom."

Patiently she explained.

"We'll need a place to come home to."

"A room off the Mead Hall will do us fine."

Tansen sighed, thinking of Halls with built-in benches where drunken soldiers slept. Of trestles littered with pots and pitchers. Of damp cloaks huddled in a corner. For a moment her mind dwelt on a High Table spread with a delightful variety of coloured glass jars, silver beakers and polished horns.

And she thought how a house meant something more to a woman than a man. If she did not have a hearth she felt she was nothing. A home was a haven. And it could be the same for a man, if it was filled with homeliness and a love that they could gather round them during the night.

She had better forget her dreams. Ean was not ready for a home. And he was not ready to father a bairn. Let there be just the two of them for a little while longer. She would ease some of the pressure off him, but in her own way, bringing them both release and fulfilment. She would change the tenor and tempo of their love-making.

"Will you give me some of these gold coins you throw away so freely?"

"Why?"

"You'll see."

At the next village she bought sweet oils from a Wise Woman. That night she made him lie down while she caressed every part of him with her oiled fingers. With her lips and her tongue, she worshipped his body, feeling her love flow towards him like a balm, finding a strange sense of fulfilment in giving him love with no thought of return.

"While you're with me you won't think grim thoughts," she whispered.

So she warmed him with love-words, pouring out her caring in images of colour and sound. She teased his body until his member stood out swollen and distended. She cupped her hands round it as though it was the stamen of a flowering plant and sucked like a bee, tasting his nectar till his honey spilled over and he was at rest.

"My mother, my Queen, my lover and my Goddess," he would murmur then, half-asleep. "With you beside me I can conquer the world."

She lived in a strange contentment, fulfilling herself entirely by giving. It was a queer way to love, she thought. Not natural to a Pretani woman who expected as much from her man as she gave. Yet sweet, like fine mead with an after-taste that lingered.

They reached York early in the day and settled into quarters that overflowed with hot water and slaves with warm towels. And feather beds and laundresses and barbers brandishing blades as though they would cut throats as cheerfully as they would trim beards and cut toe-nails.

Almost at once a deacon arrived sent by Bishop James to invite the King to the Church of the Apostle Peter.

"Don't go," advised Theobold. "He's a chum of Paulinus. He'll only show you the mummified head of Edwin tucked in a box."

"And he'll conduct his pupils in Gregorian plain-song till your jaw hits your knees," put in Beofric.

The ealdormen of Jorvik had prepared a royal feast of swan pie to be eaten in the sportsground beside the river Ouse with the prows of the fishing boats rearing on the bank and the mast-lights of the traders bobbing and twinkling. Afterwards the field was invaded by glint-haired giants, lighting huge bonfires, drinking and sporting, sporting in earnest, with muscles and sinews. And with knives.

And Ean, stripped to the waist, his skin blotched by the chill wind, seeking a challenge, seeking to prove that he was ready to conquer the world. He wound a cloak round his arm and caught up a knife. Wulf leapt to face him. Knees bent, grinning, they circled, feinting, stabbing, slashing.

The field was alive with straining bodies, whirling arms, tossing hair. Feet scudded and slid in the squeaky-wet grass. Eager bodies gleamed and gambolled. And, like a voice crying out in warning, the trees whined in a sudden wind.

Ean had Wulf's arms in a grip like a vice and they stood, eye to eye, foot to foot. Wulf's arms bulged, straining to break Ean's grip.

With a whoosh the wind changed direction, curling the flames of the fire in a sweeping curve so that the watchers had to run with streaming eyes to the smoke-free side.

Beyond the waiting shadows, lit by the cold eye of the moon, Tansen glimpsed a lone figure, hooded, swathed in a long black cloak, watching, one shoulder hunched as though to hide his face. Curious and apprehensive she scrubbed at her smarting eyes. But the figure was gone when she looked again.

CHAPTER THIRTY TWO

Above the yelling and grunting Tansen's ear caught and held Ean's roar of defiance. Fire painted his naked body with streaming gold. Then Ean's heels dug in the ground and he pushed, an almighty shove, that sent Wulf flying backwards, thudding on the earth.

And Ean stood crowing, skirling like a fighting cock, arms high in triumph, looking for another opponent.

And there was one, a smallish youth, and slender. Part of the rag-bag of the mercenary army by the look of his supporters, shaking his head at the knife, holding up his fists. But sharp of eye and swift of foot, as he danced round Ean, searching for him to drop his guard for a second, and then his fists thumped and buffeted Ean on thighs, body and shoulders. His canvas shoes held the grass better than Ean's leather boots as he swayed and side-stepped. And it was obvious to Tansen that every swing from Ean was being parried and used against him. Little urchin-tricks like clipping heels or gouging eyes were confusing Ean.

The youth gave his King no quarter. One vicious blow took Ean on the chin, jerking his head to the side. Ean staggered back, shook his head to clear it and launched himself, arms flailing, to meet another blow that almost felled him.

Then with an uprush of pleasure Tansen saw that Ean was learning to watch, trying to guess where the next move was coming from. And side-stepping out of range. And back-heeling, feinting, pursuing and trying the odd underhand trick himself. His breath began to labour, his feet to stumble and one eye was decidedly swollen. And Ean hooked a finger in the fellow's belt, thudded into his ribs with his elbow and as the fellow's feet left him, flung him to the ground. And then he was helping the fellow up and they clung together and called for ale. And when they had drunk it they blundered into the shadows to relieve themselves.

And there he stood again, a hunched silhouette against the dark, dark sky, the lines of his cloak gilded with fire. And where his face should have been, a darkness. There was a swirl of a cloak, or a puff of smoke, and he was gone..

Skeletons of trees forked brittle fingers across the face of the moon. Then a scudding cloud cut off the moonlight and the scene changed from blue-silver to red-gold. And the beauty of the fire was in its light and warmth and colour and the curl of the flames as they curtseyed and bowed and danced to the wind.

Ean was trying his strength with another on the far side of the fire. A shadowy man, black-bearded, and a peculiar slant to his lean spare body. Stabbing, slashing, gripping and breaking away to stab and slash again, low and high so that both men were leaping and crouching and swaying and breathing hard. And Ean, being too impetuous, exhilerated by his last victory.

The wind roared through the bonfires. One collapsed with a thunderous whoosh. And another, nearer the river, and another. And the sparks caught in the frenzied branches of the saplings at the river showering over the fishing fleet. Little spritely flames danced from boat to boat. Over a net here, a spar there. And everyone ran to help push the boats out and dowse the flames.

All except Ean and his dark opponent. Their arms locked high above their heads and Ean grasping the knife-hand of the stranger. But he could not break the lock and his body was arcing back like the bow of a hunter till it must surely crack. And Tansen was running, elbowing through the crowd, letting out little moans of horror, her eyes fixed on the struggle. And it seemed she would never reach them they were so far away from the circle of light and their bodies ebbed and flowed and their limbs flailed and sank like logs caught in the tide.

The stranger placed his foot at the back of Ean's heel and clipped it. As Ean lost his grip and collapsed the knife flashed downwards. A scream tore from Tansen's throat. For a blinding second the man with the black face looked towards her. Then once, twice the knife rose and slashed and then flew, dripping into the trees. And a tornado rushed past her. It was Wulf, his mouth opening like a bleeding gash in his face. And Ean's retinue, dripping, storming from the river, roaring orders.

Ean lay staring up at her, asking questions she could not answer. And she held out her hands to help him rise. But his arms lay limp and curiously shortened.

"Oh, Bride, no! no! no!"

She threw herself down beside him, calling to him, raising his head, his shoulders, embracing the warm flesh, tugging at the ribbons she had tied at the neck of his tunic that afternoon.

"You planned this! You and that Cymry butcher between you!"

She looked up into the face of Theobold, distorted with rage. And saw the muscles bulge at his shoulders as his sword began to descend. She threw herself sideways, rolling among the feet of the retinue. Someone, his eyes wild and desperate, came down hard on top of her. And she clutched at the undergrowth as her world turned over and over.

She came to herself standing calmly looking down at Ean. Someone had closed his eyes. And the shadow of a tree, like the antlers of the Whetstone stag branched across his naked breast. And in her hand, someone had thrust the knife, ruby-red, and on the handle, the shape of a dolphin.

"So this is what you were plotting with that murderer, Cadwallon." A fierce grip lofted her hand high so that all could see the dagger. Torches sprang to life.

"You're wrong! I loved Ean! This was Dale, the Briton! This is his sign, the dolphin."

"Aye, Dale, the man you hid in the retinue of your husband. And took to Lleyn to receive his orders."

"The Prince of Clyde?" It was a new voice, one of the sherriffs from Jorvik. "That one was fostered in Lleyn. Joined his father, Maddern, as a mercenary under Cadwallon. Last I heard he was leading a contingent of wild Irish mercenaries. That's your cuckoo in the nest all right!"

"And here's his accomplice. Fools that we were to heed her! I say cut out that treacherous tongue of hers now."

"No, burn her along with the man she betrayed!"

"Aye, burn her!"

And the journey back behind Ean's bier, riding slack-limbed through the heather, her hands shackled. And venom in the eyes of the guards. And a thatch lit by a single lamp and sobs and groans tumbling from inside her. And her whole being filling with a slow consuming hatred. For Dale, murderer and spy, for Wulf and that impotent retinue, for the merciless Anglian nobles. Even for Verna who had tugged off the gold ring with the spell on it Ean had given her and dipped it three times in a bowl. And held the steaming potion against her mouth. Hatred at herself because she drank. And slept.

Then her eyes opening on a roof-tree of lime-washed timber flooded by the long low winter sun. And a foul smell invading her nostrils, the stench of a cess-pit, or a prison cell where the straw was never renewed. And she guessed she was imprisoned in Yeavering Bell, the name that had rung so sweetly once and now tolled like a funeral dirge through her mind.

Then a guard leaning in the doorway, taunting her till she could bear it no longer. And threw the worm-eaten bread at him. And the plate and the cup. All that was left was a ricketty table so she threw that too for good measure. But it broke and a splinter gashed her hand. So she went after it, kicking aside the fallen pieces, beating at the guard's leering face until he retreated, laughing and clanged the door shut.

And she lay down on the rank straw and wept.

CHAPTER THIRTY THREE

The sun had not yet sunk over the crown of the moor when a long line of torches began weaving to the crest of the escarpment. It had been an unusually cold day and the evening showed promise of a hard frost.

Ean's body was to be burned in a ship. It sounded very grand. Ean would have liked that, Tansen thought. And she was to be burned with him, branded with the guilt of his murder. The guards thrust her past the line of staring folk.

"Waste of a lusty wench, lads!" cried one. "Keep her for yourselves!"

The guards growled and hacked their way upwards through the throng.

Towering over the men who sweated at the ropes was the Royal Vessel that had brought Ean and herself from the Forth, her great ring-prow outlined against an amethyst sky. Beautiful and graceful she glided forward on rollers as if breasting the waves. Once more she surged forward and stilled as though poised on the crest of a wave.

"The broad-bosomed ship, ringed with ice, weary from the sea, clothed with the brightness of the sky that shines from the south," sang the poets. The rollers creaked and groaned as they were withdrawn one by one. The sun was sinking beneath an island of cloud. The ship floated in mid-air, sparkling with diamond ice-crystals, held by silvered ropes.

"The ring-prowed ship measured the sea-paths, plied the ocean streams, threw aside the sea, brave to the wind." Slowly and with supreme majesty, the ship began to sink into her grave.

Amidships was the wooden cabin where Ean and she had sheltered, and from where she had been thrust out into the storm. Its roof had been newly lined with gold leaf. Now Ean lay there alone, his face hidden in the comical prim-mouthed helmet. Was he afraid, waiting for the fire to melt the silver cord that chained him to his body? Was he remembering the joy she had been guided to give him in their last few days together? Was he waiting for her to come to him in white-hot ecstacy?

The men of the Witan came, weighed down by Royal Emblems. The ill-omened Standard with the antlered deer, puny and powerless now, its duty done. Until they stuck it in the earth of the mound. And the last rays of the sun sent out a separate star of light from each antler to enter Tansen's heart like a dagger.

Leading the procession round the lip of the grave walked the King's three horses in plates of gold with plumes of peacock feathers dyed deep mulberry.

"Heroward, the war-horse," intoned the minstrels. "Herowulf, the hunting stallion, Herogard, the riding mare."

Heroward who had carried Ean to that ill-fated meeting in Gwynedd. Wulf sat astride him, hollow-eyed.

By now the whole high ridge of the escarpment flowed with moving lights like a river circling the lonely island where Ean lay.

The ealdormen laid the ceremonial war-corselet of silvered gold, his shining belt, his great sword in its scabbard beside his spear-hand. These she could look at calmly and dispassionately. At his other hand, they laid his personal things. And each one held a memory. First his cape, the one with the fancy shoulder clasps he had thrown over her beside the river. His supping spoons with the Christian symbols on them. And the auroch horn he had shown her so proudly as he set off to be acclaimed. There was his lyre that he used to play in the Garden of the Wise One. It was funny how they looked the same, his things. It didn't seem right that they should still exist when he was gone. Yet after the fire they wouldn't exist either. And neither would she. And there was Wulf again laying down the purse with the gold coins to pay the steersman and forty oarsmen who would row him to Valhalla.

The thanes lifted well-fed arms in bright padded sleeves, displaying their funeral gifts to people whose threadbare tunics lay flat on empty stomachs. Thanes held up flashing rings, enamelled brooches, buckles and clasps to show to folk with calloused hands and chilblained feet. Thanes with maplewood bottles filigreed in silver, laying them in the bow or the stern, proclaiming how they had loved and honoured Eanfrith, the King. But not how they had despised his youth and weakness and used him as the whipping boy for Cadwallon to vent his spleen on.

Silver bowls and hanging cauldrons engraved with Christian crosses. Getting rid of the evidence of their conversions until they could test the temper of the next King. And no Paulinus to accuse them. For while they were at Lleyn the Bishop had taken ship for Kent with Edwin's Queen and Edwin's Cross and all the Church gold and silver.

And Tansen asked Bride would she be happier decked in jewels than in fruit and flowers? Would the Moon Maiden rather be hung with pearls than with stars? And, more urgently, were the Loved Ones there, waiting for the spirit of one, Tansen, who had hoped to be Queen?

Even the poorest were giving something. Walnut cups full of mead, bone combs, a pair of leather shoes newly-made. A man, his feet tied in sacking carried a battered bowl filled with a gruel that his children could have used. And she signed to the guards but they would not allow her to follow him. So she kept hidden in her cloak the small articles that Verna had smuggled into her prison. The flint to spark the Fire of the Radiant Ones in the little lamp filled with beeswax. And the Water of the Life-Giving Ones in a tiny clay pot.

The King's Archer hauled a silver-tipped bow from its place on his back. And dropped it on the deck of the ship.

"No more will the hunter draw his bow. No more will his arrow fly to the mark." He drew crimson-feathered arrows from his quiver and broke them. And threw them after the bow.

And there lying gleaming against the bare planks was the crescent of the bow and across it the sign of the broken arrow. The sign that the Pretani clans were united? Or a sign that Grannie Bea was calling for her to escape and fulfil her task? What unseen hand had guided the fall of the woods? It had not been chance that had formed them into a sign that held meaning for her. That etched her mind with hope.

Until a careless foot stepped on the arrow, crushing it and kicking the pieces aside. And she did not care what the signs meant any more. And was filled with such terror that she tore between her guards and down the earthbank to where a tree leaned, scarred and aloof with the dignity of age.

They caught her and twisted her arm up her back.

"Your turn next, traitor!".

Her body arcing with pain, she was forced to watch the twelve warriors cover the cabin with bracken, fill the ship with sand and finish the mound with turf.

"We have built a barrow, high and broad,

Look from afar all you sea-farers and travellers."

Another twelve warriors built a beacon on top of the mound and set a torch to it.

"We have lit a beacon for that brave young man, Prince of Treasures.

"Twelve sons of heroes, we ride round it, sorrowing, mourning our King, chanting an elegy,

Our hearts grieving, our minds mourning for the promise that was in him."

That was the line that twisted Tansen's heart and brought tears flooding from her eyes.

"The heart lies low that was ready to be a comfort to his people, a warrior among heroes, a ring-giver.

"Where shall we find solace for our woes."

All they wanted was a ring-giver. But her true love lay dead. A lifetime of exile stretched in front of her, bleak and barren, without him. She had no kin, no home, no gladness without him. She could bear the waiting no longer. The heat from the flames seared her cheeks. Now she must die. But she would do it in her own way, with dignity, a Queen going to join her King in the Otherworld. She brought her knee into the groin of the man holding her and ran towards the beacon, holding out her arms to welcome the moment of searing ecstacy that would take her to meet Ean.

When through the flames leapt a golden figure, gilded in metal from head to toe. It was Ean's spirit, coming to fetch her. She ran faster. The song of the iron rings of his corselet chimed in her ears. She held out her arms as she ran. And against the yellow radiance of the flames, she saw the face of Ean. Yet as she neared him it was not Ean but a man with a shoulder twisted by some battle-wound and soot mingling with the sweat running from his beard. An icy finger touched the nape of her neck.

With a scrape that curdled her blood, he drew his sword, and the sweep of his arm threw her unnoticed to the ground. And she saw him flourish his sword against the fire-bright sky.

"I come amongst you, girded by fire and glory, Ecfrith, first son of Aethelfrith. Ecfrith, your rightful King!"

It was monstrous! It was unreal! And she knew then without doubt that the murderer had not been Dale. Nor Cadwallon. It had been this man, this jealous man who had killed his younger brother, to set himself in Eanfrith's place.

Brightened by fire, the faces of the people, turned towards him. The name of Aethelfrith rang in the air, above the crackling of the timber.

He would be acclaimed as their saviour! She must not let it happen! She sprang up, looking round in disbelief.

"Ecfrith, Ecfrith, Ecfrith!" It began as a whisper and grew to become an acclamation. Their hopes for Eanfrith had been shattered. They had set his spirit free. Now, out of the sacred fire had stepped his brother.

"It's a miracle."

"The gods have sent him."

In the smokey air the stony faces of the Witan wavered and then cracked asunder. Churls began to cheer. A thane pulled the King's Standard from its mound and ran through the smoke to present it. With a forceful sweep of his arm, Ecfrith sent it crashing down the hillside. He held his sword high before his face.

"The sword, Halogal, shall be my standard. Halogal who cuts through the shield-wall, hacks the limestone wood. He will demand tribute and will flourish in honours. And I, Ecfrith, will surpass all other Kings in valour. I will become Breatwalda, King of all Britain. I will give rings to my chosen warriors in the Hall. Only then will I be throne-worthy and my under-kings will row me to my Acclamation!"

The crowd gasped and cheered and the guards roared their approval, suddenly eager to be led by a man with style who knew what he was about.

Tansen began to scream.

"He's the murderer! He's the one who killed your King!"

Ecfrith heard the voice and his gaze homed in on her joyfully.

"There's the Picti, lads!" he cried. "Take her! She'll serve the Hall Goblet tonight! Spoils of war, Picti! Eh!"

Small dark men surrounded her, his mercenaries, the hated Scots, from Dal Riata. Their hands lifted her and bore her aloft down the hill-side into the Citadel. Her guards led the way cheering, back to her foul stinking cell.

She faced what lay in front of her now. For Ecfrith would surely despoil his brother's Queen. Ecfrith dare not let her escape in case she carried Ean's seed. For his brother's seed coupled with her Royal Blood might take his head and his throne from him some day. So he would spawn his own filth inside her first.

'Spoils of war, Picti!' he had cried. How could he have known who she was if he had not recognised her at Jorvik?

There was a squeak, a creak of a timber. Her eyes flew round the cell. Rats or assassins? Up near the roof was a glint in a hole. It blinked.

She stared back, leaning against the slimy wall, wondering if it was Ecfrith, gloating.

Perhaps he would kill her instead. For he knew she had seen him kill Ean. To kill to reach a Kingship was common. But the murder of a blood-brother, was a foul deed most Kings wanted to hide. No matter how folk cheered him now, his reign would be ill-omened unless he killed her to break the curse that was upon him.

And she thought of the vows she had made. To rouse Garnard against the Angles, to make a praise-song of Maga's death, to lead the Clan Mothers, to win the Queenship from Reatta. And how she had thrown it all away to love a lad.

She had thought she was so clever, tricking the Embassy, persuading the nobles, cajoling Cadwallon. She had thought she was beloved of the gods and chosen to do their bidding.

The hole above her head was dark and lifeless now. There were other eyes in the darkness, kinfolk accusing her. And hard black eyes, filled with triumph. And she pressed her hands to her head and fell, rolling over and over in the reeking straw, weeping.

And then a tingle passed over her hair, like a hand. As though the love she had given to her kin and to Ean had not been wasted and was being given back in abundance. Calm now, she sat up and took the water and fire from her cloak. She struck the flint until the wick in the beeswax lamp caught alight. She poured the water into a hollow in the floor where a drip had eroded the stone. The reflection of the flame burned steadily on the surface of the black puddle. And she sank her mind deep down into darkness and gave herself into the keeping of the Wise Ones.

Then came the familiar nudge at the base of her skull and she opened her mind to the Beings who were there.

And the knowing came, that the Ones had not forgotten her. That this was a test. All life was a test. And she would survive and learn from it. What she would learn she would not know until long after. For it was not time for her to go through the tunnel and reach out to the light and love that waited beyond. Instead she must go forward. And she would need to be strong. For they said that when you gave yourself fully into the hands of the Wise Ones, that was when the real testing time began.

A sort of peace fell on her. She faced the guards calmly when they came. She ignored the sneers of the drunken Angles who pulled at her filthy robe and knotted hair. And the jeers of the Scot who thrust the Hall Goblet into her hands so that the mead slopped on her feet.

She went humbly past the servant lasses, just scrag ends of waifs sold into slavery by starving families, giggling and flaring their skirts. And the men were having them, under tables, on tables, against tables, it was all the same. And she cried in her heart to Bride. Not for release from the degradation she was about to undergo. Because the kitchen wenches had little hope of release either and she was no more worthy than they were. But for courage.

Ecfrith sat at the far end of the Hall with a lazy leg hooked over the arm of the High Chair.

"Aha! My little brother's Picti!"

He upended the Goblet into his mouth and threw it from him. And while two men held her, his hands roved hot and questing over her body and her face was rasped raw by the coarse hairs of his mottled beard.

And she willed herself to be calm, that it would ease the pain, that it would soon be over. But she couldn't breathe for the acrid smell of him. And when he flung up her skirts like a blanket over her head she felt suffocated. And pulled them from her face. And that was worse. For now she could see. He was like a beast mauling her with red savage eyes. And she was shamed and sickened and her body struggled against her will. But she would not let the horror of it seep into her mind. Be calm, she told herself. Think of sand

and the plash of waves, of the sunset flaring gold on the water, of the wild sea and sky in the storm.

It would soon be over! Soon, soon! Let it be soon! She would not let the foulness of it pollute her spirit. She could cleanse her body. She could wipe the stench of him from her skin. She could cleanse the contamination from within her body. But she would not let it enter her spirit to become a canker that would destroy her! She would not! Oh, Bride, when would it end?

His men cheered him to the echo as he yelled his final spasm. She lay inert till he gripped her clothing and shook her upright and dragged her face close to his. Hairs sprouted glistening from his nostrils. The pink pouting lips of a recent scar blossomed along his jaw. His eyes, storm-blue islands in white red-veined seas lanced into hers.

"And we still have our little secret, eh, Picti? Shall I kill you now or save you for tomorrow?"

Sickness rose in her throat and she fought it down, every nerve strung tight and screaming with effort. He flung her to the floor.

"Till tomorrow, Picti!"

And he was drinking again, toasting her as the guards, skirling, swung her aloft and threw her back in her cell.

Diamond-sharp stars wheeled across the darkness of her mind. Under the din from the Hall her ears caught the creak of the door. A beaked nose, two sharp eyes, glinting from under a hood. An old crone showing her toothless gums and gathering up the putrid straw in claw-like hands. And rubbing it all over Tansen's face and hair till she was almost retching. And then the crone was stuffing the straw into baskets till they overflowed. And slung a basket over Tansen's shoulder. A claw beckoned.

Then they were out into the lamplit night filled with drunken song. And Tansen, hunched and bowed,followed the old woman.

"Hey, you two! What kitchen leavings have you tucked under your cloaks?"

They thrust the baskets under the noses of the two guards.

"Feuch!" One staggered back. A cudgel cracked his skull. The other grasped Tansen, his eyes bulging in recognition. As he opened his mouth to yell, two hands appeared from the darkness behind, clamping over his mouth, twisting his head backwards till his neck broke. And women, flowing round her in a silent stream, carrying her with them as if she was in a tide-race until they were out beyond the gate where the ruts in the ground were hard with frost and the tufts of grass crackled under their feet.

A hump rose out of the heather and stretched out its arms and hugged her.

“Praise the Compassionate Ones we were in time to save you,” came Verna’s whisper.

“And praise the fact that human dung smells worse than a farmyard.”

They left the torches and bonfires glowing behind them and the laughter of the soldiers sounded like nothing more than the cackling and squawking of a field of feeding geese.

They used a raft to ford a river they called Glen. A queer name for a river. And there were stars in the dark of the water for a maiden to tell her fortune by. Too many stars for one who had no dreams left.

The sleeping circle of hills lay dark, a fitting rim for the bowl of the sky. Yet despite all the strange and terrible things that had happened, the night with its stars was still the same, the silent night on the verge of dawn, and the feel of the Mother. Unchanging.

And with the first pale lightening of the sky, the first faint breeze that lifted her hair to life and the first pipe of a blackbird, she felt that old familiar yearning. And the blood warm in her veins. And the first faint flicker of hope. And she knew she was still that same young maid that had counted stars with a lilt in the beat of her heart. Even though there was nothing in front of her except a cold journey back to Pitcarlie. And a black horror of men for ever in her heart.

CHAPTER THIRTY FOUR

While Ecfrith's men scoured the countryside, Tansen and Verna lay in an underground corn-store hidden by dead scrub and a fallen tree-trunk in a darkness full of the ripe rich sleeping smell of the All-Mother.

They hid for days which they did not count, numb with cold, wakening at night to the call of a snipe signalling that it was safe to come out to relieve themselves and take in food.

And each new awakening was another mountain Tansen had to climb carrying her burden of grief.

She began to tell Verna what it had been like, that bright day she had met Ean beside the river Leven. About the young girl she had been then, so foolish, thrilled by gem-strewn Queens and warrior Kings and the glittering pageantry. But how she would do it all again and go with him gladly. For a love that had flashed like lightning in a summer storm. Oh, how sweet it had been!

And those days would come again! For she would awaken tomorrow and Ean would come, with hands all fresh and wholesome, to wrap his cloak around her and lift her on his horse and carry her through the Gateway into the Citadel. Then she was moaning and shaking her fists and calling Verna a fool for saying it was Ean who had lain ship-shape among his treasures.

Later when her sorrow was spent and she was back in her mind again, she told how he had loved her but he had loved the Kingship more. How she had had to close off whole areas of herself because she could not share them with her bonny prince.

When the snow came no one dared to leave food and a trail of footprints. They were forced to eat the roots that thrust through the roof of their hiding-place. And Tansen talked then of how long ago, yet it was not seven cycles of the moon, she had thought she was special, that Grannie Bea and Marten and the Great Ones would always protect her. How she had found that no one could protect her against her own emotions.

She told how the young girl, fresh from a massacre, had been afraid. Afraid of the mission that Grannie Bea had sent her on. Afraid of the judgments of the Council of Elders. Afraid of competing with the hard-centred Reatta. Fooling herself that she had the courage of a Caterin. How she had turned her back on them all. For love of Ean.

Now she would go home, back to the place where she had been born and whatever kin she could find. She would give her labour to feed the bairns of Pitcarlie. She would lock herself into the rhythm of the seasons so that soldiers and statesmen could fight their wars and weave their plots without her. And she would girn and grumble into old age with no one to love her and no one to judge her. Except herself.

She saw herself sitting beside the hearth with bairns clamouring for stories. And she would be able to tell them how heroes were made. They were given a task to perform. And although they knew the perils they were brave and bold. But how some were sent forth like golden arrows and betrayed their people.

When the snow melted food came again but it was either salty or rancid, it was all folk had left. It made Tansen and Verna sick. And mornings, noons and nights were all one, dark and cold in the womb of the All-Mother. And Tansen felt neither terror nor hope. But a grey dead feeling about the awful thing that was to happen.

Once the burbling call of a night-owl invaded their darkness. It was a trick to entice them out. Then a whisper. Wulf's voice.

His nose wrinkled at the sour smell of sickness but he folded Tansen's filthy hands in his own.

"Where have you been?" she asked.

"In hiding." His mouth twisted grimly. "Trying to get near Ecfrith to kill him."

She closed her eyes. In her weakened state she could not summon enough strength even to wish for Ecfrith's death. A hoof stamped outside.

"You must leave here quickly! Ecfrith's on the move again. With more Scots arriving daily to join his army. He's hanging hostages to force folk to tell where you're hidden. Some woman's going to tell what she knows to save her babe from the spear or her man from the rope."

"And go where?" It was an effort for her to think.

"North, of course. Though I reckon Ecfrith won't be far behind. Unless he decides to deal with Cadwallon first."

Tansen rose then, the ingrained soil on her face setting into hard grim lines. Wulf had brought three horses, finely-bred, two stallions and a mare who sniffed the air and arched their necks and went straight into a gallop across the moorland. Straw-coloured grasses flared against the dark brown of the heather. And here and there a tarn, peat-coloured or black with the reflection of a hill. And a lonely tree, making lace with its bare twigs against the sky.

For the first time in many moons she felt her mind lifting and expanding into the distance, to the north where black hills waited in mist. To the east where a long swathe of grey cloud hung over the Danish Sea. To the west where a raincloud came sailing, tinged with orange, heading north-east to cut in front of them, trailing wisps of vapour. And the wind that came in the wake of the cloud whipping her cloak and the free-flowing mane of the horse. And the heavy smell of the earth claiming her senses. And the wide wide sky claiming her spirit. For she had been imprisoned too long in the citadels of men.

They stopped at a farm and ate hungrily. New-baked bread. And ale, for the milk was not yet flowing. And she threw back her hood and told them she was the Picti, fleeing from Ecfrith. So that Ecfrith would hear and no bairns would be left fatherless and no woman left childless because of her. And Wulf, red with rage, almost hit her. And again they fitted their aching muscles into the backs of the horses and went hurtling on.

It was a strange feeling, clinging low on the back of the stallion, urging him with her knees, fleeing from a murderer, listening for the drumming of hoofbeats at her back. Yet her body was coming curiously alive. And it was not fear of Ecfrith that set her blood pumping. It was something to do with the bite of wind on her cheeks and the questing call of peewits. And the pull of her native land.

She was beginning to find her true self again. And the dewy air was helping her to reach down into the essence of her being.

The wind was coming in sharp gusts now, the dark clouds racing low over their heads ever-changing, ever-passing. Like life. The horses braced themselves and planted their feet more firmly on the never-changing immoveable earth.

She whacked her horse's rump and he jumped to obey her.

"Hold on!" Wulf called out. "We're near Two Fords on the River Twide. We'll rest there."

"No," she cried. "I'm not tired."

"No, but you're bloody selfish! You'll kill the horses and Verna too."

"Ecfrith's men won't rest!"

"Ride on by yourself then!"

Contrite, she slowed her pace. Verna who had done nothing to deserve this, was swaying with weariness.

At the travellers' rest the icy water from the pump stung her wind-roughened cheeks.

"Eat quickly and don't attract attention," ordered Wulf.

They huddled at a corner table, eating pigeon pie with their heads down and their damp cloaks steaming. Wulf ate, sunk in his own brooding anger, sometimes pausing to stare at the ground as though a chasm had opened beneath his feet.

"It fair riled me, the waste of good gold that went in that burial ship."

A big straight-backed churl with firm bare arms was holding forth over his ale and tafl. "And all the gomeril ever did in life was to bow his knee to Cadwallon."

Tansen cringed into her seat as the churl twisted about looking for an argument. In a dark corner he spied a brown-habited monk, whose thin face looked tired to the point of exhaustion. "Kings and priests, they're all kittled from the same bottle of leeches, right, Coel?"

He planked an elbow on Coel's table and leered into his face.

"Hey, tell me! What kind of God allows a thane twenty hides of land when a churl has only one hide to feed his family?"

The monk struggled with his weariness.

"Don't blame injustice on God. He sends the blessing of air and rain and sun to both men. Is the air purer, the sun brighter, does more rain fall on the rich man's field? No. Only man is unjust."

The churl's arm swung round the room.

"So your God tells us we've to bow and scrape to priests in purple night-gowns, that eat lark's tongues while our children starve, eh?"

The thin-faced monk sighed.

"Sadly these priests share in the sins of rulers instead of attacking them."

Blood throbbed in Tansen's temples. It seemed to her that the churl had the right of it and the monk sat there calmly, mouthing words without pity or passion.

"Eternal torment if we don't pay our tithe and let them dunk us in the river, eh lads?"

A toothless old man sniggered.

"And kneel in their great buildings where their God lives. And where is he then? Curled asleep in a silver chalice? Or tucked under the golden altar-cloth?"

A blacksmith thumped the board with a hand puckered with burns and pitted with charcoal.

"Shut your coarse mouth! You're talking about Romish priests. Coel's a Columban from Iona. He sets his shoulder to the plough when it's needed. Where are you making for in this weather, Coel?"

Coel's voice was low.

"To the Farne Islands, far away from war and turmoil, where I can build a ditch round my hut and see only God's sky."

"You'll still have to look to your back, man, since the King's peace fell with Edwin." The blacksmith moved a piece on the tafl board. "Go to the Jarrow monastery at the Goat's Head. There you'll be happed in kidskin and fed milk and cheese."

The churl roused himself again to give a drunken bellow.

"You reckon? No monastery's safe from a King." He spoke thickly, but with conviction, stabbing the air with his finger. "Every hide of land a monastery sits on is a loss of tax. Every new monk's a loss of a labourer. Or a foot-soldier." He spat out an oath. "Or maybe Coel just likes being with men and boys, is that it?"

The monk seemed undisturbed by the guffaws of the churl and the old man. He lifted his long slippy whip of hazel and his brown hempen bag.

"This new King may be different. He was baptised by the monks on Iona. He might surprise you yet. God might still make a saint of him."

"Saint?" The word exploded from Tansen's throat. She was up and facing him, her hood falling back. "Your future saint murders and rapes like the rest of his breed! While you prattle and prate and hide in your ditch!"

Coel turned eyes in which the suffering of mankind was laid bare as if sliced with a scalpel.

"War breeds misery and disease and famine and vengeance. It resolves nothing. My way is harder. And takes longer. It is the way of peace, of prayer, of turning the other cheek. But some day people will have suffered enough and will draw back in horror from the chasm that the war-mongers have opened in front of them."

Tansen felt her emotions streaming out of the dark cave that had protected them and it was both agony and relief to scream out the words that tumbled from her mouth.

"You want me to bare my neck to the axe of the invader? To open the legs of my sister to their filth? To offer the body of my child so that they can hack his bones into toothpicks?"

Coel's eyes were strange and terrible.

"No, I expect nothing of you." And he looked through her and beyond her as if across aeons of remorseless time. "Many innocent souls will die before the lesson is learned and people will finally say 'This is not the way'. Then the sacrificed souls will look down from heaven and rejoice."

He turned his pale cheek away from her and unbarred the door.

"And when that time comes, it will not matter which god they call on. So long as the Name of the God is Love."

He slipped out into the night. As Tansen pushed her stool aside to go after him to argue Wulf slammed the swinging door in her face, his fist clamped on the bar so that she could not draw it.

CHAPTER THIRTY FIVE

"Let me out!" cried Tansen.

"I haven't brought you all this way to lose you to the dancing bog-lights or a drunken herder."

The men were chuckling, turning back to their game.

Tansen faced Wulf squarely.

"You brought me?" her lip curled. "I don't need you! What do you care about me? You always hated me!"

"If you're harmed what excuses can I offer Ean when I meet him in the Beyond? Go up to bed, woman! I've paid for a room for the night."

His words infuriated her. She had had two bodyguards. Yet neither had prevented Ean's death or her own rape.

"Oh, go and find someone else who needs a bodyguard and make a better job of it this time!"

Her voice died in her throat. She saw by the hurt in his eyes that she had wounded him deeply. Wulf had loved Ean with his whole heart. He must be weighed down with guilt knowing he had failed Ean in his hour of need.

His answer came low with a dangerous slowness.

"Don't treat me like a serf."

Suddenly it came to her that Wulf would never give such love and loyalty to a man again. He had lost everything when he lost Ean. She at least had her own land to go back to and could maybe turn her hand to making it strong again. She wanted to say something to comfort him. But she dare not. She was a woman, not a milk-brother.

She lifted her gaze to his and met a new look, hot and ardent and tender all at once. It was swiftly masked. Bewildered and with a feeling of revulsion, she went swiftly up the ricketty stairs to what was little more than a loft where Verna with a candle was muttering over the bed-covers.

From the window Tansen looked through the silvered elbows of the oak-tree at the Moon Maiden. She had always assumed that Wulf's hero-worship of Ean had an element of sexuality in it. Yet his eyes had been dark with a sudden desire for her. And the knowledge sickened to her core.

Was she going to grow old and sour, wounding others because of her own hurt? Why could her emotions not sink into oblivion and be at peace. Like the Moon Maiden, sailing serenely in a sea of stars? Why did her mind toss and turn, in a sea of queer questions that had no answer that mattered?

"You shouldn't have flown at poor Coel like that," said Verna.

Poor Coel? Tansen let the silence go on. She had met men like him before. They came from Columba's Isle of Io where they lived in cells and kept bees. They came with their healing stones and supped with folk and told stories about the One they followed. He was a Healing One and a Wise One, they said. He did not ask for special buildings nor gold nor jewels.

Coel had touched some deep chord within her. For a moment she had looked in his eyes and had shared his grief at the failings of mankind. And the glory of mankind's aspirations. Coel was a man with a vision and the strength to proclaim it to others. His spirit had spoken to her spirit. Yet she was bound by the present. Bound to a homeland that was ringed by invading armies and being plucked over by men with new-fangled gods.

"Do you need a brand-new god in your life, Verna?" she asked and threw off her cloak.

"Which one? The Bishop's? It's all the old stuff dressed up like a crystallised cherry."

She pounced.

"Got you!"

"Oh, leave the poor beasties in peace! We won't sleep anyway. Not with Ecfrith at our heels."

Verna huffed and puffed, making a bed with their cloaks on the floor.

A horse stamped and snorted in the stable below. Tansen's ears pricked. She let her breath out after a moment.

"They make a great song about their healing miracles. But Grannie Bea could do a dozen in a morning."

Tansen fitted her head into Verna's shoulder.

"Women," said Verna quietly, "suckle all they need to know from their mother's breasts."

They tossed and fidgeted for a bit, before they eased up to sit against the wall in comfortable silence, wrapped in the steamy warmth from the stable.

Verna became so quiet Tansen thought she had fallen asleep. Her whisper barely fanned Tansen's cheek.

"What do you think about the man who was nailed on the Tree of Life?"

"I'm not strong on these foreign gods but I think that was Odin of the Northmen, Verna."

"But there was another. He died and came later and talked to his friends. Paulinus said ... " she stopped and darted an apologetic glance at Tansen ... "Well, you were busy and I had nowhere else to go ... The Bishop said it was a miracle, that he came back. And one friend doubted and had to touch the nail-marks on his body for proof that he still lived although his spirit was now in a higher world."

Proof. Tansen knew that first elusive spirit-scarring moment of proof.

The wonder of it would stay with her for ever. Skipping like a lamb along unfamiliar rocks her mother's face had suddenly been there in front of her, warning her. And she had stopped. And her shoe had fallen off and gone gurgling down into a quicksand. Oh yes, it was one thing to hear about the spirit living on and to believe. But when something happened, suddenly like that, there could be no doubt.

A tear, just a single tear, edged out from Verna's eyelid and slid into her hair. She gave a long shuddering sigh.

"I saw my son crucified," she said. "And when the light was fading they lit a pyre under his feet to see his suffering better."

"Oh, Verna." Their arms, their hair, their tears mingled.

"I've never doubted that his spirit lives on. But oh, I miss him."

Tansen tucked her cloak further round them both. Like the mantle of protection Grannie Bea asked for before she opened her mind to the Wise Ones.

"There's a knowing that us pagans have. It's just a way of life. It doesn't need preaching about."

But where was Marten's flame in the pool that was to give her strength to go forward? She had had to find her own strength. Maybe that was the point of it all. Oh well, the Generous Ones had given her royal blood and green eyes and a quick brain. How could she expect any other gifts?

But Coel was right when he said that injustice came not from the gods but from man. In that case injustice could be fought. She needed a goal to fill the emptiness of her life.

What a big word was injustice, Tansen thought sleepily. So easy to say. So grand to stand up and fight for. When all that really mattered was to care. So long as your God was called Love. Coel had said that too.

And there came the knowledge that did not bear thinking about and injustice was a silly word when she thought of the enormity of the pain she was carrying.

"Where are you heading for?" the inn-keeper asked next morning leading their horses from the stable.

"North," said Wulf shortly, mounting.

"Aye." The man held Tansen's rein, his sliding eyes taking in the fine breeding of the stallion, the lack of saddle, the fine stuff of her cloak with no insignia brooches. "You'll have heard that the King of the Pretani is gone, then."

Tansen gasped and masked her shock by arranging her hood.

"Dead?" she asked.

"Skipped out. In a Kentish ship. Wrapped in sable and spitting venom, they say. Some Prince from Strathclyde has been named as Heir."

With Wulf's furious gaze upon her Tansen bit back a host of questions. How had Dale wormed his way into the Kingship? And where was Reatta? She mounted quickly. Why should she care what went on in Dalgynch? Yet she did. Passionately.

"If anyone asks we're going to Traprain." Wulf's horse struck fire from the cobbles.

"Aye. Well, watch out for the screeching Daughter of Llyr in the Gorge."

Ignoring his warning Tansen followed Wulf. Every rushing torrent had its evil spirit. And every traveller had a bit of iron and a spell to go with it.

Back there in the hole under the tree she had wanted to be like Coel, to bury herself away from the world where the Peaceful Ones, the Compassionate Ones were all around in every blade of grass and every pebble. Now her mind and body were coming back to life. She was no longer numb. She was thinking and feeling again even though it hurt. She was back in the turmoil of life, rising to meet the challenge.

But what challenge? She desperately needed another flag to pin to her mast. Her horse pricked his ears, sensing her frustration, and quickened his pace.

Swans made decorative patterns in the river where it joined the Northern sea. The far-stretching brown moors did not look inviting. As the sun exploded over the breast of the horizon Tansen gathered her reins and splashed across the ford.

CHAPTER THIRTY SIX

It was well after noon when they heard the distant drumming of hooves. Around them the silver bark of birches slashed the purple darkness of firs. The insistent beat resounding from trunk to trunk came at them from all directions. The horses reared, snickered, and bolted, slashing through the undergrowth, threatening to catch their legs in the bare curling roots.

After a breath-taking plunge through thinning trees the horses broke out onto a wide plain of toneless grey and galloped on, their flesh quivering.

Only wind-gnarled hawthorns, shaggy birch and black alder broke from the dead bracken like hulks of wrecks thrusting up through the surface of a dead sea. All life seemed to have gone from the landscape. It was an empty place, haunted by the breath of spirits. And although no wind, no bird, no creature stirred in it, a restless place. And still the hollow reverberation beat all around them, and echoed back from the low dense roof of cloud.

The horses suddenly reared as a hidden gorge opened beneath their feet. It was deep and dark and narrow and bare. No fern hid in a crevice. No birch clung precariously to a ledge.

The thunder stopped! Stopped dead! The silence was even more terrifying. They looked back the way they had come. Nothing! Only the stunted trees, lop-sided and leering.

They swung from their horses and gentled them, slithering downwards until they met a river. Here they paused, looking at one another in the eerie dimness, uncertain whether to turn east or west. Verna's hand shook as she drew the hair back from her brow.

Tansen's skin felt chill and clammy. And then, above the throb of her heart, there came a rhythmic rushing like the patter of tiny goblin feet spewing out from their bottomless mounds at the stroke of Samhain.

And an unearthly screeching, striking off the dank stone walls and shrieking like the Furies Tansen thought they had left behind.

The horses reared again, white eyes rolling, forelegs flying. Verna screamed. Wulf twisted his hands in her tumbling hair as the mare, mad with fear, plunged neighing into the current. The arching brown neck appeared once and vanished in foam.

The screeching stopped. The silence throbbed. Had the sacrifice of the mare in the cauldron of death appeased the Baleful One?

Tansen froze.

High in the rock-face something hovered. Pale and ghastly. A shrouded figure, taller than a man. Headless.

It glided along a ledge. Palpitating. A mist of long draperies trickling downwards, trailing, green and slimy, in the water.

Tansen, swallowing, held her dagger with the iron infill before her face. Still the thing flowed onwards, spitting out a volley of curses now in an ancient tongue that stirred Tansen's memory.

Wulf's arm went back and his dagger flew. Straight to the heart. Straight through the body, taking the empty cloth with it.

A cry shattered the pulsating air. The howl of an animal wounded to death. A sobbing cry of loneliness and longing. It fragmented in the heavy air and fell like shards from a broken pot, down the trembling rock-face.

The shroud shuddered, empty, a nothingness, held aloft by boughs. A veil fluttered downwards like a wounded moth and lay crumpled on the surface of the water.

And the cry came again, thin now, bewildered and heart-stopping, the cry of a spirit in anguish.

The branches swayed and collapsed. Wulf threw his reins to Verna and strode towards the pitiful heap of rags. Two feet bound in docken leaves twitched at his coming. He fumbled for an opening. A dark pointed face, upsidedown, bat-like, peered out at him.

Verna hastily made the sign for protection. Over and over.

The face was hairy and hideous. Long lank hair writhed from the skull. Sunken eyes spilled out a terrible hate. Withered lips opened, dark and moist as a loathsome cavern. Yellow fangs snapped at Wulf's hand with frightening speed. With a superhuman effort the figure righted itself and flew at Wulf, clawing at his face, mewing like a buzzard.

Tansen, running, thrust Wulf's raised fist aside and imprisoned the wasted figure in her cloaked arms.

"Leave her be! She's sick!"

Wulf grabbed the pitiful wrists and threw her down, straddling her with his long legs so that she would not attack again.

"Nonsense! She's faking, the old witch!"

The head fell to one side, exposing skin, leathery through exposure, and Tansen saw with pity the grey pallor of it. There was no more strength left in her. Cowering she clutched her rags to her bony breast.

"On your way, woman." Wulf stood back.

Her body convulsed and she rolled over onto all fours. She began to crawl back along the ledge, stopping once to snarl over her shoulder. Tansen followed, leading her horse.

"Come back!" cried Wulf. "She's mad!"

Tansen found her collapsed beside a pool where the river dallied.

Clawing hands, bristles of chin-hair quivered upwards towards a cave partly screened by shrubs. Tansen lifted her and her body was as weightless as a bird. She laid her on her bed of bunched bracken. Scattered curses wafted up to her on an unclean breath.

"Hush, old Wise Woman," she said. "You can stop pretending.".

The walls of the cave ran with slime but near the back on a dry ledge Tansen found the jars and potions she had been looking for. The old woman snickered in alarm as Tansen sniffed them. The hanging bunches of herbs were rotting in the damp. Some pots held messes she could not even guess at and did not want to. Then she took the stopper off a jar and found a smell that was like something Grannie Bea used to give women for strength after childbirth.

"Wulf, Verna!" she called from the mouth of the cave. "Light a fire! Heat some water."

Wulf stared at her.

"You're a witch yourself," he said and there was accusation in his voice.

"Witch, Wise Woman, it's all the same," Tansen snapped.

Unwillingly he tethered the horses and followed Verna up out of the chasm to find firewood.

The Woman's eyes had closed. Tansen opened the laces at the old woman's neck and swallowed her sickness at the stench that came at her. She drew the sign of peace on the furrowed forehead. And the eyes blazed open upon her, recognising the age-old sign.

"What drove you to this place, Honoured One, away from people who would serve and shelter you?" asked Tansen.

The Woman began to tremble, uttering little soft moans like an animal in pain.

"Priests," she breathed. "Told the people ... my powers ... came from the Devil. They would burn ... those who fed me."

"They were afraid of you," Tansen tucked her cloak round the withered body. "They worship the power of the spirit but they are afraid when they see spirit at work. They don't understand."

The seamed forehead was icy as Tansen smoothed back the matted hair. Hunger and cold and fever had drained her body. Rejection and loneliness had sapped her energy. Tansen thanked the Compassionate Ones for guiding the horses here to help with this passing.

"No hope ... for the ... Folk of the Old Faith now," came the cracked voice.

And Tansen sensed the Caring Ones all around, waiting to welcome the released spirit, and their words came tumbling through her mind.

"The Great One that set the living Universe in motion is not troubled by creeds that spring up in the night-time and die in the dawn. For that is how it appears in the vast millenium of time."

The tight lips softened.

"You have many ... gifts, little One."

"There will always be folk who see more than others," said Tansen. "Folk who know that the Natural Law must take its course and cannot be altered."

And as she soothed the fluttering hands Tansen felt a glow of warm light fill the cave.

"Mankind's temples will empty," she heard herself say. And her mouth formed words that pained her to speak. "And when folk turn back to the All-Mother for succour, they'll find her waters polluted, her land poisoned and the sky rent with holes."

Then she pushed back the spirit beings who crowded at her back. And cradling the wasted body in one arm, held to her lips the warm brew that Verna had brought.

"The old ways will stay in the folk-memory, Mother," whispered Verna. "In a charm made from a gem-stone, in the salt thrown, in the healing wells, in the Hallow's Eve bonfires and the mistletoe."

The Woman sipped and lay back. Eyes, calm and content as crystals in water, opened full on Tansen.

"I see an arrow ... flying ... falling ... I see a pool ... a flame in it ... glowing ... "

Her breath was like the rustle of dry leaves.

Tansen felt rather than saw Wulf standing, his eyes boring into her back. His harsh whisper betrayed his fear.

"Arrows and pools! Empty, everyday things. Don't let her fool you there's a hidden meaning there."

But the trivial words of a Wise Woman always held significance for the one who was meant to hear.

"And the babe ... a boy ... King ... some day ... "

She let out a little slow sigh and her chest did not rise again.

Tansen felt for a pulse in the scraggy neck but there was none. She looked up. Wulf stood, his eyebrows lifting from horror-stricken eyes, sweat glittering on his forehead. Verna's hand fell from her charm, her mouth opening and shutting

"It's true!" Tansen rose from her knees, lifting her cloak from the lifeless body. "I'm pregnant."

Wulf's breath hissed between his teeth.

"Ean's?"

In the leaden silence that fell between them the green boughs in the fire at the entrance fizzed and popped.

Verna let out a little moan, her hands twisting together.

"We need stones for a cairn," Tansen said.

Wulf brushed past her, enveloping her in cold air with the violence of his passing.

"Signs and portents and the meaning of things." He kicked at the fire, as if the roar of the flames would erase the unthinkable from his mind. "It all comes to the same in the end, a hole in the ground and a smell in the air."

He built the cairn, massing the stones quickly but with care to leave no space where something could burrow in. Or thrust its way out. Verna helped, glancing up at the uneasy sky.

Tansen poured the water of the libation and said the incantation, her voice crackling with anger at the blind ignorance of those who had reviled the Wise One. At the injustice of it. At the injustice of the fact that she was to bear a child. And she would never know if it had come from the love of Ean's body or the filth of his brother's lust. Even when she looked on its face, there could be no feature that might not have come from either of them, brothers as they were.

The flames of the little fire flared on skins stretched taut between dead branches and on long thigh bones hanging from outcrops of stone, terrible in the fading light.

She caught up a great white bone, knobbed at both ends and swung it. And the sound boomed down the gorge and resounded in her blood. And she sprang and leapt and swung, wilder and wilder, battering at the drum-skins with a brutal ferocity. And her rage at the horror within her erupted in a torrent of savage sound and action.

The flames, lancing off ripples in the pool, broke into slivers that stabbed at her eyes and entered her mind and her heart. And she saw Ean coming towards her carrying a bairn, a boy, with rosy limbs. And she beat out the glory of their love that had been wild and exciting and beautiful. And then she was pounding at the skins again, hammering out her despair that the child she had longed for was tainted for ever in her mind with the savagery of his father's murderer. And the great bleached bones above her head swung and rattled, sharp and staccato, as white as only burnt bone can be. Then it was Ecfrith, holding the bairn aloft. And he threw on the flames. And laughed as the rosy limbs curled and blackened.

And the earth shook beneath her feet and the walls of the gorge stirred and trembled like a monster awakening from some primordial sleep. And above her head the rock split open and a giant stone, long and rectangular, hurtled downwards. The shock waves as it thudded on the ground threw her sideways. Sparks, dust, gravel engulfed her. And when she raised her head, the entrance to the cave had been sealed, neatly and precisely.

Then she was riding, riding until she found a place where the horse could ford the river. And as her head lifted over the gorge the stars dazzled her with their brightness. So she rode through the night, over ice-hard cart-tracks, hardly aware of Wulf at her side with Verna perched behind him.

She rode hard for two more days, following the coast-line, locked within her thoughts, stopping only to fall exhausted and sleep, huddled between Verna and Wulf for warmth.

They came to a circle of stones bedded deep in peat. Some leaned, some had toppled. Yet some still reared upwards in lonely grandeur. And Tansen thought of the folk who had taken time from the sowing and reaping to plant giants to probe the secrets of the skies. How these folk had gone, and passed and dissolved like mist. Or so it seemed. Yet did their blood not still run in the bairns? The bairns that grew in the bellies of the women who dug peats from this desolate moor, their skirts tucked in their waistbands.

This was the land that the Lothian Chiefs squabbled over, calling themselves Kings and raising great broods of offspring. And after each skirmish, young Princes would lie dead in the ditches and the Kings would gallop back to breed some more. First Edwin and now Ecfrith thought this land was worth owning. To become a stepping-stone to her own land beyond. She could not shake off the feeling of terrible sadness that hung in the air.

Then a field-lark fluttered upwards beside them and hovered high in the rippling light, trilling its liquid notes. And Verna came abruptly out of her deep dark dream.

"I can make you a potion to get rid of it," she said.

And Tansen considered that thought for the last time and shook her head swiftly.

"Each day I scream inside my head to the gods, Why me? I know that Reatta's curse, that I'd never have a child by Ean, arose out of jealousy. But if it's not Ean's then it will be Ecfrith's."

"So drink the potion. The spirit coming to life within you will withdraw and choose another unborn being to inhabit."

"I know all that! I know! Yet there's a time when a certain spirit is destined to come into the world. A time when all things are in harmony for its destiny to be fulfilled. When the child must be allowed to live, whoever fathered it."

"You're thinking that the Daughter of Llyr saw him becoming a King."

"The hand of the god is on this one, Verna. I would give it back to the Other World if I could! Believe me, I would!"

Then Wulf's mount began to limp. Tansen sat calm and still while Verna and he examined the hoof.

"There's nothing wrong with him."

And Verna cried out suddenly.

"You crafty scamp, Wulf! You stole the King's horses! That's Heroward!"

"It's his pride that's hurt." Wulf agreed, stroking the long flaring nose. "Too young to have seen battle. But trained as a war-horse. And once he was dressed in plates of gold and carried a King to his Acclamation."

"We'd better barter him for a pack-pony," said Verna, glancing at Tansen's stiff face.

"Who'll want a dejected war-horse?"

Wulf shaded his eyes to look across the plain.

"I wonder if Morfael's at Traprain. He stole back to his fortress while Edwin was busy with Cadwallon. I used to lodge there when I carried messages between Ean and his kin."

Suddenly the air was alive with songs of ancient heroes. The Selgovie people on Eildon and the Votadini on Traprain. Eildon in the south had not survived the Romans but Traprain further north had allied with them and prospered.

So now they cut inland to the great hulk of rock that rose like a stranded whale from the plain.

"The ramparts might be crumbling but there are flags on the palisade." Wulf stroked his chin.

Wan faces of women appeared at the doors of homesteads. Cattle lowed softly, locked in byres, hidden from marauding armies.

At the gate to the fort they met a train of travelling people moving south for the cold season. They shook their heads at the limping war-horse. But Heroward pricked up his ears at the snickering of the mares. Then one trader fixed a calculating eye on the rearing head and twitching nostrils.

"In exchange for a pack-horse, you say?" Heroward sidled away from the probing hands with an eagerness in his step that had not been there before. The trader blandly detached the baggage from a sturdy hill-pony and grinned after them as they made for Traprain.

"Now what's our story for Morfael."

"Tell him who we are!"

"And he'll serve our heads on a platter to Ecfrith to save his own skin!"

Wulf shook his head. “I’m a ship’s carpenter looking to buy trees for masts. You’re my women.”

The Guards were suspicious, drunken and unkempt.

“Bed and bite? You’ll be lucky. What’s the news down south?”

“Ecfrith’s marching west!”

“Oh aye! And I’m the callant that blows his war-horn.”

But they were allowed in. And found Traprain, once the richest Citadel in the land, its power extending from the Forth to the Humber, now a place of weary waiting where flies bred in piles of horse-dung and men relieved themselves openly in the drains.

“Splendid he was in battle, with his nine hundred horse, Cunedda, the Lion.” Wulf was quoting from an old bard song. “He left a gap here, right enough, when he took his Votadini and went to change the history of Wales.”

CHAPTER THIRTY SEVEN

They bedded down in an empty stall lulled by the warm steamy air and the soft snicker of horses.

And in the night a sweet trickling melody on a keening harp came to Tansen, wakened by the movement of the life inside her. And a voice bore upwards with the piercing sweetness of a lark.

"Cadwallon's hall is dark tonight
No candle burns, no bed is made.
I weep awhile and then am quiet.
Cadwallon's hall is still tonight
Where once I sat in honour held.
Dead is my lord, yet I am alive."

Only by the light of the Moon did she find the cloaked figure, in the curve of the stone-faced turf rampart, his foot wedged on a rock to support his silvered harp.

"He's been slain, then?"

The man turned and looked at her along his shoulder.

"Surprised by Ecfrith at the Wall of Hadrian."

His melody took a sudden downward swoop to keen on, thin and remote as a tune heard only in dreams, pulling at the heart with its loneliness.

"You'll find another master to give you board and rings."

"I'm not welcome in any Hall. I sing only of what might have been. It's not Cadwallon I grieve for so much as the death of the dream that was in him. I know the worth of what was lost."

He turned his empty eyes southwards as his fingers brushed the strings.

"High is the mountain,
Thin is my hempen cloak,
Hard is my goatskin bed,
Yet once I was drunk
On the mead of Brynn."

A jangle of discords told of hidden emotion.

"Thin my legs, bare and uncovered
Brothers I had who never lost heart
Brothers I lost like fine hazel saplings
The dykes endure
Those who built them are no more."

He laid his hand on the strings to silence them.

"Britons no more will be Kings in Britain. They'll be Cymry, foreigners, exiled to the bleak unlovely hills. Since Arthur, King has fought King until few of the ancient royal houses survive. Flawed as he was, Cadwallon could have united us in our dream."

"There are still free men in the north," said Tansen, pressing on her lively stomach. "Dale, another Briton, has taken command there."

"And what dream will spur him into battle? He has no kinship with the Pretani, no obligation to the land. Only a hatred of the Angles and a personal vengeance to exact from them. Once his sword is sated with their blood what will motivate him? Power, ambition?"

"And why not?" Tansen was stung to reply. "Without power there can be no progress, no going forward in peace. Without ambition there can be no achievement in the end."

Yet the bard was right. Dale, a mercenary, a spy, who had disappeared without a trace from Lleyn. If he had done his duty then, Ean might still be alive. Dale must have heard that Garnard had left and had swooped north to see what he could gain out of it. He and Reatta were well-suited!

The bard's scrip lay open at his foot, some crumbs of bread spilling out. A fieldmouse whisked away at Tansen's sudden surge of anger.

"Your verses are pale beside the praise-songs about Bridei. He was a Briton, like Arthur. He knew the clans were weak in beating off the enemy yet strong in fighting one another. He welded them into one great unified force by the sheer power of his personality. Garnard has dishonoured the Pretani. But a new Bridei will arise! Dale the Briton, or another! And I'll be there to see Bridei's Hall at Dalgynch bright with a thousand lights and filled with the praises of a thousand bards."

At that the baby in her womb gave a great leap. And as she bent over gasping, horns blasted from the look-out posts. And Morfael, squat, low-browed, shifty-eyed, grey-faced in his night-shirt, leaned from a high window, bawling to be told the news. And the messenger yelling over the clatter of his foam-flecked mount that Ecfrith was rampaging north again.

At the door of the stable Wulf tried to wrench the reins of their animals from the grasp of two struggling men. A bundle flew from an arm and exploded at their feet, showering the earth with silver. Chalices, candesticks, bowls, someone's booty pressed flat ready for melting. The thieves lunged after the silver and Wulf forced his way through with the horses. They rode west for Dun Eidyn with Wulf on the hardy hill-pony and Verna seated behind Tansen. They did not journey alone. Carts, like hump-backed beetles, scurried west to the ferry.

While the salt wind stung her cheeks and the shadows of clouds raced with them across the landscape, Tansen felt stunned, dazed that there were men still marching and slaying while her breasts were swelling and her belly rounding with new life. A child who would march and be slain in his turn.

Yet to be a king if the prophecy of the Daughter of Llyr came true. For there were many paths in front of a person and a seer saw only one. Yet how the child had leapt at the name of Bridei! And she cried to Bride in the anguish of her spirit, "No! We need a saviour now! The Pretani cannot wait until he grows to manhood! And neither can I!"

And it came to her that her body would go on, despite her, changing to fulfil its new purpose. While her mind and spirit withdrew from the task. She was merely a channel for the being that grew inside her. It had its own destiny to fulfil. There was nothing else that she could do for the bairn that might be Ean's. Or Ecfrith's.

Yet high on the hurrying wind came that old yearning that had aroused dreams in the young Tansen. Dreams that had been swept into oblivion by the harsh winds of reality as she had learned about the world and herself.

Never again could she live in a farmstead and content herself tending animals and fields. She had lived in the centres of power and studied how the minds of the leaders worked. She could laugh a little at the simple chit who had rung Caterin's Bell and thought she might be Queen. Yet she had tested herself against courtiers and Kings. And won! Having gained that experience she knew how much more she still had to learn.

Oh, but her fingers itched to touch the corners of that web of power again. She knew she had the will to change the pattern of people's lives. She was different to those who bowed their heads and accepted their lot. It was her abundance of energy that made the difference between them and her. A new energy that danced through her limbs carrying a feeling that she could conquer the world. Now at last she was tied to no man and no kin and no Court. She had ambition and the freedom to pursue it. She had flirted with danger and enjoyed it. It had exhilerated her. It was like seeing how close she could go to the hearth-fire without being burned. For the first time for many moons she laughed aloud for the sheer joy of being alive.

The sight of the Law at Berwick and the Bass Rock erupting from the waves brought Tansen's gaze north. There snug in the mist lay Fib and Dalgynch. And a mark to be made there. Like a tide-mark on the shore.

The monk Coel might bide tranquil in his sanctuary. The tides that ebbed and flowed over his causeway would leave no trail but a frond of seaweed. While she was born to be a fighter. Dale was the elected Heir. But Reatta was not yet Queen. Grannie Bea's arrow was still winging on its flight-path to fate.

The houses on the Dun of Eidyn showed sharp and clear against the clouds, no hearth-smoke hazing their outlines. Only the rumble of hand-carts rose from the mist wreathing the reed-beds of the Nor' Loch and sending the wildfowl flapping. Tansen, cantering through the bracken past the slow stream of fleeing folk, was filled with a vast anger that Ecfrith's Scots would wanton through Dun Eidyn's steep cobbled lanes before nightfall.

Would Ecfrith remember the army of Mynyddog that had feasted there for a whole year? And had set out to divide and defeat the two kingdoms of Bernicia and Deira? And how only three men had survived. Along with the song of Aneirin to tell how they fell in battle, unmanned by mead in the hall and the beverage of wine.

Would Ecfrith stand on a thick stone tower and look towards Fib? And follow the long twin-coned ridge of the Lomonds, eastwards, until his gaze fastened on the roof-ridges of Dalgynch.

At the river's edge they brushed through the crowd who wailed across the rain-swept Forth at a ferryman who had shut his ears and beached his boat. Riding westwards they plodded through a swathe cut by woodcutters among the bare jointed oaks, skirting the monastery at Abercorn.

"That House boasts a fine Pretani name," Wulf gritted, wet tendrils of brown hair ringing his cheeks. "But the monks cut their tonsures in the Roman way and will welcome Ecfrith. We'll go upriver to where the Bannog Burn joins the Forth in the land of the Manau."

And Tansen, pausing to look south, saw an orange glow reflected on the low cloud, the flickering glow of a hundred burning thatches.

CHAPTER THIRTY EIGHT

The Miathie lived in the plain between the two rivers of Cluith and Fiorth, plumb in the path of every plundering army that coveted the fertile lands to the north-east. The Miathie had the fiery Scots and the stolid Britons to the west and the crafty Lothian Kings to the south. But they belonged staunchly within the Pretani network of clans. And none would deprive them of the pleasure of the first crack at any enemy.

And so, trotting quietly, head high, with the crisp clean air running fresh through her cloak, Tansen crossed the Bannog Burn and entered her homeland. On the watch-towers of Dun Miathie lanterns were coming alive, glittering on metal, sliding across the high grey windowless walls and flaring on the blue and silver standards.

"Maybe I'll hear word of my kin here," said Wulf.

Tansen turned towards Wulf with a face that was suddenly sharp-featured and bleak.

"The travelling stone-masons?" she asked. Wulf nodded, averting his eyes. Verna, silent, bit hard on her bottom lip.

One trumpet call, echoed by another, halted their approach.

Tansen recited her lineage and saw the eyes of the Guards meet and slide away.

"Daughter of Beatha, the Healing One?" asked the one in command. "Tell Fodthur."

Closely guarded, they climbed the steep beaten track, dismounted, and entered within the thick grey walls.

A big fellow dressed like a leather-worker, his broad peasant face enlivened by a ferocious squint in one eye, strode out of the stables. A fleshy muscle-padded arm smacked the rumps of their horses and they disappeared smartly into the dark interior.

"We might need them for the pot before we're done!" he cried, his russet beard splitting open in welcome. "You're Beatha's girl! Good! We'll need all the healers we can get now that the Angles are on their way!"

It was Fodthur, the Chieftain, loose-limbed and joyful.

"We can't stay. We're making for Dalgynch," Tansen cried urgently.

"You'd do better to wait awhile. Dale the Briton's on his way here. We'll face the Angles on the border near the Bannog. There's a few folk here anxious to see what our new Heir makes of Ecfrith."

A thought brought him wheeling round.

"Married onto the young Eanfrith, weren't you?"

His gaze hardened at the sight of Wulf's yellow hair and long bony Danish face.

"And who's this?" he asked. "Ecfrith's spy?"

A Guard sprang forward and caught Wulf's sword arm in a bruising grip. A sword-point pricked his throat.

"No! He's half-Pretani!" Tansen cried.

"Half-Dane, more like!"

"He's spent all his life at Dalgynch."

The Chieftain snorted.

"Taking a trip now and then to Bernicia with a message in his mouth. And thinking to take up the same trade for a new master."

Wulf stood foursquare between the Guards, colour running high through his cheeks.

"What can I betray that Ecfrith doesn't already know about your defences from his Scots mercenaries? That man murdered my milk-brother! I'd kill him before I'd serve him!"

"Would you now? Is that why you're fleeing from him, louping low over the heather?"

Wulf jerked and a sword slashed his dagger-arm from shoulder to wrist. He steadied himself with a deep breath.

"I've brought the wife of my milk-brother back to her homeland," he said, breathing heavily. "Until she's safe I'll be at her side to defend her."

Drop by drop a ruby puddle was growing on the slabs at Wulf's foot.

"Fine words, half-man! So I'll give you a sporting chance! March with your half-kin to fight against your half-kin." The squint eye, sharp and bright, slewed round them all. "Survive tomorrow and you're free! Till then, half-man, you're under guard."

"There's no glory in it for me," Wulf ground out. "And if I lay down my life, it's for the safety of my brother's lady! Promise me that at least!"

Fodthur spat out an oath.

"Guard the lot of them!" he told the soldiers. "On the eve of battle, Beatha's lass, I study what lies under every bent blade of grass."

In a bare room near the barracks, with a guard posted at the door, Verna begged for water while Tansen tore the sleeve from Wulf's arm. And suddenly she could not bear to touch his flesh.

She bent her head and asked for the healing touch that used to soothe the greeting bairns and wounded birds. She had never had to ask for it before. It had always been there, just a thought away. Now there was no tingle in her arm, no warmth in her palm. And she knew that her mind was putting up a barrier. And why. For her flesh shuddered from contact with this man, any man.

But Wulf was not any man. She swallowed back her nausea and began to press the edges of his wound together. His skin, still sun-brown, warmed under her touch and the soft brown hairs quivered. His blood, a living spring oozing gently from a beating heart, began to congeal. A muscle in the wind-fresh flesh tightened as she smoothed on a salve from her pouch. She bound a strip torn from her shift, over and under, down to a sinewy wrist where his life-blood pulsed in blue branching veins. She tied it at his hand, leather-stained from the reins, thin and strong and capable, maybe a stone-mason's hand, after all. And dared not meet his eyes. For Wulf was no longer a shadow at Ean's side. He was a man of flesh and blood. And the maleness of him still repelled her.

She pushed herself from his side and went to grasp the bars at the cell window, sick and angry at the turmoil of her emotions. At first Wulf had despised her because he thought she would bring harm to Ean. Yet from their mutual love for Ean had grown a certain companionship. She had always known that Wulf was the better man of the two but she had loved Ean because he was handsome and merry. Yet the day would surely have come when she would have found Ean wanting. Would she have turned to Wulf then? Would he also have found Ean wanting and turned to her? How could she be thinking this way? For all their care neither had been able to halt the knife that sent Ean to his death.

Lit by a dozen fires the cleaning and oiling and sharpening of weapons went on in the courtyard. The battle was real to her now, a noise and a heat and a darkness that threatened not only her homeland but this man, Wulf. In the days before Ean's death she had been guided to give him a wealth of love. Surely now she could do the same for Wulf. Oh, Bride, was this all a woman was created for? To give of herself so that a man could go happy into battle? But no! Love freely given was never wasted.

Now death clanged and whistled and stamped in the courtyard. Behind her, Wulf reached for his scabbard.

"Rest," she said and, scooping the grease from the eating-bowls, she began to smooth and polish the long sword-blade, aware all the while of the lean lithe body on the couch, that might soon lie wasting beside the Bannog Burn.

Despite the fairness of his cropped cap of hair, his eyelashes were dark and thick and lay quietly on his cheeks. She knew then that, if she could overcome her revulsion, she too needed love. Not from a boy like Ean. Not from a man who wanted to protect her. But from a man who would share the risks and the good times. A strong man who knew when to keep silent and think within himself. And when she saw he was looking at her now through deceptively lazy eyelids she glimpsed a sweet sadness.

She saw him in her mind's eye as an oak-tree, black-brown and solid, his feet firm in the soil, unchanging. A trunk that a woman could lean on and gain strength as Ean had done to her. And Wulf's spirit, branching towards the sky, bursting with buds and leaves and acorns and sheltering a host of birds and creatures and giving succour to tiny plants? And finding fulfilment in the natural law of the changing seasons? She seemed to have known him always and yet not known him at all.

When Verna came with a candle, Tansen saw the blaze in Wulf's face, quickly quenched. And she held her breath at the quiet flowering of glory in her heart. And listened to the sweet song of the blood in her veins. When the guard brought stew, Tansen saw with a rush of gladness that Wulf could use his sword-arm to eat and would not go injured into battle.

"I couldn't bear ... I couldn't bear to lose you now," she said. And her voice was rough and breathy with the depth of emotion that shook her.

Wulf saw the betraying quiver of her lip and how her teeth pressed on it to bring it under control. It was beyond believing that she could feel anything more for him than a surge of sisterly tenderness. And a need for that which she had lost with Ean. He rolled to his feet and stood, his back to the window, watching Verna untangle the long wet sweep of Tansen's hair.

"She is royal and taboo." The words beat like a drum-roll in his head. And who was he? A nobody without Ean. More than that she had been foully used by Ecfrith. He had seen her shudder away from him. What would it mean to her if he told her he loved her? Nothing but torment! Wanting to give comfort out of the kindness of her heart. But unable to bear the touch of his body.

Yet tomorrow he would most likely die. His first battle. His battles had all been fought in the night, trying to blot out the picture of Ean's caressing hand on her breast, the sound of the carefree laughter of a girl in love. They had thought he was jealous of her place in Ean's heart. How they would have laughed if they had known the truth. How her shining courage beside the river Leven long ago had stilled the beat of his heart? And what would happen to her now if he was killed? He turned angrily, needing to break the throbbing silence.

"You'll be fine in your own land with Beatha's name to shield you."

She stared at him with wide distended eyes, not understanding that he was assuming his own death.

"I've fashioned my own shield." She smiled and he saw a dimple he had not noticed before. "Wulf, you can step out now from the shadow of Ean. You can become the man that Ean never was. The man whose heart was big enough to love both of us."

A flutter passed over her hair as if Ean had heard and approved. She met Wulf's gaze where he stood opposite her, silent, wary, a curtain drawn over his expression.

"Loving Ean was like loving a bright shining star. I'll never love that way again. That blaze of glory is a once-in-a-lifetime thing."

Wulf waited, rigid, his face white.

"A brilliant love like that is like a shooting star that fades and dies." She forced herself to go on, steeling her emotions against rejection. "There's more to love than that. There's a knowing in your hearts and minds that you're going in the same direction. There's a love that creeps up on you when you think the same way about things that matter. When you comfort and help one another and share in the pain."

She stopped and bowed her head again, suddenly shy of this warm comfortable love that she had found in her heart for Wulf. Even if he rejected her she would always be glad she had known there was such a love. Then his finger rested under her chin and tilted it. There was a great tenderness in the light in his eyes and in the gentleness of his mouth. And the sick distaste she had felt at his touch was no longer there.

"From the beginning, that day at the river, you were a red rose that I hid in my heart."

Her smile blossomed up at him, warm and uplifting as a golden sunset.

"And high time, too," muttered Verna to herself, wondering, as she slipped out if there was a guard somewhere that might relish a chance to boast about the deeds he would do on the morrow and let her share his brazier.

For a long time they kissed and touched one another and held hands, and gazed into one another's eyes. And while the dusk deepened outside, they felt bathed in a warm glow.

Then they gave their love to one another, a slow and unhurried love, warming and comforting, taking and giving with the deepest of enjoyment lasting long into the night and ending with deep throat-catching sighs of pleasure.

Later they talked about the battle, knowing that the Miathie did not have the numbers of men to stop Ecfrith nor the resources to withstand a siege. Even if Dale and the Pretani army arrived, it would not be enough. So they spoke of what they would do after the battle, knowing that sharing a dream was sometimes more fulfilling than having it come true.

Wulf told how he would travel north to find his kin.

"I imagine they'd be in the north-east where things are more settled and chiefs have time to think of employing them," Tansen said. "Do they work in wood or stone?"

"Both. You've seen their work at Gefrin."

"Edwin's Mead Hall? I thought I saw a Pretani scroll or two on the pillars. But when I asked about the sculptor it was a Danish name, Bjorn, they told me."

Wulf smiled, shy and proud and yet sure as though he had found the place in life he was looking for.

"My grandfather, Bjorn. My Pretani father came to study under Bjorn and married his daughter." He grinned. "So that's why I used to travel down to Gefrin. To visit the old man. He died in the last cold season. So that severed my link with Gefrin. And now that Ean's gone I've no allegiance to the Angles. In fact I'll be a half-breed no longer. Like my mother I'll follow my Pretani father. And my lovely Pretani woman."

Later, drowsily, she spoke, wanting him to sleep so that he would be quick and strong in the morning.

"Would you like me to ask for warmed wine?"

Wulf had been listening to her heart-beat in the silence, to the quick intakes of breath that betrayed that she was not asleep. He had angled his head on the pillow so that he could see the fine bones of her face and how the lustre of her skin glowed in the lamplight. Her full lips that quivered now and again as she thought of the morning.

"I don't need false courage," he said. "I'll neither yell nor beat on my shield. I'm going into battle because I'm forced to. It's the way things are decided. I'll kill the man in front of me unless the axe at my back gets me first."

And Tansen lay listening to voices droning, bodies heaving and tossing, a whole citadel waiting. And she imagined a flame reflected in a pool. But no flicker of life nor ripple of thought disturbed the image. And she thought of promises and threats. Made by Marten, by Reatta, by Dale. And knew there was no place for her at Dalgynch however the battle might go. Unless she carved out her own niche.

CHAPTER THIRTY NINE

Long before dawn the barking of dogs, the smell of cooking, the jangle of metal, revealed that the army was up and about. Tansen knelt to tie the thongs of Wulf's sandals on his bare legs and fussed with his brooch-pin, bent by the coarse cloth of his cloak until he folded her close to his body.

"I'll be safe, wedged behind a bulwark of shields."

But her crushed breasts and seeking arms felt how vulnerable he was with only a light stitched leather tunic to protect his flesh.

"Guard him well," she whispered, exploring with her fingers the dents in the square wooden shield at his back. He lifted the borrowed pike and tried an upward and a downward thrust. And tested a well-worn javelin for balance. She fastened on his sword-belt and scabbard.

"Do not fail him, bright blade." She slipped her own dagger into his boot.

"We'll take them with the dew still on them," he called, his eyes already remote with the business of the day, and left with that swinging stride she remembered but had never noticed. While all unknown, tears fell like a curtain over her cheeks.

Fodthur's chariot led the army out. Its wheels bristled with blades, nails, and hooks. The iron-capped charioteer waved his goad, a yellow circle on his forehead to distinguish him from his master.

"We've met greater odds than this! And sent them reeling into the bog." Fodthur was in a layered tunic of waxed skin plates, a tanned leather apron hanging from his battle-belt and on his back a dark curved shield with flint-sharp edges. He postured with a five-pronged trident at his women, his bards and his Druad. On his helmet was a boar emblem borrowed from the Veniconie to lend ferocity to the attack.

Women with flat blank faces who had done it all before sent the bairns to the cellars with bowls of hot broth in their hands. In the courtyard where the wounded would be brought, Verna was laying out bandages and medicines and tending the fires under the cauldrons. Tansen toiled under bales of hay, taking them to the courtyard under the lower rampart, half-rock, half-earth where the beasts, newly herded in from the fields, lowed and squealed and bleated. Then up the winding worn steps to the high rampart bearing bundles of arrows, spears and rough-hewn rocks for crushing skulls.

After her first glance over the wall at the empty homesteads and fields in the plain, she did not look again. For her mind and body toiled grimly on, numbed by the immensity of the task before them. When the arrows had been laid in neat foursquare shapes, the light throwing-spears and javelins angled against the palisade, and the rocks settled into cone-shaped piles there were flasks to fill with water and place in racks.

Behind the racks the wall was pitted where it had melted and bubbled in great heat. And she saw by the black glazed stonework that there was no need to dowse the timber-laced walls against fire. For the fort had been set alight so often that the intense heat produced by the draught channels of the burnt timber beams had vitrified the stone and turned it to glass. And so the sacrifice of those who had suffered defeat before had built a priceless defence for their descendents.

Older children stood on boxes to look taller, poking painted wooden helmets over the parapet in a pitiful effort to fool the enemy. Now they set up a cry as the first horseman came flying across the plain. The women caught hold of his bridle, thick with foam and blood. And he threw back his cloak and held aloft a severed head. At first the folk cheered till the familiar squinting eyes skewered them into silence.

"Behold Fodthur, generous and famous, pillar in battle, shield to his land!" the rider cried. "My heart thunders in my breast!" And the keening began, softly like a harp behind a singer.

"Woe to my hand for striking off the head of my master! Woe to the Dane who would have carved signs on his cheeks! Woe to the Angle who buries none except in the belly of beast or of bird. Woe to Ecfrith who has bared Fodthur's breast to the raven."

The burgeoning wailing, the beating of breasts stopped. Over the craning heads Tansen saw, reeling in at the open gate-way, a man, blood-soaked and dazed. And as he dropped, more, holding their crushed and gaping limbs. And the women ran to carry the wounded in their arms to the ramparts where their exhausted comrades began to gather, checking weapons, watching over the parapet for the spears of the enemy.

Tansen searched every face as she bathed and bound and fed the remnants of the army that had crawled back to die on the ramparts. No one had seen the young man with yellow hair and would have slain him if they had. She felt strangely calm, as if she had known and it did not matter.

"What happened?" she asked.

A man tilted a wine-flask to his mouth, while his gaze still scanned the darkening plain where every rock and tree might hide an army, drawing silently closer.

"Ecfrith put slaves, Britons, armed only with short-swords in the centre of his line to tempt us to attack at his weakest point." His voice was raw with despair and exhaustion. A boy, gulping at the stench of blood, fanned the red-bandaged legs to keep the insects off.

"We saw through his ruse, all right. But Fodthur gambled that the Britons would turn on their masters. Yet the vermin ran and the horsemen caught us in the middle and slaughtered us with no room to turn or lift a spear."

He slumped suddenly into sleep. A woman rolled him over and took his place, shading her eyes with cupped hands.

"Dowse that torch!"

In the last gleam before the steam rose hissing from the bucket Tansen saw a face, blinded by a river of blood. Yet still his neck stretched, every other sense attuned for the sound of a rustle or a scrape of an enemy boot.

"Where was Dale in this?" She strained her eyes over the palisade, cursing the Moon for her absence, wondering vaguely how long they all had to live.

"The Briton?" It came out as a groan. "He came. You could see he'd been training his men. The shield-wall stood firm. The javelins flew, nicely timed and all. But too light. Garnard left him a sorry legacy in weaponry. The Angles brushed them off their fire-hardened iron like midges. Fought well, he did. But ten to one was too much for him. For all of us."

There was a long aching silence. Tansen staring eastward with gritty eyes, saw the pink glow of the dawn outline the low hills. And heard the creak of stiffening joints as hands felt for bows. And a child urgently making water against the wall and the clout of a hand on his ear and a stifled yelp. And a shuddering moan from a woman finding her man had died in the night. And a slow slurring step as someone dragged his wounded leg to peer over the wall beside her.

"That's no' the dawn," he said. "It's Dalgynch."

Slowly Tansen turned disbelieving eyes and looked in his face.

"It can't be!"

"He's followed the Briton to his Citadel and fired it. You can smell it on the wind."

Folk were fighting to get to the parapet. A long indrawn breath. And then the shouting, weeping, cheering began. Children began beating on their shields. Setting off the dogs and the uneasy beasts in the yard. Their lives were saved! There would be no siege! Not this day, anyway.

But when the stars paled with the dawning, when they saw pillars of smoke jet-black against the lightening sky the tears poured down their faces for the kin that suffered in their place. And Tansen, absently rubbing the cuts and bruises on her hands and arms, went to her cell.

As she drew near she heard a voice singing softly.

"My mother once told me
She'd buy me a longship
A handsome-oared vessel
That would breast the broad sea.
It would circle ..."

It was Wulf's voice. Her heart lifted and she began to run, weeping and breathless, and threw back the door. He lay on the cot, bloody, filthy but alive. And very tipsy.

Verna, her face beaming, lifted the bowl of ruddy water, the cloths and the empty mead bottle and left.

"Ah, my Queen, my Princess, Odin didn't call me to feast in Valholl tonight."

She knelt, kissing the dust from his face and hands.

"Hush! You're Pretani, remember!" She closed his mouth with her lips. He struggled free and raised a strangled gurgle of a shout.

"Tonight I'm Frey, lusty and iron-hard. Tonight I'm Sigurd, the Dragon-Slayer ... "

"Tonight you'll slay no dragons, man-of-mine."

She cradled his head between her breasts in case some passing soldier with a sword already crusted with Danish blood would hear him. And she rocked him until he whistled gently into sleep.

CHAPTER FORTY

"We saw it all! Ecfrith laying a circle of gold on the head of a young Angle and calling him King of the Pretani."

Two Miathie youths had bribed a Scots slave to pass them in to Dalgynch through an underground passage.

"His hair's too brown for a Dane. Must have a tinge of Pretani blood in him though they say he's in Aethelfrith's line."

"Ecfrith knew enough of our customs to marry him to Reatta, and give him a Pretani name, Talorc. Ecfrith boasted that Pretani Princesses were hot for the Royal House of Aethelfrith."

Tansen ignored the sly looks directed at her.

"Where's Dale, the big Briton?"

"Took off northwards with the remnants of the Guard. Didn't last long, that one."

"And the clansmen scattered back home to defend their own pits."

A tall man, gaunt with years of seige rations, combed his beard anxiously.

"And we're left holding the front line again, a leaderless bunch of wounded men and mourning women."

Well, they could count on being rid of two women and a wounded man shortly, decided Tansen. If there was to be a rebellion against the Angles it would begin in the north.

When at last the three of them achieved the outer gate of Dun Myat, Tansen clapped her heels to the stallion and swung eastwards towards Dalgynch.

"Not that way!" Wulf's startled shout rang after her.

"For Bride's sake go north," Verna cried over Tansen's shoulder, her teeth chattering to the beat of the hooves. "Keep the Ochils between us and Ecfrith."

"I want to see if it's all true!"

She was gambling that Wulf would follow. If he didn't, she would go herself.

The whooping of swans and the first light of morning came sliding silently across Loch Leven lying at peace to the north. A wisp of smoke rose from the cells of the holy men on St. Serf's island. She leapt from the horse and ran, climbing up Ben Arty, slowed by the weight in her womb. And a hard arm caught her round the neck, swung her off her feet and laid her gently behind a rock.

"You're crazy!" hissed Wulf, pressing her down with his arm "What are you playing at?"

"I have to see it with my own eyes."

"Then look!"

There to the east where the red-tiled roofs of Dalgunch should have risen proudly to meet the sky, there was nothing. Twenty-four nights since it had been fired. Not a look-out post, not a parapet remained.

"Why was it never properly fortified?" she demanded.

"Because it was ringed by defensive Duns. And the Kings were strong. Until Garnard."

Since her eyes could not pierce the morning haze, Tansen sent her mind winging across the tops of the trees. Where was Reatta? Had her low-lying chamber escaped the fire? And there came a knowing that the Dark Force was still in possession of Dalgynch.

"I can't believe it!" she whispered.

"You'd better! Ecfrith's scouts have seen us."

"She stared where Wulf pointed and saw the glint of mail passing a clump of trees by the water."

"What should we do?"

"You're going to your kin. You've Ean's bairn to deliver. On your mount and ride! And don't wait for me!"

She knew then that Wulf was going to divert the horsemen on a tough barrel-legged garron with a heart as big as his own.

As she and Verna distanced themselves from Dalgynch, there were few signs as yet that the Angles were over-lords. Except that folk straightened from their field-work calling for news, as anxious as the ewes that bleated to their lambs across the foothills.

Next day at the start of a long slow twilight, sick with constant riding, every bone in their bodies aching, they rounded a hunched hill and saw the thatches of the Pitbervie farmstead and heard the grind and thump of a butter churn.

Nain, plump and pregnant, bustling out of the dairy, saw them and a load of cheeses went flying.

"You!" she cried. "You've a cheek to come back here, you Dane-lover!"

Tansen stared at her out of eyes dazed with exhaustion and slowly pushed her hood back off her head.

Then the bairns came running and there was a flurry of dismounting and hugging and kissing and marvelling at how they had grown. And two sisters, bright and blossoming, yet drawing back shyly as they recognised her.

And one face that was missing.

"Where's Fawn? Where's my doe-eyed Fawn?" Tansen cried, looking round.

Fionna, a bundle of fun, a roly-poly body on unsteady legs, that used to trip her unfailingly into the nearest cow's pancake.

"She's dead!" Nain said bluntly, straightening from gathering the cheeses. "She kept crying for you at night. Then it went into a cough." She held her hand at her back, pushing her stomach forward. "Did you not hear her call on you with her dying breath? Did you never think of us in those great Feasting Halls down south?"

Tansen reeled as though she had been struck.

"I had to go!" she cried, spreading pleading hands towards them. "You all know that! But I loved Fawn dearly."

"Then where were you when it came to the washing of linen, the sponging and wiping and feeding. And holding a wee bairn's head while she coughed up her lungs!"

"Oh, stop it, Nain! I'd have come if I'd known." Her despairing hands clutched her head.

"You were too busy kicking your legs up to a Prince! Little you cared!"

"You could have sent for me!" she moaned.

"Tansen?" It was Deva, drawn from the orchard by Nain's shouting, her face pale and etched with bitter lines. "It is you. Why have you come back?"

"To drop that yellow-haired brat in her belly! Why else?" Nain threw over her shoulder.

"You're my kin!" cried Tansen, stricken by the venom in their voices.

"Kin!" Deva spat out the word. "You chose the Queen for your kin. We don't want you and your Dane-spawn here! You'll bring the Angles down on top of us!"

And Tansen ran blindly into the night gulping in deep quick breaths to still her sobbing. She followed the sound of the stream, sure-footed on the familiar banks in the silvery darkness. In the water-meadow beasts blundered away from her, panicking as the wet mud pulled at their hooves. And she flung her arms round a great sycamore tree and screamed her anguish and guilt into the night, tearing her throat raw.

And she called on Fawn, on Leone, on Grannie Bea. On Baran, on Çynon, on Dela and Maga and Malorc, all her loved ones on the other side to witness her grief at the great wrong she had done in deserting them for an Angle.

Her tears flowed like rain. Then when the weeping had stilled she felt a sort of peace invading her body. A sort of healing creeping up through the soles of her feet from the humped roots, seeping through the stuff of her cloak from the unyielding trunk. A sort of promise as she looked up through the black tracery of boughs above her head. As though the sap was rising and the buds bursting and the seeds falling. And all would pass in time. And her lost kin were still there. And the Guiding Ones. And the love of the Great White Spirit.

All the vacant places of her body became filled with a strange calm. Even when a hand descended on her shoulder and she glimpsed silvered gold hair and two arms crossed over her breast imprisoning her.

"Lucky I came scouting on foot," Wulf's breath feathered her ear.

"We can't stay here." Her words came out on a long deep sigh.

"I suspected this would happen."

He turned her in his embrace and she felt she could look deep into his heart through his moonlit eyes and read there an understanding and warmth and love that needed no words.

"They despise me," she said as they walked back together.

"They're shit-scared! Can you blame them?"

"You're right. I should never have come! I don't belong here any more. I can't stay."

"You can and will. Take it on the chin, Tansen. Until they've said it all. But they'll find they need us here as much as we need them."

"How?"

"Too much land and too few workers. Am I right?"

"They took over Grannie Bea's pit for extra land to feed our bairns."

"And they'll need a good harvest to pay the new tithes that'll come," said Wulf grimly. "I'll talk to the men."

"Deva's the Clan Mother."

"Then you talk to her. You need somewhere to rest until Ean's son is born."

At that she pushed him away and began to plod back alone. Maybe for her sake, maybe for his own, Wulf had decided that the child was Ean's. But he was talking sense. Until she was delivered she could help to repay Deva for her care of the bairns. And she pushed the thought of the birth from her mind. For her hatred of Ecfrith lay ripening alongside the babe in her womb.

Back at the homestead, Verna stood waiting, leaning at the head of the big stallion.

"A peaceful night to you and yours," Wulf greeted Deva cheerfully. "I see a house there beyond the compost mound and it's needing a thatch. Will you let us use it?"

"And a stretch of fallow meadow below the old homestead that we could work," added Tansen.

Deva looked dubious. Nain opened her sulky mouth.

And that was the moment Verna chose to slide neatly down the stallion's foreleg to the ground.

"Sheer exhaustion!" snapped Nain. "Ill-treated till she can bear it no longer!" And she carried Verna gently in to lie beside her hearth.

So Tansen locked herself into the wheel of the days and the needs of the land. And now and again she would hear the laughter of her sisters rise from the meadows. And she would rear her head to delight in the wide space of light and sky and would long to dance in a whirl of skirts and plaits again. And knew she would never again slip away at the bright coming of the moon to meet the lads from across the stream, for all that she had only seventeen cycles of the seasons behind her.

When she felt the first pain of labour rip through her womb, she was filled with gladness that her time had come. She leaned on her hoe, waiting till the sharpness passed. Below, Wulf, warm in the noonday sun, had thrown off his new pigskin jacket and whistled as he cut through the fresh soil with the simple wooden ard he had made himself. A bonnie mess he had made of ploughing at first!

A growing need came upon her to move and she chopped fiercely at the dry earth. If only Deva had let them have a goat to eat the thistles. But at least she had let them stay. As well she might. They had repaid her ten-fold in labour. Tansen glanced along the neat rows of curling greenery, their roots swelling in the deep dark earth. And pressed on the growing ache at her back, exulting, before the next pain hit her.

This son was in a hurry. Thank Bride she would soon be free of him!

Verna came, lazing along from the bee-skips, swinging a bucket in either hand. Tansen had found Grannie Bea's old bee-boles in the dykes and had inserted new plaited wicker skips. Now Tansen leaned to breathe in the sweet smell of creamy wax cut from the skip and the dark oozing syrup.

"That should sweeten Deva's temper." She dipped in her finger.

"Frothed whey with ripe fruits," she sighed, remembering. "Mead fermented with meadowsweet, plantain and mint. Salmon baked in honey."

"We'll be lucky if she gives us the wax for a candle."

Verna saw the sweat gleam on Tansen's lip and brow.

"Is it time?"

The next spasm brought Tansen to her knees, gasping, her head straining back. And when it lessened she rose, gripping the hoe till her knuckles showed white. And set out, pacing along the line of beans, thinking that they ought to be staked soon, step by slow step towards her bed.

As she lifted the cauldron to set it on its tripod, she yelled out at the tearing agony inside her.

Then Verna was there, looming out of a darkness that came and went. And later Wulf, holding her arms. And in her pain he became Ecfrith, wrenching her legs apart while a monster tore its way out of her flesh. And long afterwards she awoke and found herself clean and fresh. And felt her abdomen and cried a little with relief when she found it was flat.

And from beyond the wicker partition, Wulf singing a Danish lullaby. And she cried out weakly.

"Don't ... sing ... that!"

The song stopped. There was the creak of a rocker. Wulf's face slipped like a rising moon over the partition. "Are you ready! Here comes Hagnar Hairybreeks, son of Eanfrith!"

And she screamed out "No! He's an Angle! Take him away!"

"His mother's Pretani so he's all Pretani. You'll have to feed him. He's hungry."

And Ecfrith came again pawing and slobbering over her breasts. The tide of revulsion that swept through her brought a wetness flowing between her thighs.

"Don't you want to see him." Verna came, opening a hole in a squirming bundle.

"No! Take him away!" she cried again, sickness spurting up into her throat.

"I'll take him to Nain. She's bulging with milk."

And Tansen turned her face to the wall and wept. And slept.

And only woke when the partition was pushed roughly aside and the brightness of the sun filled the house.

"A fine squawking you made in the end!" Nain stood there, her lips twisting, a boy-bairn on each arm. "And now you want to be like a Queen and have a wet-nurse. When are you planning to ride off again?"

The sooner the better. Tansen shut her eyes. She felt the mattress sag as Nain sat on the edge.

"Which boy is it? Wouldn't you like to know?"

A faint smell of mingled milk and sweat made her stomach revolt.

"Is it the big bouncy one that yells and gobbles at my breast. Or the little runt that mews and spews."

Oh, Bride, so he was puny and sickly. And his own mother could not bear to look on him. Tears rained out of the corners of her eyes and wet her hair.

If he was Ean's and had gone full-term he might be small because of the days when she had hidden hungry under a tree and eaten roots. Her breasts ached with unshed milk.

But if he was small, he might be Ecfrith's and had come early, not fully grown. Her heart thudded violently.

Even if she could bring herself to look on his face, the family features would look back at her and she would never know which son of Aethelfrith had sired him.

Nain stirred and rose, angry at her lack of response.

"You're unnatural, you are! Not fit to be a Clan Mother. far less a Queen!"

The babies fretted at the malice in her voice.

"Time you got up and shook yourself." Nain paused at the door. "The geese are back at the loch! So there's plucking and pie-making to be done. And eggs to be found for the Beltane caudle. Unless you and your fledgling want to starve."

CHAPTER FORTY ONE

Tansen rose from her bed and made sure she was there, balancing a tray of Beltane bannocks, when the beasts were rounded up to climb the rutted path to the Beltane hill. From far and near the festive folk and their herds converged on the flattened ridge, stepping over the ditch and into the Circle of Unending Life.

Until the Circle seethed and bubbled, dust steaming upwards, enveloping the two towering Beltane fires and their topmost crowns of greenery. The Beltane Festival was always the same. Chaotic and joyous, riotous and merry, unruly and rumbustious.

Three long-stepping Druad had come loping over the hill before dawn. Their practised hands swiftly kindled the fires with the magic twigs of nine different trees. Their incantations were drowned in a snarling, yelping, bellowing turbulence as cattle, tails high, blundered through the Saining Gate. A scatter of sheep and goats, bedraggled and bleating, daubed with dye went next. Crates that squawked with a feather-brained frenzy. Five trundling sows and their squealing piglets. Seven mares who had seen it all before, nosing their foals through. And Ean's hunting stallion following, composed, swishing his tail.

Now the dairymaids, giggling, faces fresh-washed in dew, ladles and cans clanking from their belts, slung their bed-rolls on their backs and set off to the grazing grounds. And the young hunters, fishermen and farmers, chaffing the youngest girls, new to maidenhood, leaping before them to help settle them in their bothies. And cocky herdboys, rending the sky with their bear-horns and wolf-bells, inspired by the presence of their youthful heroes.

Ignoring the smell of stewed goose and the pedlar with his dolls and bells and rattles, Tansen stood, hand on hip, where two metal-workers had set up a wooden bench. Their practised tongues unrolled the latest news along with their packs.

"The sherriffs are out. All over Fib. Measuring every pit of land and putting marks on tablets."

"Counting every seed as it goes into the ground, so the folk can't hide half the harvest at tribute-time."

"Reporting it all to a Bishop Trumwine from York, sitting safely across the Fiorth at Abercorn."

"Fearful to come himself in case he raises his crozier some day and comes face to face with his own head stuck on top of it."

That brought a grim laugh from the Clan Brothers testing daggers and spear-heads and fish-hooks.

Tansen elbowed her way through.

"Will the Veniconie in Fib not make a stand?"

"Ach, they're too near Dalgynch to rebel. The Angles have rebuilt the Citadel and surrounded it with five thousand men to keep the Boar Clan locked into the Howe of Fif in case their breeks get too big for them."

"Ecfrith's gone back south to keep tabs on his earls. But his brother Owin remains in Dalgynch to command the army here. 'Druad-killer' they call him." He gestured with his thumb at the reciting Druad. "Yon spell-makers had better kilt up their skirts and hop smartish back into hiding. Their pals at Pitversie were thrown into the Room of Writs and burned."

"Only the Pillars of the Halls of Learning were left, standing up like sticks of charcoal."

"The Arch-Drui? Now there was a thing! How did the Angles know about the sanctuary at Dunino? First place Owin went. And the Druad waiting, calmly and serenely, gathered around Marten."

Tansen pictured them, illumined by the knowledge that this savage death would be but another milestone on the road towards spiritual attainment.

"Singing spears, whistling arrows, biting arrows. And in the end, Owin had a Christian Cross carved into the wall of the Gorge at Dunino. So that the blame of the massacre would fall on the Church and not on himself."

It was no use asking why, Tansen knew. The Angles would devastate every place that might become a centre for rebellion. Yet what would happen to the knowledge the each Druad laboured for twenty years to store in their memories? What would happen if the living tradition disappeared? And she saw Pitversie like a smoking desert beside the waters of the Tay. And a desert in the hearts of the humble folk.

Tansen's mind fastened on the one person who knew every Drui haunt in the land. Reatta who had sworn to learn their secrets and then destroy them.

It was as if a spark from the fire at Pitversie had lit a flame inside her. It burned steadily, white-hot hatred at its centre, red-tinged with anger. Calm and still, reflected in a pool. Fire and water. The flame within the pool.

Tansen knew then that she must go north to find a place where the seeds of rebellion could grow. And she must leave the child.

The Druad were having difficulty lighting the need-fire so that folk could rekindle their hearths and dispel the Dark Forces for another cycle of the year. Sweating they twirled the axle pole, feeding the sparks with agaric from old beech trees. The fire which usually sprang up strongly as a gift from the Fertile Ones was sluggish this Beltane. Women moved within the Circle to make sure all legs were uncrossed, laces untied, hair unplaited, all knots that would impede the free current of Power. And Tansen turned away wondering if it was her dark thought about leaving the child that was hindering the flow of power.

Verna stood rocking the bairn in a fleecy shawl made from wool that she had plucked herself from the sheep, washed, dyed and spun. Tansen stood a little apart.

"I can't describe how I feel, Verna." Her voice came out in breathy broken spurts. "It's as though he never was a part of me. Never came out of my body. I try to love him but I only remember the pain and the darkness. And Ecfrith." She wrung her hands. "I feel so helpless. Caught in a tide of pain and guilt that will darken my heart for ever."

And softly, so as not to wake the child, Verna spoke to her.

"Women feel guilt more than men. It's because we're the life-givers, I suppose. We try to look ahead. To shield our loved ones from harm. And when they're hurt, we feel we've failed. But everyone has to do the best they can at the time."

She paused to hush a fretful wail.

"But don't let me hear you say that you're helpless! You're stronger and wiser now. Through your own grief you'll understand better the burdens of others. And you, with your gifts from the gods, must work for others. Doing more, giving more to folk, than those of us who sit rocking a cradle."

"But our future lies in the cradle!" cried Tansen.

"Stop tormenting yourself! Nain's tongue is only sharp for you. Wulf and I understand why your love for the bairn is tainted. The boy will never know. Nain's heart will embrace him, never fear."

Verna was right! The boy was better with Nain who could give him heart-whole love. Maybe in time the guilt would lessen. If she held his well-being in her thoughts for a little time each day.

"Will you come with me?" she asked Verna.

Verna smiled, the sun glinting in the fluffy strands of her hair, silver like the bonds of friendship that had been spun between them.

"You don't need me. I'm tired of travel. I'd hold you back from whatever you have to do."

"I'd like to give you something for all you've done for me. But I've nothing left to give."

"You took me from Dalgynch and brought me here. You gave me my freedom. You've given me a child to watch over. Go on your way and may the Guardians guide you."

Tansen stepped away, an unbearable sadness slowing her steps, until she found Deva and her brother Aith standing in her way.

"It's time you moved on," Aith announced flatly, setting his foot on an outcrop.

"And leave Deva with the burden of bairns to feed and tithes to pay?" Tansen still needed to be sure.

"Bairns? Your sisters went up with the cattle. The boys are herding already. They're earning their keep."

A sudden rush of loneliness overtook Tansen. She was an outsider now looking back into the Circle of Life. If she stretched out her fingers there was no one who would clasp them, no one who needed her.

"We need to plan ahead to pay this tribute. Our seeds weren't counted. We can still hide a good half of the harvest underground."

"And the fewer adults to feed, the more we can store."

Wulf and she had done the hardest work, breaking new ground. And her kin would reap it. It was fitting.

"Besides when the sherriffs come they'll know who you are. And that man." Deva was crumbling a bannock, throwing every second piece over her shoulder to keep wolves and foxes from the hens for the next year. "They'll know that's Eanfrith's bairn. And what King in his right mind is going to let a nephew grow up to rival him. If you go, Nain has twins and none to say different."

"If you stay we'll all suffer for harbouring you. Think on it." Aith stamped away to begin the ceremony of Breaking the Caudle Cake.

"There's one thing more," said Deva drily, placing her hands on her hips. "Your sisters will never know from me they've royal blood in them."

"But you must tell them, Deva. They'll find out. Folk remember Grannie Bea. They ought to know their ancestry and have pride in it."

Deva's shoulders wriggled with satisfaction.

"Knowing didn't bring you any happiness!" And she ran to whack a randy young goat who was jumping on the nannies.

They all wanted her gone. And fast. She had heard the half-muffled whispers about her pert sulky face and proud gait. It was because of what she had become. Somebody different. She had reached out beyond the world as they knew it, following a star that was hidden to their eyes. They would never understand her. She didn't belong here. She had no kin any more.

The cone of one of the fires collapsed with a burst of flame and it was as though all the pain and joy she had known merged in one upward flash, a rising flame, clear and bright-edged. And she knew she still had the white-hot ambition within her to be another Caterin. And the opportunity if she could bring herself to take it.

She raised her eyes to the horizon. And turning followed it round. For the horizon was also the Circle. And wherever she would go, she would be within the Infinite Circle, the source and the ending, like the cycle of the moon, the day, the year, the cycle of time itself.

She found Wulf, handing out his ale-bottle as custom demanded, talking with the Bull-man, newly come from servicing the cows of the Taezalie clan in the north.

"Did you hear any word of the stone-masons on your travels?" he was asking, somewhat thickly. "The clan of Fael?"

CHAPTER FORTY TWO

The Bull-man wiped his mouth on his sleeve.

"Fael, you say? The chiel that carves Ancestor Stones? Now what did I hear?"

He screwed up his eyes, till they were almost lost in round rosy clean-shaven cheeks and studied Wulf through the slits.

Wulf offered his flask again.

"Aye, that's it. They were lacking customers. No bed and board for us travelling folk when there's tithes to pay come Samhain. So Fael's growing his own food." An eyebrow quirked at Wulf. "Thinking of having a stone carved, are you?"

"I could chisel it myself. Fael's my father."

"Your father, eh?" He swigged again, a wary eye on Wulf.

"And he has a parcel of yellow-haired Pretani sons like myself," Wulf agreed. The skirl of pipes had drawn the crowd away.

The Bull-man edged closer, rosier than ever below his gleaming white pate. "All I'm saying is there's something brewing up Burghead way. My guess is that's where you'll find Fael." He melted away leaving Wulf looking at Tansen, his face still and careful.

"If I went now I'd be back in time for the harvest," he said.

"Oh, come on, Wulf! I'm coming with you."

"Not with a child! Oh, I see. You're leaving him, casting him off, glad to be rid of him?"

"Nain wants him! And Verna's staying." No, she thought, I'm not going to feel guilty. "I warn you, Wulf! Don't push me any further."

Wulf swung through the festive crowd and stopped to look down on Nain, sitting smiling on a mound, an infant on each arm. It could have been his own mother with himself and Ean at the breast. And what a bond had been forged between them then! Gods, he would have liked a hand in bringing up Ean's son. He would have liked to be the one who threw him up on his naming day to catch the breath of Dagda.

He turned away, clenching his fists and striking them on his forehead, knowing he was fooling himself. Ean or Ecfrith? The question would always torment him. That base secret ought to be lost in the darkness of time. Better to leave the boy where he was wanted.

Yet the old Wise Woman had foretold that one day he'd be a King. And he could believe it. The boy was in the line of Aethelfrith, whoever was his father. And he'd have a milk-brother of his own. Yet here he'd grow up without a smear on his name. Better that Tansen and he should cut loose from the past. Maybe have a child of their own some day. And bring him up to be a stone-mason.

He saw that Tansen was watching him, her head tilted in that challenging way of hers. He was fooling himself again. She'd never stay with him. She was born for greater things. Aye, but it would be something to have her with him for a little while yet. To share in her boundless love, her exquisite body, her enchanting sense of fun. He strode across, pulled her into his arms and kissed her.

"By Thunder, my brothers are going to stare when I arrive with my milk-white swan with wreaths of rowan berries for hair."

So when the horse-traders came by next day it took one, no two, no three gold discs from Wulf's purse and Tansen scarcely saw the twinkle of the hand that whisked them under a cloak. It was arranged that they would ride north at first light.

The sleeping hut was awash with Verna's snores when they crept out to find places in the traders' cart. They followed the Tay to its mother loch dotted with islands built by the crannog folk. Tansen and Wulf left the dealers arguing over a pair of mules with the men on the loch-side and waded across the causeway to where the women beckoned.

"What's new? Any sign of the sherriff yet?" they asked, looking askance at Wulf's yellow hair.

Nothing that they could tell was comforting.

They were offered bannocks with beakers of milk. But the sheep and goats that grazed on the lochside had left their stink in their night-time byre that surrounded the living quarters.

An old woman laughed.

"You're not the first to wonder why we live out here on the loch beside our beasts. But listen."

Water gurgled and slapped on the stones.

"We were all suckled to that sound. And the reek of beasts is the smell of home."

Home.

Tansen offered her tainted bannock to a staring bairn that yelled and ran, straight into a clip round the ear.

"Wheesht! The Wild Red Man of the Mountains'll play hurley with your head!"

"Liath? Liath of the Fiery Thatch?" Tansen asked, instantly alert.

The woman caught the glance that flashed between Wulf and Tansen and her eyes glazed with studied vacancy. She shrugged.

"Och, no, no. His body's a queer red shade but they say his hair's green as seaweed and he rides on the White Kelpie."

Outside the breeze came hurtling straight up the loch sending rippling paths across its surface. The hills that rose on either side were not high enough to keep the sun out. Jubilant curlews trilled on the far shore and nearby a mother eider chuckled cosily to her brood. And Tansen knew it was not only safety from bears and wolves that kept the folk on their crannog. But this feeling of confidence and space she had that would vanish when she and Wulf reached the shore.

Barely stopping to dry her feet on the grass she gripped Wulf's arm.

"That's twice we've caught a whisper of rebellion. Liath, the Caledonie, must be plotting in the north!" Her words tumbled out breathlessly. "Maybe he's at Burghead! But folk will never breathe a whisper of it to you with your yellow hair."

"And you're itching to join him." Wulf shook his head. "It's too chancy. He and his clan can't do it alone. They'll be decimated. Then what happens to the folk who cast in their lot with him."

"The clans will rally. They need someone like Liath to lead them."

"He's too rash. Fine for surprising a few tithe-collectors. But Ecfrith's learned all about ambushes in the glens of Dal Riata. And he's leading a trained army now, for all it seemed like a rabble at first."

What Wulf said was true. Yet Tansen felt hope stirring in her heart. Hope was such a little word yet if you had no hope, you had no motivation, no dream, no inspiration, nothing.

Tansen paused to wave back at the crannog folk.

"So many different kinds of folk we are," she said. "Individuals and proud of it! With a healthy dislike of being told what to do and how to do it."

"Don't take pride in that," said Wulf. "Caledonie and crannog-folk, hunters and farmers will have to learn to take orders before they can unite to throw out the Angles."

Tansen was silent, thinking of Burghead, sure that if the gods had a task for her, she would find it in Burghead.

The next day while the traders went about their business Tansen and Wulf borrowed ponies and followed the ruts of an old cart-track. They came out above the tree-line, high on top of the world, on grass with patches of brown heather cut by deer-paths and pony tracks. The white band of a river flowed far below broadening into a loch shot through with silver ripples. A curving sickle of pale-gold sand brought the land round into a wooded spit.

"This is the kind of countryside that can be used as a weapon!" she cried.

"It was done before. In Roman times. They hid a cow in a bog. And as the invincible legionaries sank slowly up to their necks, Whoops! the hills came alive with arrows and their supper was whisked away."

Wulf sat as if entranced. And Tansen fell silent, knowing he had forgotten her in a sudden awareness of a oneness with the whole vast panorama.

From the far side of the valley mountains rose, grass-green at their bases and patchy with dark-green trees soaring to purple-washed, majestic heights. Beyond more and more peaks reared and dipped in clear strong lines against the sky, slivers of snow arrowing downwards from their summits.

Wulf dismounted and stretched his arms wide as if to encompass the whole sky.

"This place is timeless." He spoke as if to himself. "There's a knowing here, a certainty that the land will go on for ever. Even the wounds left by quarries in the hillside there are healing, hidden by dark straight-stemmed saplings."

Tansen breathed in air that was as clear and cool as spring water and looked down into glens that were deep and shadowed by the great peaks.

"The day we send the Angles packing," she agreed, "they'll go without having left any mark on the land."

Deer browsed, seemingly standing still yet moving with incredible swiftness across the grass until they were hidden by the fold of a stream that leapt downhill in a series of eager waterfalls.

Wulf caught her hands and drew her to share his newfound happiness with him.

"All my life I followed Ean. Trained beside him, served in his retinue. Never once did I look around and know my place in the landscape and say 'Well, here I am! This is me! What do I want to do with my life!'"

They laughed together at the joy of it and watched the shaggy red cattle, far below, drinking knee-deep in a quiet curve of the river. Yet these same cattle would be culled for tribute soon.

Tansen did not have the timeless patience of the true-born peasant. Not while Reatta betrayed the Druad and played with her fake magic and Ecfrith and Talorc prepared to grind folk beneath their feet. And there came such a wild jumping of the blood in her veins that she wanted to shout her frustration to the sky.

She caught Wulf round the waist and swung him.

"Let's take off now and find your kin. These horse-traders are too slow. Let's cut across the mountains to the Garry and north to Burghead. Even if we go on foot, let's go."

"We'll do it," Wulf cried, infected by her exuberance. "The weather's fine. There are salmon in the streams and grouse on the moor. I'll take a net in my pack."

So they left, striding out with pleasure in a rhythmic glide of limb and muscle, with only the sun to guide their path.

Then one day they came over the brow of a hill and saw the Moray Firth stretch from west to east with the broad rocky headland of Burghead jutting out before them in a curve, protecting the few ships that lay at anchor in the bay. One, two, three massive walls at its neck cut off the headland from the land. There was a fourth wall with an entrance gate, two enormous towers tapering inwards at the top, solid faces without entry or outlet like the great brochs the cheiftains used to build, partly for protection, partly from vanity.

"What price Dalgynch? Or Gefrin?" cried Tansen when she found her voice. "This fort beats them all!"

"It's massive! Must be built on solid rock!" Wulf sounded impressed. "And look, on the seaward side! Men strengthening the ramparts. That's where I'll find my kin!"

"Look at the pennants!" she cried. "Moray and Ros, Catness and Orcades. They're all here! And a dolphin!"

Tansen drew in her breath. Twice she had seen the dolphin sign. Both times it had been Dale who had used it. Now a shiver trembled across her skin. She had sped north with Wulf, believing there would be a welcome from her Northern Taezalie kin, that now was the time to proclaim herself a Daughter of Caterin, a Queen to lead an army against the Angles. But Dale was here. A man whose very presence spelt treachery and failure. A cold hand seemed to close round her heart.

Exhilerated Wulf ran, following the contour of hill and stream eastward with Tansen following step by slow step. When he stopped within sight of a few fresh-built timber houses, she stopped and waited. A woman sang as she worked a loom, a bairn at her feet. A lanky-legged, long-tongued puppy yipped a warning. The heddle stopped, setting the loom-weights shuddering. With her toe the woman urged the toddler by his backside into an open doorway before she turned.

Wulf cupped his hands round his mouth.

"The peace of the All-Mother this fine day. Will your man be wanting a fine sturdy plough-horse?"

"My man is his own sturdy plough-horse," she cried, screwing up her eyes. Three women came to cluster at her back, knives glinting, half-hidden in their skirts. A boy scudded out of a back doorway, fear at his heels, to warn the men.

"I know that voice!" An older woman elbowed the others aside. "That's my son! Wulf, is it really you?"

"Ragnie!"

Wulf went leaping over the tussocks into her outsretched arms. Tansen picked up the net and the two plump ptarmigan he had thrown at her feet. And waited, thrusting aside the bleak memory of her own home-coming.

There was a smell of fresh lime-wash about the houses and fine knotwork carved on the lintels. The women ran to feed the fires and swing the cooking pots round to catch the heat.

Up from the harbour came five young men. And stood astounded. Then came leaping and yelling, twirling axes round their heads. And an older man, Fael, it must be, came more slowly leading an ox cart that held new-cut timber. But his slowness was not due to illness or old age for he was well-built and bronzed. It was his way, a steady plod. The lines of his face were strong as if hewn like an image in granite. Granite with a glint of wetness, deftly flicked from his cheek-bone by a finger.

And there was Ragnie, apple-cheeked, smiling a welcome at Tansen, holding warm water in a washing bowl and a cloth.

"So you're farmers now," Wulf said after supper, loosening his belt and laces and stretching back. "Did I see a cow and goats in the ruck of the cliff?" "Farmers? My men?" laughed Ragnie. "We manage!" Fael stopped her next remark short, rubbing chisel-scarred hands together.

Wulf had told his own story in great bursts between mouthfuls of ptarmigan. But nothing about Tansen or how they had met. Ragnie smiled encouragement at Tansen.

"Maybe you can teach us travelling folk a thing or two about growing crops?"

"That she can. And she makes the best harvest bannocks in Alba."

The tender secret look that Tansen threw to Wulf warmed Ragnie's heart.

"We'll make you our Clan Mother come Lugnasad," said Ragnie to honour her.

Ragnie watched the girl with the proud calm bearing slowly turn her head. The green eyes of a certain family were honest and clear, fresh and vital as a new-opened leaf, but shadowed by sorrow past. Tansen shook her head.

"Lug's Festival honours the foster-mother," she said.

Ragnie gave a slight nod. This was Eanfrith's woman, right enough. And Royal. She wouldn't stay. Yet Wulf would remain. And maybe it was better that way. But she gave the time-honoured welcome to a son's woman.

"You and I will not let the grass grow between our two houses."

Wulf gave up contemplating the myriads of stars and rolled on his side.

"So! It's all happening in the stronghold down there, is it?"

The ale-cups went round. A crunch of shingle in the darkness below and a young man threw his plaid on the grass, his eyes straying towards Arnie, the prettiest of Wulf's sisters who ran with a brimming flagon and a cup.

"Finlae, son of Horn, chief of the northern Taezalie," announced Fael. "He'll tell you."

Tansen folded her hands round her knees and kept quiet about her kinship with the Taezalie.

Finlae shot a grin of pure delight at the newcomers and drank in quick eager gulps.

"Ecfrith's next move must be to capture all the strongholds on the eastern coast-line and round the shoulder of Alba."

"Hold on!" Wulf sat up. "Cadwallon didn't leave much of a fleet for Ecfrith to inherit."

"True. It's his brother Owin's task to refit it. And Talorc's to provide timber from the King's Estates. Give them the cold season to build a fleet. By Beltane they'll be ready to sail."

Finlae rose and with his toe drew the huge shoulder of Alba in the dust and prodded it with a stick to show each stronghold on the line north.

"Dunnottar?" queried Wulf. "They'll not take that one easily. It's perched on top of a sheer cliff."

"And joined to land by a narrow path of stone. If a hundred Angles encamp on that neck of land, the food in the fort will run out in a week. Then one after the other the fortresses will fall to the Angles like ripe plums. Only Burghead's strong enough to withstand a siege."

"And we daren't fail!" Eirik, Wulf's younger brother, stopped whittling great chunks out of a log held between his knees and raised twinkling eyes. "Burghead's the gateway to Moray and the North. If it falls nothing will prevent Owin from taking Craig Phadrig and sailing down Loch Ness. And then Ecfrith has all Alba in his grip."

"I'm hoping you'll stay and work with us, lad!" cried Fael. "Look down there! We're adapting the natural terracing at the end of the promontory to make an upper and a lower enclosure within the fort. Must be done before the neep tides and northerly gales force us to stop."

Wulf rose, his back turned to them, and looked down at the torches that flared on the walls of the fort.

"I've no building skills, Father. You know that." But there was hope in his voice.

"Then give us your labour till you acquire them." Finlae tweaked Arnie's plait for more ale. "There are new jetties to be built and extensions to the store-rooms."

"Tomorrow you can start on the wall of the upper ward." Fael said. "I want them fitting till there's naught but a hairline crack between them. And when it's finished we'll embellish the face of it with the symbols of the great northern clans. And the Bull, the great Royal Bull."

"And where's the Eagle of the Caledonie?" Tansen asked. "I didn't see their pennant. I thought they were here with you."

"Not them! They're safely tucked away behind the White Mountains. A day's ride from where the Garry joins the Spey. At a place called Lynchattie. And I can't see the Angles going louping up the Spey after them. Discount that clan. Our business here is serious. We don't want the Caledonie charging over the mountains on shelties, every man thinking he's Cu Chulainn born again."

"It beats me why they trust us dandelion-heads anywhere near their defences," said Wulf.

"Man, they have to," Fael chuckled. "I've worked there on and off since I was a lad. And you'll note Ragnhild's disguised her fancy Danish name by chopping it in half. But you wait till you see inside that fort tomorrow. Walls so thick there's ample storage space inside them for ships' gear. Last time I was here we extended the space right inside the fortress with massive oak beams as thick as a man's trunk." Fael clapped Wulf on the back. "I'll make a mason of you yet, boy, like your brothers."

"Maybe he likes wood better!" cried Eirik. "There's a whole fleet of ships, waiting to be repaired!"

"A fleet? Where is it?" Tansen, elbows on knees was listening avidly, missing nothing. "There's just a pickle of small craft in the bay. Yet this is the finest harbour in Alba."

"Old Mal rounded up the twelveand fourteen-benchers and herded them off to the Orcades."

"Why? There's no timber there for repairs."

"So it's the last place Owin would look for them. They slip across here in the darkness to be re-fitted."

"And there's a couple duc tonight. So I'll be off." Eirik sheathed his knife at his belt. "For you. To say welcome to Burghead."

He handed Tansen his wood-carving, a bull on a plinth, still rough and unpolished, but unmistakeably the Royal Bull and the symbol of the fortress at Burghead. The firelight glinted on the bulging sinews and on the horns of the lowered head. She looked at Ragnie and there was a sadness in Ragnie's blue eyes. As though she could read Tansen's heart. Tansen set the bull beside her bundle.

"We were told you lived in some sort of cave," she said.

"It was our summer home when we used to travel," said Ragnie. "Come I'll show you."

They climbed down to a little cove where a cave was set well back in the cliff.

"The locals call it the Sculptors' Caves. But this time I said, since we're staying for a spell, we'll have proper houses well away from the blare of war-horns." Ragnie laughed. "It's the tap of hammer and chisel that's music to my ears. It's the dust of stones that runs in my veins. Not the blood of the North Humbrians."

"And the sherriffs will have a long road to travel to tithe us," Fael chuckled.

The cave was roomy, the walls dry. Here and there apprentice stone-masons had tried their hand at drawing, low down, but reaching higher as they grew tall. In the middle was a hearth and an iron stand with arms.

"It'll still move freely once the rust's scraped off and a bit of sheep's grease rubbed in."

Stone instead of wood had shaped the furniture. Great upright slabs divided the cave into cubicles for families. Four slabs made a bed with a niche cut in the wall for a lamp. A huge dresser on one wall to hold clothes and another near the fire still holding pots and bowls.

"I'd like fine to sleep here with the sea air blowing over me," said Tansen. She needed to distance herself from these caring folk and the longing for her own hearth was strong.

"Sea-grasses make a fine springy mattress. We've enough extra fleeces and eider cushions to make you snug. Look, Fael, my draughtscreen's still here."

Ragnie threw her plaid on a seat at the back of the cave. Slabs were set on either side for armrests and a larger one to shield her from the wind.

"I used to sit here and sing my grandchildren to sleep," Ragnie said wistfully.

Tansen was already opening her bundle and setting the Royal Bull on top of the dresser.

CHAPTER FORTY THREE

The next morning Tansen stood at the door of the cave and bared her arms to the warming air. Wulf's eyes followed her gaze towards the fort.

"I knew it. You're leaving me."

"Some day. Not yet." She felt light-limbed as though she stood in the palm of a goddess, a Fateful One who was waiting to waft her in the direction she was to go. "I've to find a way inside the fort first."

"You, a green-eyed Taezalie woman from the south, descended from Caterin. They'll welcome you with flowers."

She shook her head.

"Then why don't you take a hoe and work with Ragnie in the turnip strip?"

Tansen seemed not to have heard him. He threw his jacket over one shoulder and went with a heavy heart to find Fael. No man would ever bind her. But some day she might need the quiet love he could offer her.

Tansen, swinging her sandals by the straps, half-walked, half-waded along the shore to Burghead.

At the first rampart wall she was stopped by a guard. The Entrance Gate where the dolphin pennant swooped and dived seemed very far away

Yet when she asked for Dale, the Briton, she was directed to a door just inside the outer perimeter wall. A huge barrel-bath took up all the space in the tiny room. Softly she took the rough woollen drying wrap and the brush of birch twigs from the waiting lad and sent him out.

"Who's paying you now?" she whispered. "Someone who likes his spies to smell of mint and honeysuckle?"

Dale grabbed the cloth and rubbed the suds from his eyes. He looked up at her and his jaw widened. It was clean-shaven again, the black beard had gone.

"Was your last pay-master too mean?" she went on, trying to rile him. "I suppose, for a mercenary, a change of lords is the only way to promotion."

"Do you know," he said blandly. "They had to bring this water up the cliff-face pail by pail? There's not a well in the whole of this vast fortress."

The water ebbed and flowed at his dark chest-pelt leaving a tide-mark of green mint leaves. His body had matured since she had seen him last, yet it was still lean and honed to athletic perfection.

As he leaned over to take the birch brush from her hand she saw again the signs of his past, the lash-weals on his back, the pale slave-mark at his neck.

"You took a long time getting here." His teeth flashed as he scraped at his skin.

She was glad he was using the brush or she might have thrown it at his head.

"You lost no time," she snapped. "It's a wonder they allow you to fly your dolphin pennant. Defeated at the Battle of Bannog Burn and turfed out of Dalgynch. You leave a fine trail of failures behind you. Or are you paid to fail?"

At that he rose from the bath, his nakedness commanding the entire cell. Rivulets ran down the planes of his body. Beads of moisture winked from his body-hair.

"A warrior needs time to serve his apprenticeship. Mine was cut short."

"So was your post as bodyguard to me." She threw the wrap over the scars on his back. "At Lleyn you just turned your cowardly back and fled."

There was a brave display of flying limbs and drying cloth and falling moist leaves.

"Actually I was sharing a prison cell with a rat called Onecipherous Philaritus the Fifth. You won't believe me, of course."

"Why should I?" bitterly.

"Because." He stood before her, his naked body compelling her gaze. He had grown in stature. And he was filled with confidence, his movements and voice cool and assured. He had lost the vague and innocent expression that masked his thoughts. Lines of authority were beginning to mark his cheeks and tighten the long linear mouth. Yet the great yellow eyes were the same. Shining a lamp into the hidden places of mind and brain. A dallying soldier would quail before that searing gaze. But was the light in his eyes the glint of greed or ambition? She could not tell.

"Because," he said again, softly. "I'm learning strategy here. How to prepare a fortress against siege. How to build a force that will strike the enemy at the right time. And defeat him."

He was dressing quickly and deftly in a wide-sleeved white tunic and black leather jacket and leggings. His dark hair had grown and as he combed it, it fell into soft curls on his shoulders. Carefully groomed, the shame of his scars hidden, he suddenly looked what he was, a prince from a great family, a man of authority, perhaps even a man of destiny. An explosive combination of youth and vitality.

He lifted her arm and laid the drying wrap across it.

"And you have come in time to be proclaimed Queen of the Northern Pretani. Think how the clans will rally to your pennant."

"I haven't come to be used by a mere mercenary."

Laughing, he straightened from pulling on goatskin half-boots and tying them with scarlet laces. He fastened on a scarlet belt and a sheath holding a fine ivory dagger. With no dolphin on the handle.

"Come, Princess Tansen, and meet Horn, Chieftain of the Taezalie, Commander of Burghead."

"I'll meet him on my own merits. And I want no trumpets blown for me."

"Why? That's always been your ambition, hasn't it"

"Ambition, no," she said. "But when the time comes and someone is needed to stand against Reatta and her Angles, I'll be there."

She left him and went slowly back to the homesteads. Somehow that morning she had been given a sign. And she couldn't lay a finger on it.

Ragnie's tasty rabbit stew, laced with herbs and beans, was eaten out on the grass in the long light evening. Later they left the bairn-minder with her charges and everyone climbed down to where there was a cove lined with sandstone slabs and sand that was grey with stone chippings.

The women settled to one side and unfolded their sewing, holding up tunics, trying them on, embroidering them, gossiping. It went without saying that each stitch held love for a bairn or hope for a lover. The men tapped and chipped and pecked, making the slabs that would decorate the walls of the stronghold once the extensions were finished.

Fael sat on a stone under a tattered awning with a piece of sandstone between his knees. He slanted one crooked eyebrow to where Tansen stood apart watching him as he brushed the old flakes away with his fingers.

"Do we show her the secrets of our trade, Wulf?"

It was the old story. Stone-masons married stone-masons' daughters to keep the craft secrets within the family. And Fael was asking if Wulf and she was going to make a pair-bond that would last.

Without looking at her, Wulf struck a spark and a flame sprang up in the tinder within the square of blackened stones. Ragnie came softly to sit with her new-found son and ply the bellows.

"She knows how to make a man happy and she's true to him," Wulf answered quietly, talking about her as if she had already gone. The charcoal at the heart of the fire glowed on the planes of his face. "But she'll go from me when she has to."

Tansen had felt a hint of the warmth that would enfold her if she forgot who she was and stayed with them. How she would be happed in love and laughter and would rear healthy bairns. And she would have kin and a home and peace at her breast. And have Wulf look at her with that same long slow understanding smile that he now gave her. But a deeper yearning came on her. And she whirled her skirt and climbed over rocks. Until she could no longer feel the bonds of love tugging at her heart.

For she had to leave and go to live in Burghead. There was something waiting there, calling to her in words that she could not make out. She did not know what it was. Only that it must happen.

The air was filled with that magical light of the sweet bright evenings of the season when the day never ends. And Dagda waits beyond the rim of the horizon to catch his ball of light and throw it back again into the sky.

The waves nudging at the pebbles seemed to whisper tales from beyond the sea about men and women who had changed the fate of a people. She pressed her hands together, wanting to make things happen faster, to shape something better out of this disaster that had fallen on her people.

And then she saw it! Far out, a flash from a sleek wet back. And then another. Seals, she thought. Until she saw the fluked tails. And black bodies with white under-bellies thrusting out of the water, hurtling themselves skywards and rolling over and splashing down again in an ecstasy of delight.

"Dolphins!"

And another shoal, closer. She watched, longing to share their joy in the thrust of their fine bodies through the cool cleansing water. And before they had gone from view another shoal, further out, rolling over and over. And another. And they rolled on and on, out to the North Sea, till they were gone. And she was left, pressing her hand to her breast to hold the leap of her heart. An omen! Dale and his dolphin sign? She held her breath, waiting for an answer from the Wise Ones. None came. Only the melodious calling of the shore-birds down by the promontory.

She told herself that an omen did not work unless the opportunity was there to make it work. And went back to where the air was white with a thin dust that settled on hunched shoulders and in the lines of faces, startling white against the sun-bronzed skins.

Fael was flexing his fingers, stiff from wielding the axe. Wulf was laying out a cloth and arranging the chisels neatly graded into sizes.

"I don't know what it is with Kings and Queens," Ragnie said bitterly. "You'd think the seasons couldn't turn without them."

Tansen bowed her head and bit her lip. Why was she different? Why did she have to hurt others to tread a path that seemed to be leading nowhere.

Fael chose a chisel. Wulf laid it on the charcoal and spoke without looking up.

"An army going into battle needs a pennant to follow. A leader, a Queen. A symbol of what they're fighting and dying for."

The fire blurred as Tansen's eyes filled with tears.

Ragnie thumped the bellows until a cloud of smoke and ash set them all coughing and flapping their hands.

"If it's acclamation and fancy robes she wants, forget her, Wulf," Ragnie said with all the anger of a mother whose son is hurt.

"I'm not seeking power," Tansen sought to explain. "I've been a Queen already and paid for it with tears."

Wulf was watching the chisel turn to a coppery-grey.

"She has ambition and energy," he told Ragnie gently. "And skills you cannot understand. And she learns more, all the time. I'll not stand in her way."

Tansen came and looked down on the two fair heads.

"I'm not going as a Queen. But I've work to do down there."

"And none here, I suppose." Blinded by tears Ragnie left, treading on the bellows so that they sighed and squeaked after her.

"I'd have liked it here fine, Wulf. But I have to go. You can come with me, if you want."

Wulf took the fire-hardened chisel by the handle and dropped it on the ground beside Fael to cool. But the dull red that burnished his cheek was not from the glow of the fire.

"I worked stone at Pitbervie and learned to enjoy it," he said abruptly and went to sit with his back against the cliff, absently scratching his fingernail on a piece of sandstone till the crystals crumbled.

"So that's the way of it," said Fael sighing.

The slump of Wulf's shoulders accused her. She could feel his loneliness like a deep sorrow inside her. But she could not feel guilty. Not while Burghead called with the sweet plaintive song of the seal.

"I can't hide myself in a fishing creel while Angles rule our land." Tansen plied the neglected bellows."But later, a Queen will want to understand the needs of the craft-folk in her land."

Fael thoughtfully caressed the length of a long granite slab with stubby fingers..And Tansen sat hugging her knees, prepared to watch and listen and learn while the long evening darkened into amethyst twilight.

"What do you know about the making of an Ancestor Stone?" he asked her.

"Not much." She had been more interested in using their power. "Except that the one at Dun Nechtan is rough and humped while my clan stone is tall and flat and smooth."

"Aye, the old ones were shoddy, mere signposts on the path of life. It was my forebear, Derelei, who first taught his sons to choose slabs that would stand tall and proud. He taught them to peck the stone all over with a chisel, so that the surfaces were smooth and the symbols would stand out clearly. Pecking's the apprentice's job, Wulf lad."

Wulf still sat with his back to them. Tansen was aware that although he was a grown warrior, he would have to go back to the beginning to learn his new craft. He would spend many hours getting the feel of his father's tools. Only when he was allowed to make his own kit of tools would he be a craftsman in his own right.

"I'm leaving the back of this stone for clan symbols," went on Fael. "Maybe there's still a chief somewhere who's bold enough to display his clanship. Help me turn it over."

"It's a fair size," Tansen said, blowing on her dusty hands.

"A good third of it will be planted in the ground, lass. You don't want your grand stone to topple over the first time a cow scratches its rump against it."

A deep rectangle had been cut in the stone as a frame for a scene. Fael closed his eyes and let his fingers wander across the surface. Tansen waited, knowing he was opening his mind to the in-built spirit.

"I'm asking the Powerful Ones to work through my hands to turn the stone into silk." There was a long silence broken only by Fael's even breathing and the tapping of chisels in the background. "Now I can see shapes forming and floating in my mind."

He sighed deeply, bringing himself back from the vision he was holding.

"It takes time. Imagination. Subtlety. And humility, so that I may not offend the spirit of the All-Mother."

He selected another chisel and held it out to Tansen. There was warmth in his eyes and a genuine eagerness to make her understand. Honoured she placed the tool carefully on the charcoal.

Then with the cooled chisel and short sharp taps of his hammer Fael incised the outline of the shapes he would follow. Tansen placed another fine chisel on the fire.

"Huntsmen, two on horseback with a couple of hounds. And a fleet-footed deer."

And he began to shape the strong springy haunches of horses, the fine arching necks and dainty high-stepping legs.

"Why huntsmen?"

"It's the beginning and end of all myths. The lure of the white deer, the quest of the hero, the search for fulfilment."

The women chatted softly at their backs. Someone let out a sharp gust of breath to blow away the dust.

Fael began chipping on a lower panel and murmuring.

"Through my fingers the Ones create the finite shapes of the magic of the Infinite. Sometimes swirls and spirals like the rolling colours in the landscape of meditation. Sometimes the symbols of the Universal Power, sun and moon, lightning, rain, wind and rainbow. Sometimes I reach into the folk memory for a powerful happening. Sometimes I make a calendar of the twelve partitions of the yearly Cycle, with the symbol of each star as it comes into its full power and fades again."

"I thought," Tansen said hesitantly, "that the Symbol Givers had ruled against making a decorative Stone?"

"They're imprisoned by their own laws! They're blind to the presence of the Beautiful Ones in the Stone. But they'll not step up here to stop us. We're free to follow the vision of Derelei."

"I heard once," Tansen cut in again, "that Derelei worked a praise-stone for Queen Caterin and he died before it was finished."

Fael laid by his chisel and looked into the misty blue distance.

"He wrought a picture of the Queen with her King and trumpeters and retinue. And then it was lost at a time when the Scots were flaring out of control. Maybe it's propping up an old hay-cart for a chicken roost by now."

They said Derelei had loved Caterin. How inexpressibly sad that even his praise-song to her had been lost. For although they were a society of Clan Mothers, only male hunters and warriors were depicted on stone. After Caterin's time the Symbol-Giver had ruled that it was taboo to carve a woman in stone. For the stone itself was All-Mother and All-Woman. She glanced at Wulf's rounded back. He was working at something on the ground between his legs. Perhaps some day Wulf might picture her in stone.

"Haven't you hurt him enough?" said Fael softly, reading her glance and her thought.

A sudden chuckle erupted from Wulf catching them both by surprise.

"I'll survive. How's that?" Grinning he held up his piece of sandstone. Fael pursed his mouth in disapproval.

"Don't say a word, Fael," warned Tansen laughing. "That's talent of a different sort. Folk need a laugh now and again."

The glum eye of a mule and one long ear were cast back in mock trepidation at his rider, a fat farmer with a bald head and bushy beard who drank freely from a horn. Even the bird decorating the end of the horn looked on aghast at the farmer's capacity. The picture stood out clear and unmistakeably comical.

"Ach, I'm no good at it!" said Wulf, carelessly throwing his chisel on the ground. But his eyes met Tansen's in a long deep look and she saw he was pleased that she liked it.

"You'll never find a taker," cried Eirik. "Who wants a picture of a drunken farmer above their doorway?"

Wulf cuffed his ear and they rolled on the ground wrestling. Cousins and uncles and brothers came, stretching their stiff muscles, washing the dust from their throats with ale and stood in a circle egging them on.

"Ah, give me a plank of timber, new-cut, where I can feel the sap of the All-Mother flowing." And Eirik snatched up his bundle of tools and went to the bay for his night's work under the torches.

Two women came holding up a tapestry for Tansen to see. And no longer did Tansen want to be a picture in cold dead stone. For the women in the tapestry were a riot of colour with flying feet and swirling skirts and slim bodies bending and swaying in the dance.

Fael laid aside his beaker and rubbed his hands together.

"Now, you might think I'm going to start cutting that outline into the stone," Fael told her. "But I'm not. That's child's play. Rough and ready. Watch."

The others gathered round in a good-natured circle while Fael chipped away at the background till it began to recede and the figures began to stand out in relief, clear and strong and full of movement. Bold and catching the eye. As each chisel grew blunt he threw it down and Wulf had a new fire-sharpened one ready with the same timeless patience of his father.

Tansen felt honoured to be here, watching a master at work. For this was a new style of Ancestor Stone being created under her eyes. No longer would the Clans be content with a hump of stone and their insignia scratched roughly wherever there was space. There was a precision, an orderliness, an artistry in Fael's touch.

Even the everyday image of the hunter and the deer took on a new meaning. For these figures in stone would endure and be true, on and on into the future and would tell of the Pretani, even if the Angles toppled the stones and the wind and rain blurred them.

And she wondered what the folk of the future would think of the Pretani. Would they be known only as the painted barbarians that the Romans had sneered at? Would they hear of the Pretani only through the books of the monks from Eirean who despised the Druad and the Ancient Truth? Would the Ancestor Stones alone be left to tell of the existence of the folk of East Alba? Would their descendants remember them only by a word passed down in their tongue or in the name of a farmstead or in the red hair and white skins of their bairns?

A sense of despair made her fling off her sandals and run along the shore, her skirts fluttering, her eyes turning this way and that, looking at the empty landscape, faraway hills rising from the grey mist to smoulder in the fire of the sunset. And she cried in her heart to the Splendid Ones that folk should not forget the Pretani. And the answer came in a flash, clear and blinding, not from the turmoil of her own mind but like the cutting edge of a sword.

What did it matter if folk in the future thought of the Pretani as savages? For the Pretani, would live through their descendents. And the teachings of the Infinite Ones would be there in the future for those who chose to listen. And what would it matter if the folk did not know their blood was pure Picti so long as it sang at the sight of the hills and the sea and the flowers?

And she stayed to watch the night wheeling in from the east trailing its cloak embroidered with stars. And the breath-taking immensity of the glimmering darkness made her feel small and yet a significant part of it. And her despair quietened and became calm and she heard Wulf's call with a sure deep pleasure.

She knew a peculiar stillness within herself. The Wise Ones were with her, teaching her, guiding her, waiting for the right time.

And because she was not striving for it, the answer came sliding into her mind. Dale, the dolphin man, had said the fort had no well.

And she went to the cave to take farewell of Wulf.

In the morning Wulf kissed her and lifted her bundle, the last little service he could do for her, he thought, and went with her down to the Gate of the Fort.

She ran from him and found Horn, astride the outer wall, putting a dozen young horsemen through their paces, alternately swearing and praising. Before his guard could throw her aside she had yelled her lineage at him.

"Hi - yup!" Horn yelled. His sword went up and the line of horsemen turned on a pebble. "Daughter of the Taezalie, you say? Proof?"

"Dale, the Briton!" she cried.

"Hi - yup! Chancy proof that!"

"Liath Caledonie!"

"Even chancier! Hi-yup!"

"And I can dowse for the well that you'll need in a siege!"

The sword came down. The riders galloped onward. Horn turned a strong face, boasting a black moustache whose points swept his chest-plate.

"Start today. I'll give orders you're not to be disturbed. You can live with my women in the fort. Hi - yup, ya dolts, before you tumble over the cliff!"

CHAPTER FORTY FOUR

"Hang them and stick their heads on the gate! I'll have no raping of farmer's daughters! We need all the goodwill we can get!"

Tansen had waited until the training was over and now came to confront Horn while he ate his noon meal. A couple of soldiers had been tried and found guilty first. Now she had to wait while the Masters of the Trades gave their reports. Carpenters, tanners, farriers, charcoal-burners, smiths, the conflicting smells of their crafts mingled with the fish pie and all of them demanding more raw materials.

"And where do you expect me to find them?" Angry and frustrated, Horn swept the clutter of beakers and bowls from the board in front of him. Dale at his side, swiftly rescued a lone bread-roll and bent to speak in his ear. "Aye!" Horn nodded. "If you have to, use old shield-rims, horse trappings, or strip the metal off chariot wheels."

Horn's red-veined eyes raked over Tansen.

"You girl, clear up that mess or your head's a hurley-ball for the lads!" he yelled.

"I came to find you a well!" Tansen shouted back. "Not to wash your dirty cups in it."

Thoughtfully Horn combed his long greasy moustaches with his fingers.

"Right!" he barked. "Keep clear of the buildings. My men won't thank you if their quarters are dug up. Mind, I don't want a trickle of last week's rain. And I can't spare diggers for false alarms."

Tansen slung her bundle over her shoulder and went to work. Most of the rivers in Moray flowed towards the north-east so she followed the line of the walls starting from the west to try to locate a spring, using a twig of willow she had cut on her way there.

"A source of water," she told the under-part of her mind and began to cover her chosen path methodically. It was hard to concentrate. Wulf's brown eyes swam in front of her filled with sweet love and understanding. A line of men brushed by carrying loads of stones. In the distance Dale yelled orders to a group of trainees. Had the gods really used him and his dolphin sign to bring her here?

She rested her arms at her side and found she was looking up at the inner Gateway. High above the entrance in all his glory blazed the Royal Bull, carved in stone by Fael, now painted black with its sinews highlighted in gold, his head down, ready to charge. This was the emblem under which the chiefs would unite to throw off the Danish yoke. And it was the emblem of the Queen!

"I want flowing water that's not too deep," she began again, knowing she had to be precise or it wouldn't work.

Soon she was enclosed in her mind and her task, her arms thrilling to a light surge of power. And then the twig was pointing strongly downwards.

"Which way does it flow?" she asked, turning slowly. The twig died in her hands and she knew it was only a puddle seeping under the wall.

She went on again feeling the tingle of knowledge in her hands but unable to pinpoint it. A late-nesting tern began to dive on her and she lost her concentration again. But something told her to retrace her steps. The downward movement of the twig was slow and hardly perceptible until she came to a spot where the twig was almost vertical. It was at the junction of two high-banked walls and far enough inside the ramparts to be safe.

A broken arrow shaft lay nearby and she pushed it into the ground as a marker. She approached the spot from another angle and got the same response. She threw away her twig and held out her hands, trying another tack and another until she was sure she had the source of a spring and she followed the flow north-east until she was hard up against another of the high banked walls.

Horn snorted when she reported to him.

"There's nothing but solid rock under there. These walls were dug into the headland."

"If we start digging, we'll have both walls down about our ears," put in Finlae.

"There's no rock underneath the junction of these two walls," she told them firmly. "I can't tell what's there. It's a chasm of some sort. It's a wonder the walls haven't subsided before now."

Horn glared suspiciously at her but at last he ordered his men to dig away the covering of earth.

"Be careful!" She felt she had to warn them.

"They'll be careful all right," said Horn. "We'll have Fael and his boys shoring it up as they go."

That was not what Tansen had meant. How could she explain to him that there was something there, unknown, long unseen, left over from the past.

Then a spade struck rock and the men stood back to await orders.

"Fool of a woman!" grumbled Horn. "This is a wild goose chase."

"Wait a bit!" cried Dale. "See! It's a shaped stone. And it moves!"

Then she knew she had divined more than a well. She could feel a great empty space between herself and the water. No, not empty, but waiting.

The digging resumed and two more shaped stones were uncovered.

Dale curled his hands round one and heaved it out of its bed, leaving an awesome black space. He put his head into the hole and his soft whistle echoed eerily within.

"It's more a chamber than a well!" he cried. "But the air stinks like a vixen's lair."

"Move over!"

Horn pushed Dale aside and lay on the ground to survey it, wrinkling his face at the rush of sour air. Then he turned his body round and began to lower himself inside feet first.

Tansen closed her eyes and in her mind saw what he was seeing. A rectangular chamber with well-rounded corners. Lit by candles in branching stands. And on the walls stone carvings of men and women performing strange rituals with beasts and birds. And in the centre a smooth bowl cut into the rock. And a crack in the rock where spring water bubbled. And a walkway round the basin. And niches at intervals where bowls cut from crystal and marble and jasper flashed sparks of light in her eyes. She was seeing it as it had been in the past.

She had come believing that the gods had sent her to find a well for military reasons. Instead she had found a shrine.

By this time Dale had gone down and the diggers were revealing more of the roof and clearing a stairway. A crowd gathered, peering in, stirred and excited. One man threw down his spade. He ran to where a cluster of sea-pinks had taken hold in a niche.

"For the Lady of the Well!" he cried, kneeling and offering the flowers to Tansen. And she felt a dark cloud rising in her mind and a shiver of fear along her skin.

"No!" she cried, scattering the pink heads on the grass. "It's not the will of the gods that it should bear my name. You must have a Drui to dedicate it to Bride."

It was as though a hand had come down between her and the well.

Dale came out, smiling and lazily wiping his mouth with the back of his hand.

"Clear and cool as the purest stream."

And Horn, spraying drops of water from his moustaches. They were laughing, slapping one another on the back, cheering her along with the others.

"I knew she was a Wise Woman when I saw her divining with her bare hands."

"She came with the green eyes of Caterin and brought us sweet water from the snows of Thetil."

"No! No!" Tansen cried again. "It's the Guiding Ones who work through me."

"She communes with the Life-Giving Ones!" The cry was being taken up by others.

"I'm one of you!" she cried again. "I'm here to work with you. To carry stones and lay out arrows."

"If the women decide it's your well then it's your well," said Dale.

But when she heard the word 'Queen' become a chant in the cheering, she grew deeply afraid. This was not how it was to happen. She turned and fled to the women's quarters.

The word had spread before her. The women looked sideways at her out of their eyes. And took her to a cubicle they had made for her, strewn with fleeces and bright cushions. Before they started bringing bairns for her to heal she drew the curtain and lay down as if to sleep.

When she opened her mind to the Guiding Ones, they were not there. Why then had they pointed the way with the dolphins and the dolphin man? Any dowser could have found a supply of water. No kind of knowing came, only an emptiness with none of the thrill of the power that burgeoned as it was used. There was a deeper reason. And she was not to know of it yet.

CHAPTER FORTY FIVE

One thing Tansen had learned as the days went by. Maybe it was not worthy of one who was being guided but she had seen the advantage of a dramatic happening. One day she might need that knowledge. But she would use it honestly. For although the gods worked with her, they could always accept a little help.

During the next few days she walked the ramparts watching Wulf and his brothers in a cloud of dust laying bare a staircase to the well, uncovering the vaulted roof whose strength had kept the walls from subsiding. And she waited for the gods to answer.

One evening she saw Dale on a high slope looking out across the heat-hazed Firth. She climbed and stood below him, scanning the horizon, letting the warm breeze trifle with her loose hair and the frayed edges of her robe.

"This is a fine site for a beacon to guide in your paymasters some moonless night," she said.

Dale continued to gaze peacefully over the calm water, his feet mired in charcoal brands and black ash.

"It's a fine spy I am, on a borrowed mount, with a borrowed emblem." His laughter was soft yet insolent and disturbing.

"Can you swear you were never in the pay of Cadwallon? Did he put the slave-ring on your neck and hack it off when you promised to work for him?"

"Not really. It was one of his under-Kings, a petty mean man." He glanced down at her, a raw flush deepening on his jaw. "Think what you will of me. But speak softly on this sacred site."

He saw her look of astonishment and his eyes lit like lamps.

"You of all people should be aware that this is no beacon rock. But an ancient holy place."

He turned with his last words, revealing a great monument sunkissed and glowing with a warm amber as the sun sank in a rosy mist. Her breath caught in a surge of wonder.

"It's the resting-place of the Clavie," he said.

The upthrusting rock was topped by an iron basket. The black iron and the grey rock had been overlaid by rivulets of hardened amber. It was a beacon in itself, gleaming, shining against the amethyst sky. Dale laid his hand on the rock in a kind of caress.

"One full Moon-cycle after the longest night the folk here carry a barrel of burning pine branches on a pole round the houses. Each household is given a blazing brand from the Clavie to light their need-fire. They let it rest here to burn itself out. And the pine resin flows and cools and solidifies, spreading the news that soon the Mother will be stirring."

Recollection of the story came to her in a bright sweep of colour.

"I may be a foreigner and a mercenary," Dale went on."But I set myself to feel the pulse of the folk I'm among. For our pulses throb to the same rhythm no matter what pennant flies above our heads."

There was a moment as he stood there in his black leathers that Tansen saw him, not as the awkward lad she had first met, making clumsy efforts to impress, but as a leader of men exuding a powerful force. He broke the spell by moving towards her, kicking the dead charcoal from his path.

"I reckon we'll still be here at the turn of the year to see the grand fire it makes. The lot of us, still reeking of sweat and squealing about lack of meat and hay and ore and everything."

She shook herself and came back to the present and answered.

"The chiefs don't think that." Her arms swung to include the brave pennants and the bursts of activity around them. "They say Owin is sure to come before Samhain."

Dale brooded. "No. he'll not come before the winter. He's bound to know about this season's work."

"Who would tell him? You?"

The words were out before she could bite them back. The great amber eyes turned on her and, like a lamp being snuffed, the light in them died.

"You saw how weak they were after Cadwallon defeated them," was all he said.

"Yet how quickly they rallied and overthrew him."

"That might be their downfall. They can't hold on to these vast tracts of land that fell to them at Cadwallon's death, Gwynnedd, Reged, Lothian, Clyde. Add to that list Fib and the rest of Pretani-land and their communications are stretched to breaking-point. They'll consolidate their gains down south first if they're wise."

Tansen narrowed her eyes against the drifting smoke from the turfed mounds of the charcoal-burners and felt strongly that he was wrong.

"So you're betting on them coming next year. Is that why you're dawdling up here instead of breaking your back with the other workers?"

Solemnly he brushed aside her barbed words as he would a fly.

"No. The Angles will wait till they're sure they can take this fort and hold it. But by that time we'll be ready to attack south ourselves."

"Is that why you wanted me to stand up as Queen? Do you see yourself back in the Kingship?"

Dale's mouth tightened. And it was only the long beams of the low sun that set his lantern eyes afire again.

"A fishing-boat came today," he said. "Slipped out from Dysart. Reatta's ordered every tree on the King's estates to be felled for timber for new ships."

He knew that she would rise to that, Tansen told herslf. The estates were granted to each elected King by the people. The revenues covered the expenses of his Household and his Guard and the entertainment of visiting nobles. In her mind's eye she saw the rolling landscape lying bare and the soil running before the wind with no roots to hold it and cattle huddling together for shelter from the northeasterly. And another two hundred years to go before saplings would grow and the land lie drowsy with treasure again.

He was tempting her to make a stand against Reatta with himself at her side. There was a silkiness in his voice she had not heard before. Yet she knew surely, with every bone, every sinew, every breath in her body that the time was not ripe.

She gazed down at the Well, where women scrubbed at the cracked steps. Maybe the answer lay down there. But she would not go near it until the folk were venerating the Spirit of the Well and not herself.

"I know how Reatta's mind works," Tansen said bitterly. "She'll have picked over the People's Treasure for the best pieces. The rest will have been melted down into silver bars for trading. By now they'll have all the credit they need for weapons and ships and men. I think they'll come. And soon."

There was a ceremony at the Well at Lugnasad. Tansen hid in a cell with an old fletcher, whittling rough arrow-shafts for him to perfect and feeling guilty. She should be there with the others praying for a harvest of yellow heads.

During the next days she became deeply afraid. Her dowsing skill had brought a quick reward. Her farming skills were not needed. She would have to wait until Owin attacked before her healing skills would be required.

As she studied the preparations her heart grew sore. If, as Dale suggested, the attack did not come soon, how would Horn keep this force together. Samhain was coming fast, the end of the Year, the start of the Season of the Ice-Misted Moon. Just now there was plenty of fodder. Game, fish, berries and honey for those who could take time off to hunt and gather. But where were the barns to store the hay and the meal and the malt? Where was the salt for the slaughtering to come from?

What about the men from the north when the season of ice-grey seas came upon them? And no fine raiding and booty to show for it. They would melt away, back to their women, taking their new weapons with them.

She walked among tradesmen sitting round the smith's fire, waiting to see Horn, and listened to their talk. Fael was there to ask for time off for his men for a late harvest.

"Time off, is it? So that you can feed fat this winter. Who's going to guarantee our bite and sup?" the Master Smith grumbled.

"I need seasoned timber from Nor' Way," put in the carpenter. "They say there's eighty odd ships still for refitting."

"You'll have to wait your turn!" the Master of Smiths shouted at him. "I'm short of ore. My lads have picked the beach clean of iron-stone. That's the last of it, in that basin there."

The powdered stone, mixed with charcoal, crackled and spat in the cauldron.

"There's plenty iron in the peat if you look for it."

"Oh aye! And no men to spare to hack it out. And no pavement wide enough to fire it to get at the iron. There's only a puckle of iron to get that way." The Master kicked a broken mould in disgust. "And where's the copper and tin to come from?"

"Trade," said Dale's voice at Tansen's back.

"And what do we trade with?" The tanner's face and arms were as dark brown as his apron. "Skins? I need all the skins I can get for shields and jackets and boots."

"What did the folk round here use for trading?"

"Food, man, fish, fowl and fruit. But the fort takes it all. And the farmers are geared for war, too. They're not weaving or trapping or making fine tableware any more."

"Melor in Dublin has some fine Breton swords for sale. And a few Frisian spear-heads I'll be bound." Dale stroked his wide strong chin.

"Even if you get Horn to give you a ship that doesn't leak, what do you trade with?" The Master Smith went back to poking gloomily at his cauldron.

"Silver," Dale said. "We need silver. There must be many a man or woman would give their silver to see the threat of a Danish raid removed." He rounded on Tansen. "You're doing nothing. You could persuade the women to give up their earrings."

"Not me! I'm not going begging!"

"Not even for a Queenship?"

Then one evening at the meal-time, Horn pointed his dagger at Tansen.

"Get some decent clothes and a brooch or two. Go round the steadings and persuade the women to part with their silver. They'll trust you to repay them when you're Queen."

Tansen whipped round to accuse Dale of prompting Horn and found he was missing.

"If you're looking for the Briton, he sailed for Eirean with the last of our silver. The Kings of Connaught, Munster and Leinster will trade."

"If folk are wise they'll have buried their treasure before the Angles come," she protested.

"And the Wells," said Horn. "I've seen a glint of silver already in the one below."

"I can't rob Wells! These are offerings to the Spirit Ones!"

Horn leaned forward and spoke gravely.

"These are desperate times for us all. The Far-Seeing Ones know this is the only way."

It was true, Tansen knew. Another fishing-boat had limped in with news that Donnottar had been besieged and had fallen.

Tansen went humbly northwards with an escort, foreboding nibbling at her garron's heels and sharpening her pleas to the women. And came back one noonday with a lean bag of silver and bronze.

Nestling the bag in her arms, she hurried from those who would have escorted her to Horn. It was only fitting that the contents were shown first to Bride with a request to add her magic to the meagre offerings.

Tansen stood hesitating at the top of the stairway leading down to the Well. The side walls had been built up long ago with boulders. The steps were worn by countless feet. A black hole yawned before her. The muscles of her neck went rigid with a nameless terror. There was something down there, waiting for her. The bag began to slide from her nerveless fingers and she clutched it to her breast.

"Oh, Bride!"

The words ripped from inside her and she began to go down, counting the steps to keep her from turning and running.

"Seventeen, eighteen."

She stopped, an eerie green glow, a glimmer on water. And two more steps to go. Twenty steps. And she had counted on her tally-bone that it was only twenty nights till Samhain and the season of the Ice-Misted Moon would begin. Twenty nights left for the Angles still to descend on them from their high-prowed ships.

"Nineteen, twenty."

She stood on the walkway, letting her eyes adjust to the gloom. If there had been carvings they had been obliterated. By humans, because the walls were dry. There were no marble bowls in the apertures, no branching lamps. Yet the water glowed, casting a pearly dawn-like radiance on walls and roof.

Garlands of flowers and leaves had sweetened the damp sour air. A scatter of polished gems, agates and carnelians, amethysts and jasper lay quiet and twinkling in the crystal pool. At first she hated those who had recited their incantations and had drunk the pure water from her Well in their cupped hands. Then all resentment and fear left her. It was as though she stood between one world and the next, between the past and the future.

Then she heard it. The soft rustling of feet walking round the walkway. And Bride let her see dim shapes, bending to scoop the water into their mouths. And she knew they were the Attecottie folk who had welcomed Cruithne and Cruithna and their seven sons who had founded the seven great clans of the Pretani. And their eyes told her she had disturbed the rightness of things before they passed into the dimness.

Then the whisper of armour and the pad of sandals and Roman soldiers came, brushing their foreheads and lips with the water. For although they were only passing through, they knew the rightness of things.

Then her own people came dipping their charms in the water. And their sorrow filled the chamber, pressing on her mind. And she was sharing in the surge of prayers for healing, for peace, for love, for hearts' desires. Cries from the grieving and the wounded going out to the Great Spirit who encompassed all other gods.

She stood on the rim of the walkway and in the deep stillness of her mind she called to Marten.

"How long must I wait for a sign?" she asked. "How long must our people suffer? How long must I wait before I can serve?"

When she opened her eyes there was a flame in a basin on a pedestal that she had not seen before. And the reflection of the flame pointed across the dark pool to her feet, like the line of a spear. Or the flight of an arrow. Marten's flame. Grannie Bea's arrow. And the flame glowed brighter until its light filled the cavern.

Marten had answered! Her heart leapt with joy! Now was her moment when she must lead her people to victory! She closed her eyes and heard the clash of weapons, the groans of the injured, the screams of the dying, resounding backwards and forwards off every stone in the curved roof. And asked the Guiding Ones for strength in the battle to come.

A shadow fell across her face and she opened her eyes on a giant with a golden helmet on his yellow hair standing with the blue of the sky behind him. He leapt down and caught her by an arm and her hair and swung her up after him. And threw her on the ground outside while he whipped the bag from her arms and ripped it open and yelled his triumph to the skies.

Weapons flashed and flared around her. She screamed to the bodies slumped on the ground to rise up and fight. And screamed again to Dale who was not here to see another of his failures! Or was it a triumph and he had escaped in a ship before the onslaught he must have known was coming?

She was borne like a straw on the back of the soldier, her body bruised by his mail. And wept as she saw him step over the Royal Bull stone, cast down from his proud place and split in two. And in a blinding flash of insight knew that if she had lent her name to the Well, Princess Tansen's name would for ever have been connected with the slaughter at Burghead.

CHAPTER FORTY SIX

Within the Hall of Horn Tansen was thrown into a room of keening women. At first she held onto the image of the flame beside the pool, unaware of time passing, just knowing that if she lost that vision she would lose herself. Above loomed pale drawn faces seeking loved ones. None came from Wulf's kin. She did not say the unlocking spell that might open her mind to the Cave of the Sculptors, afraid of what she would find.

When the women wailed, soldiers came and beat or raped them, and came back again and again until the women learned to hold their peace. Tansen's mind had retreated from her body and in lucid moments she could not be sure if she too had been beaten and raped. And did not care. Then they were being moved, stumbling over pebbles, wading, crowded into a swaying hold and rolling to the buck of a ship as it reached the open sea.

When she heard the name 'Dunnottar', she came to herself, thigh-deep in icy water. They were in a haven sheltered by cliffs. Along the crescent shore-line boats unloaded their cargoes, soldiers and booty. And, towering, all-powerful, dominating land and sea and humans, a stronghold reared into the sky. Roofs and crags bristling, menacing.

Although there were steps leading up to a gateway they were herded towards a rough-hewn hole in the cliff. Tansen cast around for a way to escape because once they were forced into that hidden entrance under the fortress there would be no way out. But freedom was a wild thought while her body was filled with a grinding weariness and she stumbled on with cut and bleeding feet.

Up narrow stairways, dank and dripping, cut into rock, past dark fearsome caverns that smelled of guano. In one room, ruined by the siege, they surprised a gull, gorging on something horrible. It spread its wings and lurched and fell back on its swollen stomach. And tried again in a panic and fell back. Even the gull could not escape. Wind and sun hit their faces as they came out into the busy hub of the stronghold. Then they were inside again, huddled at the end of a Long-Hall.

There for the first time Tansen saw Ecfrith's army commander Owin. Tall, fair-haired, broad and muscular with a narrow face.

"We did well, that's a fact," Owin was telling his men, ale-beaker in hand. "Eh, Erling Wry-Neck?"

A short brisk man with a furrowed pouch under his chin danced and punched the air.

"A three-pronged trap! Always works! A surprise crack in the jaw where a man's expecting it. And wham! Two more either side of the body. Doubles them up!"

"I drink to your fine ships, Talorc, and the sailors that man them."

A young man, wearing both the Danish gold circlet in his brown hair and the Pretani Chain of Kingship, grinned. Talorc's down-drooping moustaches gave him a hang-dog air. But there was nothing hang-dog about the way he cuffed Owin on the shoulder.

"Told you we could do it! I spent many seasons raiding in the Moray. Know the river-mouths like the runes on my sword."

Sickened, Tansen learned how they had set out from the great Beach of Kilrymont at the Tay and sailed south as though retreating to Wearmouth. Far out from spies on land they had turned and sailed north. How at night they had disembarked Erland's army at the Lossie Mouth and Talorc's men at the Findhorn. And how, when the look-outs on Burghead had warned that an enemy fleet was sailing in, the Burghead folk had forgotten why their ancestors had built ramparts to shield them from attack from the south. They had fled inland into the arms of two armies coming at them from the south-east and south-west.

"And while I waited for your pennants to show on the walls, I sank a couple of ships sneaking in from the Orcades. Then I was in, right into the harbour I went, smashing their hulks to firewood and setting them to the torch."

Owin's eyes strayed to the huddle of women.

"The old hags to the kitchens," he ordered. "The wenches for serving, handy for using later."

In the days that followed Tansen quickly learned how to dodge the Angles in drink. She lime-washed her hair and screwed it into three spiky braids and rubbed her face with soot to make herself look repulsive. She slid in and out of the hall like a shadow, listening to their talk. But in the night in the kitchen, happed by the warm fug of female bodies, she cursed Marten for his flame and his pool that had raised her hopes and then dashed them. And cursed Dale for being a traitor. And thought of ways to escape, knowing she would rather die, ice-rimmed out there on the moors, than here in this stinking rat-hole.

Talorc was the first to leave, back to Dalgynch to oversee the stocking up of the King's Barns, to hunt on the King's Muir and to breed on Reatta. Owin planned to go next, leaving Erland Wry-Neck in command.

"Since Ecfrith's caught Cadwallon with his trousers down, I've a notion to give him a hand in plundering Gwynedd." Owin settled into his seat for his last night's drinking.

"What about the Picti woman Ecfrith told us to look out for?"

"Forget Eanfrith's filly. The Church historians have scraped out his pagan reign from their books and slipped Ecfrith's name in after Edwin. That's security enough." Owin opened his shirt to the waist and belched. "When I'm finished in Gwynedd I'll bring my brother back here to view his strongholds."

"The sherriffs can take those glad tidings to the Chiefs and Mormaers. And an order to present themselves to their Liege Lord." Botulf the Stubborn grinned.

"There's only one that might be disposed to hold back," went on Owin. "That Liath, Chief of the Caledonie."

With her sleeve Tansen mopped up the wine splashed by the tremble of her hand.

"He's tried snatching the Taezalie cow-gelt and herding it back where it came from," Owin went on. "Axe a few farmers and he'll stop his tricks."

"Ach, he's too scared to venture out from that cursed eyrie of his in the hills."

"He knows when he's beaten. He's ringed in by manned fortresses like a treed cat." Owin leaned forward, glittering. "Erling, lure him here one night with the promise of a Kingship."

"And what pretty surprise will we cook up for him?" asked Bjarni, the Gold-Browed Poet.

Owin expanded his broad chest, smiling.

"Feast him like a King," said Owin. "Tell him what a jolly fellow he is. Have some fun at his expense. Set a wench to find out which road he's taking back. Then ambush him and kill him. We'll have no further trouble from his tribe after that."

Tansen had often eyed the daggers that lay carelessly on the board. Now she could hardly stifle the temptation to use one as she passed with a brimming jug at Owin's back. Somehow she must escape and warn Liath of the danger.

She had studied the layout of the stronghold. The tunnels and caves in the rock were too well guarded. Glancing from slits in the walls she saw that Donnottar was much higher than the squat Burghead promontory. On three sides the cliffs fell steeply to where the North Sea lashed and leapt around jagged rocks. She was seldom allowed near the east side but there lay the only chance for escape. Two small lagoons nipped the land into a spit as scrawny as the thrawed neck of a chicken. That spit leading to the top of the steep towering cliffs was too well guarded. It would be suicide to try to escape along there even in darkness. But the southern lagoon looked promising.

Then she noticed a glint of water far back in a fold in the cliff-top. A waterfall by all that was brave! The gorge it fell into was a narrow black thread among the grasses. Yet it must fall down to the sea. And surely a slim figure could disappear up there at night. If only she could find a way down to the southern beach.

Days passed and she could find no break in the wall that gave her a sight of the mouth of the stream. Her hopes grew. That meant that few sentries overlooked this side because they thought it was unassailable. It was when she was at the squatting bench one day that she looked down into the gaping hole and saw the slippery slope plunging down to the beach. The smell of it and the thought of it made her want to retch. But she would take any means of escaping. She was so thin and ill-nourished she could squeeze easily through the hole. Her threadbare clothes did not matter. But it was a pity the squatting holes were always busy.

The Moon had waned and waxed before she glimpsed the carrot-head of Liath glowing in the Hall. Her heart gave a great lurch at the sight of his blue eyes dancing with a fierce delight.

"King of the Caledon Mountains?" he was crying out. "By the White Thighs of Thetil, that name has a merry ring about it!"

He cocked his head at Erland and slapped him on the back with a staggering insolence till his neck wobbled. And Tansen knew Liath's tongue was firmly in his cheek. For to Liath the title of Cheiftain was supreme over any Kingship. She cast around looking for some excuse to go near him to warn him about the ambush. And some way to use him as a means of escape.

CHAPTER FORTY SEVEN

The Steward's iron-tipped wand prodded Tansen to the far end of the Hall where the foot-soldiers sprawled. Liath's rakish laugh sounded from the High Table.

"If I'd known you were naming me King I'd have worn my fine hat with the three sea-eagle feathers. And my best tunic with the ten fox-tails round the collar."

Liath smoothed down one sleeve of a fine wool tunic, with richly decorated borders. Tansen paused in the serving, holding her breath. He was taunting them, his eyes bright under heavy lids. For his tunic sewn with Danish designs, looted from an Angle.

"Will I have a ring of gold to keep the hair out of my eyes?"

"We've rings in plenty to fit any part of your anatomy," bellowed Erland, his blue-veined cheeks flushed with drink and anticipation.

"Not there!" protested Liath. "That's one chastity belt I'd not care for."

"Then here's a ring fit for a King!" cried Erland and the gold sparkled as it flew through the air. Liath's arm closed tight into his side as he allowed the ring to fall. Slowly he picked it up and examined it with interest in the rays of the nearest lamp.

"Worth a King's ransom!" he cried at last throwing it up and catching it fast. And the Angles did not bother to hide their laughter behind their hands.

The drink flowed long into the night. The lamps grew smokier, the jokes coarser.

The Steward retreated behind a barrel with a beaker. Tansen grabbed a jug from a passing serf and went to fill Liath's horn. As she bent close to his ear she mouthed the one word "Ambush". The sound was lost in the hubbub but Liath's head jerked round. Let him recognise me, she pleaded. But his eyes were fixed on her breasts.

"Hey, Caledonie! What's between you and the wench?" demanded Erland.

"Three spiky braids that tickle my fancy!" Liath roared back.

Erland's eyes bored into Tansen's.

To run would have proved her guilt and she would be cut down. She had to stand her ground, staring blankly at him as though she did not understand his his language.

"I'll spike her braids for her!" Erland swore softly. "And I'll have her tongue as well!"

"That's it!" cried Liath. "You and I, Wry-Neck! Get your dagger out! Three throws each to pin her to the wall by her braids."

As Tansen leapt for the doorway two men caught her and held her firmly against a timbered panel.

"And then the tongue!"

Erland wet his lips, his heavy jowls wobbling. He left his own knife lying beside his meat-plate and took a dagger from the belt of the nearest man. He raised it and aimed, squinting. In that second Tansen knew he was so drunk that his aim would not be true.

"Hold it, man!" cried Liath. "Where's your hospitality? Guests go first in this land." He lined up three daggers on the board before him. Lifting one he stroked it with long loving fingers. Merciless blue eyes looked at her from a serenely smiling face.

He drew back his arm and aimed. Tansen's eyes snapped shut. She heard the thud of the dagger in the wood beside her head. Another thud and another before she drew breath. And her three braids held her fast to the wall.

"Match that, Erland!" Liath left his knives embedded in the wood.

Tansen dreaded Erland's throw. He was angry and drunk enough to finish her off with a dagger in the heart. Especially if he missed the first time. Her eyes flew to Liath, pleading with him to make some diversion. He had turned his back and was leaning on a chair, his head cocked in mockery at Erland's attempt to focus his eyes.

Erland's knife nicked her shoulder before it pinged into the wall and hung vibrating. Tansen's terror wiped out the jagged pain. Furiously Erland cast about for another dagger.

"First a challenge, Wry-Neck! You and your men!" Liath's cool voice cut across the fire-hazed hall.

He leapt down to a table in the centre of the hall near the hearth-fire, kicking plates and bread and cups to the floor.

"We Caledonie are a barbarous tribe!" he cried. His toe hooked a bannock high in the air. "And our games are barbarous." He had the wary attention of the Angles now, ready for any ploy. "Start the music, boys! Let's show them how we make our prisoners dance."

It was a wild skirling sound that his men struck up with their mouths. Tansen, her head held rigid, slewed her esys round as far as they would go. Liath extended an exquisitely pointed toe to touch the board. A dagger from one of his men hissed through the air to thud into the wood where his toe had been an instant before. But now he was dancing. Arms curving high, head thrown back, disdaining to watch either his toes or the daggers that his men thudded remorselessly around his feet.

Now the Angles entered into the spirit of it and jostled against one another to throw their daggers and keep him moving. His feet were as dainty and swift as a fawn's among the quivering blades. Only the twinkling points of his toes ever touched the table and that only for a split second. Tansen forgot her pain and the blood trickling down over her breast.

When knives began to encircle him and hide his feet he leapt to another table and the Angles moved forward in a rush to retrieve their daggers and try again. The music grew wilder and the dancing faster.

The Angles shouted, egging him on, the lights gleaming on their daggers as they edged nearer for a surer aim. But still the music skirled and the feet twinkled. Then Erland come so close that he could not miss. The knife in his hand had a long thin wicked-looking blade and he was taking his time to aim.

Tansen held her breath. The other Angles stepped back to watch, gloating. But the mouth-music went on without a falter. She hardly saw it but she heard the hiss and the thud. And the bellow that rattled the shields on the wall.

Liath stopped dancing, one foot pinioned. Blood oozed from his leather shoe.

"Oh dear," he said softly. "I think I've lost a toe."

He withdrew the long reddened blade, his hand steady. Leaving crimson footprints in his wake he strode up the table towards Tansen. She screamed as he slashed at her. But her head was free, the braids cut cleanly near her scalp.

The Angles, surging to howk their daggers from the table found Liath's men barring their way with the daggers they had kept ready in their hands.

And then everything slowed down, like a saga unfolding its pictures in Tansen's mind. Liath, his mouth soft and smiling as a babe's, his eyes sharp with malice, held Erland's own long pointed knife twinkling in front of his face. He took a bunch of Erland's long greasy hair in his hand, and, still smiling, swiped off his head and tossed it contemptuously into the hearth-fire.

"Murdering cur!" he took time to say. Then as he hurtled past her Tansen grasped his outstretched hand. It seemed like magic when the door opened for them and slammed shut behind them, the Angles bouncing off it as Liath's men hammered a plank across it.

They paused to look down on the spit of land where torches were gathering, drawn by the yelling and the steady hammering of daggers on wood.

“This way!” cried Tansen, and led them to the squatting hole.

The serfs scattered, yelping, pulling up their clothing. Liath kicked aside the plank that rested above the hole.

“Yeugh!” he cried. He pulled off his tunic and, holding it to his breast, shot feet first through the hole. Tansen went next, slipping through and sliding down the slimy grass, faster and faster, till arms caught her and slowed her fall. Then together Liath and she tumbled headlong into the stinking mess on the beach.

Bodies thudded round them, grunting. Then no more.

“It’ll be Fat-Arsed Boab that’s stuck in the hole,” growled someone.

Then the bodies started hurtling down again and they were all up and running. Tansen led the way, through the gorge made by the stream, so narrow she was sure Fat Boab would stick again. And they climbed with their feet on either side of the gurgling water, using the walls, grasping handfuls of grass. And then the water was falling on their heads, in their mouths and eyes and they were climbing on one another’s backs and pulling up the last men after them. And they were away, still deep in the path of the stream, hearing the horns blowing and turning their heads to see the evening sky alight with flares.

They went westwards with the rain washing the slime from their clothes. A pine-wood, hushed and darkly-green, rose before them and they ran through it, crouching low, little spurts of laughter jerking out of them. The trees thinned out and they were in marshland. The ground between the tussocks was damp and treacherous. With certainty Liath picked a path for them to follow. Then they were climbing a rock-face fitting their feet into ledges that would hardly hold a nesting bird.

At last they were on a broad flat summit. The men threw themselves on their stomachs, panting and chuckling and looking back up the valley. Tansen lay on her back gasping, her heart almost bursting with joy.

“That was glorious! Oh, what a risk you ran!” cried Tansen breathlessly.

“And every man’s got a fistful of gold brooches into the bargain.” Liath lifted a kerchief from the nearest head to bind his foot. “You were too busy watching my fancy footwork to notice.”

An arm pointed due north-west to a pin-point of light.

“Right! That’s the way we go!”

Liath waited to pull on his fine tunic and they were off again, running down the steep slope and onward until they came to a farmhouse that had a torch on a pole above its thatch. And waiting, was a cart with a load of tied hay. But when they lifted out the bottom bale at the back there was a hole and they could clamber in and find space to stand and lean against one another, warm and cosy and pungent. The driver's whip cracked, the mules strained, the cart creaked and finally moved off at a snail's pace. One man started the mouth-music again, soft and appealing, till there came a low whistle and an oath and suddenly a drunken woman was singing a bawdy song that did not stop when there came a gruff order and a clank of arms. Tansen felt the men stiffen and sensed that every man held a dagger in his hand.

"Hey, come into the cart with me, you lusty young fellows, and I'll give you a taste of my fine hams."

The Danish curses and laughter had faded before the woman's cackling stopped.

"Are you for half a Danish bannock?" said a voice that seemed to come from her elbow. "Go on, it's fresh and clean. I hid it in my bonnet."

"Fifteen, sixteen, and each one pure gold by the bite of them."

The crunch of an apple in her ear, the clink of coin and metal told Tansen they were sharing out food and booty. The bannock tasted as good as when she had baked it that morning. The mules clacked over cobbles and came to a stop. The cart bucked once and an oblong of dim light appeared.

"Out with you, lads!" A voice roared. "Feugh! You stink worse than Davin's sow. You'll stampede the beasts with the whiff off you! The dung of beasts smells sweeter than human dirt. And why is there one more of you here than I brought."

Strong muscled arms checked Tansen to view her in the light of his lantern.

"A hedgehog with a nose for escaping." Liath threw back.

The driver was huge, big-shouldered. And wore a skirt, bonnet and shawl.

"You were the old hag along the road."

"The Danes had the chance of a lifetime there, Stub-leg. Jon, see to the mules." Liath led the way outside. Behind the barn, hill-ponies pulled at their tethers and shook ragged manes at them.

"Get up behind Peedie Petrie," ordered Liath, mounting.

Peedie was small and thin so his pony was the least burdened. Bannock crumbs still clung to his out-thrusting beard. She had to run to throw her leg over the eager pony and she clung as they sprang forward up the drove-road, with the fingers of the dawn unfolding at their backs.

The rising mists were friendly, twining away out of their path. Threading through winding valleys, climbing steep braes, skirting rockfalls, slanting across mountain-sides, circling woodlands and bogs and fallen trees, the hill-ponies tossed their heads, plunged over everything and drove on.

Passing each homestead tucked on a shelf of land or nestling in a shoulder of a hill, Liath gave a low three-note whistle of reassurance.

They stopped on a height to let the ponies draw breath after the climb. There was no smell of human, no woodsmoke, no cooking. And Tansen slipped off the pony to see better the land that fell away from her feet, little by little, fold on fold, pearly light on deep black shadow.

For it seemed she was on the edge of tomorrow and all those tomorrows that waited for her feet. All the dark places her path would take her, all the bright summits. And maybe somewhere a sign, a golden flame in a deep dark pool.

And the great wide sky encompassed her. Clouds, pink-tinged from the dawn sailed overhead and the wind that steered them picked at her rags and cleansed and dried them and blew ice-cold on the back of her bare head. And she watched the clouds as far as they went, beyond the land towards the ocean still hidden in dark-blue night where a faint star lingered.

She longed to swing skyward and go forward with the clouds. At Dunnottar she had been like Coel the monk and had built an earthbank around herself for protection. Now the bank was crumbling and tumbling down the hillside and she was free and looking upward and beyond to a sky that was free and a land that should be free. And it was as though a torrent that had been dammed up inside her had burst forth and she laughed aloud that she was free and was going to join the rebels.

Liath lounged forward to stand beside her, shadowy, with the sheen of dawn on his hair, the planes of his face and the creases in his tunic. His eyes opened wide on her and gleamed with a luminosity all their own. Her spirit leapt to meet his gaze as if their two natures had suddenly locked in some silent recognition that they were birds of the same feather. Then the small movements of men and mounts penetrated the sudden glow that encompassed them. Liath broke away, mounted and held out his hand to pull her up behind him. She clasped his waist as they took the down-slope at a canter, her body aflame with joy.

Later in the morning they saw a great coiling river still dark on the floor of a plain, flowing through an ever-widening vale, fair and green with cornlands and hay. But in the west the river emerged from a deep wooded cleft in the mighty shoulder of a hill. And that was where they made for.

CHAPTER FORTY EIGHT

As Liath and his men turned into the narrow cleft a startling series of curlew cries went before them. The path narrowed and turned back on itself once, twice.

Then the curlews were yelling a welcome. The rock-faces fell away and they were in a vast open space crowded with tents and campfires, horses and shelties, busy folk in bright plaids who paused smiling to wave a greeting to their Chief. The smell of roasting meats fought with the reek of dung. Sparks flew from a grinder's wheel and from a corner came the sharp clang of a blacksmith's hammer on iron.

There facing Tansen, seemingly lodged in the sheer face of the rock like an eagle's eyrie, rose a gaunt stone fortress.

Tansen slid to the ground and gazed enchanted. It was a glorious setting for a wild Caledonie Chieftain. Her father must have known this place well. At once she felt at home, a daughter of Oengus, ready to stand with Liath and lead the clan to victory over the Angles.

A man with flashing teeth and a red woollen cap planted himself before Liath.

"And was it a fair exchange?" he asked. "A dozen useful horses in return for a bald female?"

Her face flamed. She had forgotten how ugly and bedraggled she looked. On neat but purposeful feet she stepped forward and, lifting his cap from his head, planted it firmly on her own. He grabbed it back.

"Ye'll no wear Tam the Toorie's bunnet," he said.

Liath, dismounting, paused with one hand on the pony's rump.

"Your dozen useful horses are lodged with the Danes' horses in a stable down the coast from Dunnottar. But a couple of braw serfs that can't count are nesting on a ledge in the cliff. You'll have your horses back and a few extra before the Maiden shows her crescent." He slapped his pony off in the direction of the pack and turned to Tansen with a light smile. "As you see, we're a parcel of scoundrels."

A girl came beside him, dainty as thistle-down, tawny-skinned, amber and bronze clasping her neck and wrists. She rested her net of loch trout at her feet.

"She should never have thrown in her lot with us, should she, Flam?"

He turned into the ready embrace of the girl's arms. And Tansen wondered if she had imagined that moment of kinship that had sparked between herself and Liath on the mountain.

"But will she stay?" A soft whisper whose gentleness was belied by the fire in the burnt orange eyes that smouldered on Tansen.

"I saved your lives, didn't I?" Tansen flung back at Liath, angry and hurt.

"So she did, Flam. We were spewed out of the fort like drunken soldiers from a brothel. But, as you say, Flam, will she stay?"

A curious crowd was gathering leaving Tansen forlorn in its centre. She was aware of being thin and ragged and bald. She put her hand up to her head. No, not bald but definitely bristly. Liath's eyes taunted her, stripping her defences bare, as if he knew exactly what she was feeling. And did not care.

"I want to join your clan."

Flam laughed deep in her throat and tossed long russet hair shot with gold.

"I hope she's no' brought lice with her." Tam peered into his cap thoughtfully.

Tansen drew in a breath trying to hold onto her temper.

"I want to help you to clear the Angles from the land."

"Then you were in the right place back there to put poison in a cup or a knife in a rib. And an escape route handy," said Stub-Leg.

Tansen turned her head sharply to stare at him.

"I see I was mistaken. I thought you were a proud and loyal people. All I find here are the ill-gotten dregs of a barbarian tribe."

"Not half as ill-gotten as the company you kept at Dunnottar," snarled Stub-Leg.

"Or when she supped in the Halls of the Angles at Gefrin with silver spoons cut with a cross," said Liath.

So he knew who she was. She met his eyes squarely and did not answer.

"You're a pretty prize, Prickles," said Liath. "But we've enough cooks. What else can you do apart from sliding down slippery slopes? Can you butcher a cow? Can you throw a spear? Or maybe an axe is more in your line?"

Tansen let her temper fly at his mocking smile.

"You know full well I hate Angles. And why!" Her furious gaze swept round the hard faces. "And I'll never betray you. For I'm the daught... "

"Enough for one day!" Liath's voice cut in and rounded on the crowd. "We tucked Wry-Neck into the arms of the Furies. And we picked up a hedgehog with ambition. Saddle up, Peedie. Drop her off at the first homestead that takes her fancy. Now, Flam, what's for eating!"

"I want to know a bit more about her before I take her at my back again."

But Peedie Petrie pocketed the carrot he was chewing and trotted off.

Liath was already swallowed up by the crowd. She found him resting one foot on an upturned barrel and Flam bringing him barley brose in a bowl.

It was a tall man with a fine curling creamy beard who stood at the cauldron and flourished a ladle. She took a wooden bowl from a stack at the side and held it out. A sweeping eyebrow, thick enough to adorn three men swivelled in her direction but the grey eye beneath was as cold as a pebble. Still, the ladle was large and dripping gravy. She lifted the bowl to her mouth and gulped ravenously. Liath on his second bowl surveyed her calmly. Beyond, Peedie waited on a garron in the haze of another campfire.

"I'm not going," she told Liath.

"You should, you know."

"Why did you rescue me then?"

"It was a joke. A rib-tickling magnificent joke! Unfortunately we don't need a princess of the royal blood here." He spat the words like rotten nuts from his mouth.

"No, the Caledonie were never keen to be classed with the rest of the Pretani." Tansen answered with deliberate contempt. "The other clans are handy folk for you to know in time of famine or plague. But join with them to defeat the Angles? That's not your style, is it? You go your own way, playing brigands in the mountains."

"As you say, daughter of Oengus, it's not our style."

The silky acknowledgement that she was half-Caledonie stemmed her flow of words.

"Go back to Dalgynch, Prickles, where you belong. Back to the fluted bowls and a drunken Angle to lie in your silken sheet. A wig from a mare's tail and they'll never guess you were the greasy scullion who was spiked at Dunnottar."

"Scullion or royal, Dalgynch would be death for me. I'll stay."

"Oh no, I gave you the chance once before and you chose the Angles. How can I trust you now?"

So that was it. He was mean enough to want his revenge. And she had thought him a hero. Tansen's temper snapped.

"And that was a fine stirring speech you made then. About having a place at Lynchattie where free men and women could gather. Where you'd launch an attack on the Angles. And what do I find? A rabble. Petty thieves. Pathetic cattle-raiders. And there'll be another Wry-Neck at Dunnottar before your next dinner."

He gazed at her, his head cocked. Then roused himself, picked her up and planted her at Peedie's back and bellowed.

"Peedie, for the sake of my poor beleaguered lugs will you get this scold out of here."

But Tansen was off and running lightly back to the fire with folk cheering and children and dogs yelping round her legs. She stopped with her back straight as a birch-tree, her glance sweeping the grinning faces with sharp-edged defiance. Peedie made to dismount but Liath's hand stopped him.

"Stay here," he warned Tansen smoothly, "and I promise to barter you for a jug of wine and peace to enjoy it."

"I'll stay!"

Liath's eyes gleamed with a sudden blaze of light. And she knew he had gambled that she would indeed remain. He was testing her to the limit. As he would test all who came to his eyrie. Liath raised his voice.

"A second-hand Princess to any man that thinks he can take the Kingship and needs to make it lawful."

"I'll buy that." The sonorous voice was deeper than she remembered. She froze. It couldn't be Dale the Briton!

"O, gods of my fathers, preserve us all from the ambitions of fanatics." Liath's voice lilted back from among the crowd.

It was Dale! Leaning on a tethering post, golden-eyed, his wide jaw cracking in welcome, and a ragged Caledonie eagle winging awkwardly across his tunic.

"Do you paint on a new insignia every time you change masters?"

He laughed.

"This isn't Liath's eagle. It's supposed to be an osprey, a trifle crooked, I grant you."

"Suits you!" She answered and wished she could sense what lay behind that mask of warm innocent friendliness. A superb self-confidence, she guessed, that no matter what master he served he would never be around when battles were lost.

She turned her back on him to rid herself of his presence and listened for the crank of a well-handle.

"We could set up as Warrior King and Queen of the North, you and I."

She caught the creak she was waiting for.

"You tried that gambit at Burghead," she threw back savagely. "And it still doesn't tempt me."

She cut directly across the arena to the well and found, nearby, a bucket and a lump of grease and ash that smelt sweetly of heather.

She filled the bucket. In the earth-house she stripped and scrubbed at her skin in a fine fury at her father's kinsman who was trying to humiliate her. And just at the very moment when she had thought they had something special to share. At the low entrance she caught a sudden flash of amber and a swirl of tawny skirt. Outside on a stone lay a tunic and overskirt and a shawl in bright greens and yellows. She rubbed herself dry with the shawl slowly, remembering with dismay how Flam had subtly made clear that Liath was her man. It was strange. She had not considered that Liath might have a woman of his own, with hair like leaves just turning before the fall and eyes like fire.

Tansen caught her lip with her teeth to stifle a sob. Already she was missing the scent and swish of her own long hair when she turned her head. She put up her hands and found the limed bristles were gone. Instead there were the beginnings of soft curls all over her scalp. Now she was clean she could face the world, however hostile it might prove to be. And Tam the Toorie was waiting outside, holding out a roomy orange cap with a green toorie.

"Take it. It's no' been worn." He shuffled off at speed, turned and added. "It was meant for feast days and festivals. But the Chief's no' one for rest-days." He shuffled again and turned. "I made it myself."

The strands were coarsely knitted with hands that were rough and calloused. They were a strange folk, suspicious of strangers. But kindly, it seemed. She had been far too full of her own importance coming into this close-knit community. Liath had been wise to play down her kinship with the Clan. Instead he had tested her as a person in her own right. And, for one man in the camp, at least, she must have passed the test. She tucked her head into the cap and pulled it at a jaunty angle.

Liath rose out of a scramble of bairns, tucked a lass with a wasted leg on his shoulder and their fiery thatches merged. Without a glance at Tansen he made for the steps cut into the rock-face, the child clinging like a newborn kitten.

Every fortress is different, Tansen thought. This one was tucked cunningly into the natural lean and dip of the rock. She swallowed a chuckle. She was becoming an expert in strongholds. Maybe with good reason, came the chilling thought. As she climbed eagerly up the steps the air changed and became scented with leaf-mould and pines and wood-smoke and even a touch of frost.

The rough wooden door to the great Hall lay open and Tansen stopped on the threshold in surprise. Apart from a long blackened iron tray that was their winter hearth, this place was an arsenal and smelt of sheep fat and leather. Arranged neatly round the walls were row after row of leaning spears, box after box of swords and daggers, pile after pile of horse straps and blankets and boots. Both men and women worked at tables, oiling, cleaning and mending.

I've been monumentally wrong, thought Tansen with delight. This is not just a clan of rievers. There's a force here that can change the fate of our people.

CHAPTER FORTY NINE

When Liath entered the great Hall at Lynchattie, the folk seemed to come alive as though caught up in the swirl of his vibrant energy.

The child untangled herself from Liath's neck, climbed down his clothes and ran, limping, to an old wisp-haired man who bent to hear her tale.

Tansen watched Liath as he strode forward his head turning, calling out greetings like a well-loved father returned from the hunt. At the far end, huge ox-tongues turned on a spit. Flam laid a basin of water on a table for Liath.

"Where's Griff?" asked Liath.

Two lads straightened from a table laden with broken straps to answer the Chief but a grumbling voice from a bench in a corner cut in.

"Off to the Moray, like ye told him." He was a sturdy man with a high colour and an air of restless vigour, held in check by a leg bandaged from thigh to toe.

"But not back yet?"

"With his own Black Isle glowering across the water? He's likely rowed across to check his wife's bed's empty."

"I'll deal with him when he comes skulking back!" Dale spoke from the doorway.

Backs stiffened and turned. The easy familiarity vanished and a new tension crackled in the air.

Liath's grin froze. Silently he threw off his upper clothing and rinsed his tanned body bitten with old puckered untended scars.

Dale sauntered towards the boxes of axes, seemingly unaware of the hard eyes that followed him.

Flam handed Liath a fresh shirt.

Dale wiped his sweaty hands on his tunic, chose an axe and weighed it in both hands.

Flam belted a green plaid sash on Liath and clasped it at the shoulder with a huge cairngorm brooch. And Liath stood, legs astride, facing Dale, flaunting his Chieftainship.

The bitter enmity that flowed between these two men could almost be touched. And Tansen's whole loyalty surged towards Liath who was so like her father, lithe and virile and proud, Chief and Father of his clan and leader of this well-armed band that would surely bring success to the Pretani. There was a sudden thrashing of air as Dale whirled the axe round his head, once, twice, three times. And stilled, mocking Liath out of his great mild eyes.

The full-bodied warning of curlews trilled through the open windows. A woman ran to the window.

"It's Fod's men," she said, her toneless voice denying the tremor of fear. "Three dead. Five, six wounded."

A woman here and there left her work and went out.

"You still want to join us?" Liath asked Tansen. "This is the price we pay. We die in bogs daily."

A man hurried in, sweating, blowing his cheeks out after his climb and swearing mightily.

"That sherriff, curse him!" Fod spat on the floor. "There he was riding as cheerful as you like, with two covered carts behind him and a smell of kippers in the air."

"And when you fell on him the carts opened and troops sprang out," Dale interrupted drily.

"And there he sat like a rose in a thicket of swords. How did you know?"

"Ha!" Dale lovingly placed the axe back among its fellows.

Liath walked to look from the window, his fist beating lightly on the wooden sill like a caged bird's wing.

"Who have we lost?"

Fod's whiskers twitched.

"Bay's two lads and Cadel."

"See to Bay and his wife." At Liath's glance some women picking over bog-cotton in a corner went quietly out.

He's a compassionate man, thought Tansen, in spite of seeming reckless. And, strangely, remembered the injured foot that no one had bound for him. She rose and went to join Liath at the window. If sides were to be taken between the two men she would show from the start where her sympathies lay. Yet her natural curiosity made her speak out.

"I heard you'd stopped attacking sherriffs because the Angles were hanging the farmers in retaliation."

"If they hang all the farmers who's left to pay the tithe?" It was Dale who answered. The cool insensitivity in his voice filled her with horror. Liath gripping a lone leaning spear watched the unloading of the bodies.

"Besides it keeps the lads on their toes," Dale went on cheerfully.

Liath's long bony fingers tested the cutting edges of the spear. Tansen guessed the soldier in Dale was mocking the traditional habit of the Caledonie, to wear down a stronger enemy by ambush and raid.

"There's a new pattern emerging now." The calm voice at her back was nearer. "Too many sherriffs have been robbed of silver and skins. Now they're only sending out recorders. 'Name of Pit and amount of tithe, please'. Later the army collects the tithes."

Liath swallowed noisily. Blood dripped from the hand that held the head of the spear. He turned from the sight below and forced out his words as though Dale had not spoken.

"The ones we should go for now are the serjeants. They'll collect the gelt. But only at Festival-times, says my man at Dalgynch. Imbolc, lambs. Beltane, calves. Lugnasad, grain. Samhain, winter-kill."

"Not to mention salmon, venison, hares and the rest," growled the invalid, shaking his birch crutch. "And Trumwine's Bishops? How can we relieve them of the tithe they levy? Coming up here, taking men's labour to build churches instead of growing food for their children. But for this leg I'd be roaring for vengeance."

Fod sucked in his cheeks.

"Talking of vengeance, Chief, Talorc's after you now for lifting the head off his commander."

"Aye." Liath's voice was warm and loving. "And if they come and we were timing it right, lads, one fine night, we could lure both Angles and Scots, sighting the camp-fires of each other and thinking they had us ... "

"The Angles would be fools to venture this far where they might tangle with Dal Riatans!" Dale strode to the door. "It's fine and handy to have a clan full of young lads willing to throw themselves at Scots daggers and Danish axes for the fun of it!"

Carefully Liath leaned the reddened spear back against the wall.

"Make no plans in front of that one" muttered Tansen. "He'll sell the information for a bite and sup and a safe corner while the battle's on."

Suddenly Liath roused himself.

"Hey, Garna! This is Prickles. Take her. She's yours."

A cascade of copper hair rippled and turned from a group sitting at a table. A strong bold profile emerged paling into insignificance as Tansen met the full impact of her eyes. And what eyes they were. Large liquid brown eyes that stripped away all pretence. Slowly Garna rose and her hair fell away. She was immense, instantly dwarfing the room and those in it. Magnificent bare shoulders, immense copper-tanned breasts, oiled and glittering in the firelight.

"My, she's a scrawny one!" It was a deep melodious voice with hidden undertones of passion.

Garna walked over, thick hips sliding sensuously under skin-tight leather trousers and looked down on Tansen from her great height.

"Feed her up and you'll find there's a fire in her to be Queen." Liath taunted.

The liquid eyes were suddenly laced with scorn.

Tansen drew in a shaky breath. Deliberately Liath had laid her aspirations bare at Garna's feet.

"Queen?" There was a gurgle of laughter, a harsh note of contempt. Garna moved to the cauldron, throwing her hair up into a coil on top of her head and fixing it out of her way with huge bronze pins.

She ladled out a bowl of stew and came with it, as magnificent as a goddess dispensing a mystical sacrament from a magic cauldron. The venison had been cooked long in herbs and wine until its texture was silky, tender and succulent. Tansen sniffed at the beaker that came with it and smelt herb-brew.

"What did she expect, Chief? Mead in a silver chalice? A room with a feather mattress? A servant to wash her bowl?"

Tansen's cheeks reddened with humiliation. And Dale came in, carrying across his arms a lad of barely twelve summers whose hair and breast sprouted blood-red. He laid the dead boy at Liath's feet.

"Your handiwork." His voice sharp as grinding ice. "I warned you not to send fledglings against trained soldiers."

An explosion of rage from Liath and swiftly Garna was across, gripping his shoulder, her arm across his chest. Tansen gathered her dishes and fled to sit by the well below. There was something desperately wrong here. Wild passions flickered like lightning through the air between the two men. It was evident that Liath was planning some future uprising and that he had the makings of a strong military leader. Then why did he suffer a foreigner to humiliate him in his own Hall? Was it possible that Dale fitted in to some subtle scheme that Liath was hatching in his mind.

Friendly camp-fires lit the dusk in the arena. Folk with hair as bright as their plaids milled between hearths and wattle huts. A man and a chuckling bairn kicked an air-filled bladder between them. A burst of easy laughter came from the group round the story-teller as he acted out the latest legend of heroic clansmen who tormented greedy sherriffs.

Ignoring a lad and lass who kissed under the trees, Tansen untied her knife and cut several willow stakes. Without even stripping them properly she stuck them round a patch of soft earth. Tomorrow she would weave a proper screen, find ferns to lie on and moss for a pillow. She pulled her over-skirt round her shoulders and curled into sleep, fiercely glad to be free and to be near where Liath slept.

Incredibly the sound of pipes and horns, the beat of dancing feet, the skirl of dancers in the fortress above woke her once. And nearby the keening of a lone woman. And Garna's voice filled with an infinite compassion, crooning somewhere in the night.

She knew then the awful price they all had to pay, the folk that lived at Lynchattie, every man, woman and bairn. And how they each dealt with it in their own way.

In the morning she woke to the smell of sizzling pork. Garna, hair and breasts milk-white in the dawn, sat on a tree-stump tearing pork off a foreleg with her teeth. Tansen stopped the spit and sliced off a hefty chunk, holding it sputtering in a leaf. With the pork halfway to her open mouth she paused at the sight of Liath striding towards them. The clack of ivory pieces from a camp-fire checked his stride.

"Where there's gaming there's treasure to play for." His short-sword flashed and he hooked a leather bag from between two enormous feet.

"It was a sherriff," crowed the giant, not in the least put-out. "All agog to spill his ill-gotten gains to save his life-blood." His long arm seemed to stretch out to an impossible length to snatch his pouch back. But Liath had tossed it in the air and caught it and emptied the contents onto his hand.

"And where did he find gold coins hereabouts?" he asked.

"Must be Danish gelt," grinned the giant.

Liath threw him three gold pieces.

"I'll keep the rest for the lass in the glen that's suckling your bairn. We might need lusty lads like him yet before we oust the Danish scum."He tied the bag on his belt.

Tansen tensed, waiting for the giant to throw himself at Liath. Instead the man scratched his chin.

"Ach, I'd only lose it anyway," he said with resignation. Then his face beamed as a thought struck him. "Here, d'you think the lass is ready for another one yet?"

He has a kind of charisma, Tansen thought, that draws men and women to follow him. And remembered the dance of the knives and knew. No matter how much they dared, he would always dare more.

"Don't think to tempt him into your willow cabin." Flam's husky tones came from behind.

Tansen looked boldly round at her.

"Where does he sleep then?"

"Between silken sheets no woman's ever lain on." Flam's eyes melted as she watched him. Yet Tansen knew by her air of contentment that she and Liath were lovers. "He has a secret core no woman's ever pierced."

"If he has a core," Tansen replied.

Flam gave her a wide smile.
"Be sure he has."
"Now!" Garna came at her briskly. "Today you start your training."
Life here, thought Tansen, would be a constant challenge.

CHAPTER FIFTY

Tansen balanced her brand-new spear and aimed at a leaking straw sack.

"Slam your whole body into it, woman!"

Garna was at her back, tilting her elbows till her muscles screamed.

That first morning she had trained under Garna, exercising for balance, for suppleness, for speed. She had followed through with her dagger-hand practising up-curves and down-thrusts. Her arrows had flown straight and true. Her pebbles shot from a catapult had clipped the dead twigs off the trees. She was tired and hungry and wanting to rest and cut her own notch-sign in the shaft of her spear.

Garna came again to watch her jab and stab at the straw sack.

"It's not a scarecrow, girl! It's an Angle with an axe!"

"Don't tell her that! She'll only tickle him in the ribs." Dale shot at them as he passed. "Pretend it's me there, unarmed and at your mercy."

Tansen stabbed two-handed, viciously, her heart hurting wth the memory of raw and bleeding bodies at Pitcarlie that still haunted her.

"Why can't I just be a cook?" she complained to Garna.

"Because you've ambitions to be Queen, my lass."

Tansen had discovered that life at Lynchattie was lived on three levels. A grinding programme of training for everyone led by Garna, like a legendary warrior Queen, with a hand that felled and a tongue that flayed. And Dale, they said, was worse on the days he was present. Then there was a gallant ostentation when folk dressed in their best and danced the night away. And underlying both, moments when a lone pipe sounded in the night and wept and tore at the heart-strings as it echoed from crag to crag, singing of men and women who fell because it was the way of things and they could do no other.

As each hungry healthy day went by Tansen grew strong and rounded and firm-muscled again. Soon she earned the right to her own shield and a heavy-handled dagger. So one wet raw day she went to Tam to collect them from the store he guarded so jealously.

"You're a right bonny wee Hedgehog getting!" he said, handing her a round leather shield that had never been fashioned in Alba.

"Flattery won't get you your bonnet back." Tansen laughed. She turned sharply as riders entered the camp, her eyes sparkling, her cheeks vivid with an outdoor bloom, looking for Liath.

"Forget him! You and I would make a better King and Queen of the Northern Pretani: We have the gifts for it."

Dale, indolent in black supple leathers, drew his dagger across the nearest whet-stone.

Tansen had tilted her shield to hide her disappointment. Now she let her eyes mock Dale over the rim.

"Or will you again betray your people for love of a fine lad."

She drew in a long hurt breath and let it hiss out in warning.

"You should be at Dalgynch." Dale wet his finger and tested the blade. "A new Commander stormed in there after Erland. Bjorn Blood-Axe, bringing more men. And following Reatta's beckoning finger into her bed. You could have made a fine-handed gesture of it. With the slow sweet breath of a lingering poison in his bedtime cup."

"I have to face my enemy, fair and square. I couldn't force my body to do what my mind doesn't believe in."

"Don't tell me you believe in Liath? After Imbolc and the ice-melt Bjorn will be after him, leaving an avenging trail of murder and rape, fire and pillage behind him. Your Chief of the Name and his piddling raids will have a lot to answer for."

He played with the dagger, tossing it and catching it by the blade. An emerald winked in the handle and Tansen saw that the lop-sided osprey from his shirt had become a harbinger of death, its outstretched wings forming the handle.

"Liath risks his life daily." Her contempt at Dale's cowardice and spying was clear in her voice. "While you only interfere and hinder his training scheme."

"To mould this rabble of thieves needs a certain force of character that Liath lacks."

At that she lowered the shield.

"It's strange to hear an opportunist like yourself maligning Liath. I've never met a man so brave."

The lantern eyes glowed on her eager face for a moment and dulled.

"This enemy must be met with discipline and endeavour, not heedless raids and extravagant gestures that bring wanton carnage in their wake."

"He feeds and clothes you and supplies you with weapons. He gives you a place to hide. You'll not undermine his authority in a year of moons. No one here heeds your jealous carping!"

He rose, the dagger glinted. He drove it at her with such force that she fielded it with her shield only at the last minute on the edge. She heard the blade slash through the leather and stared at the point quivering in the wooden frame before her eyes. She threw the spoiled shield at his feet and it cracked under her foot as she strode away.

She sought refuge in her cabin. There was nowhere else to go on a day when the training ground was a sea of mud both over and under the walkways they had plaited so laboriously. She shivered, longing for a fine supple bed-blanket of skins.

Yet she was warmed by the blaze of wounded pride that had flamed in Dale's eyes. He was a man who prized his self-control and he had lost it when she accused him of undermining Liath's authority. But his words had made her thoughtful.

She picked up the thick wooden soles Tam had fashioned for her to lift her feet above the mud. Thongs threaded through the holes he had bored would bind two rabbit skins snug round her feet. As she worked she pondered. Was Liath really throwing away young lives? He was always off scouring the countryside for news of sherriffs and serjeants. And finding few about in this weather. And lately bringing back more wounded men than booty. But his strategy was to keep the Angles busy while he built up an armoury. Was there another way?

The stew that night was wersh and watery. A dearth of game? Or was the bitter taste in her own mouth? Should she have gone back to Dalgynch? Could a Princess with a Danish boy at her breast have triumphed over Reatta? And stirred up a rebellion in secret? It was useless to think such thoughts now. She gave her bowl to a hound to lick and took him back to her cabin to keep her warm.

So she went back to filling her days with training and her nights with sound sleep.

One raw blustery day just before Imbolc she and her comrades came from training to cup icy water to their mouths and sit in a sweaty huddle round the well. Arrin, the bard, came among them and sang of the old days of Chieftainship and warfare. Of the boasting and chariot-beating, the charging in a straight yelling line, and the Chief standing up as champion to fight in single combat on behalf of his clan.

"Battles aren't won by grand lungs and fancy trews nowadays, Arrin," Liath joined them, setting one thigh on the well. By the way he avoided looking at her, Tansen hoped his senses vibrated to the same tune as her own.

"No," she said boldly. "They're won by stratagem and raw courage. By men with a vision! Like our own Chieftain." And not like Dale, she might have added if they had been alone.

Liath's swinging boot knocked flakes off the wall for a moment.

"I'm forming a band here that's different. Each man, each woman. We depend on our individual skills. Use our own initiative. Each one is a warrior, a champion."

Tansen felt the stir of hero-worship around her and stood to face him, forcing him to look at her.

Liath met her eyes lazily, his face closed. She tilted her head, covered now in close bright curls and saw the crooked line of his lips part as if his breathing troubled him.

"Nowhere else in all this land is there an arsenal of weapons like ours. Or a training scheme like ours. We'll have the best fighting force in Alba soon. And a leader to match!" She challenged him with her eyes to set her at his side as his partner.

His face shut on her, tight as a prison door. And he flung himself off the wall to relieve Flam of a bag of meal that was as light as a feather. Hand-in-hand they ran, with Flam's tawny skirts swirling, laughing, up the steps to the fort.

"What did I say wrong?"

Tansen turned in hurt bewilderment to Garna. She sat with a bare foot resting on one knee, watching them, the great liquid eyes filled with a soft, tender light. She loves Liath too, thought Tansen with a sudden shock.

"You'll not come between those two." Garna resumed her rasping at a broken toe-nail with a rough stone. "There's a kinship there. Liath's passionate, flamboyant, undisciplined. Flam suits him with her wild animal beauty. She'll never leave him to go back to wander with her kin."

"Whereas this lusty lass might take flight tomorrow behind another adventurer with a cockade in his bonnet."

Tansen drew in a sharp breath and turned viciously to where Dale sat idly on the parapet.

"I'd rather be lusty and succeed than be a jealous tom-cat howling over his failures, like you."

"You don't know what you're ... !"

Garna spluttered into silence as Dale raised his hand, his great eyes flaming.

"It's better to have self-control than to shed bairns like a farmer sows seed."

A tide of scarlet shame flooded Tansen's body. How could he know about the bairn she had left at Pitcarlie? Only Wulf, Nain and Deva had known. Why was he always there, churning her emotions, lashing her with his cruel tongue.

"Why do you follow me? What are you? A professional scavenger in other folk's middens, picking over the filthy rags of gossip," she threw back.

He slanted a sudden brief smile and laughed softly, undisturbed.

"You sounded a Bell once. Remember? You had the makings of a fine woman then. Like an arrow shot from the bow of the gods. Yet still you trail your pennant in the dust before every glad-eyed rogue."

"You two-faced scoundrel!" Fury, hatred and a sick hurt almost choked her. "You're not half the man Liath is!" She turned to appeal to Garna to defend the Chief they both admired. And loved. Garna stared owlishly back and shrugged her bare shoulders indifferently.

After that Tansen took her new weapons to the Hall to find companionship among those who sharpened and oiled their weapons, fondling and cherishing the iron, the bronze and the leather as they would the sweet flesh of a lover.

CHAPTER FIFTY ONE

Time began to slip past in a welter of warmer days with sudden showers and gusty winds. Tansen pointed her toe in the reels with the best in the Hall. Dale took detachments of men out on exercises. Liath slipped quietly in and out with a chosen few. And always Flam was there glowing like a willow-the-wisp waiting to pull his boots off. And to dance for him later, all fluttering skirts and pinpoints of toes like a moth round a flame. Then Garna promoted Tansen to be a scout.

The daily stint was a lonely one but Tansen welcomed the chance to roam the hills on a brave little sheltie. One evening she was returning, thinking longingly of her wattle cabin, her soft springy mattress that smelt of bracken and heather. She had been scouting westwards all day looking into glens from the summits of mountains, her horn ready to blow a warning to farmers, two short notes for bad weather coming in, one long blast for raiders. From a height she had seen the ships manned by local fishermen, left on guard in Loch Ness by Liath. And she remembered the purple skirt she was weaving on a loom made of twigs. And the pleasure she would have in handing back Flam's clothes.

Suddenly a lone rider burst round a clump of trees. By the three pheasant feathers in his cap she recognised Liath. Her sheltie sensed the leap of blood in her veins and bounded towards him. Liath turned a pale ravaged face as she drew near and savagely kicked his horse into a gallop away from her. Shocked she drew rein. Then some welling instinct urged her to follow.

He led her a wild ride. a feverish search for danger, veering from side to side, mercilessly setting his mount to jump at anything that loomed, a fall of rocks, a clump of gorse, a scuttling sheep.

Now she knew there was something far wrong. Her sheltie scrambled up the slopes taking them ever higher. Until they were locked within a ring of mountain peaks dark against the sky.

Far ahead she saw his horse stumble and Liath fly through the air to fall out of sight. Breathless now she clung with her knees and came to where his horse stood, blowing through his nostrils. Liath was rolling on the ground, pressing his hands to his face and groaning in anguish.

Before she could free her hands from the twined reins, he had heard her and was up, bounding from her, to stop at a stony crag. With his eyes he followed the unbroken plunge of the nearest dark-green giant to where a silent loch waited, its tree-filled arms open in cold everlasting welcome.

When she saw the tears washing unheeded down his cheeks, she knew it was his mind that was hurt. And she stayed where she was, aware that this was the core of the man. Something had wiped away all pretence, all bravado. Something had cut deep into his great heart.

"They knew!" he cried suddenly, lifting his clenched fists to the skies. "How well they knew!"

He was facing northwards, through a cleft in the mountains towards Craig Phadric at the head of Loch Ness. The armies of the North had fled from that fort after Burghead. Now the Angles had another haven for their new fleet to hide it from their former ally, Penda of Mercia, who was harrassing them in the south.

She waited, not daring dismount in case he ran from her. But trying to love him better as she had done to the birds and animals who had come to her as a child.

And she thought of Wulf and his gentle kindliness. With him she had felt safe and warm and unafraid. But none of this headlong exciting emotion of falling in love that gripped her now.

And Ean, the boy. And how she had learned that men and women mature at different times and to different levels. And how as life went on and people grew and changed, so love grew and changed. And if two people did not move in the same direction and change together, love between them could be lost. Any one who fell in love would have to take that chance. That their love might not last for ever. That they would not love only one person in their lifetime. That there was more than one kind of loving. But love was unique while it lasted and brought a special quality that should not be missed.

Night was sifting in. A golden cloud gleamed forth and lit a thread of a river down in the glen like a shining rapier-blade.

As the gleam faded Liath spoke, his voice low and edged with roughness.

"I'd had word of raiding parties going out from Craig Phadric. I lay on a hilltop watching for movement but I saw nothing. So I rode east, across the moor at Culloden."

He stirred briefly. Then words came tumbling out of him, seeking an escape. "I must have been spotted! I saw smoke in the distance. My mother's homestead! They'd fired it, knowing I was nearby, tempting me to come to her rescue."

A shiver shook him.

"She was waiting inside knowing I was coming. She always tied a blue veil high on the thatch if it was too dangerous." His voice came in a whisper. "Even from afar I could see the veil, curling in the flames. And I saw the glint of weapons around the house, men hidden in every thicket. I had to choose. My fierce proud mother, my bonny mother! Or the clan, the folk who live by my word in mountains and glens from Tay to Ness. And I turned my face towards Lynchattie. What kind of man am I? I left her to burn!" And he threw himself on the grass and shuddered in an agony of remorse.

Only when his limbs had stopped threshing and he lay exhausted, face down, did Tansen speak.

"I often wondered what kind of man you were. Now I know. And your mother knew. From her came your fierce courage, your staunch loyalty, your great compassion. She knew what you were and what you were doing. Yet she lived elsewhere, knowing the score, even as the enemy crept closer. She was a woman who thought and felt as you did, Liath. She left you free to make your own choices. And she trusted you to choose for the clan."

"I should have saved her!" His voice surged from the depths of his sorrow.

"You were too late," she said steadily. "She was a brave woman. You'll miss her. But she ought not to be mourned. For she wants you to take up the challenge again. So that her death has not been in vain."

He turned a tight-lipped mocking face to her.

"And what do you have that will wipe this blight from my spirit?" he asked bitterly.

"Nothing," she said. "All I can offer is a love of freedom and a winning way at tafl."

He turned his back on her, leaning on the rock.

"And an inside knowledge of Burghead and Dunnottar," she added.

He took her words into himself and rose, slowly at first and then stretching his limbs as if trying to shed a pain that could hardly be borne.

"Always the clan," he said bitterly.

She dismounted then and let the horses graze. A new understanding had come to her. A Clan Mother could mourn and it was proper. But here in the Caledonie mountains the folk needed a champion, one who rode out confident that the gods had made him invincible. Yet he was also the Father of the Clan. And Liath loved them like a father. And every death in his service had to be fought through within himself till he could emerge strong and fearless again.

"Now you know my weakness." The tough bronzed face had hardened and grown pale.

She came then, face to face with him, laying her hands on his shoulders.

"No! I've seen the compassion in you. And compassion is the fountain of all strength."

Slowly she drew his lips down on hers and kissed him deeply and passionately, forcing her body against his. His body began to tremble. He held her away and looked into her face as if seeking the spur he needed to go on living. As she kissed him again she felt desire kindling in his body .

Wulf and Ean had always let her lead their love-making. It was the Pretani custom. Now she let him tumble her onto the soft cool grass.

He bared her heated breasts and she felt no chill from the air as he fondled them. Quickly he unclasped her belt and loosened the laces of her trousers. Then in a sort of fever he slid the leggings off her long slim legs, trailing his lips over the firm flesh as it was revealed.

The mountain peak behind his head thrust forth from its cloak of mist as he read her eagerness in the arching of her body. He drove into her with a desperate need, a wild hunger. And she met him with an explosive desire. And let his superior strength control her for that was what she needed too. Only this barbaric plunging could satisfy her own hunger, could bring the Life Force that had been lying dormant, to flood through her, searing her with its heat. Their need swept them into a mindless shuddering explosion of passion. And a pleasureable ebbing of ecstacy. And a moment of stillness, as though the world held its breath while they searched one another's faces for signs of pleasure.

"I knew this would happen." He laughed softly. "You should have gone when you had the chance, Prickles."

He held her close and rocked her in his arms.

"Oh, daughter of Oengus, since I first saw you at Dalgynch I wanted you." "Why did you wait so long?" she asked.

"In Dalgynch you were a Queen, distant, aloof, exotic in your rich silken gowns."

"Borrowed finery."

"You were a statue of bronze with a Danish King at your feet and skin like foam waiting for the circlets he would place round your throat, to hold you in thrall. What besotted fool would ask you to live from day to day and risk your neck with me?"

"Yet you brought a slave in rags from Dunnottar!"

His mouth curved.

"Stately and proud, you came from serfdom, slender as a sapling, with your crystal eyes and your skin like flowers and your strawberry-coloured mouth. I tried to drive you away. But you stayed."

Suddenly he laughed, joyously, and together they rose and ran, throwing their arms upwards, sharing their gladness with the dark sky and the fierce mountains around them.

Before the last light had gone Liath picked up his fallen bonnet and threw the broken feathers into the wind. He captured their mounts and led the way back at a fearsome pace.

Flam, reclining on the stairs, saw Tansen come with the fulfilment of love blazing in her face. A flash of brown leg and she was up, poised, her back arched. Tansen might have expected a dagger. Not the steady amber gaze full of a thousand timeless curses. Not the quick cat-flick of her sand-striped hair. Not the poised pad of feral feet as she climbed the stair. And certainly not Garna's voice from the heights.

"Come with me, my precious. That one's a Queen with the chain of Kingship in her hands. But silver tarnishes in time."

Now Tansen lived with Liath within the fort and rode like a wild thing on raiding parties at Liath's side. No more training for her, or for the young men Liath picked to follow him. One hectic adventure followed another. They revelled in danger, riding high on the tempestuous wind, their blood singing with exhileration, their nerves vibrant with life, their senses attuned to the secrets of mountain and glen and sky. Savouring every sweet moment, knowing that it might be their last and making a praise-song of it. Yet, when she thought about it, all they seemed to do was to chase a few Scots back to their coracles on Loch Ness.

She came striding into the warm Hall after one such raid, frustrated and furious.

"When do we stop practising on Scots and turn our blades on Angles?" she cried to Liath. She sat on the bench beside him and flung back her cloak.

Liath unpinned his huge clan brooch from his plaid and fastened it carefully in his jacket.

"What else is there to do?"

"Hunt game for a change," grumbled Moran, banging down a pot of greasy liquid.

"Scottie skins are fair game." Liath bit into a round of hard cheese, grimaced and threw it at Moran. "I'd starve rather than let Domnall Brecc so much as sniff at the air I breathe."

"The Scots under Domnall are as weak as this stew." Tansen sniffed at the mess in the ladle and returned it to the bowl. "But we're outlaws here in our own land, hunted fugitives. Our heads off if we're caught." She found a stale roll and bit into it.

"Next year we'll burn the tithe grain before the Angles can take it. Moran, my stomach's as flat as a burst bladder."

Tansen turned to Liath speaking earnestly and quietly.

"That's not the way. The Angles are not any hungry marching army. They and their horses are fed in strongholds provisioned by their fleet. It's time to plan organised attacks on the Angles." She paused and added quietly. "When will you avenge the death of your mother?"

Liath in a savage burst of anger ripped his dagger from his belt and held it before her.

"Could you do better? Nineteen Scots already have paid the penalty!"

"Scots killed your mother?" She stared open-mouthed. "Then you were spying on Scots that day, not on Angles."

"I'll kill ninety and nine Scots before she's avenged!" His boots thudded on the reeded boards as he stalked out.

"It seems we've both gambled on the wrong horse." Dale's great voice rumbled from an alcove. "He'd barter the rest of Alba so long as he can keep his wild mountains free. And why should he face an organised force like the Angles, when he can boost his vanity routing out a few half-starved ill-armed strays."

CHAPTER FIFTY TWO

It was past Imbolc when Tansen and Liath and twenty rollicking lads rode out to plant a couple of spies dressed as girls with fishing creels in the Cave of the Sculptors at Burghead. Dale was not in the crowd to see them go. Tansen wore a home-made kerchief on her head in the Danish style and each man had found some item of looted clothing. They rode sedately, shouting a muffled word that sounded like a password to distant scouting parties of Angles, too cold to be curious.

In the cold dawn of a day chilly with sleet they reined their horses to a stop on a hillside and scanned the countryside to the north. It was distressingly clear that the fertile river systems now flowed between deserted meadows and ruined homesteads.

The shocked men grunted or whistled and fell silent.

"Fiends!" Liath hissed. "They're taking the skin off the Mother! How will she breathe?"

"I see it now!" said Tansen softly. "In North Humber Land the Angles took tithes from the local farmers. Up here, it's our land they want! They'll put their kin in these derelict steadings. Dale was wrong when he said they wouldn't hang all the farmers. They've plenty farmers waiting back home. Come on, let's move!"

Ferociously they kicked their mounts and went down the slope. If they had met a party of Angles then they would have forgotten their disguise and fallen upon them.

Just south of Burghead they left their horses and swords with Runn, a trapper, spending his off-season snug in a bearskin, mending his snares. That night Tansen led them past the fort, ablaze with torches and bright as the Clavie Barrel. Inside the Cave nothing remained but broken stone slabs in grey dust and Ragnie's draughtscreen. Sadly she wondered what had been the fate of Fael and Ragnie and their clan. And Wulf. What had become of him?

While the spies made themselves comfortable Tansen climbed down to the sculpting platform. It had been scoured clean of chips of stone and dust by gales. But broken slabs lay strewn about. And there leaning against a rock she recognised Wulf's comical picture of the drunken farmer and his mule. Not a careless drawing on sandstone now but carefully and boldly pecked out on hard stone.

The bald farmer with the bulbous nose had grown a paunch. The lean-shanked mule with its splayed forelegs looked even more downtrodden.

The drinking horn had grown to an enormous size. And the long beak of the bird curled in a sarcastic leer.

Wulf must have worked at it after she had gone to Burghead. Fael would not have approved of this departure from tradition. But Wulf, missing her, uncaring about custom, maybe even drowning his own sorrows a little, had put his heart and soul into it, perhaps laughing a little at himself.

The call came for her to hurry. On the journey back the men began their mouth music. Low and fierce at first and then rising, hurling out a fury of sound to the tops of the tall pine trees. And their throats worked as they cried their pain at the devastation, and from their lips, tongues and teeth came the beat of the marching army that would one day launch its challenge. It was a bold and spirited gesture and could have only one end.

Even when they heard horsemen, riding through the dark-wood in pursuit they still sang their despair. And did not vary the long steady lope that came as naturally to them as walking.

Then the music stopped as though a whip had cracked. Not a sound but the splash of a stream. Like shadows they turned and began to climb, scrambling over rocks and scree where horses would be useless.

Suddenly Liath was far below, crying 'Caledonie' into the distance. And they lay low on a high plateau, faces pressed on ice-cold rock. It still amazed Tansen that Liath issued no orders for his clan knew their country and how to cope with it.

"They're surrounding us!" Liath had stolen up unheard to lie beside them. "Come! I don't fancy dangling from a ricketty gibbet in this weather."

They pushed with their elbows till they were on the edge of a gorge that fell sheer to a river. It was a narrow river, heavy and dark, shouldering its way sternly past constricting boulders. Strands of vapour steamed from the lichened walls. And a rainbowed mist hid a plunging waterfall.

Someone's sharp eyes saw willows and a gentler slope and they made for it. Loose scree slowed their pace and the men gathered fallen branches and stripped them as they ran. On a rocky platform they paused, listening, sensing, eyeing the maelstrom below while fingers plaited twigs into ropes and bound branches together.

"We can't!" cried Tansen staring downstream where cliffs rose straight up from the water and she knew there would be rapids.

"Why not?" Liath flashed a sardonic eye at her.

"Because it flows north. Away from Lynchattie. We'll be going the wrong way."

"Sh, don't tell the Angles, my sweetling!" He tossed down a rotting log. "Watch and learn. See what happens in that white water!"

At once it was caught by the swirling froth and held rigid, pointing upwards like a tree growing out of the river, till it smashed on a jutting rock.

He set off past the rock, long legs pumping, and hefted another branch.

"See that innocent-looking flat stretch. There's a fearsome pull underneath. Watch!"

The branch flowed strongly just below the surface until it was pulled into an eddy, swirling round and round before it was sucked underneath.

"Aye, we can do it," said Ban, stuffing his stockings into his shoes and tying them round his neck. "Five pairs of hands paddling each raft and we're clear of that whirlpool."

Fear rose strong in Tansen. I needn't go with them, she thought. I could hide from the Angles in the scrub.

A shout from the summit told that they had been sighted, At once she was heaving logs and lashing them in place and plunging downwards into the river. Suddenly she was in her element, filled with exhileration, ready to pit her strength against the awful force that filled the gorge. She tumbled into a raft after Liath, tucking her bare feet into the corded twigs that held it together. They were launched into the boiling, bubbling water and three more bodies thudded on top of them. Then they were paddling, leaning half over the sides, punching the water in time to Liath's grunts.

Icy water streamed over them coming straight from the glaciers at the source. At times she could see nothing above her head but frothing green water. Then the raft would be sucked downwards and suddenly spewed upwards to land in mid-air tilting, ready to capsize. Then down and round and up and round again. And black jagged rocks leaping out at them on either side.

The raft shuddered as it struck. A log-end sprang loose and neatly swept away a man with a red kerchief, sucking him beneath the foam. There was no way they could save him. They were fighting for their own lives. The same thing could happen to any one of them. It was terrifying. Yet through the terror a growing excitement as survival became the only and ultimate struggle.

They were tossed into an eddy. For a heartbeat they had a respite from the buffeting and booming. Then the craft began to swirl, slowly at first and then faster and faster.

They did not need the cry from Liath. They strove against the water, muscles cracking, trying desperately to keep away from the dreaded centre. With agonising slowness, the straining branches beneath their bodies began to respond. Tears of pain mingled with spray on Tansen's cheeks. Cramp knotted her legs as she strove for leverage. An ice-cold numbness weighted her arms.

Suddenly they were flushed out and racing downstream, flung forward by the impetus of the water tumbling down behind them. It was as though a giant hand dashed them around among the huge boulders it had sprinkled in their way. Liath unhooked his feet and hurled himself to the front of the raft. Tansen found that a high shout meant 'paddle left' and a low roar meant 'paddle right'. So that if they were engulfed by water they could still hear him.

Then they were in deeper water. But still at the mercy of the current. Time and again Liath chose a surge of water and tried to ride down on it. Time and again the raft tilted alarmingly until Tansen stared into white foam curdling beneath her. Then the brave ones would take their feet from their anchorage and lean their weight on the high side to bring the craft level again.

The gorge was narrowing!The rocks on either side were coming closer! With the force of the water behind them they could easily be smashed on one side or the other. With oustretched hands they fended off the rocks. Yet it seemed that the water itself was determined to force them straight through.

Then they were out of the tunnel, and plunging over a series of small waterfalls. They stopped paddling to cling on like limpets with the roar of water deafening them and taking deep breaths when they could so as not to drown as the water crashed over them.

A mighty heave and suddenly all was still. Silence resounding in Tansen's ears until she shook her head and became aware of the gentle grinding of gravel and the gurgle of the small waves that washed over her feet. It was as though the god of the river had had his fun and grown tired.

Tansen disentangled herself from the lashings and the muscled legs of a grinning Conal. When she rubbed her numbed arms she left trails of blood from hands torn by rocks.

She looked back at the dark glowering gorge with a growing sense of wonder. They had fought with the elemental spirit of the river and won. She was filled with exultation.

"Yahoow!"

Suddenly they were all stretching their limbs in an orgy of dancing and yelling. More rafts tumbled in besidc them and half-drowned men crawled out and lay catching their wind. The last raft swirled past into a lower beach.

They splashed downstream to help the men, laughing and hugging them. Then Liath held up his palm and with his eyes took a roll-call.

"Brioc? Aban"? Cet?" No answer from these three. Cet was the son of the cook, the gentle Moran.

Tansen shifted her thoughts into the ancient silent language that is the only way to address the spirit world and paid her tribute to the three men who had been sacrificed to the spirit of the water. Liath turned from halfway up the bank and saw her hand move.

"Make no whim-wham signs over this black-hearted ruffian when he goes!" he cried. "Forget me and get on with the task ahead!"

They lit a small fire in a cave and slept. And woke to a world white with late snow. They went single file, stepping in the footsteps of the one before, the last one sweeping their tracks with a branch. So it was late after noon when they loped into Lynchattie with the curlew calls sounding.

Liath strode before them, shoulders wide, his bonnet appearing from nowhere to sit jauntily on his head. And the women and children crowded round, eager to touch him for the magic to rub off on them. Men turned their heads and stopped work, but stayed back.

"Tell us where you've been, Father of the Clan," cried a boy, hip-high to Liath.

"How many heads rolled in the grass?" cried another, tugging at Liath's belt as he crossed the yard.

Out of the fort-gate came Dale, in his black leathers, his sword sheathed at his side, down the stairs, step by step matching each step with Liath's stride until he was two-thirds of the way down. There he stopped, astride the narrow steps, waiting.

Liath came to a halt, head tilted, questioning.

"No man bars the path of the Chief of the Caledonie into his own fort." Liath's voice was pleasant but dangerously low.

Dale scanned the bedraggled band at Liath's back.

"Three men lost, and all to plant a couple of fish-wives at Burghead?"

"My prerogative."

"You plucked the best men from training and lost three in a mad escapade! What can your spies tell us that we can't guess? You've left twenty horses, the gods only know where! And a track a bairn could toddle after."

A hush fell on the yard. Tansen pushed forward to Liath's side, her eyes dark. Liath's bodyguard closed in on soft hunter's feet.

"Until you learn to curb your animal antics you, Chief of the Name, are barred from leaving this fort."

CHAPTER FIFTY THREE

Liath's hand paused where his sword should have hung. With his eyes fixed on Dale, he gestured with his empty hand at his back.

Tansen sprang to a scabbard left carelessly on a bench. Adfothla, his beard curling and frothing like whipped cream whipped, swung it from her grasp and she met the full impact of timeless authority in his ice-blue eyes.

"You can't leave him defenceless!" she cried.

"This matter's better aired without weapons."

Liath laughed as he overheard, flinging his empty palm eloquently in the air, supremely confident in the men and women at his back and the vulnerability of the lone figure before him. And Tansen knew by the thread of excitement in his laugh that he had been waiting eagerly for this showdown. Dale spoke again.

"And since you make a habit of casting off weapons and horses at a whim, you will remain unarmed and unmounted until I give you leave."

Cries of protest came from some of the women. Stub-leg stumped across to stand at Adfothla's side, in silent support.It seemed to Tansen that Dale was making a fool of himself in front of the whole Clan.

"We'll see who gives the orders in my fort. Disarm yourself, my rowdy cockerel. Come down and wrestle it out with me!"

Liath moved sideways to the bottom of the stairway, his eyes glittering, lean hands inviting Dale to come to him. Dale made no effort to unbuckle his sword-belt.

"Not while there's more to be said." Dale's eyes flickered ceaselessly over Liath and his men, watching for a move to unleash a hidden dagger.

Flam stood smiling at the top of the stairs, her tawny overskirt curled up like a shell over her bare arms and shoulders. Behind her, heads wagged and bobbed.

Tansen swung her gaze over the faces of Laith's clan, faces she knew well by now. And stopped short at Adfothla.

"Are we going to stand back while our Chief's insulted?" she asked him, half-amused. "You're not going to let this thieving spy squirm his way into our leadership?"

"Be quiet! Bite hard on your toorie," growled Tam. He had appeared in the middle of the young men returned from the raid. "They've a wheen of talk to do, these two."

"Leadership?" Dale answered her, smiling faintly. "A leader of any worth would havè rallied the Chieftains of the North at once after Burghead.

He threw away that advantage for his obsession with the Scots."

He appeared to be measuring the men in the yard with his eyes, reading the answer to some question that only he knew.

"He let the men of the North flee back to their homesteads. Now they quarrel over fishing and hunting rights, kill one another over the damming of a stream. They're settling old scores. Petty jealousies are becoming clan wars. Isn't that so?"

"Better than bickering in our backyard!" It was Conal whose legs had tangled with hers on the raft. Tansen gave him a quick grin of encouragement, although Dale's words were making her uneasy.

Dale's voice boomed forth.

"For a hundred cycles of seasons the Clans shared the harvests of the Mother in peace. And the Clan Mothers could do so still with a strong King and Queen at the helm."

Tansen's mouth slowly opened for Dale was making sense. Memories of phrases she had used herself came back to taunt her.

Liath leaned on the edge of the steps. It was a subtle move for now he too faced his Clan. He gave a quick ironic scan round their faces.

"The man blames me for a natural upsurge of human greed."

A low uncertain laugh from the crowd greeted Liath's sally.

"No, for wasting the advantage that you held in your hand." Dale sat now, laying a negligent elbow on a knee, as though they were having a pleasant fireside chat. "For standing back while the Angles foment trouble by promises of protection. And bringing fresh kin from across the sea to fill up the homesteads they've emptied." His steady voice bludgeoned on. "I foresaw it all and warned you, you blind fool."

Liath's smile stiffened. Tansen stared from one to the other. Did Dale not understand how much Liath had done already in gathering and arming and training this force? Ready to launch an attack when the time was right.

"And for all your raiding and stealing back of tithes, the farmers haven't enough food to see them through till the geese come from the icelands and the grouse breed in the moors."

"That's the fault of the Angles."

The young men beside Tansen growled and shifted their feet.

"Yet the farmers blame you, Liath. Funny that! Saying that you didn't have to pay tithes, so why have you no salt meat or meal or animal fodder in store. Try to find one homestead who'll offer you bite and sup willingly now."

Liath's face went white and slowly filled up with blood. Tansen gripped her hands together tightly. This dogged listing of minor faults must end soon. Or Liath would be forced to defend his honour by the sword.

"You think to shame me before my Clan." Liath's voice crackled with derision.

There was a roar from the young men of the rafts.

"He's only one against all of us! Let's rush him!"

And Liath was up, arms outsretched, sinewy legs braced.

"You'll not touch him!" he cried. And softly, turning, "He is mine."

"And still they follow you blindly." Dale sat unperturbed, his jaw wide, his eyes like burning coals. "You throw away men's lives. Men who used to know nothing but rising from the heather in a yelling bunch. And who were beginning to act as an organised army under orders."

"I've a band here that's different as the Caledonie have always been different. We use our heads and our countryside." Liath's voice rang with pride.

"Admirable. A useful trick to have in your armoury. But not enough."

"No, not enough." Liath agreed amicably. "Let's see what tricks your sword can play then. Adfothla!"

Dale must realise he's gone too far this time, thought Tansen.

"Hold, Adfothla," said Dale. "I'll not fight him till he's rested and eaten."

"And let the proud blood of my fathers cool in my veins? No!" Liath exploded.

Adfothla leant deliberately on the long ornamented scabbard.

"I'll give you the sword, my Chief. This conflict of words has bitten too deeply. Only a shedding of blood will satisfy."

"Let me feel the welcome of cold metal in my hand, Adfothla." Liath strode forward, hand outstretched. Adfothla raised his palm.

"Yet before you grasp this hilt and smell blood, my Chief of all the Caledonie, you will acknowledge that this sword was not fashioned here in Alba, nor looted from an Angle. You are turning it against the man who brought it from Ireland. Along with all the axes, daggers, shields and spears in the Hall above."

Tansen, her feet rooted in the scuffed dust, felt the blood rushing to her head.

Liath gave Adfothla a crooked grin.

"All bought with Burghead silver. Where else should he bring them once Burghead fell?"

"Dale, Prince of Strathclyde, is still in command of the men and the ships that wait in Loch Ness. The Scots, Angles, Irish, even his own Britons would have paid dearly for such a force. Yet when he found Burghead had been taken he offered his force freely to you, so that you would lead them in the fight against the Angles. I was there when you gave him that oath, O Chief of the Caledonie."

And he dared Liath with his eyes to deny him, to forswear his vow and drag the proud name of the clan for ever in the dust.

Tansen closed her eyes on a wave of dizziness. Her mind, her senses cried out that this could not be true. Yet it was Adfothla who was speaking, an elder of the Clan, and round him had gathered the older men, the experienced men, condemning Liath with grieving eyes. Liath, the Father of the Clan.

"This training which he organised, whose rules you have flouted and incited others to flout. It could be the making of the Caledonie. It could make our clan the leading force in the battle to unite the clans and free our land."

Adfothla's voice carried like a whiplash. Folk listened and stirred uneasily, yet on their faces Tansen read pain. The same pain that was like a cold lump of stone in her breast.

"The men and ships Dale left in Loch Ness were sufficient safeguard to keep the Scots from our back door. Yet time and again you have failed to turn your face towards the Angles."

Tansen felt herself reeling from one blow after another. She had praised Liath's armoury to his face and he had not told her the truth. Yet for all his faults, a Clan would never desert its Chief. And she was a daughter of Oengus. Her heart lifted as she saw Liath stand proud, confident, his Cheiftainship plain on his face and in every taut line of his body.

"You, Adfothla," he said, softly and with sorrow. "An elder of my father's Clan. Yet you join with my enemy and accuse me of cowardice, of failure, of misjudgment." He thrust Adfothla aside, grasped the scabbard and drew the sword.

"But of all men you stand alone!" he yelled. For a breathless moment the sword hung high and purposeful over Adfothla's calm and creamy head. Then Jon was between them, his neck invitingly bare. And another, and another. Old men and not-so-old. Liath's eyes slowly widened. He sucked in a huge quick breath and swung round to face Dale, snarling.

"And while I've been gone. You've even turned my clansmen against me."

"No, never!"

The young men would have surged forward but for outflung arms. Adfothla's, Tam's, Stub-leg, Jon's.

Dale began to rise, taking his time, with a certain reluctance about his movements.

Slowly he unbuckled his belt, unsheathing his sword as with a lazy foot he tipped belt and empty scabbard over the side of the steps.

The space before the fort cleared like magic. Dale came slowly downwards, his feet meeting each step with an elegant sense of purpose. Liath, pale yet resolute, backed until both men stood, widely separated, within a circle of onlookers.

"Shield? Dagger?" Liath did the honours of a challenger. Dale smiled at the irony and shook his head, his eyes steady on Liath's face.

Liath's favourite hound lolloped out of the crowd towards his master. And Liath took that moment of diversion to launch himself forward, his long blade aloft and gleaming. A clash and rasp of blades. Dale had side-stepped and parried. And the air was filled with a bright curtain of thin blades flashing in the weak sunlight. And the yelping of a rapidly retreating hound.

CHAPTER FIFTY FOUR

Both men were in their prime and born swordsmen. At first, Liath lunged and thrust, full of aggression, determined to wipe out the insults that had flayed his spirit to a white agony. Dale, moving easily but steadily backwards, parried and ducked. Liath, probing Dale's defences, soon had inflicted a mass of small bleeding cuts on Dale's bare arms. To everyone and eventually to Liath it became obvious that Dale was holding back, respecting the exhaustion that showed white at the corners of Liath's mouth. Liath dropped his guard.

"Attack will you!" he cried. "Give me a fight of it!"

With a flicker of movement and a click, Dale had the two blades locked together in a cross above their heads. Sinews bulging, muscles straining they remained until Dale began to force Liath's blade downwards.

"There's one more mark against you," said Dale, pleasantly into Liath's face. "You treat women like chattels."

Tansen, crushed between Adfothla and Stub-Leg knew he had used this as a lever to spur Liath into a face-saving show of action. It worked. With an inhuman effort, Liath swung his blade round and freed it.

"I knew it!" he cried, springing back. "It's my woman you're after!"

His eyes sparked in his pale face. This time when he launched himself forward, his back was straight and firm, his wrists strong and supple and there was skill and power behind his blade.

"You always wanted her, didn't you?"

Now both swords were instruments of death. Liath rained a hail of blows so fast the eye could not follow and only the clash, whine and rasp told of their fierceness, and the quick accuracy of Dale's reflexes.

Then Liath drew back, breathing harshly.

"You followed her to Gefrin. You killed her husband and then lost her to a travelling mason. Yet it was I who took her from slavery in Dunnottar!"

Again they engaged. And there was a deadly power in the thrust of arm and blade, And a grim beauty in the flashing curves and spirals of the sword-play. Brains, eyes, arms and bodies in one concentrated interplay of brilliance and balance.

Tansen, frozen, only her eyes moving, saw first one man, then the other gain the ascendancy, meeting lightning strokes of fire-hardened iron and falling back. Liath's blade streaked like a curtain of falling stars in a display of spontaneous inventiveness.

Dale with his solid athletic frame and constant practice was no less nimble and creative. And yet it seemed he was not being stretched to his limit while Liath was steadily tiring. Aware of his growing weakness Liath went for the kill, time and again seeking Dale's heart. While Dale's blade point shifted at the last minute, slanting away from Liath's vital organs towards his limbs. Behind the great yellow eyes, Tansen suspected, he was intending the fight to end with a slash to Liath's leg or sword-arm.

A sheen of sweat on both faces, their hair lying dark and lank on their necks.

It was Liath's exhaustion that brought the fight to an end. As Dale lunged, Liath's ankle buckled on a stone and in the nick of time he flung himself backwards to fall against the wall at the foot of the steps.

An indrawn moan of horror arose from the women. The flat of Dale's sword on Liath's hand sent his sword slithering across the dust. Dale's foot instinctively stamped hard on the open hand. His blade, poised and intent, steadied on Liath's throat. Liath half-lay, half-leant, calm, waiting, only his ribs moved, quick and ragged, with his breathing.

Tansen, hovering on a silver-edged abyss of fear, sensed the working of the mind behind the great yellow pondering eyes. He must not kill Liath. For Liath was the Chief. The Caledonie clan might respect Dale but their ultimate loyalty lay with the Chief of the Name. Yet if he did not kill, he offered Liath a greater insult that any Chief could bear. And Tansen's knowing eyes saw Dale's right foot position itself for a strategic stumble. Then two-handed, Dale drove forward, straight at Liath's exposed and sweating throat.

A flutter like the wings of a tawny moth. A scream echoed and was caught up by other tense throats. Flam lay in the curve of Liath's arm, tawny, vivid, alive, her hands curling protectively around the hilt of Dale's sword impaled in her breast.

It did not matter then that Dale had deflected his blade towards Liath's shoulder. Dale, stunned, drew back in horror. Tansen ran to kneel beside the girl. A red poppy had bloomed on her breast. The dark eyelashes fluttered and opened. The great tawny eyes lit on Liath's face. The red lips opened and drew in a tiny breath that ended on a gasp of pain.

"Hold me," she whispered.

Tenderly he moved so that his arm and shoulder hid the hilt with its large rounded pommel from her sight. And she was enclosed in his arms.

She touched a lock of his bright hair and it curled itself round her finger.

"Sun of my seasons, star of my nights." Her arm fell like the white broken wing of a dove. "I could not live without you. Now I can live for ever in your heart."

Her eyes, lit from within, glowed on his face. The amethyst beads rose once. A soft sighing breath as life left her body. Another moment of suspended time and her spirit soared free. And the beautiful body was empty.

And Tansen knew that she had not met a man she could love like that, enough to give her life for him.

Liath laid his face in Flam's hair. Behind his back, Garna took hold of the sword and withdrew it gently so as not to move them. A little spurt of blood came with it and stopped. Granite-hard, like a priestess at a ritual, Garna held the blade upright, two-handed, before Dale. His face convulsed fleetingly, before he bowed his head and accepted it. And with it, his guilt.

"She thought to save his life," he said softly. "She did much more. She saved his honour."

Garna nodded. Laying her arms on Liath's shoulders, she lifted him away. At first his grip tightened until he looked in her face. And saw the naked suffering in it. Garna gathered the girl to her breast. Only Tansen heard her whisper.

"My little tawny moth. My little love." Slowly Garna mounted the steps to the Fort with her precious burden. The tawny hair swung in a lively caress over Garna's bare shoulder. Here and there a woman keened softly under her breath and a man cleared his throat loudly, breaking the silence.

Liath's restless blue eyes swept the arena, lingering on no one. His men came warily grouping around him, their eyes narrowed on Dale. Grey-faced Liath burst through them and ran towards the stables.

"Leave him!" Adfothla stopped the movement to go after him.

A despairing wail rose from the women. Children, echoing their mothers, sobbed, their eyes frightened. Men's voices rose, protesting, demanding. Liath careered round the shed, bare-back. The lame girl screamed, hobbling after him. A flurry of hoofbeats. And he was gone.

At that moment, Tansen saw clearly that someone had to take the lead. And it could not be Dale who had defeated their Chief and left them fatherless. She stood on the steps and read their faces. Faces blotched with anger, sallow with resentment. Scowling, bewildered, sorrowing, anguished.

"He'll come back!" she cried. "But for once let him be himself and suffer alone."

Dale came swiftly, thundering at her side, his feral eyes glinting dangerously.

"He'll be back! And he'll demand an accounting! From you! And you! And you!" The sword pointed, one after another, at the ragged retinue.

"For Talorc has taken the Scots into his heart," he said slowly, with a suave satisfaction. "He's settled Dom, son of Domnall Brecc, King of Dal Riata, and all of his cenel snug in the heart of Fib. When your Chief comes riding home, there will be battles to be fought!"

A wild anger shuddered across the faces of Liath's men.

"Then let's get to the business of eating and sleeping. For tomorrow you start training like never before!"

"Aye!" Tam led the first shout. "Aye!" came the answer. Fists beat at the air. The crowd began to break up, back to being practical and purposeful, the bairns to playing, the dogs to scratching. But a long low lament seemed to swell from nowhere and the folk fitted their steps to its beat.

Tansen turned to seek the privacy of her willow cabin to mourn for Flam and for Liath and for a lost love that had never been enough. Yet the shock of Dale's news brought her swirling round again.

"Why?" she asked Dale. "Why would Talorc take our enemy into the heart of our Kingdom?"

"Why?" Dale thrust his sword into the hard-packed earth to clean it. "Because he's afraid!"

"Of us - s - s!" She whispered on a breath of wonder. "Talorc feels threatened by us?"

Dale's eyes glowed like harvest moons.

"Ecfrith's hard-pressed in the south by Penda. He might have to recall Bjorn Blood-Axe. Talorc's looking for allies. But Talorc doesn't know Domnall Brecc. He's allied himself with a sewer rat. A bladder full of wind and water, wearing out his cenel and himself to imitate the great Aiden, his grandfather." He sprang up the stairs to the fort and turned at the top. "I think perhaps Liath's star is in the ascendancy again."

Tansen found herself gazing at the spots of blood on the steps where Flam had died. Her anguish and guilt and confusion were too much to be borne. And now battles to be fought against men drunk with ambition and power.

A lad descended the stairs towards her his arms filled with blankets.

"From the Prince of the Britons," he said.

She took them smiling wryly. She was being thrown out of the fort also. She turned to where the hound lurked. And when she clicked her tongue he rose on his hind legs and gave tongue to the world that his mistress wanted him again in her bed in the willow cabin that he had guarded alone for far too long.

CHAPTER FIFTY FIVE

That night, sleepless, Tansen crept silently out into the moonlit dark, her hand on the hound's broad head. The air around Lynchattie had warmed and filled with the mingled perfume of broom and hawthorn. She knew where a cherry tree blossomed and she silently told the spirit of the tree about the ill she had done to Flam, the little wild thing, blooming for so short a time and blown away like a poppy petal. And how she had not guessed at the pure and undying love at Flam's heart. And she cut a flowering spray and laid it on the step where Flam had died.

Shadows flickered, folk laying turves on fires, murmuring uneasily.

A fire on the far side had not yet been tamped down. Someone stretched a branch, lifting the body of the fire until it glimmered with new life on the planes of Dale's face.

"What will happen to the Clan now?" she asked him. "How long can you go on walking a tightrope?"

The dancing firelight lit on a widening jaw and eyes blooming with childlike joy.

"As long as it takes. The elders are solidly behind me. They know that raiding and rieving belong to the past. They need an army if the Clan is to survive."

"And the youths who are crying out for action?"

Dale embedded an iron beaker in the heart of the fire.

"They'll have no time to spare for resentment. Not till I've welded them into a strong fighting unit."

"You carefully didn't tell Liath about the Scots in Fib."

Dale loosened the laces at his throat.

"He'll hear soon enough and come back with his honour shining high. And a willingness to go forward with me."

"You made sure of that when you fought him. You neither killed him nor destroyed his pride."

"No. He's man enough to work through what happened today and to build on it. He needs to recover himself. It's a need that comes to us all. When only an escape into freedom and space will serve. And we need to attune to the new person we've become."

"When he returns he'll be a mere figurehead."

Dale did not answer. Tansen drew a rush stool forward with her toe and sat while the fire crackled and curled between them.

She should have guessed there was a steadying hand behind the Clan.

Liath hadn't misled her, she argued with herself. But she should have drawn her own conclusions from his silences. And his nature. Instead of being blinded by love. And building her own picture of a braw Chieftain like her father. Her mother had adored Oengus. Yet lived day by day with Suen, the kindly lame potter.

Love between a man and a woman was queer, she thought. Ecstacy and despair in one twisted strand. Powerful and fragile. Yet even as she recognised that her love for Liath had changed, it was still there, and always would be, like her love for Ean and Wulf, part of her being, tucked in a corner of her memory, among the strands that had made her what she was.

And what was she? A woman ready to take her place in the forefront of the campaign to free our land of Angles. She needed no signs or portents from Marten. It was a quiet knowing in her bones that she recognised calmly and with gladness.

"There is a way forward," she said. "We can rally the whole of the north under one leadership."

A sudden gleam lit up Dale's magnificent eyes.

"And who can we spare to persuade them?"

"A Queen of the Royal Blood." She tilted her chin defiantly against his expected derision.

Dale stretched his long booted legs lazily.

"I wondered when the Warrior Queen would grasp the nettle."

"I'm sick of killing. Yet I know it's the warriors who'll free the land."

"You fought and killed Angles at Pitcarlie," Dale reminded her. "You may need to do that again."

"I fought to survive. But when a great issue is at stake, I wouldn't reach for a weapon to make my protest. There are other ways."

"So what do we do about the Angles?"

It was a hard question to answer for had not the Great Spirit implanted in everyone the instinct to survive.

"War is the way of folk in this world we're set on." He hoisted his bubbling pot from the fire and laid it on a slab to cool. "Some warriors fight for glory. Some because they see the peace beyond the carnage."

"Druad and monks withdraw from war."

"Good men need only to stand back, for the killer to triumph."

"Yet what if all good men, united and together, stood back and refused to fight?"

He emptied some dried minty leaves from a pouch onto his palm and stirred them into his brew with a twig.

"In time that idea may take root. But we live in the present. In this little corner of the Mother the balance is on the side of the killer. I'll challenge that and somehow restore the harmony that should exist between folk and the land they feed from. It's the best I can do in this life. We're only human. Sent here to fail but in failing maybe to learn."

Once I taunted him with being a failure, Tansen thought. Yet the person who fails and tries again and again may succeed next time. It's the one who stops trying who fails.

Dale sipped slowly from his iron pot and spoke his thoughts aloud.

"Folk breed and need more space. And have to fight for it. The weak fall and the strong survive and breed some more. And so the strongest become dominant. And poets sing of the courage of heroes."

"And praise women only for their beauty."

"Yet these are the songs that will ring down the pathways of time. For there are no women bards."

Smiling she clasped her hands on her lap.

"Oh yes, there are. Around the hearth. Lullabies and love-songs will live in the folk-memory longer than war-songs."

It came to her that she had never really spoken with Dale before. They had always traded insults. Yet here they were letting their thoughts range together in an easy comradeship.

"I sometimes wonder about my folk, the Pretani, holding on to our tradition of Clan Mother and Queen, yet we still need a Warrior King to defend us. Some day perhaps we'll be engulfed by these same Warrior Kings."

"Killers and creators. Warriors and healers." Dale said. "Does it matter whether they are man or woman? We all share the same spark of the Infinite One within us. Some of us have to take on certain roles that don't fit us. Yokes that chafe till the pain drives us mad. Yet some of us see beyond to the kind of peace we want to make. Some day I hope we'll learn to choose wisdom before pride." The heavy sigh he gave seemed to bring him back to reality. "Would Liath accept the Kingship?"

"Why not yourself?" she asked. "You'll stick to your purpose. Someone has to take the lead."

"But not anyone. Only someone who could set up a Northern Kingship to rival the flawed one in the south. Only a woman with Royal Blood can do that. You're the only other Princess in the land. Only you have the power to make Kings." He paused, watching her. "And to topple Queens."

She heard the words she had longed to hear and they brought her no joy, no leap of the heart. She would have to think it through. The good laid in a balance with the bad. The possible with the impossible. And all for the sake of the weak, the starving, the enslaved. She let his words sink into a recess in her mind to deal with later.

"Have I misjudged you all along the line?" she asked gently.

He rose and with an iron-heeled boot stamped out the last of the fire.

"There's only one judgment on a mercenary." He drank off his brew and slipping to the ground rolled himself in his cloak.

It was the first time she had heard a note of bitterness in his voice. He had always seemed above envy and personal pride. Even the awkward youth in Dalgynch had always looked self-contained, purposeful, had never thrown himself wholeheartedly into the wrestling and ball-games but kept his energies for serious ploys. What emotions lurked behind that wide moonish face, those yellow eyes?

She rose and stood still, proud and sure. A woman, dipping her bucket in the well, paused in wonder at the white night-robed figure, rosy with reflected firelight, regal and graceful.

"There's an elderly mare in the stable that won't be missed," she said softly.

He stirred at that and grunted.

"Training starts at first light."

"I'll not be at training. There's a journey I must make first."

He watched her go, wondering at the queer intent look on her face.

Next morning she sensed that a new fury of purpose had descended on Lynchattie. The thought of Angles dining and wining in Dalgynch had roused the Caledonie to anger. But squalid Scots lording it in Fib! That was the ultimate insult. Few would need the whiplash of Dale's tongue to rush to obey his orders.

Twice the elderly mare kicked out at the hound frolicking at her heels. By the end of the day they had decided to tolerate one another. The mare grazed by a stream. The hound crunched the bones of a hare he had caught and she had cooked over a fire.

Tansen replete, drowsed beside the dying fire, thinking of nothing.

"Folk give gifts to hansel a new venture," she murmured as the hound nuzzled in at her side. "You're the only hansel I'll get, my friend. You'd better learn to come to your new name."

Next morning when she opened her eyes on the first hint of sunrise behind mountains whose dark folds were not yet alight, her mind was light and clear. It was as though everything had been made plain overnight. And all she had to do was to remember it, to draw it from the sleep-drowsy corners of her memory.

She let the mare meander alongside a lazy stream on the floor of a wide upland valley between mountains, smoothed and rounded when Dagda had warmed the Earth Mother with his fire-ball. And Her blanket of ice had glided slowly from Her body and she had roused from her cold sleep to mate with him. And the Mother had laboured and brought forth her fruits. To each animal for his need. And only one animal fed also his greed.

Despairing she urged the mare upwards and over the shoulder of a hill. An eagle soared with matchless grace, gloriously detached from the mobbing of a pair of merlins. Below from a tussock a head with a russet crown appeared. A tiny yellow body with brown markings ran out, stumbled, fell. The eagle fixed it with his fierce regal stare and passed so close she heard the beat of his great ragged-tipped wings. As he swooped his shadow fell across the tussock and he snatched the baby bird to feed his own young.

Higher and higher she climbed. Till they were in another valley where a stream tumbled and chuckled between boulders. Unlike the last valley the stream had been master here, wearing down the steep sides of the mountains into a V-shaped cleft. This was water with vitality and purpose. A stream with a powerful goddess. And it did not flow towards the lochs in Dal Riata, but towards the east and Pretani country. It was one of the seven springs of Tatha that fed the great loch and the river of Tay.

She wound the reins of the mare round a stone and, leaving Hansel to guard her bundle, clambered upwards. A burn hurtled downwards between two ribbons of yellow saxifrage, and she felt a strange need to find its source. The water, gushing from a spring guarded by three huge boulders, was clear and translucent. Yet on its downward path it had left mineral deposits that blazed forth in vivid colours. Tawny orange like the glorious hair of Flam as it caressed Garna's shoulder. Glowing scarlet as though the heart of the Earth-Mother bled for her uncaring children. Brilliant crimson, like a great moist tongue, thrusting out of a jeering mouth.

She leaned back against the mossy cushions that burgeoned nearby, fed by the iron richness of the water. And closed her eyes and fell into a reverie, thinking of the folk who toiled and fought and died. And the Great Spirit sent them back again and again to complete their journey towards wisdom and understanding. Only the joyous gurgle of the brook came to her, the voice of Tatha, telling how it would be once folk learned how to live in harmony with themselves and the Earth. How they were all part of the Great Spirit and had only to ask for healing and light and peace. And how often they forgot. Or set up barriers of pride.

And in the dark dim corridor of her mind there came a flash. And a ripple. A gilded ripple. And she found her inward mind looking downwards into a pool, black as oak-gall ink. And shining within it, the reflection of a flame, pear-shaped.

She knew then that she had been mistaken to seek signs in the outside world. When all the time the pool was a darkness within her being and the light was a reflection of her own spirit. Her own spirit and yet not her own. For what was it but a spark from the Radiant White Light, the Sun of Life, the Great Eternal Spirit. And it was from this flame within that she would draw strength. All she had to do was ask.

And there on the top of the world, she saw her way forward. There was an army to be raised in the north. And she must raise the pennant of Queenship. There were plans to be made and battles to be fought. And she must fight them. And there was a Queen in the south who must be vanquished. And she must vanquish her!

The cliffs resounded with glad curlew-piping as she turned into the cleft that led to Lynchattie. A lump came in her throat at their welcome as she waved to the unseen watchers and the bairns that came to lead in the mare. And she went looking for Dale, walking tall, free, at peace with herself and the world.

She found him, his bare chest and legs gleaming with sweat, helping a family of smiths newly arrived, to dig their fire-pit. He gave his spade to the lad waiting to line it with clay.

"Pheasant?" He laid his hand on the leather bag at her back.

"Healing plants. I used to be a healer. But the gift has left me since I've not used it for so long."

Dale frowned.

"What became of the Warrior Queen?"

He followed as she took the path to the well and dipped a cloth in the water.

"She's here now, waiting to hear how long before this motley army is ready."

The golden eyes lit and fixed on her like an eagle sighting his prey.

"I've a solid core ready now. Too few to succeed in an attack. But enough to be the deciding factor in a battle between Angles and Scots."

She raised a startled face from her washing cloth.

"We'll set Angle and Scot at each other's throats." The intent yellow eyes burned on her. "I brought men from Leinster, Munster and Connaught who swear that Domnall Brecc is the dregs of a particularly unsavoury beer-keg."

"This will make sweet music in Liath's ears."

"It did. He's here, piping a grand tune himself."

Calmly she went on patting her face with her cloth long after it was dry. But her heart lurched and bumped and her mind exploded with ideas. It was action at last. Bright with possibilities. Yet still she wondered how she would feel about Liath when they came face to face.

"Put that rag away and come and eat."

He took the steps to the fort three at a time and waited for her at the top.

"My Irishmen together with Liath's men can convince Talorc that this viper's nest between his knees is going to hatch out into a hundred little Domnall Breccs. Already the Scots are setting themselves up as landowners. And Talorc's sitting none too easy in his High Chair. He'll be ready to listen and ally with us."

Her mind leapt ahead as she ate.

"And I'll go north." she said. "Leave me Peedie and Tam and Stub-leg. And when you come back to Lynchattie, I'll have an army for you."

As she watched his smile widen she wondered about Liath's taunts that Dale had wanted her for his woman. As if he guessed her thoughts and wished to fend them off he said quietly.

"I rather think you'll find Liath at Flam's cairn."

To find the cairn she had to thread her way through a number of clefts in the rock. She stopped within one, where she could see onto the open hillside. Liath had laid a yellow blossom on the cairn.

She made no sound. Yet he sensed her and came with long slow strides, his hair grown longer and blowing in the breeze, his face softer, sadder.

"She was right," he said softly. "She still lives in my heart. But only as a memory. I know now she felt caged in Lynchattie. And I want to set her free, for she was like a wild and untamed bird. That's how I want to think of her now."

Tansen took his hands in hers.

"In life she chose to be with you in Lynchattie. And though her spirit roams the mountain-tops, she is only a thought away, after all."

Tansen saw him turn his head back and wondered if he had heard and if she had said anything that might help him in his sorrow. For she could remember when she was grieving for Ean and Fawn and for her kin at Pitcarlie. And she had had to grow a shell to shield herself from the unbearable words of sympathy. So she plunged straight into her offer.

"Yet we must go on, Liath. I'm going north to declare myself Queen. Will you take the Kingship?"

His smile was crooked.

"The Kingship? No. I want to remain the reckless Caledonie Chief that Flam loved."

And I still love him too, thought Tansen. Flam's death did not change my love for him. Even the knowledge that she had grown beyond him had not changed her love.

"But we'll always be friends, Liath. Always loving friends."

He gave a little grunt or maybe a sob and drew her close.

"Always that."

He kissed her forehead and teased back a curl that had strayed. And was gone.

She stayed, leaning against the tree-trunk, absorbing the eternal calm of a living being that had seen an infinite number of cycles of the Earth pass. And had weathered them. And she saw the dawn gently brush with pearly light the shape of a man, Dale, poised and still on a crag, alone.

It was a radiant morning with all the world alive and brimming with energy when Dale and Liath and a small force of one hundred men rode for Pit Lochrie. Adfothla, his silken hair and beard giving him the age-old dignity of a Drui had gone before to invite Talorc to meet them there in peace. And had sent a messenger swiftly back to say that the meeting had been arranged.

And Tansen prepared to face her three unwilling escorts.

CHAPTER FIFTY SIX

First Tansen sent out a bevy of fleet-footed runners to take the paths over the high mountains to every homestead to announce her coming.

"Tansen, daughter of Beatha, daughter of Caterin and Queen of the Northern Pretani."

She made them recite the formal recruiting message over and over till they had it right.

"The Black Bull bellows! When the last Corn Maiden is dressed, the last sickle thrown, the last reel danced and the last pipe blown. At the start of the Season of Fire-Bright Mists. At Hilton of Cadboll in Easter Ros."

There was a fire-bright ring to the words as though they had taken form and colour and music. And when released into the air, they danced.

Peedie, Tam and Stub-leg shuffled their feet and grumbled when she cornered them at last.

"I'm too wee," Peedie argued. "I get trampled on in fights."

"It's your tracker's eyes and ears I'm after. And you make an awful good stew."

"It's only another fine cap you're wanting," Tam grunted.

"Not till you've made me a bow like your own that flexes like the Crescent. And a quiverful of arrows that fly on the wind. And Stub-leg." He looked round sourly. "Bring your sling."

They stamped off, hiding their pleasure that she had noticed their skills. And that night for her meal, a whole ptarmigan, caught by Stub-leg, cooked by Peedie and stuffed with bread and ham and juniper berries. And beside her plate a new cap with a fanned spray of speckled yellow-brown ptarmigan feathers.

No messengers came from Pit Lochrie. Since few travellers found their way to Lynchattie, Tansen sent Tam out to scout for news on the one old mare left in the stables. When he came back, he shook his head, caught a fresh-baked bannock thrown by a lass and scooped a cup into the water-pot.

"Not a faint feather of a rumour."

"That's good, though," nodded Tansen. "It means they're negotiating with their heads down."

She hoped it was true. It would need one of Paulinus's miracles if she was to raise an army up north. With herself riding and the three men and Hansel loping at the mare's side they went north across the moorland. Tam had not batted an eyelid when Tansen had mounted wearing his cap and the matching plaid she had woven herself. Now I know where my left-over wool went to, she thought.

But he had nodded when she pinned on the big round amethyst brooch Liath had given her to signify her Caledonie kinship.

Stub-leg went scouting ahead and met them at the Boar Stone, an ancient rough symbol of a Veniconie sept that had since moved south but their symbol still stood at the meeting-place of the paths.

"We'll cut east here. The Angles in Craig Phadric are edgy."

A group of three women, two old men and a boy stood a little apart from the stone, grey-clad, grey-faced, the boy's leg swollen from some infected wound. They stared at Tansen, bewildered, despairing.

"Remnants of a smashed clan," warned Tam. "If you stop to help every group of refugees we'll never raise the banner."

Ignoring him she opened a bag at her side. The boy limped forward quickly.

"I'm sorry we've no food. That's to make your leg well."

He sniffed at the jar and spat and threw it into a bush.

"And what do you give the next lot? And the next?" Tam snarled as they moved off.

Stubleg knew a man with a coracle who took them across the Ness with the mare swimming behind. Then north to where the land was a yellow sea of stubble between islands of dark green and orange and red woodland. And more groups of hungry homeless folk, bairns and old folk, gleaning, roaming, scavenging for the last unharvested berry.

Then Tansen was riding on the North side of the Moray Firth with the Black Isle sliding behind her. And she raised her eyes from the grim unhappy land to skim over the water looking for a glimpse of the free unfettered dolphins.

"Homesteads ahead!" cried Peedie. There were seven houses, an unusually large number to crowd together. Nets hung to dry and from a shed came the smell of smoking fish. And further east several tents and shelters huddled near a burn. Tansen dismounted and gave the reins to Stub-Leg.

"You go and greet them. I'll walk."

Hansel went lolloping down to the water's edge and splashed in, barking to invite her to play. But she was silent looking east across the Firth to the mist that hid Burghead. So many had died there. And the wheel of the seasons had turned. And she was here again, missing the folk who had passed, seeking to find her destiny. And that great yearning blossomed like a bubble inside her. She'd thought it was a childish longing, that it wouldn't come again. But it was there, fiercer, hurting more than ever before. Bringing with it a cutting awareness that it was her hand that must rise to give the signal for another battle to start.

Hansel raised his nose to the wind and gave tongue. She had not heard the footstep. But there was a man, walking towards her along the line of the waves. A man in a plain tunic and leggings. He stopped, as if unsure. And as he placed his hands on his hips a little puff of dust rose.

"Wulf," she whispered. And began to move. Hansel ran between them, growling a warning and barking a welcome, unsure of the signals he was getting. Until they ran into one another's arms. And Hansel found an enticing scent on the wind that might hopefully be rotting seagull.

"Word went round that you were coming," Wulf said against her hair.

"Ragnie, Fael and the rest? What happened to them?"

"I was off with the cart fetching new slabs at the time. Fael and my brothers were killed, Except Eirik. We got the women and bairns away. Found them a welcome with our uncles. All except Ragnie. Her heart gave out."

No words could fill the void. They clung to one another tightly, sharing comfort by the touch of their warm firm bodies, and the sweet knowledge of love once shared that could blossom again if the soil was right. Later when her tears had dried they walked hand-in-hand towards the homesteads.

On the shore Peedie had a meal cooking on a fire of driftwood.

"There's a Clan Mother up there with muscles like the Burghead Bull and a voice like a cow-horn," he said, nursing a darkening bruise on his jaw.

The folk in the homesteads and tents were busying themselves round their fires and turning their heads suspiciously towards the newcomers. Once the Pretani had been a hospitable race. Now there was hostility in their faces, voices were low, and bairns did not wander far from their homes.

"This is a foretaste of what we'll meet up north," said Tansen.

"Remember Cadwallon?" Wulf said. "You'll win them round fine."

"Of course I will."

Outside the tents a shuffling group of men had gathered.

"Who are they?"

Wulf grinned.

"Outlaws and thieves! Men who've killed in the heat of passion. For a woman, for an insult. Men who live on their wits, by dicing or robbing a rich farmer of all but his trousers. And sometimes not even that."

Wulf waved an assurance. The men muttered, heads weaving.

"But they heard there was a Queen coming. With an amethyst brooch and a job to be done. nd they told me to ask you. Will you have them?"

Tansen drew in a deep breath.

"I can't pay them or feed them."

"They'll fend for themselves. They've nothing to lose and everything to gain from Danish bodies on a battlefield. Eirik and I came with them. We've a tent up there by the burn."

When they had eaten, although the evening was still warm, Tansen dressed in plaid and cap and amethyst brooch. And went purposefully towards the homesteads. The Clan Mother met her, a thick untidy braid of dark hair falling between her bare breasts, her clan in a semi-circle behind her, silent and hostile. Stubleg had already announced her lineage. And her mission. And paid for it with a black eye.

"Is this your welcome for the Queen of the Northern Pretani?" she asked, stopping where the golden bracken gave way to the cropped grass between the houses. A low growl from the men. A woman laughed scornfully.

"There's an army gathering at Lynchattie, home of the Chieftain of the Caledonie."

"The man who's raids brought us to this sorry pass." The Clan Mother turned aside and spat.

"These raids told the Angles and Scots that we exist," said Tansen. "Up to now we're the only Clan with the courage to stand against the Angles."

"And scurry back into the hills leaving the folk on the plains to the vengeance of the Angles."

"Even now the first step has been taken. Liath's gone to rid Fib of a colony of Scots."

"What do we care about Scots in Fib," said the Clan Mother bitterly. "What do we care for a self-styled Queen, empty-handed, with a mouth full of words that blow on the wind."

"I had nothing to bring."

"But you'll take. The last of our game. And our young men!" The Clan Mother was shaking her fists, shouting now over the outcry from the folk. A stone flew. Tansen stood her ground, head high.

"After the next ice-melt, when the earth softens and the springs gush, the army will march."

And from the tents Wulf came striding with the outlaws behind him. The clan sullenly slunk back to their homes.

Despairing at ever making them understand Tansen turned to Wulf.

"You'll win them," he said. "You have it in you to turn failure into success. Leave it tonight. Tomorrow I've something to show you. Something wonderful that will light up those bonny green eyes."

Next morning the new-risen sun dazzled those same green eyes as Wulf threw open the flap of her tent.

With warm creamy milk in her cup stolen fresh from a cow's udder, and biting on a stale bannock, she stepped outside with him through a lush meadow where once cows had browsed half-hidden in buttercups. And under an oak-tree, roughly walled off from the curious, she saw a long dark length. Silently Wulf peeled off the sacking to reveal a stone slab dappled by sunlight filtering through a nearby oak.

"What is it?"

He sat on the wall and she stood between his knees. His eyes were soft and brown. His mouth tender.

"There is a song about a stone-mason who so loved a Queen that he made a praise-song in stone in her honour."

"Derelie and Caterin," she breathed and promptly choked on a crumb of bannock.

CHAPTER FIFTY SEVEN

It was the longest slab of stone she had ever seen. There were four central panels, two still empty. One with the double discs of the sun, the rising sun and the setting sun. And the crescent of the Moon Maiden, all infilled with carving. And overlaid on the crescent was the broken arrow, finely decorated.

There as Fael had described her was the Queen, side-saddle on her horse. Tansen turned away, overwhelmed with wonder, savouring the moment, before looking back again. A hood framed the Queen's face. Her cloak rippled back in folds from an overskirt and a glimpse of her boots. Dainty gloved hands held the reins of a horse with high-stepping well-bred feet.

"I found it while you were dowsing in Burghead. It was shoring up the wall of a ruined earth-house. We didn't raise it then but kept it hidden."

Trumpeters in flowing draperies proclaimed the Queen's passage. Her retinue, with shields and spears and stiff lime-washed hair. Her hounds snapping at a deer.

She heard in her mind the words of Fael. The beginning and end of all myths. The lure of the white deer. The quest of the hero. The search for fulfilment.

Half-hidden the profile of Caterin's husband, the warrior Gort, renamed Brude, whom Caterin had saved from the ill-fated Battle of Catterick. Everyone knew the story. Yet not a bard had praised her courage as the Wise Woman had foretold.

"She's too prim and formal," said Tansen disappointed. "I always thought of Caterin riding wild and free."

"And so she did," said Wulf. "But Derelei who loved her as a woman, chose to praise her as a Queen. I would have done the same."

Tansen heard the longing in his voice that he tried to hide with a laugh. And she thought of how warm and comfortable their love had been. And could be still if she would stretch out her hand. Wulf broke in abruptly on her thoughts.

"I'm glad it's been under cover all this time, safe from the weather."

Around the outside of the stone there was a scroll-work of intertwined birds. The curving beaks, the pointing talons were Pretani and familiar. But the intricate weaving of elongated bodies was new. Or was it? She had seen something like it before. On the pillars at the entrance to the Mead Hall of Edwin.

"Fael?" She lifted a face rosy with wonder.

"He worked on it in secret, meaning to raise it at Burghead one day. When I heard you were coming I brought it here to be a standard for the gathering of the Northern Clans. I'll raise it to face towards Burghead in memory of the folk who died there."

"I know the very spot. Just above the shore-line where we met yesterday," she said.

A feeling of immense excitement was building up inside her. This was the miracle, the happening and it felt right. She went to bathe and wash her clothes so that she was ritually cleansed for the ceremony. Later Wulf took her to the grassy knoll where a pit had been dug. And lying aslant on the edge of the pit was Caterin's Stone.

"We levered it up bit by bit with wedges and inserted boulders covered with sacking so as not to damage it. It's ready for the Standing Ceremony."

Wulf stood looking upwards. There was pride in his face at the work of his father, joy that he was now able to show it to the world.

"We must have a Drui, a fire, a libation and a feast," she said, happily, her heart lifting with love for him.

"Done! We've a Drui coming tomorrow at the zenith of the sun. The rest we'll scrounge somehow."

"What's on the back?"

They moved round and she stopped in horror.

"No!" she cried. "No! Not Caterin's Stone! She can't have a Christian Cross defacing the back!"

Her feeling of revulsion was so strong that she was almost wept. Mindless unbelievers! Vandals! This venerable Stone would be a symbol of the age-old Truth. It would be a focus for adoration, deference and devotion. Folk throughout the ages would come in humility and reverence to pay homage to Caterin and the Mighty Ones whose signs lay clear in the morning sunlight.

"I don't know how it got there. Not Derelei for he was a Drui." Already Wulf had a chisel and hammer in his hand. He paused.

"Are you sure? Round here a lot of folk pray with the monks. They're poor men. They live quietly and help folk."

"Maybe they do. But how long do you think these strange new beliefs will last? Not as long as Caterin's Stone!"

Wulf shrugged and began chipping away unmercifully. There was no time to leave a smooth surface.

The next day it was clear that Dagda had burnished his fire-ball for Caterin.

The Mother led her clan from the homestead, their shabby clothes hidden under gaily-coloured flowers, their sun-bleached hair smooth and shining. They might scorn the woman who had come empty-handed. But they had never had a Stone Raising in their midst before, and a powerful one at that. There was even a Drui, a round rosy little man with the weather-signs on his cloak, eagerly trotting along with his lamp and water-bowl. It must be a long time since he had Raised a Stone. For all that, the folk stood well back. Who knew what magic the woman might conjure up.

"A libation, Peedie," she whispered in dismay. "I forgot."

He grinned and tapped his nose. Suddenly there was a drone of bagpipes and two of the outlaws came marching from the tents with a drummer picking up the beat behind them. They marched three times round the meadow scooping up flushed and excited bairns on the way.

Wulf was there, anxiously testing ropes, placing his men, lost in a busy world of his own. A little girl came to him with a garland, all yellows and blues, and he halted. Suddenly he looked up, becoming aware of the surge of the music, of the glory of the day. His face shone. He lifted her and kissed her while she laid the flowers round his neck. Over the flaxen head his eyes sought Tansen's. She caught her breath in a half-sob. For his face, open to joy, said plainly 'If only you were mine again and this our bairn'.

Suddenly that was what she wanted, a man who created instead of destroying. Her arms wanted to reach out to him. But she was here to raise a Stone that would bring men flocking to join an army. And she must lead them to glory or death. She turned from him and stood by the Stone, her eyes clear as crystal, a little pale but tranquil, and sent a plea to Caterin to come winging through the blue bright air.

The moment had come. Wulf signalled to the musicians. They stood by the bonfire and played long slow notes, swelling and dying, with a mighty hammer-blow of a beat to them. The Drui lit his flame and spilled his water and mouthed an incantation that no one but the Highest Ones could hear.

Wulf's men caught up the trailing ropes and slowly and easily the slab slid into its slot, steadied itself, and settled upright among the in-filling of small stones as though it had come home. As the men lifted spades to pack soil into the pit, a young woman ran forward with a pathetic cloth bundle, a still-born lamb or a babe, and laid it in the earth with care and reverence. Peedie put a jar in Tansen's hand.

Caterin's Stone stood firm and proud. It was more squat now, hardly higher than a doorway, with a good quarter of its length rooted in the ground. Fael's scroll-work round the edges gave it some semblance of being finished. Someone would complete the blank panels some day. It was usual.

Folk went on adding to the story for as long as there was space.

Tansen became aware of a quiet ripple of movement. Folk were edging back, slowly, fanning out, leaving her alone with the Stone.

Wulf had chosen the spot well with only the sky, blue and speckled with fluffy clouds, as a background. And now it could be seen that the green land fell away in folds on all sides, leaving it alone in splendid isolation. The grey grandeur of stone against the blues and greens, cool and serene in the hot midday sunlight.

The silence was more potent than the noisy clamour of acclaim. Tansen stepped forward and laid her hand on the side of the stone where she could not rub off one precious grain of dust from the carvings. She waited, not knowing if the Stone had made contact with the Mother yet.

The jar in her hand smelled of fresh water. It was all they had. She splashed it across the face of the stone, leaving a dark stain.

Only then she felt the prickling in her thumbs, a triumphant tingling in her palms, spreading up her arm and throbbing through her body until she had to hold both sides of the stone to stay upright. It was the Mother accepting the water and the stone back into her bosom.

Leaning her forehead on the stone Tansen framed a plea in the old language for Caterin to come and dwell within. And felt no impact, no answer, no feeling of Caterin's presence. Only a great emptiness. And she cried out from the anguish of her heart.

No one stirred to break the spell that was on them. They were watching in wonder and a little fear. And Tansen sensed they were waiting. As she was waiting.

And in the breathless stillness they heard the beat of a lone rider coming fast. Along the shore came a figure, Dale in dusty leathers, waving. A lad caught the reins of the foam-flecked horse.

"Victory!" Dale cried. "The Scots are out of Fib! And when Domnall Brecc attacked we chased him back to his capital at Dun Add and fired it!"

The unbelievable had happened! Tansen turned a radiant face back to the Stone. And suddenly Caterin was there, calling to her and the flame of her spirit blossomed in answer, searing her with joy. And she was filled with an immense sense of power, expanding her whole body, stretching her spine. And she vowed with all her heart to Caterin that she would free their beloved people from bondage. And when she turned, her face radiant, she held out her hands to the hushed folk, her head high, her shoulders wide, feeling her flesh strong and supple, her sinews taut yet flexible, and every nerve-end quivering, eager to fulfill her need, her dream of freedom.

The Clan Mother planted her bare feet on the grass before Tansen and studied her.

"It's Caterin come back to us!" she yelled. "She has the green eyes of Caterin."

It began as a soft whisper among the women.

"Caterin's come. It's Caterin." It became a quivering murmur. And because the spirit of Caterin filled her Tansen half-believed it herself. It was the Well at Burghead all over again. Only this time it fitted.

A sigh shuddered round the group and then the air shook with an outcry of wonder till the seagulls rose squawking and the pipes took up an old jubilant battle-song. The Drui was beside her striking her head three times with his wand. And Dale, hoisting her on his great broad shoulder so that all the folk could see her.

And Wulf standing apart, frozen, his face like chiselled granite, his shining joy quenched.

A woman raised a starry face to Dale and called him Brudei, one of the King-names, and lifted her high clear voice in a song of triumph. And only Tansen wondered if he had done his usual trick of disappearing before the battle. Or if he had earned the right to taste the joys of victory. Yet he had come, or had been sent at just the right moment.

In snatches he told the folk how they had marched to Dalgynch, how Talorc had listened with his rising ambition clear in his face. How they had routed the Scots from Fib and how Domnall Brecc had attacked. How they had chased him back to his own Citadel at Dun Add. How Talorc had besieged the Capital while Dale and Liath using the bog and the river and the night had crept nearer until they were clambering all over the Rock. How they had left Talorc with the glory of firing it.

The folk shouted and wept and exulted at that. Till he calmed them and told how this had been their first chance to test their army. How with their few resources they could never have done it on their own. How Talorc still hoped to use the Caledonie to free himself from Ecfrith. How with an army raised in the north the Clans would defeat even Talorc in the end.

The women ran in feverish excitement to bring a brave pathetic show of barley bannocks and honey cakes. And lads were sent to other homesteads for the folk to come and wonder.

In the amber twilight of the evening Tansen went from the jubilant crowd to where Wulf stood by the Stone. With the sun slanting across from the west the figures carved in relief sprang out from their background.

"Don't let anyone paint it, ever," she said softly.

"The story repeats itself," he said and turned a bleak face. "The Queen's Stone parted Derelei and Caterin for ever. If I had thought before I raised it ... "

She laid a finger on his lips.

"You would still have raised it. This is not a time for pairing and mating. Go to Lynchattie with Dale and the outlaws."

He kissed her palm tenderly. But there was no hope in the sorrowful look he gave her before turning towards his tent.

So Tansen went north on her muster. The awesome tale of Caterin's Stone had gone before her. She hardly needed to stir up northern Mormaers lurking in well-fed neutrality with barbed allusions to Bridei and Brude. And vivid pictures of the devastation the Angles would wreak in the north unless they were stopped.

She went further north until she met the Pentaland Firth and looked across at the Orcades. Some spirit from the past or maybe the future called to her across the water. But she did not answer for she had a lurking fear that if she sailed across she might stay and lose her hold on the army. So she sent Stub-leg and Tam across.

And came back to Lynchattie with faith given and allegiance pledged and the core of a nice little army at her back, each man self-sufficient with only the odd chicken maybe missing from a homestead on the way.

CHAPTER FIFTY EIGHT

The story of the Raising of Caterin's Stone had gone before Tansen to Lynchattie. The curlews in the crags announced her arrival with a joyous trill that changed to a skirling mouth music whose rhythm matched the beat of the feet of the three hundred men and women loping at her back. And the music changed to cheers and tears as folk ran from hearth and Hall to greet the newcomers. Garna herself, regal and bare-breasted, came to hold the rein of the mare.

"Well, Prickles," she said, grimly. "You've been climbing high mountains."

Tansen dismounted and they faced one another, both threadbare and none too clean, yet as fierce and proud as legendary warrior Queens. Garna's mouth softened which was as near to a smile as she could summon.

"Queen of the Northern Pretani, welcome," she said. "Let us drink mead in the Hall."

Their hands met in the clasp of friendship. Their eyes, meeting, said that titles meant nothing more than a means to achieve the downfall of the Angles.

And real mead it was, waxy, golden and sweet as honey, fermented secretly by Garna. And just enough to share with Liath and Dale.

Yet as she settled in again Tansen found that folk had changed towards her. They made way for her so that she walked alone. They looked into her eyes and wondered why they had not seen Caterin in them before.

The Caledonie welcomed the mix of recruits from northern clans. And others came, not all Pretani. Dale's name attracted Britons and not a few Welsh. There was an unspoken acceptance among the clan that, although Liath was their Chieftain, it was Dale and the Queen who would lead them against the Angles. And the way would be hard but it would happen.

Liath, who used to caress her shoulder, her neck, her cheek in passing, now treated her with a reverence that held both pride and humility in it.

But Dale had not changed. He set himself to develop a striking force the like of which had not been seen since Bridei. A force as organised as Ecfrith's army and as mobile and speedy as Liath's guerillas. So far the Mormaers themselves had not openly joined them although offers of support poured in. In one way that was a bonus. For without their clan leaders the men accepted Dale's authority and trained willingly under his command.

Time went by like a tide-race. Their sights were always set on the Angles but they had to watch the Scots at their backs. If Ecfrith linked with the Scots at the head waters of the Forth, Lynchattie would be isolated, trapped in a ring of enemies.

Tansen had the smiths make her a fine short sword that she called Bright-Fire in the Danish way after she had seen it plunged, white-hot and hissing into water. She practised her skills mercilessly. She took troops of eager youngsters out over mountain paths, worn by runners in ages past and trampled by deer, to teach them scouting and hunting and ambushing skills. Or to catch and tame the wild garrons that ran free on the hills.

Wulf, red-cheeked and weather-beaten, trained exhuberantly, finding a new comradeship among the men. Eirik produced his tools and set up a bench to train the exiles as carpenters, knowing that ships would be needed to win back the strongholds on the coast.

"Half-Angle, aren't they?" Dale asked Tansen one day. "The sea's in their blood then?"

Tansen grinned, reading Dale's thought.

"And they know where the remnants of the Pretani fleet are hidden."

"Do they now? Could it be recovered under the noses of the Angles at Burghead?"

"Wulf and Eirik, working together could do it. Eirik knows the ships and the islands but he'll need the wiser head of Wulf to guide him."

So before the cold Season began Dale sent to the training ground for Wulf and they stood talking round Eirik's bench.

"Of course we can do it!" cried Eirik eagerly. He spread a mound of sawdust over the table and began to draw the outlines of islands as he spoke.

"See, the ships are in Scapa Flow, between the Isles of Hoy and Flotta. Give us a contingent with our outlaws at the core and we can sail it out with the steep cliffs of Hoy between us and Burghead."

Wulf wiped the sweat from his brow and spoke carefully.

"The Orcadians won't give up the fleet willingly. They feel it gives them some protection. And the few sailors who man them are mostly Orcadians."

"They must see that the ships are just rotting up there. Surely we can persuade them to let us work on them nearby," cried Eirik.

"So we need," said Dale then, "firstly to assure them of future protection. And secondly, find a place to hide the fleet where the Angles can't touch it."

"Eriboll," offered Wulf. "The River Eriboll on the north coast has a wide mouth and sheltering hills. And it's near enough the Orcades to protect them in case of attack."

"And I know some ship-builders and sailors whose skills are rotting too," mused Eirik. "They'll be louping aboard to join us once they know what's afoot."

With Eirik and Wulf gone and the Cold Season coming, the troops began to spend more time hunting than training.

They went hunting, deep into Scots territory, not for heads, but for food. Yet when the first sleety gales hit them, despite all their preparations, food was scarce.

To save firewood they deserted the camping ground and lived and slept in the Hall, army, bairns, dogs and all.

They gobbled up any crumb of news from the outside world as eagerly as dogs and bairns pounced on a half-eaten rasher held in an unwary hand. But in this season news was as short as food. And when the curlew cries announced a batch of new recruits they could hardly splutter out their antecedents before the bairns were at them for leftover food.

As the Chief Clan Mother, Tansen prepared an alcove where the increasing number of women could meet. There was water in basins so that the women could cleanse themselves and keep their bodies healthy. Their own Wise Women gave healing and advice and delivered babies. There they talked together and learned from one another and told stories to the bairns, stories that taught them their history and their counting and how to compose a poem with a simple rhythm. And how to march to it, or dance to it.

And one day the round and rosy Drui from Hilton of Cadboll came stepping calmly into their midst as though he was returning from his morning walk. Ronan, he said his name was, and, once he had made a cell for himself in a shallow cave in the rock, he too began teaching from his great store of learning. And into this fort geared for war and killing, he brought the presence of the Compassiomate Ones and communed with the Wise Ones and blessed the new bairns with their Spirit Names as well as their clan names.

But Tansen kept her mind closed to the call of the Other Ones. For until the Angles were defeated there could be no peace in her heart. And in the land of the Pretani there could be no real harmony between the Eternal One and the Mother and her children.

She and Garna and the young women warriors sat with the men endlessly making arrows and talking tactics. And drinking water for there was nothing else.

It was a time when even the hardiest grumbled at doing battle with the wind in the training ground on days when arrows and spears veered dangerously.

"It'll sharpen your eyes and your wits," said Dale and kept them at it.

All but Liath whose restless energy took him out in all weathers, in the threadbare habit of an old Columban monk he had once found frozen to death by the wayside.

Every morning Tam looked at the weather and shook his head. And took out his tally stick to count again the marks of the nights from Imbolc, in case he had miscounted.

The younger son of a British chieftain watched him and chuckled.

"I hear the clerics have got their calendars in a twist. They've a Festival they call Easter and its date jumps about like a flea on the lid of an oven."

Tam brooded over his tally marks.

"Ninety-one nights between Imbolc and Beltane," he said shaking his head. "And when Beltane's over you start counting ninety-one nights towards Lugnasad. It's so sweetly simple."

"It's Rome against the Columbans. The Romans met at a place called Whitby, thumbing their noses at the Columban monks across the water in Lindisfarne. And they made some complicated arrangement to fix the time of Easter. Ecfrith says he and his retinue will still troop over to Lindisfarne to celebrate Easter. But fourteen nights later his Kentish Queen will ride to York for Easter with her superior nose in the air."

"And they've to shave their crowns instead of across the top of their heads," said his dark-browed comrade.

"A different hair-style threatens the whole fabric and unity of the Roman Church," Tam chanted, pursing his lips and wagging his head sarcastically.

"Maybe they thought the Celtic way was too sexy."

Tam paused and reflected.

"I never thought of that. Peedie, a dip in my next platter if you'll cut me a swathe from ear to ear."

At last the weather changed with the startling suddenness of the season and the air blew warm. And there was an outpouring of people too long cooped up and voices too long hushed.

Tansen needed to fill her lungs with air and her eyes with distance and her spirit with space. The pony took his own direction, higher and higher where once he had roamed free with his herd. Until Tansen left him pawing for heather beneath the melting snow. And stood against a lonesome ash and listened to music that was not hired for the price of a ring. And saw the leap of stags from a stream and the flash of plovers from the heath. And the familiar yearning came on the haunting breath of the wind. And she stifled it quickly and went back to the reality of the cramped fort.

There she found Dale calmly bathing at the rain-barrel, with a canvas up and she could not resist an impulse to pause to admire him and maybe to bait him a little. He was beautifully formed now, finely muscled with the heavier muscles of a swordsman bunched at his shoulders.

"King Brudei they called you up north. You liked fine the sound of that name on their lips."

He gave a low pleased laugh but did not turn.

"What about freeing your own kingdom. Surely that's where your ambition should lie?"

She watched the droplets slide down his back, dipping into the scars that cut across the smooth skin.

"We were turned out of Al Cluith when I was ten. Just when I was growing into my first coat of mail."

Tansen settled herself on a tree-stump and began to tease at Hansel's heavy cold weather coat with her fingers.

"And then?"

"My father went south with what remained of his army to enlist Cadwllon's help. Cadwallon agreed if he would first help to defeat Edwin. So my father became a mercenary."

"And you?"

"Me? I was fostered on one of Cadwallon's lords." There was both pain and anger in his voice. He thrust his head into the barrel and came up spluttering. The violence of his movement to grasp his drying cloth from the pole dislodged the canvas.

"He was a cruel and vicious man. May I never meet his like again."

And there, Tansen thought, reading behind the words, you suffered. And threw yourself into acquiring your skills as a warrior. And learned to hide your rebellious thoughts under a mask of vagueness and innocence. Almost of idiocy.

"And those are his marks on your back and neck?"

He turned sharply putting them out of her sight. His belly and flanks were lean with the shape of muscles lightly hidden beneath the skin. A line of black hair ran down from high on his chest across his flat stomach to explode in a dark cluster of curls in the angle of his legs.

"When I was old enough I joined my father as Cadwallon's mercenary. And have been one ever since. That's what you wanted to hear, wasn't it?"

She had found a tick burrowed head-first in Hansel's flank. She dug her fingers in and pulled. And studied it to make sure she had removed the head or it would go on feeding on his blood. The cloth had stopped its violent scrubbing. The canvas was back in place. "That time Edwin defeated Cadwallon." His voice was quieter, under control. There was the sound of leather sliding over skin. "My father was dead and our Britons with him. Cadwallon fled to Eirean. And I came back with him, leading a contingent of mercenary Irish."

He stepped out fully dressed.

"Cadwallon was a madman. I detested him. His ally Penda was a mindless savage, too. I couldn't stand it. That's why I came north, alone."

And appeared at Dalgynch, Tansen remembered, a rough awkward lad, used to living in fortresses and unsure of how to behave in the Court. With gangly limbs that were not quite at home with his body and a knobbly angular look as if he had been half-starved. And probably was. Yet when practising his war-skills, mind and body had come together in a kind of honed perfection.

Now with his wide jaw-line, scalloped by tiny scars, his great lantern eyes holding an expression of pleased innocence, he looked down on her from his mature and commanding height. And still he had an aura of gentleness about him.

"In those days I had a burning ambition to win back my kingdom. I'd nothing to offer but my skills. I couldn't see any way of obtaining men and support. So I'd to make my living where I could. And travel to find out who might help me. That's why I volunteered to follow you to North Humber Land."

Hansel, released from his grooming, sat looking up into Dale's face expectantly. Dale fondling his ears.

"There was another factor, though. I admired the strength in you and the way you handled yourself in the face of the danger from Danish nobles. I'm not all mercenary, you know."

"You must have put your life at risk when you came to visit Cadwallon after you'd foresworn your oath of loyalty to him."

"It was worth a try. To keep my eye on you. But despite my beard I was recognised and thrown into prison. My cousin Taudar helped me escape. He's King of Strathclyde now, did you know? Ecfrith gave him a leg up there."

"Why not you, the true Heir?"

He gave a little amused laugh.

"Taudar's welcome to it. The Kingdom's been mutilated by both Morfael and Ecfrith. I wasn't tempted. When I unleash my army it won't be from a base in Strathclyde where I'd have to meet the full strength of the Angles on ground of their choosing."

Suddenly Hansel rolled over in abject and ludicrous abandon at Dale's feet.

"My mother's Pretani, you know!"

Tansen looked up in surprise.

"A chieftain's daughter from the Strath of Earn. They're constantly threatened by Ecfrith's outposts across the Forth." Dale rubbed the dog's soft belly absently. "I've a notion that an army based beside the Earn could madden Ecfrith into taking a few risks." He stood to tighten his sword belt by a notch. "And now if the interrogation is finished I'll resume my duties." He strode off on long shapely legs that balanced his sturdy body.

Tansen smiled, and resumed picking over Hansel's long hair. Interrogation it had not been. The facts of his past had poured out of him without prompting. And still so solemn. Always hanging back from the wrestling and the games and the high jinks that Ean had revelled in. For too long she had ignored him because of the stronger attraction of the happy-go-lucky Ean and the reckless pirate Liath. Yet now he could not be ignored. Far from it.

Through the long hot months of the Growing Season Dale and Tansen trained and worked together. Amid the flash and dazzle of weapons their eyes would meet and he would give her a fierce eager smile. Above the clang and roar of iron and bronze she would make out his laugh, full and ringing.

At Dalgynch she had seen him walk the land as though he owned it, stopping to expand his chest and take in the beauty of the land through all his senses, a land he seemed to love in all its wild extremes. Outwardly he was still at ease with himself. There was a charisma about him that drew men like a magnet. And he made them work for him, not for his sake but for joy in their own achievement.

Yet inwardly she sensed a simmering fire, like a charcoal-burner's furnace, waiting for the first blast of the bellows. As though the accumulated anger of years was damped down until the right moment came for it to explode.

She recognised the feeling. For it matched the slow-burning anger within herself. That sometimes erupted in a blinding fury when the training ground would disappear in a swirling mist and she was in the past fighting for her life at Pitcarlie. Or Theobold's sword was swooping down on her neck. Or Ecfrith was grinding into her, invading her body with his juices.

Then she felt that same killing urge invading her mind and body. And, her aim went wild and her weapon was a danger to herself and others. Panting, she would stumble her way to the edge of the field and turn her face to the sky and clench her fists until she gained control of herself. Sometimes in the hall she paced backwards and forwards like Cadwallon's wild cat, stopping only to part the window-slats that caged her. To watch the great clouds sailing east. And her mind would fly with them to where the Angles rampaged and pillaged and gave free rein to their lusts.

More and more she and Dale walked or sat in private to share in the forming of plans. Tansen's scouts brought back reports of the numbers of men and weapons in each of the coastal strongholds on the coast and the timetables of the ships that supplied them.

And one day Dale and she set off to take the information to Wulf and Eirik and to inspect the Fleet at Eriboll.

"I wish you'd been there," Tansen told Liath and Garna when they came back. "What a sight as we came over the hill! Loch Eriboll spread out before us. Ships riding on the waves, more than I could count. And a training flotilla sailing in. Great sails spread out on the land while the sail-makers stitched them. And the ropemakers working with their bundles of dried heather and bog-fir roots."

Bairns who had never seen the sea crept nearer to listen.

"We rode the sea-lanes in a grand new flag-ship," Dale told them, a wide-toothed grin splitting his face. "We explored the coast-line for landing-places, dodged in and out of the sea-mists to flummox the Danish warships. We practised tactics all day on the ocean and sat up all night listening to tales of sea-battles."

Dale's enthusiasm was infectious. Every face reflected his joy. Hope shone anew in tired eyes. Stubbled chins broke apart in grins.

"That fellow Wulf astonished me with his grasp of naval strategy. I told him our plans and he was off, telling us how it could be achieved. I tell you he's made himself known in every little inlet along the coast. Places where the monks live in cells shaped like beehives, ignored by the Angles because they've nothing to steal. Nothing but a robe and a staff and a bundle of manuscripts. But they'll share a bite with Wulf and tell what they've seen. And hide a fugitive or two I'll be bound. I'm telling you, we couldn't find a finer Commander of the Fleet when the Bull begins to bellow."

CHAPTER FIFTY NINE

Curlew cries and a derisory cuckoo call announced the arrival of a rider, a Veniconie from Fib, judging by the Boar on his horse-blanket. Yet he was not one of their paid spies who lived in and around Dalgynch, part of whose task it was to foster the idea that any activity at Lynchattie was merely against the Scots.

The man wiped his face and armpits at the well before climbing to the fortress.

"It's Domnall Brecc!" he panted. "He went rampaging across to Eirean swearing he'd stretch the tripes of the High King from the Giant's Causeway to Cork for holding his son hostage."

With a wild whoop Liath erupted from the Chieftain's Chair.

"Never! He'll not fight! Columba made it taboo for Dal Riatans to go to war against his kin."

"But he did and was soundly whipped. Now he's on his way to attack Manlot of Dun Eidyn."

"You're a great gallumphing idiot, Dom Brecc! And I love you!" cried Liath. "Old Cummene of Iona swore divine vengeance on him if he dared to attack the Ui Neill. Now mine will be the hand that will wreak the Abbott's vengeance!" He turned eagerly to Dale.

Dale stood silent, thinking.

"I'd a hard job to find you," grumbled the man accepting a cup and bowl. "There's not a mouth that will open to say where you're hidden."

"And we'll keep it that way," said Dale. "You won't be returning to tell your tale to Talorc."

The man eyed the numbers of men and weapons.

"I'd just as soon stay here. I've a notion to be on the winning side."

Liath sprang to face Dale, half-crouching, fists clenched, swaying slightly.

"Come on, man! Every time we've had to face an enemy the Scots have stabbed us in the back. Let's smash 'em!"

Each heart could hear itself beating in the expectant hush.

Dale's chest expanded in a great breath.

"And why not?" he cried. "We need to test ourselves." And a wave of cheering set the weapons ringing and the dogs barking.

Once again the army marched south. Liath in red plaid headed the main body, with his pennant-bearer on one side, a drummer on the other, the Drui and Arrin the bard at his back.

Dale in black rode in the rear. Now he too had a bard. Regle had been Abbot of Bangor in Ulster where many Pretani clerics worked and taught. When the Angles had invaded Bangor, most clerics had fled south. But Regle, being half-Briton, half Pretani like Dale, had come north.

"I've no need of a Bishop," Dale had said gently.

"Yet I've a gift I'd like to practise. And you have need of a bard."

Now Regle in his monk's robe with a new harp on his back rode contentedly behind Dale.

They were going to bypass Dalgynch and take Domnall Brecc on their own. Talorc would not take kindly to that. It was a plain statement to the Angles that Lynchattie was a force to be reckoned with. They were committing themselves to a future war with the Angles. That was, if they defeated Domnall Brecc.

Tansen was left in charge. Each day she trained the young scouts with one eye on the south for a cloud of dust that meant a messenger.

In the end it was the brave gleam of a banner the youngsters saw from afar and went leaping home to arrive at the cleft in the rock before them.

They heard the drumming first, daggers on shields. Then the shouting of a victory-song, soaring triumphantly out of raw parched throats. Tansen waited with the women in the forecourt as the army rounded the cleft. Women whose eyes noted each gaping hole in the ranks and who wiped away tears before enfolding in their arms those who had survived.

"Arrin, true and trusty bard," Liath crowed. "Tonight you'll sing of how we caught the Scot when he was hardly in sight of Dun Eidyn. And laid him low." And slid gently off his horse, faint from loss of blood from a wound high on his shoulder.

Men, saddle-sore, exhausted, wounded, footsore, stretched and grimaced and washed blood and grime from their bare chests and hid their faces in beakers of water.

Soon the women came with wheaten beer and roasted silverweed, hardly a feast for champions but all that was left.

Dale was missing. Surely someone would have said if he'd been killed or wounded. Tansen pressed her lips together. Or had he done his usual vanishing trick? No, that happened after a defeat. And this had been a victory.

Yet no victory ever seemed worth while when there were bleeding bodies to be repaired. It was when she was probing for a broken arrow head in a tense and quivering shoulder that someone came and held the weeping boy's head. And it was Dale who spread salve on the cloth and packed the bandage with carrageen.

"Liath did well," he said nodding pleasantly at her. "Thinks up new tactics to suit every type of ground."

"Don't be so patronising," Tansen snapped, her overwhelming relief at seeing him alive making her irritable. She tilted the boy's head to let him sip a potion.

Dale's eyes opened wide.

"I learnt a lot from that man. I just thought you'd be interested."

And so the Queen should be, she told herself wearily. Except that the sight of torn flesh made her yearn for peace and reconciliation. And there could be none. Not until after there was more blood-letting.

Even her healing hands had deserted her. Every night and morning she made her mind an empty vessel and asked the Healing Ones to send that tingle of Power. And accepted the knowing that while she trained to be a warrior, she would not be used.

They licked their wounds and set themselves to being hungry and cold for another round of the seasons, endlessly laying in firewood and food and fodder and ore that came in ever-decreasing quantities. And waiting for boys to grow into men to take the places of those who had died or lost limbs. Tansen had a new sword forged for herself, light, slim and double-edged, with a hilt that nestled lovingly in her grip.

At the start of the next Cold Season Liath came, slamming the Hall door against a scouring gale carrying snow.

"The Scots have thrown Dom Brecc out." He spoke soberly but with an inner excitement."Too many lives lost and nothing to show for it. And although the cenel Gabran was consecrated in the Kingship by Columba, they've lost their right to that dynasty now. Ferchar the Tall's in the Kingship, chief of the cenel Loarn based at Loch Linnhe. It's hoped he'll patch up the pieces of Dal Riata. And he may walk tall, but he's keeping his head mighty low."

No one cheered. But a warmth came flowing among the huddled folk and the flame of hope in their breasts glowed brighter and stronger.

"We've come to blows before, Ferchar and I!" chuckled Liath, his eyes on Dale.

"The Scots are finished!" barked Dale. "Now we can go forward!"

"Aye, you're right, man!" Liath threw his head back and grinned at Dale lazily. "I'm like a rusty weather-cock. For ever pointing west. But I have to say, you've an uncanny patience with these Angles."

"Timing!" Dale said softly, his lantern eyes alight. "It's the talent of the commander, the statesman, the trader. And the lover."

It was the measure of the man that they listened and bowed to his authority. Only Tansen wondered at the last phrase. She had never thought of Dale in the role of lover. He seemed immune to women. Bent only on becoming a great leader.

The next news from the south came from a trader with his mule-bags packed with salt and spices. The cooks fell on him eagerly, tired of tainted meat and rancid butter.. But he waved them away and came to where Dale sat.

He swept off his rabbit-skin cap and hitched his belt to give time for the folk to gather.

"Talorc's a ruined man!" he announced grandly.

"Tell us." It was the merest breath of a whisper.

"He was hounded by that hell-cat, Reatta, to face up to Ecfrith. She swore that according to Danelaw he had a better claim to the kingship. He collected an army, a rag-bag of lads rising from the heather at the whiff of plunder."

"And Ecfrith?"

"He hot-footed it up to Grangemouth and wiped Talorc's army off the face of the earth. They say the Avon and the Carron were so full of corpses that the Angles could cross it dry-shod to catch the fugitives. Even Ecfrith's own Queen was so horrified at the slaughter that she's gone and taken the veil."

"Where's Ecfrith now?"

"He chopped off Talorc's sword-hand and spent the night with Reatta. And back home by ship with the People's Treasure for cargo."

Now! The time for action had come! The bright thought circled above their heads like a flight of swans rosy in the setting sun.

Regle struck a note on his deep-toned harp. And women, caught up in the wonder of it, hardly daring at first, began to dance, their tears falling unheeded. The notes rang out, joyful as a peal of bells. And men came skirling, whirling the women till their skirts flew. And then Dale rose, his leathers creaking. And the feet of the dancers stilled. When he spoke his voice cracked as though the wonder of the moment had taken him too by surprise.

"Send out ... the signal!"

It was between the snow-melt and the season of warmer winds that the messengers went out north and south and east, carrying the sign of unity and independence, the broken arrow on the crescent.

They cried to Chiefs and Mormaers and Clan Brothers that the Bull was bellowing. That they were to meet at Pittencrieff in Strath Earn, the land of the Venturionies, Dale's mother-kin. And for the fleet at Eriboll to follow their secret orders.

CHAPTER SIXTY

"Queens don't wear bunnets," Liath said, mounting his horse.

"This one does," Tansen snapped, fastening her sword-belt. "It goes with the frayed tunic and the plundered horse-blanket I use for a cloak."

Even if she had had rich clothes and bright jewels she would not have worn them while there was hunger and poverty IN the land.

Rain, endless rain with flurries of sleet in the wind as they rode eastward. Vast stretches of land, black in the grey light. Dark looming mountains, black twigs of saplings praying to the skies, brown empty fields, and splintered stumps on hillsides where forests had grown in beauty and majesty.

Scarecrows, wailing, staggered alongside. Like flocks of crows, white knobbled bones inside flapping sleeves, eyes like claws fastening on the firm flesh and warm clothing of the riders; eyes devouring the round haunches of the horses. Tansen would have given away her warm clothing a hundred times on the journey if they had let her.

She had known it would be bad at this time of the year. But nothing like this! Nothing had prepared her for the reality. Children with gaunt faces, swollen stomachs, limbs like bleached twigs. And eyes as old as time that endlessly asked Why? They clung to Tansen's feet with tiny whimpering cries. Babies, bird-like skeletons, clutched at empty breasts. Bairns and wild pigs rooting for acorns where acorns would fall no more.

And the sudden awareness of the lack of familiar smells of woodsmoke, cooking and dung on the fields.

It was the sacrifice of the trees that saddened her most. Her heart wept for the generations to come. Where would folk find firewood, hunt game, seek shelter?

And with the soil slowly washing away with no roots to hold it where would new seeds germinate? No shelter for the cattle, no nest for the birds. No hive for the honey-bee. No dark places for the tiny insects and bugs who started the food chain. For one tree was a little world in itself.

How long before the forests would come again. Forests, tended so that they renewed themselves and thinned to let the sunlight fall on the forest plants that fed and healed?

The stench of death and decay filled the shorn countryside, stronger at each ghostly homestead, and they dared not stop to try to relieve the suffering. And in between each homestead a silence. Where life should be renewing itself, only the silence of desolation. Half-hearted cairns over the dead. Wolves and foxes, rats and crows gorging. And getting little enough for their pains from wasted limbs.

Tansen felt as though she was moving in a grey mist, her limbs unable to function with the terrible weight of guilt that they had waited so long. And the heavy knowledge that the waiting and the long slow preparations had been inevitable. For if they had ridden forth, untrained and unready, their attack would have been doomed.

Dale, Tansen and Liath were in the lead. Dale, grim-lipped and silent, slashing in a blind fury at snarling wraith-like dogs. Liath riding negligently, as if immune to his surroundings, his tunic open to the waist, the cockade in his cap long and erect. Yet twice going aside to vomit, without shame. Tansen, filled with a growing horror, an escalating fury, and an overpowering urge to wipe the Angles from the land.

This was Pitcarlie a thousand times over. But this time she came with a highly trained fighting force at her back. They marched in formation over scree and tussocks, keeping their line, a disciplined army such as no one hereabouts had seen before unless it was an army of Angles. And the eyes of the men, wild and furious at the devastation, Shields, axes, swords, glittered. And as the lines of horsemen and spearsmen and bowmen passed, the dispirited farmers stared in awe and found a ragged cheer rising in their throats. For this force meant business. And many a starving man found the last of his strength and took his dirk, kissed his woman and bairns and followed on to be a part of this grand new army.

As they neared Pittencrieff the lie of the land brought glimpses of tents and shelters. And fluttering in the breeze the proud pennants of the Boar, the Wolf, the Bear, the Serpent, the Deer, the Horse.

Dale drew back and gestured to Liath to do the same. Both men watched Tansen come to the realisation that her moment had come. Her green eyes flared into brilliance. She blazed with a sudden confidence as though she had been born only for this moment. No one noticed her mud-spattered garments. She was magnificent as she rode forward, her cloak thrown back, her sword at her side. It did not need the lad who held aloft her Black Bull pennant to tell the army that this was a Queen. And a warrior Queen at that!

She led her men in a circle round the encampment, noting the pennants both present and absent, seeking the faces of known Mormaers, Clan Brothers and Chieftains, counting their men. Proud and fiercely independent they stared back, wary and suspicious. For the first time in their history they had been invaded and enslaved. An alien ruler and an alien Church had been imposed on them. When the woman's call had gone out they had risen and marched. But at the first hint of a slight to the independence of the Chieftains they would march back again.

On a broad stretch of raised ground Tansen flung up her arm. The tramp of feet, the jingle of harness, even the creak of the baggage wagons stopped. In the wary silence her order rang out loud and clear.

"Raise the standard!"

The bearer ran to a knoll and stood legs astride.

"Make camp!"

As her army raised their tents, tended the horses and unloaded the carts, she took her stance in front of the Black Bull pennant. Dale came to her sword-hand and Liath to her dagger-hand. The monk-bard beside Dale and the Drui beside Liath. And she waited for the Chiefs to come to her.

The Chieftains took their time. Why should they stand below a woman on a raised knoll? Yet there was a fine mix of support there beside her. And no fancy torcs of office or King-chains to spark off jealousies. Both Drui and monk backing her. Liath, a Chieftain as proud as themselves. Dale the Briton, who'd been King before he was ready for it. But he looked ready for it now. And that army from the north. Fine weapons and finer horses. And marching together as though they knew what they were about.

Even before they had all gathered before her, her anguish overcame her and she threw her arms wide.

"Oh, Caring Ones, Oh, Compassionate Ones!" she cried to the air. "Look and weep at the havoc mankind has wrought on the Mother and her children! How, in the name of common humanity, could the Angles do this to us?"

At the sound of the power in her voice and the compassion in her words soldiers paused in their work, the Chiefs stepped nearer to hear better.

But she did not continue. Instead she drew off her cap and her hair flew free in the wind, a pennant of copper. And they remembered that she was a daughter of Grannie Bea, Wise Woman, Healer, strong as an ox.

She threw down her cloak. Her body in short black leathers was straight as a shaft, lithe as an arrow. Her limbs were bare, her muscles, rippling as she moved, were honed to athletic perfection. A dagger was stuck in the thonging on her firm leg. Her sword, wicked and workmanlike, held no gold or jewels on hilt or scabbard. A spear was suddenly there in a hand that knew how to grip with a warrior's strength and a true warrior's love for his weapon.

Yet it was her face that drew their gaze. The green fire of Caterin in her eyes, the proud determined chin and purposeful arch of the neck. This woman was no empty symbol. She would be there beside them in battle, sharing the danger and the pain. And the triumph too if she led as well as she looked.

Dale, sensing the path their thoughts were taking, suddenly whipped out his sword and planted it in the earth in front of her. Liath leapt to follow suit and the Chiefs, drawing their swords, jostled to stab them into the ground, their eyes still suspicious but knowing no talk could begin until they had disarmed themselves.

"What's the plan?" someone growled, a great swarthy surly man with three warts on his nose, that no Wise Woman had ever been able to cure.

"Chief of the Cornovie Clan, from the Horn of Catness, famed in battle," Tansen addressed him formally. "No plan will be discussed until an oath has been taken. Who can tell if a Clan Brother has Danish gold hidden in his boot?"

"What oath? I'm taking no oath to the Caledonie here." Another Chief, brown hair sprouting from under his helmet and curling on his shoulders.

"Yet you've come all the way from Dornoch with your Lougie clansmen," Tansen reminded him.

"And I'm not going to lose a single one of them to put a Caledonie arse on the King's High Chair."

"He'd make a muck-up of it anyway." The bluff gruff Mormaer of the Vacomagie, from the fertile midlands, had his wild goose emblem blazoned across his chest. "The Caledonie are rare wee men at the creeping and climbing. And picking off a straggling mule train from a hidden corrie. But put them to stand in front of a wild Danish army, all yelling and brandishing axes, you wouldn't see their heels for dust."

"It's true," said Liath complacently. "But we've never been conquered yet. Can you say as much? Bowing and scraping and paying your tithes on the nail?"

"It's only your mountains that save you. Bare bleak summits where nothing grows and you've to steal to keep alive."

"You're a fool, Caledonie. It was never you we came to cast an eye at. But at the army the green-eyed Queen gathered and the Briton trained."

"And we couldn't have done it without the help of Caledonie," barked Dale. "If some of you had had the guts to join us you'd have learned as much as I did from Liath and his Clan."

"What do the bards sing of Bridei?" Tansen's tones, low and resonant, cut across the resentful voices. "That he united the clans and held our borders. Is that to be our only time of glory? Or do we go down in the bard-songs as too fond of petty bickering to unite against our common enemy. Leave then, Lougie. I'll have no trouble-makers in my army."

"Och, I'll wait a while and see how things shape." Lougie's eyes looked innocent but his voice held a hint of Celtic guile.

"The oath of loyalty is to the Queen," said Dale, smiling and confident. "To Tansen, daughter of Beatha, Royal Daughter of Caterin. In place of the woman, Reatta, who has betrayed the office of Chief Clan Mother."

"But wait!. Maybe Reatta did consort with the Danes. But so did she. They're both tainted." This came from a Chief of the Epidoie, his horse-head emblem plain on his tunic.

"Get your facts right!" barked Dale. "Your clan let themselves be chased from Kintyre and Argyll by the Scots. Now you're lost in the northern backwoods and news gets twisted on its way up. This woman saved the land from a Danish Kingship by marrying Eanfrith. She was sent to the North Humber Land on a mission by Garnard. And was in danger for her life every day she spent there. Now she's come again to save our land."

Tansen knew Dale was becoming impatient at the plain speaking of the Chieftains. Yet it was the Pretani way and if the old ways and traditions were to be brought back now was the time to do it. Or she would lose their trust and the goodwill she had fought to win on her journey north.

"You've quick tongues, Chieftains of the North," she said. And turned directly to the Chief of the Smertie Clan. "The Quick folk, you're called. Yet only a hundred men were quick enough to follow you to free our land."

The Smertie Chief came to stand grimly at her side. He faced the company.

"We're all short of fighting men in the north, it's true. The reason?" He paused and a slow grin parted his bushy whiskers. "Our lads are all with the Fleet. You can all see the grand army they've brought. But wait till you see the fine Fleet that's sailing from Eriboll to back us."

He turned and winked at Tansen. He had met her at Eriboll since it jutted into his clan land. He had admired her quick wit then. Now he knew she had used him and was well pleased to allow her to gain her point.

The secret of the Fleet had been well kept. Now Tansen could see the news spreading from mouth to mouth.

"Chiefs of the seven provinces," she addressed them. "And those still arriving. Take your time. Tomorrow name your candidates and elect the King of all Pretani in the time-honoured way."

The local Chief of the Venturionie Clan stepped forward and gave the sign of kinship to Dale.

"Dale Mac Ertha. Your mother has arrived from Forteviot. Come and eat with her in my Hall. And the Election can take place there tomorrow."

But Tansen ate with the

Keronie shepherd folk and afterwards sat at the fire of the Decantie and heard their bard sing of the Raising of the Caterin Stone.

The high clouds that filled the dawn sky held dark secrets in their tawny depths as though the gods lingered there, biding their time. Few could remember the last time there had been an election for King. The young Garnard it was, wasn't it? And the Chiefs and their clans had debated the issue for many cycles of the moon. Maybe they'd make a better choice this time, with only a night round the fires, and the voices rising and falling, sometimes spilling in anger, sometimes low and ponderous, poetic even.

Next morning Tansen joined Garna and the women warriors to watch the Clan brothers and Chiefs ride to the Election Hall. Garna's face flushed with anger.

"Men!" Garna spat on the grass. "We fight alongside them! We should have a vote in the Election of our war-leader!"

It was a strange law indeed, thought Tansen. In a land where the Clan Matriarchs had full control over the homestead, farming, trading, teaching, healing, and the settling of disputes. The Queen of the Royal Blood had great power within the land. Yet when it came to affairs of state, it had always been the Brothers who made the decisions.

"At first," she said, "I thought it was because the rulers of foreign states would only deal with men. And because war between states was a man's task." She thought back to her meeting with Cadwallon and how she had used guile to save the lives of the Angles. "Perhaps it's because men are quicker to unleash the sword. They're stronger and can kill and rape and set fire to a thatch without a thought of the folk who sat round it. And they have louder voices in the debate. Whereas women are the hearth-makers. How can a soldier who eats round a camp-fire understand the good that is done round a hearth?"

A soft rain began to fall. Garna began rubbing it furiously into her bare arms and breasts.

"It's only when we women learn to talk louder, fight better, be more aggressive that we'll gain real equality with men." Garna shook her thick mane of hair impatiently and began plaiting it.

But Garna is a woman who has never made a hearth, thought Tansen. And there are men like Dale who see beyond the battle to the peace that must surely make the death and destruction worth-while so that the hearth-fires may be kindled again.

"I think not," said Tansen. "There is an old saying. 'There is Man in Woman and Woman in Man. But the person who has both in equal share becomes a Wise One in the After-life."

Garna snorted.

"Women will always have two battles to fight. One against the enemy, one against men." She shrugged her massive shoulders. "It'll be the Briton who'll come back with a King-name and a silver chain. He chose his Election site well, in the land of his mother-kin."

"That's not why they'll choose him. It's because the hour and the man for the task have arrived together."

"Brudei! Brudei!" They heard the chant and the dirk-beat on the targes far-off at first but growing louder. And Dale riding before the Chieftains, his lantern eyes alight and his wide jaw split into a smile. He dismounted and came to Tansen. He threw back the fine red cloak of Kingship that smelled of a long waiting time in a pine-wood chest and revealed his King-chain.

And the whole plain was united in an orgy of cheering that swept all clan differences aside.

CHAPTER SIXTY ONE

Wulf leaned on the high prow of the flag-ship, feeling the surge of the sea throb through every vein and sinew in his body. Why had he not tasted this glorious exhileration before? Because he'd always had someone to look after? Or was it because he'd shunned the sea, fearing that the Sea-Dane in his blood would rise to the surface? Yet here he was, Commander of the Pretani Fleet, his ships longer, better-manned, finer than any North Humbrian navy. And who knew that better than he, the half-Angle?

He cupped his hands and hallooed across the water to Eirik, his second-in-command.

"Race you to Dunnottar!" Wulf roared. His words blew away on the wind that tugged at his sun-bleached hair. But his own men heard and cheered. Eirik stuck his fist in the air before Wulf turned to contemplate the vast expanse of the Northern Sea with narrowed eyes.

They had taken the northward path round the Orcades, missing the Pettaland Firth where the two great oceans met and battled. Some day Dale would have to deal with those Orcadian kings. First they'd been unwilling to let the Fleet go. Fine ships for hosting down the coast were hard to come by in the treeless Orcades. Then when the Angles had come harrassing them, searching their islands for the elusive ships, they'd been only too keen to point out their neutrality, even going so far as to tell the Angles they were independent kingdoms, with no allegiance at all to the Kings of the Pretani. That would change once Dale was King. And Tansen was Queen.

Fine he knew that much of his exhileration was because he was doing this for Tansen. His love for her still lay at the root of everything he did. And always would.

It had been grand showing her his fleet at Eriboll and hearing her learn from his sea-captains, as he'd done himself. She'd asked the same questions and he'd watched how her quick mind reacted to translate their knowledge into practical action.

The fortress at Dunnottar had to be put out of action first. On the sand they had drawn maps and built up the contours of the heights to be scaled. And argued all night about whether it could best be starved out by a fleet at sea or an army on land.

In the end they had decided that the fleet would hide in the Northern Sea making surprise attacks on enemy supply ships. Meanwhile the army would besiege the fortress on land. And when the army lit a beacon on the cliff in the darkest hour of the night, the Pretani ships were to beach, but on the north side of the fort, Tansen had stressed, for there was no entrance to the fortress on the south side.

Tansen had laughed then, the deep-throated laugh that Wulf loved. When she rose from the sand her hair had sparked with power in the northern lights. There was an aura about her that brought the men running. And she had told the old sea-salts the tale of her escape from Dunnottar. How she'd been pinned by her plaits to the board. How Liath had distracted the Angles. Someone began the mouth music then. Her arms lifted. The music grew and swelled. And she was Liath dancing his Dance of the Knives, her bare legs flashing, her toes twinkling.

Suddenly she stopped, fixing her gaze on an empty patch of sand. And every man in his mind could see the High Chair and Erland sitting in it. She had held her hand out. And Wulf had drawn his sword and placed it in her hand. Her eyes had glittered with hatred. Each man held his breath, seeing through her eyes the face of the Dane, vicious, drunken, savage. She pulled in a deep breath. And with a mighty two-handed sweep of her sword she had sliced off his head.

Each man had cheered and clapped his neighbours on the back, faces alight, fired with purpose and the certainty of victory. While Tansen pale and panting had stood staring with a kind of wonder at the empty sand till the men quietened.

"And then we slid down through the shit-hole and away across country," she'd cried. And then she was the drunken hag on the cart inviting the Angles to taste her fine hams. The roars of the men could have reached the ears of the Angles in Dunnottar. Every man in her fleet would lay down his life for her, Wulf thought. And so would he.

He was gripped by an overwhelming longing to hold her in his arms again. He was Commander of her Navy now. Someone of importance. She was not bound to any elected King. Yet.

She had loved him once. That bitter-sweet time before the Burghead massacre. Before she had been called to her duty. Some day once they had freed the land of Angles, her duty would be done. Would their time come again? What had she been seeing as she had stared at the sand? The past? Or was it the future?

A lively wave slapped against the ship's side, spraying him. His lips tightened. What did he have to offer her? When the time came to chose it would be Dale, the King. He had heard reports that when Tansen and Dale duelled, all training stopped to watch the swordplay of two sublime masters. Dale had a presence that matched hers. It was obvious. A mere Commander, however dear in the past, stood no chance against the charismatic figure of the King.

A shout from the look-out brought him swiftly back to the present. A Danish supply-ship! Their first kill! The long-fermented plan went into action.

The Seige of Dunnottar was swift and brutal. The small perky supply-ships were no match for Wulf's larger vessels. He could not afford to take prisoners so after the supplies were looted he had the ships sunk, their decks littered with dead and dying and running with blood. Somehow word flew south and the ships began to come armed and in convoy. They fought like heroes to save their ships, loosing arrows without pause into Wulf's ships and short lithe spears. But Wulf had three or four ships to their one and sooner or later the supply-ships faltered down into a watery billow. Wulf grinned to himself. No supply ships had got through for a full cycle of the moon. Dale would have to come soon or he would have Ecfrith to reckon with and the chance would be gone.

Each night the Fleet crept near the coast to catch any ships that might try to slip through the net under cover of darkness. And they were there, waiting, when the beacon signalled that the army was in place. Wulf gave the order to close in on the shore. Blazing arrows made fiery trails in the dark sky to light up the bay where they were to beach.

Water chilled Wulf's ankles and then wet sand was slipping under his feet as he ran, his heart hammering. The arrows stopped and in the sudden darkness Wulf could hear the thunder of running feet as Dale's army poured across the narrow neck of land that led to the promontory. A return shower of bright arrows from the Angles lit the dark figures and they were so closely packed that the archers high in the walls could hardly miss. Yet still men streamed on, each one knowing the gate or window that Liath and Tansen had pinpointed for them.

Some scaled the walls, some climbed the steep path to the main entrance but Wulf heard the dungeon gate slam open and leapt in, feet pounding on the narrow stairs, sword high. Starvation had not yet taken its toll of their bodies but their stamina was gone. They tired quickly and made fatal slips.

At last it was over. The men went wild, manhandling bodies over the walls and jeering as they tumbled into the sea. Wulf, checked that his sailors had picked off those who sought to escape by sea and saw bodies rolling to and fro at the water's edge. It was then he realised he had taken a spear-thrust in the shoulder.

In the smoke-filled Hall where men searched for loot, Dale and Wulf touched hands briefly.

"One down," said Dale grimly.

"Where's Tansen?" Wulf asked hoarsely.

"Guarding the pass!" Dale wiped his brow with a sweat-rag and passed on.

As Wulf shepherded his Fleet out to sea a plume of heavy grey smoke, billowing from Dunnottar, followed them. On his way north Wulf intended to sweep in to harass or destroy certain smaller forts on the coast. News of the plume of Dunnottar smoke had gone before him, heartening the hard-pressed folk. As soon as his victorious fleet was sighted he saw beacons sprining to life to guide him in to the nearest stronghold where Angles lay. Sailors and farmers fought together, women and boys lay hidden in the undergrowth on every escape-route to cut down fugitives.

Before the weather closed in he and Eirik sailed around every island of Orkney, flying the Black Bull pennant as a warning before they returned to Eriboll.

While the ice lay on the land Wulf took time to visit some of the cashels where the Abs lived with their twelve companions. He admired their way of life, tending the sick and feeding the poor using their own farming skills. And sometimes for the joy of feeling stone under his hand again, he would help them to raise broken walls to shelter young and old.

But as soon as the weather cleared again, Wulf was back at sea striding the billows, his yellow hair flying in the wind.

....

Liath tilted back the bonnet that hid his carrot-red hair. The sky was lightening. He parted the heather before his face and peered down from his vantage point on the ridge. His keen blue gaze caressed the broad plain of the Forth, tracing the meandering path of the river, lingering lovingly on the fords and crossing points.

He was enjoying himself. What was more he was obeying orders and enjoying himself.

"Tease them," Dale had said. "Madden them. You're good at that."

"Man, I've a flair for it!" And Liath had set off with his men, girning their mouth music blithely to themselves.

It was early yet for anyone to be about in the foothills of the Ochils. The Miathie women and children and breeding animals had gone from their homesteads round Dun Myatt. The fort lay apparently empty. Soon a few men would come yawning, scratching, making a hash of tilling fields that would never be sown, tending scraggy elderly animals fit only for the pot. And a small pot at that. For the men were Caledonie lads. And the herds were bait.

The Angles in the outposts on the southern bank of the Forth had liked the taste of Miathie beef. Except that this spring, the rustlers, creeping at night from tents and barracks, had had a bad habit of vanishing. Sentries too, had found their comrades, quietly strangled and denuded, still leaning nonchalantly on the ramparts and staring at the eerie mountains beyond. And scratched on the wall a Caledonie eagle. Or a phrase in the Goidelic - 'The Scots were here' - just to confuse matters.

Even the commander at Stirling who had gone forth with a strong guard to teach the Miathie a lesson, had returned minus guard, minus horse, minus armour and wearing only a red woollen petticoat.

Chuckling Liath signed to his captain to take over the watch and went to check the positions of his men. He scampered, four-footed, through the heather to the ridge that looked east into Fib.

"All's quiet!" Tam's toorie was heath-brown and scrub-green. "Talorc's Angles had a wee peek this morning from above the Yetts O' Muckhart. And thought better of it. With the Sea-Wulf snapping up his ships, and a great muckle beastie gobbling up his scouts, he'll not be knowing what to do, now he can't whimper for help to Ecfrith."

"Ecfrith knows fine what's happening. But he's not going to put his head in a noose for a one-armed cur like Talorc." Liath's eyes narrowed on the North Sea.

It had all begun last year when Dunnottar had fallen. Taken by Dale and that half-Angle that Tansen seemed to trust. He laughed again remembering their madcap escape from the place. Since then Tansen's half-Angle had swept the seas clean of Danish ships. When the last two great harbours, Burghead and Craig Phadric, had finally fallen to them, Wulf and Dale-Brudei had turned for the Orcades, taking the harbours by force. Now that bunch of so-called Kings jumped to Dale-Brudei's tune, welcoming his ships into safe havens and supplying water, food, recruits and the never-ending needs of an expanding fleet.

Liath took off westward, amid a flurry of startled white scuts. Always, as soon as the Pretani were engaged against the Angles the Scots stabbed them in the back.

Liath hunkered down beside Peedie. "Not even a scartin' mouse down there," Peedie said without turning his eyes from the mossy plain and the far-off mountains of Dal Riata. "Not since we trussed the Scots up neatly in their own filthy garters."

"Will you not give Ecfrith some credit for the Scots lying low?" asked Liath mildly. "That expedition he sent under Berct fair ravaged Dal Riata. The very land that took him in as a babby too. That lent him men to take the

Kingship in North Humbria. So when Ecfrith comes by to meet us, and there's no other route for a marching army, the Scots won't lift as much as a wolf-sling against him."

"So why am I here?" Still Peedie did not glance round.

"So that we don't get a wee dirk in the back while we're busy with Ecfrith, Peedie. Scots and Angles! They're all born just lusting for land and booty."

"Ecfrith's taking his time about coming," said Peedie morosely. "Maybe he's no' across the water at Dun Eidyn. Maybe he's got himself another wee war. He's a terrible man for exterminating his neighbours."

The sun had risen. Liath could feel it warm on his bare back. Barely a moon ago, his scouts had warned that Ecfrith was on the march up the eastern coast, gathering men and weapons at each of his captured strongholds. At Dun Eidyn he'd stopped.

Liath had redoubled his raids on the look-out posts. What was keeping him? They'd gambled everything on the man's arrogance, his brazen conceit, both fuelled by his decisive defeat of Talorc. Just as well they hadn't known about it. Dale-Brudei's reputation would have been tainted with defeat at the very start. The Chiefs would never have backed him. He'd never have been able to establish himself as the able military leader he undoubtedly was.

Still their whole enterprise now hung on Ecfrith's assumption that the Pretani would run like rabbits before that grand army of his. They wanted him swinging across the Forth, maddened by the loss of his coastal garrisons, tempted to stamp on the Pretani once and for all. Not to have him stop at Dun Eidyn and ponder and maybe think better of it.

Was it the thought of the weird and unfamiliar mountains beyond? Was it because his clergy on Lindisfarne, furious and sickened at the slaughter of their kinfolk in Dal Riata, were clamouring for restraint? Oh, all the Gods of Mountain and Corrie let him come soon in the full flower of vain-glory.

"Cheer up, Peedie! Better lying in the sun than penned up with Dale at Dun Nechtan, waiting."

Peedie only grunted.

"Patience, man! He'll come expecting a wee skirmish and another ten wagon-loads of loot going south."

Liath slapped Peedie on the shoulder and left. He fitted himself into a deer-scrape where he could look north to his beloved mountains. Where once he had roved with Tansen.

A brave wild time it had been then, was it not? Playing at war, as Dale had cried. Yet it was the very skills they had learned in the mountains that were going to carry the day and make Tansen Queen.

Tansen. He saw her now, soaked, sweaty, exhausted. Yet always the courage in her shining through. Her face glowing with an inner vitality. Her body lithe and desirable. Fearless and undaunted. A true Chieftain of the Caledonie, like her father. Would she come back with him when the Angles were beaten?

He had heard of her exploits at the side of Dale. Her sword flashing, her eyes glittering, her glorious hair flowing free. But Dale wouldn't have her, by all the stars! She would come with him. Back to the wild country where the spirit flowed free. For she was Caledonie through and through and he'd be a lost man if he went back without her!

A buzzard shrilled to its mate. A swift glance at the empty sky, and Liath leapt and ran crouching to lie beside his captain.

"There!"

A dust-cloud, trailing back all the way to Dun Eidyn. And the black encircling cloud of knowing scavengers that followed every army. A substantial force. Well-armed and disciplined. Cocksure and confident, judging by the way they disdained the cover that was available.

A swamping tide of exhileration and thankfulness rose in Liath. The Danish army strutted past the site where Talorc had been so decisively defeated. Brazenly they sounded their trumpets as they passed Abercorn, demanding the prayers of Abbot Trumwine for victory.

Liath wanted to rise and yell his welcome to the sky. The long waiting was over! The day they had planned for and sacrificed for was here. For a heartbeat he could hardly draw breath. Then he was slithering down to his men, sending messengers to those hidden in the creeks and folds of the hillside. And to Taudar, Dale's brother, who would follow with his Britons of Strathclyde, to make lightning attacks at the rear of Ecfrith's army. And a special messenger northwards to Dale-Brudei.

Liath surveyed his soldiers and grinned. The leaders, about twenty of them, were mounted with a motley collection of targes and spears ready. The foot-soldiers looked as bedraggled and undisciplined as though they had never endured Dale's rigorous training.

Mounted now, his bonnet shading his eyes, his feathered cockade at a jaunty angle, Liath looked towards Strathearn.

"For you, Tansen Mac Oengus," he cried. "See you at Dun Nichan, my bonny lass." And plunged with the kernel of his men towards the ford over the Bannog Burn where Ecfrith must cross into the land of the Pretani. And where unaccountably a sudden rush of dammed water was even now sweeping away the frail bridge.

"Up Caledonie!"

As if their only target was the nearby garrison, Liath and his men on their sturdy little garrons rounded the birchwood at full gallop. They stopped thunderstruck, jaws dropping open. Bloodcurdling yells of fear and warning broke out, garrons reared, sliding backwards in among foot soldiers who were scrambling, tripping, tumbling back where they came from.

A whole well-rehearsed scene of surprise and chaos erupted before the astonished eyes of Ecfrith and his army. And as the Caledonie frantically stumbled back into the forest, the leader's bonnet unaccountably flew off and the carrot-red hair of Liath the Caledonie gleamed like a challenge in the air.

Idly, arrogantly, answering Ecfrith's pointing sword, a troup of thirty horsemen detached themselves from the army to follow the louts and finish them off.

A messenger came flying from the rear. The unseasonable spate that had swept away the ford had bogged down the baggage train. And while they were struggling to free the carts a swarm of men had risen from nowhere and attacked. With the emblem of Taudur of Strathclyde on their pennant.

Ecfrith paused, sniffing the air suspiciously. The men he had sent to check that the Dun at Myatt was empty had not returned. The baggage train had foundered in the mud. And there at the far end of the valley, regrouping his ragged assortment of men, was the wild Caledonie. Where were his thirty good horsemen? Yet the Caledonie was within his grasp at last! For the first time the Caledonie had emerged from his mountains! One short sharp clash and he would be rid of the maddening fool for good. And then forward to make the dream of his forefathers come true!

Ecfrith's horn sounded the attack. The troup of horsemen on his left sprang forward at a gallop. As the fearsome line of high strong horses and raised swords pounded towards them the clansmen shot off a few half-hearted arrows. One man threw up his arms in sheer terror and the others followed, turning to flee wildly, utterly demoralised, issuing bloodcurdling howls that echoed round the hillsides. They fled northward by the Allan Water. Ecgfrith's horsemen surged after them. Yet when the horsemen returned it became clear that the clansmen had vanished into a forest of trees so thick that the horses had been unable to enter it.

Ecfrith cast an eye at the lowering sun and chewed his long moustaches thoughtfully. He feared an ambush from the wide forested hills that lay before him. Yet his army was strong enough to ward off any piddling attacks from Pretani tribes. At least he was sure of one thing. With Taudar sniping at his rear and his supplies lost, it was in his best interest to forge ahead towards the river Tay.

He followed the Allan Water till the river took a sweep south. And Ecfrith found himself on a bare hillside. With horses needing the fodder that was bogged down in the burn. With a hungry, frustrated army and not a farmstead in sight. With not a branch for a fire. And an eerie twilight hush that had the men twitching and muttering and fingering their charms.

A row of flat bonnets, blending with the curve of the hill, waited till the army had settled. And in the starlit night, a silent knifing of sentries, a muffling and unhobbling of horses, a dancing of greenish lights on the hilltops, and far away the sad, sorrowing howling of a wolf.

Liath chewing on a chicken bone at the cave where they had hidden their food was muttering, "Let's keep it nice and slow, boys! Give the Mormaers time to remember their oath and come charging south. And not too much of the wild gesturing. He's not daft, you know."

In the morning, bleary Danish eyes saw a paltry crowd of ragamuffans down in the plain, bravely jeering at them. Jeers that brought bile flowing up into the throats of the Angles. And it was "Form up! Forward march! Exterminate the rats and you'll have the rest of the day to pillage the homesteads!"

Here on the plain Liath had turned his men to make a sudden show of belated courage, standing shoulder to shoulder, beating their daggers on their shields. When they were almost within range of the arrows of the Angles a howl of terror went up. And they fled again, northwards and disappeared into the trees. Bellows of fury and the pounding of horses sounded sweetly in their ears.

For the Angles it was always "Round the next bend!" "Over the next hill!" Till it became "Over the next mountain!" "Across the next river!" And they were wet and exhausted. And sentries stood guard in threes. And if they took time off from following that ragged army to root around a homestead there was nothing there in barn or byre. Except maybe a bear-trap that chopped a man in half.

Curse Ecfrith for blundering into this wild-goose chase! And yet, the herds, the ale-pots, the women! They had to be somewhere! And by the Holy Thorn-tree, not an Angle worth his mead would stop till he'd gorged himself on all three!

Once across the Tay Liath knew his task would be more difficult. Ecfrith would have momentous decisions to make and it was up to Liath to make sure he made the right one, the one that had been planned by the Pretani.

CHAPTER SIXTY TWO

It was the Season of the Many-hued Mantle. The land of Strathearn bulged with hidden soldiers and more arriving every hour. Nearly four cycles of the Moon had passed since the Festival of Beltane when the bonfires had called to Belenos, God of Fire, to protect the well-being of humans and animals. Behind the reconstructed ramparts of Dun Nichen, Dale checked the look-outs for the fourth time that morning. And found Tansen with her face turned to the east.

"The south-west!" he barked at her. "That's where Ecfrith will come from." And stepped back from the white hot glitter in the eyes she turned on him.

"The fort's bristling with eyes. Mine won't be missed." Her voice was low, husky and intense.

"The time for battle has come and the Queen's daydreaming!" His pent-up frustration burst forth in anger.

"I'm meditating," she said quietly. "Pitcarlie lies over there. Today I'll avenge my kin-folk."

Another time they might have talked about the wisdom and morality of vengeance. But Liath's messenger had been and gone. Now each person in Dun Nichen was an island. Every mind and body was flexing itself for the kill. For each one had to maim or kill at least four Angles for a chance of victory. There would be no blaring trumpet, no throbbing shield, no beating drum, no echoing chariot, no chanting bard to fire the blood of the warrior. Each pulsing heart, each screaming nerve, each stabbing sinew, each burning brain must perform its own war-dance. Eyes that had seen horror heaped on horror were fixed on the narrow defile from where Ecfrith and his army would surely come.

Dale leant on the rampart and searched the sky. A pearly dawn, a few fluffy rose-tinted clouds, a gossamer mist on the horizon warning of heat to come. A thick shade enclosed the forests and draped them in a green web. It was a perfect day for living, for wandering in the green-entangled wildwood or the dewy glen, enchanted by the song of birds, intoxicated by the scent of blossom.

His eyes narrowed at the keen-edged ripples on the Pool of the Heron, that marshy loch that fed the River Lunan. The air was pure light, clover-filled. If he stared long enough, he could just make out the slender-legged herons among the rushes, stock-still, long bills ready to spear a fish for the fledglings in the huge untidy nests. Waiting with confidence and patience for the fish that were sure to glide beneath them. And Dale wished he could be as confident that his big fish would come swimming within range of his spears.

He pictured Liath and his gallant little band using all the tactics their forebears had used to defeat the Romans. For Liath had made sure he knew every treacherous bog and deep dense forest on the route. And had planted a few fine fat cows to kindle the fire of hunger in their bellies. It was like goading a bull. But this bull was cunning enough to see through Liath's ploys.

Ecfrith's fury and frustration must bring him pounding after Liath up to the narrows of the Tay. But would he cross? He was already too far from his base. The Tay was the last possible link with any supply ships. All his lines of communication with the south were broken. He must go on into danger or retreat in shame.

Once more Dale sent his thoughts winging towards Ecfrith, trying to pierce his mind, to read his thoughts.

Once Ecfrith crossed the river there were two directions he could take. Would he take the inland route with the Grampians to the west and the Sidlaws to the east. Even in his wrath he would be wary of that hilly countryside where the strong capital of Angus dominated. Ecfrith and his men were not familiar with mountains and glens. He chose to fight his battles on the level where his large army and horsemen could be easily marshalled and deployed. Their training and tactics and strategy were all geared for confrontation on a battle plain. And up to now he had always been the victor.

So Ecfrith must surely choose the flatter eastern route between the Sidlaw Hills and the Tay Estuary. It was a more natural route for an army on the march. It was easier for both horse and man and the sea held out hope of an escape route. Now Ecfrith must be led to believe that he had chosen the less dangerous way and that Liath was desperately trying to entice him towards the mountains.

This would be the most risky time of all for Liath. He had already angered and frustrated Ecfrith by harassing and whittling down his numbers, maddenening him into throwing caution to the winds to plunge after the cocky Caledonie.

Whenever it seemed that Ecfrith might stop and consider, Liath must flaunt himself and his insignificant little force, pretending that he was trying to entice Ecfrith to by-pass Dun Nichen and march into the ambushed mountains.

Dale wiped his brow and found he was sweating profusely, despite the cooling breeze from the sea. Where, by the Seven Singing Sisters, was Ecfrith? The day was wearing on. Had he caught up with Liath and his men? Had he left their bodies to rot and turned, sensing that he was being drawn into a trap? Had a scout told him that the deserted fort he was heading for was seething with soldiers?

If by any chance Ecfrith was allowed to approach from the south, he would have a clear view of the formidable fort of Dun Nichen. If he came from the east his leaders would plunge straight into Nichen's Marsh. Either way he would know that a trap had been set. Liath had to entice him to swing round from the north-west, skirting the base of the hill.

Straining his eyes, Dale mentally checked that there was a detachment of men hidden above every possible escape route. And went round his captains for a fifth time.

Yet there was no need for him to hearten the waiting soldiers. Each man had a fire banked in his breast ready to explode into action. And that fire had been kindled and blown to white heat by their own warrior Queen on the eve of battle.

Dale found himself re-living that magical moment. He was not a poet. He could not describe the scene in words. Yet he could picture it still with a surging sense of wonder.

The sun, sinking in a sea of lemon, pink and azure. A crescent moon riding like a brooch in the dark blue mantle of the night. And Tansen appearing, walking with quiet dignity among the men and women, in a long white robe, a high-collared green cloak fluting behind her. And himself hiding a swift grin as he recognised his mother's clothes and his mother, Ertha, following behind her. And when Tansen stepped up on a hillock, tall and regal against the amethyst sky, men and women had gathered as if drawn by some magic silver thread, until there was a wide quiet sea of heads around her.

Dale, standing between a Veniconie spearsman and a Taezalie archer, wondered at the sudden plummeting of his heart. For there was an ethereal beauty about her tonight that set her apart from mankind.

The folk stirred when Ertha unfurled the Black Bull Pennant. The still air brooded, heavy with untapped power. And Tansen spoke, her voice ringing like a bell till the birds at their evensong fell silent.

"What is this filth that fouls the glens and contaminates the mountains of Alba?" she asked, the lilt of a chant sounding in the carefully-formed words. "What is this darkness that invades the spirit and sucks at the breasts of the mothers? What is this blight that strikes at the hearts of our poets and withers the laughter of milkmaids?"

The air crackled around her charged with tension. And she continued, using the three-line song of the Drui and the bard.

"Every axe that bites breaks the chain of a slave. Every spear that thrusts saves the life of a bairn. Every sword that slays heals a wound in the Land of our Kin."

Out of past defeats, Dale thought, she is painting a picture of the victory that will come.

"Soon the billows will roar and the birds will sing glory and the sky will light up with the joy of the planets!"

And then it had happened!

Dale came swiftly back to the present. The memory was still too amazing to be believed! And too spiritual for his mind to encompass!

No enemy in sight yet. He took off his helmet and rubbed at the sweaty mark it left on his forehead. To be sure, he'd always felt akin to the land, could feel the sap flowing in the trees, could feel life springing in the soil. And had grown used to the calm and courage that this contact always gave him. Yet his life was based on reality. His thoughts and actions were rooted in the everyday world he could feel and see and hear. These things were part of the Natural Law. That the Natural Law extended to a spirit life after death he was inclined to believe because it made sense. It gave purpose and meaning to the happenings around him that both gladdened and grieved him. But he trusted in what his senses told him. And so far he had had no experience of supernatural happenings. He had seen Tansen influence folk before and had assumed she had a natural gift for it. But to say that she was aided by a Force that could make the sky light up, that he could not believe. Yet he had seen it happen!. And not he alone, but all the others.

A brightness rising in the east, a glow brighter than the Moon. Not a sound, as though the Earth was waiting. A pulsing light that lit the dome of the sky as it grew, that paled the broad landscape and the tiny watchers into insignificance. For now the whole sky was alight with blue fire. Dale felt it flicker across his face. The Veniconie spearsman made the sign of the Cross before his face. The Taezalie archer drew the sign of his clan, the two orbs and the lightning arrow, across his breast.

Behind Tansen's head a flaming orb, lovely as red-gold under hoar-frost, at its heart a ruby, deep red and perfect, that could draw the spirit out of a body. And a fiery plume behind it like the robe of the Sun-God. Magnificent, as it cleaved its bright path over their heads and out into the dark blue universe, leaving a trail in its wake of streaming stars, scattering the jewels of heaven, a throng of crystals in the dark wide sky, golden sun-dust drawing the silver stardust after it.

For a heart-stopping moment, the white-robed figure on the hillock blazed with the powerful blue force of the gods. And as if she had not seen, had not known of the wonder, she spoke again, low but clear.

"Cold is the heart in my breast for the depth of my grief. Woe is to me for the fate of my kin. But victory is ours. And this is the pledge of the sword-blade of your Queen. From the Seven Provinces the Sons of Cruithne have come. Bear battle gladly, fierce and full of bold purpose. May no man of the breed of Aethelfrith set his eyes again on his home-land!"

Her words had struck deeper than a battle-cry. They would carry the folk through the waiting, through the battle, to death or to victory. Yet it was the glory of the thing they had seen that still shone in their eyes. And it was the Great Eternal Spirit, the Great White Light, the Father-Mother Godhead, the Son and Holy Ghost. It was all of these Beings. For it was a manifestation of the Natural Law that had created the Universe. And the folk had experienced it for themselves without benefit of priest or drui.

The folk went to rest. And they slept. Unusual on the eve of a battle. For they were filled with a calm exhaltation that would rest their bodies and quieten their spirits. And on the morrow bring them to victory.

But Dale had not slept at first. He had no doubt about the outcome of the battle. He had prepared for it and he knew the army was ready. But he had seen something that his mind could not deal with. How could Tansen have known that a comet would cross the sky that night? What Force could have brought it swishing by the earth at the very moment when she was invoking the aid of the gods and talking of the joy of planets?

And it had appeared at her back and she was utterly unaware of it, he was sure. Then as he lay with his head on his saddle looking at the stars he knew that he loved her. And the wonder of it shook him. A deeper wonder than the sight of the comet had invoked. For the Sky was an Immensity. But the love he had found within, warmed him like a flame.

After the first shock of surprise, he had accepted it, as though it had been floating like a bubble between his body and his heart for a long time. And now it invaded his mind and body and spirit with delight. And then he had slept and wakened in the dawn with Tansen's name on his lips although his eyes were already searching for signs of the foe.

Yet when he had come upon Tansen in her battle leathers, her lashes sparkling with tears, he had burst into angry words. For he did not want her to be a Wise Woman in touch with the Radiant Ones. And he wished with all his heart that she had never loved before. For she had loved many times while this was his first experience of an emotion that had exploded in his brain and heart and vitals all at once.

Noon came and passed. Three hours passed yet not a man moved to ease his limbs, not an eye wavered. When at last, Liath and his bonny men came charging down the defile in full flight, Dale and his army swallowed them up and stood on the brow of the hill to meet Ecfrith.

Ecfrith came at full gallop, red-faced and panting, and slewing his horse to a sudden stop at the sight of the bristling ramparts of the fort looming above him. Swiftly his retinue surrounded him to steer him away from the reach of the shower of arrows already darkening the sky. And their horses slowed and sank at the marshy edge of the Pool where startled herons rose on great striped wings.

With his army still pouring from the neck of the defile and meeting slanting spears from the lower crags, with his spearsmen stumbling and his archers dying before they could raise their bows, there was nothing for Ecfrith to do but to face Brudei, in full sunlight on a high vantage point and the Pretani host prepared and ready for the onslaught.

CHAPTER SIXTY THREE

"Today Brudei fights in battle for the land of his ancestor." Regle had found an unmanned look-out post. It was his first real test as a bard. So as his eyes followed the battle he sent his mind winging towards the Flow of all Inspiration. And softly, sweetly the thought patterns came. And he wove them into words and rhythms, the bardic phrases beloved by the folk of his time and era.

"From the high ramparts, feathering the sky, the flights of arrows, deadly of purpose, arcing and falling. From the low crags, glinting like rain, a shower of spears, whistling, whispering of death. From the wide hill, bare-chested and free, like their fathers before them, the men of Pretani, yelling their clan-call, seeking the life-blood of the enemy Angle.

"Ploughing a furrow across the bright army, smiting the enemy, each man a giant, four men to one. Red is the burn trickling into the lochan, red is the grass and the sword of each man. "High in Dun Nichan, emboldened by havoc, swords at the ready, spearsmen and archers, leap to the plain.

"Brudei, Pretani, King of the brave lads, cleaving the billows of enemy heads. Liath, Caledonie, wild in his fury, a tempest in battle, a gale in a storm. Queen of the Comet, hair like a fire-trail, blazing a passage through helmets of gold.

"Skirmishing Angles, seeking escape routes, spurred on by terror and the will to survive. Finding the horsemen, all fresh and eager, sweeping from hiding to cut off retreat.

"Throughout the long twilight, the battle continues. Ecfrith still fighting, retinue-ringed. That which began at three hours after midday, on the twenty-sixth day of the Moon they call May."

At first Dale had found himself following Tansen, protecting her back. Her sword was a curtain of fire as she fought her way through the foot-soldiers to where Ecfrith fought, at the head of the main body of horsemen. Time and again she was beaten back. Always there was a semi-circle of enemy soldiers round her, as one fell another sprang into his place.

Then she was gone, swallowed up in a sea of swords and axes. And with a surge of exhultation he saw that the finest warriors in the land were there with her. Clansmen who would have fought in separate groups, each attacking under the leadership of their Chief and defending him with their lives. Now they were united in protecting their Queen.

As the day wore on it seemed that neither side was gaining. But at last Ecfrith's exhausted and ill-fed army began to fall back.

Slowly Dale became aware that the noise of battle was becoming less. The proud disciplined army of Ecfrith had become scattered groups fighting back to back. Bands of fugitives were being cut down whichever way they turned to flee. And in the centre of the field, carpeted by Danish dead, Ecfrith's bodyguard had formed a protective circle around their King, making their last stand. The battle had been won. It was a decisive victory. The Pretani had followed his orders as one united people.

And at the edge of Ecfrith's bodyguard, Dale caught a glimpse of Tanen's flying hair.

Wild and magnificent, Tansen still fought, leading her self-appointed bodyguard, whittling away at the edge of the fearsome thicket of deadly iron.

Dale held up his hand for the trumpets to sound the 'Stand to'. He saw Tansen turn an incredulous face towards him. And an Angle raise his axe above her head. Then Tansen was hidden by the press of men and he saw only a fountain of blood and the axe, flying in an arc.

Gradually the clash of weapons fell silent. The monotonous scream of a horse was cut off by a sword-blow. Dale faced Ecfrith's retinue standing stolid and unmoving and searched for the face of Ecfrith.

"Ecfrith, King of the North Humbrians," Dale shouted. "The King of the Pretani calls upon you to end this needless carnage and submit!"

"Never!" came a roar.

"Never!" roared the retinue and the eager swords flashed once more.

"Fool of a man!" cried Dale above the noise. "There is honour among Kings. I will not harm your retinue or your own person. Submit now! Save their lives and your own."

All eyes were now fixed on the centre of the field where Ecfrith's bodyguard was being wiped out slowly but surely, one by one.

Somewhere Tansen had found a horse. Guiding it with her knees she was wielding her sword two-handed in the middle of the retinue, surrounded by the bluish glitter of tempered iron. Dale drove his own horse into the circle, slashing at the diminishing wall of bodies, making for the King. Ecfrith saw him coming and the two men stared at one another across the battling men.

"Peace!" shouted Dale. "You are my prisoner!"

The word was drowned in a blood-curdling yell. Tansen took the chance that was offered. Her mouth distorted, she sent Ecfrith spinning from his horse with the flat of her blade. His helmet rolled in the dust.

Suddenly Dale knew! He spurred his horse forward. Not soon enough! Tansen leaned dangerously from her horse. She grabbed Ecfrith's long hair.

She raised her sword. A red mist gathered before Dale's eyes. Then Tansen was holding her spouting trophy and her red sword aloft. She and the clansmen uttered an ear-splitting yell of triumph, shivering the water in the Pool of the Heron, rising to shake the walls of Dun Nichen.

Tansen cast aside her sword. She planted her grisly trophy on a handy spearhead and rode to confront Dale. The eyes of Ecfrith stared, unbelieving. The jaw sagged open. The golden locks, streaked with blood, drooped over her hand.

"Peace!" she cried scornfully. "There could be no peace while this monster lived! King Brudei, I present you with the head of your enemy!" She held it out for him to take. Grim-faced Dale took time to sheath his sword. Then, ignoring her, he yanked savagely at his rein until foam sprayed from the mouth of the horse as it turned.

"He'll lust no more after our land and our silver and our women!" Tansen's voice echoed after him. And her deep-throated laugh followed him, echoing loud and long in his ears as he rode blindly towards the fort on the hill. A soldier testing a looted sword hailed him, saw his face twisted with fury and quickly began studying the unfamiliar runes. The burial parties stopped to cheer. Some of Liath's men roared a greeting and danced rings round him. Exhausted men roused themselves to throw their caps in the air. Even the wounded raised their heads to see him pass.

Dale did not see them. His brain, his body, keyed up to the highest pitch of battle were thrumming now with the knowledge of victory. His eyes were still alert for the flash of a spear, still tuned to the flight of an arrow. All those years of preparing and planning and waiting had led up to this day. He had climbed the highest mountain in the world. This was the pinnacle of all success.

He knew without self-conceit that this had been the most momentous battle ever fought in the land of the Pretani. Not only had he broken the hold of the Angles on the east coast of Alba, but he had freed the Britons and the Scots from constant attack and slaughter. His name would resound in bard-song and in the histories of the Church clerics.

Someone threw him a flask and he drank the raw brew in one long swallow. He left his horse with a lad and stood leaning his hands on the rampart, looking over the gory plain. He saw limping men carrying their wounded up to the fort and jovial riders coming back from hunting down fugitives.

It grew on him that Ecfrith's entire army had been wiped out. What was the matter with him? He should be dancing on the ramparts, singing, drinking. Like Liath there, his bare chest and arms cut and bleeding in a dozen places. Or like Wulf who had been drawn to leave his victorious fleet to share in this momentous battle and now stood grinning, dusty and dishevelled, his salt-encrusted jacket hanging in strips,

Yet Dale's chest had tightened as though a band of iron held it in a vice. And his heart beat heavy as though a lump of stone lodged there. It was something to do with his honour. With the code he had always worked by, yet never put into words. And still could not. He should have made provision for Angles who had wanted to submit. He should have offered terms to Ecfrith sooner before the whole Danish army had been slain. He should have offered Ecfrith himself a safe-conduct up to the fort. It would have been fitting. But now his name would stink in men's nostrils. Like the savages, Penda and Cadwallon. Because of Tansen.

His heart twisted with a queer exquisite pain of its own. In one day he had found love and lost it. When she had held aloft that head, her eyes exultant, her teeth bared, her hair bristling with power, his mind, his body, his spirit had convulsed with a sort of sickness. She had killed an enemy, a King. A King who had refused peace terms. Why should it revolt him?

Dale found he was sweating under his padding and mail.

Tansen's savagery had shocked him. It was the ferocity of the blow that had beheaded Ecfrith. And that barbarous act of impaling his head on a spear. And that wierd exultant look on her face.

She came now surrounded by jubilant men, rejoicing with their Queen. And walked straight past him to the highest point where there were holes in the rock for the pennant poles. And she ground in the spear-shaft and straightened the trophy with both hands before yelling her triumph to the crowd.

"Drink, man!" Wulf thrust a bottle at him. "Take the sour look off your face! We've just won a mighty victory, remember?"

Tansen, her hands dripping blood, strode past them, her eyes glittering green in her white face. Dale, stunned and silent, watched her go.

"So that's it!" Wulf punched Dale on the shoulder, forcing him to meet his eyes. "You don't like what the Queen did back there. It turned your warrior's stomach, did it?"

Dale fell back a step. The last thing he wanted was a drunken brawl with the Commander of his Fleet.

"Shut your mouth!" he rasped. "There should have been an honourable ending to the battle."

Wulf thrust his face into Dale's, forcing him to retreat again until he was up against the wall.

"It's your honour that's wounded, is it? What's honour but a game for the Mead Hall?"

Dale was surprised to find there was no stench of wine on Wulf's breath.

"What's Ecfrith ever done to you?" Wulf punched his chest and Dale sat suddenly on an outlying stone.

"Have some sense, man! Keep your voice down!"

"I repeat. What's Ecfrith ever done to harm you, that you should train an army and build a fleet?"

"He devastated my father-land and threatened my mother's dwelling-place."

Dale said irritably trying to rise.

"Oh fine!" Wulf sneered and punched him back down again. "And you come out of this with a Kingship, your brother safe in his Capital, your mother in her finery offering you the Cup of Welcome."

Wulf dragged the bottle from Dale's hand and drank.

"I'll tell you what Tansen's got now. See that marsh there. It feeds the Lunan River. Tansen was born beside that river. But the Danes came. She fought for her life beside that river. While they raped and plundered and burned and wiped out her kin."

"I know all that," Dale interrupted.

"Then you'll also know that it was Ecfrith who killed and dismembered her husband. And raped her. And sent his soldiers plunging their swords in the snow to find where she was hidden?"

Dale was listening now.

"She wouldn't tell you that. She's not a woman who looks for pity."

"No, she didn't ...

"And she wouldn't tell you that she bore a son, did she? A son whose face she could not bear to look upon. For he was a Dane in the line of Aethelfrith. But had he been conceived in love or in lust? I was with her. I helped to rip him from her body. I wanted to love him, the son of Eanfrith, my milk-brother. And I wanted to dash his brains out, the spawn of the brother-murderer, Ecfrith. And you talk of your piffling honour." Wulf gripped Dale's tunic and snarled in his face. "The whole of the coast from the Humber to the Orcades is yours to command! What does she have? Tell me?"

Before Dale thrust him aside, the torchlight gleamed on the tears coursing down Wulf's cheeks.

Dale strode to look over the wall, his stomach churning, his brain whirling. His feeling of revulsion overwhelmed him. No matter what Tansen had suffered at the hands of Ecfrith this battle should have brought glory to the Pretani, not shame.

A cluster of prisoners were being escorted up the path to the Fort. He snatched a cloak thrown carelessly on a wall and strode to meet them.

"Follow me and bring the prisoners," he told the surprised guards.

He led them into the battlefield. The bodies lay pale and glistening in the twilight, stripped of weapons and clothes. Crows rose at their approach and settled again to their task of stripping the bodies of flesh.

Brudei took them to where the bodyguard lay sprawled. The headless body of Ecfrith lay alone in the centre. He turned to a grizzled veteran and saw that tears poured unheeded down his cheeks.

"Wrap your King in this cloak," he ordered in Danish.

He led them with their shrouded burden to a bothy low on the hill.

"Leave them here to guard their king," he told the guard. "Bring them food and have the body prepared for burial."

The grizzled head turned in enquiry.

"You'll have his head," Brudei barked. "Tomorrow you'll have the honour of escorting him to his burial ground on the sacred island of Iona. He spent some time there, I believe. It is the burial ground of Kings."

Before the words of gratitude flowed, he turned abruptly to leave. With his hand on the low lintel he paused.

"You'll have to ask the Scots for permission, of course. And hope that they'll overlook your assaults on their people."

Still he waited. There was an idea germinating in his mind.

"What's your name?" he asked the veteran.

"Egil of Bernicia." The man squared his shoulders.

"Well then, Egil. There's a man born into the line of Aethelfrith who dwells in Iona. A peaceful scholarly man, I hear, called Aldfrith. A man who has spoken out often against the wanton aggression of your rulers."

The eyes of the veteran soldier showed only wary surprise.

"Seek him out," said Brudei. "Tell him I'd like to meet with him. And soon. He'd make a welcome change in the Kingship of the Angles."

A low growl escaped the throat of one of the prisoners. Brudei swung fiercely round on him.

"Or shall I take the Kingship myself and enslave you as Ecfrith did with us?"

The man hung his head. Brudei's soldiers looked on impassively, understanding nothing.

"See that it's done!"

Dale swung outside and stopped to breath in the evening air. Already the smell of blood and bowels and vomit was receding as the Mother Earth absorbed the terrible sacrifice. High on the crag the army was rejoicing. He could hear the clatter of dishes and the music. He could see the lights and hear the laughter.

He walked slowly up the rutted pathway. It was his right now to take the overlordship of all the eastern seaboard from the Humber to the Orcades. That had been the dream of every King of the Angles. He could bring peace to four kingdoms shattered by war. To the Pretani, the Scots and the Britons. And it would subdue for his lifetime the aggression of the Angles. Yet it was not the way of his father-kin nor his mother-kin. They had never sought power and land. It was madness to think that a ruler could extend his power over all that land and expect to hold it without using force. It was time the spiral of warrior-domination ceased.

He would leave the blood-stained Queen to celebrate with her people. He would travel to Iona himself with Ecfrith's body and seek out Aldfrith, this man who had earned the respect of the Scots, who was esteemed by the monks in Alba and by the clergy in North Humber Land.

For when he returned he had a bleeding land to heal and a peace to shape, a drawing together of the rulers whose people were sick of war and devastation. And he would base himself in his mother-land of Strathearn. Never again would the Kings and Queens of the Pretani live in the tainted southern Capital of Dalgynch.

CHAPTER SIXTY FOUR

Tansen had not celebrated in the Hall with the victorious soldiers. Instead she had lain awake and had risen with the sun, filled with purpose. Dalgynch must be destroyed. Kings and Queens would never again make it their Southern Capital. It was polluted with the Dark Force that had hung over the land while the Angles made slaves of the Pretani. Dale-Brudei would never understand. So while he rode west with the head and body of his enemy, Tansen rode south with a hundred volunteers.

The walkways of Dalgynch were empty, littered with rags, half-eaten fruits, bent nails. Councillors, advisers, traders had fled. Here and there a pale face peered from a window and drew back hurriedly. Deserted slaves. Or looters. Caterin's Tower was a bundle of firewood in the Courtyard.. The Great Bronze Bell had gone, melted down to make weapons. A sudden scurry of rats. Tansen soothed her rearing horse.

"Wait here!" she told her escort and dismounted.

The King-House doors lay carelessly ajar. An overturned chair, a broken bowl, an empty scabbard lying in the Reception Hall. A scatter of beads and a veil abandoned in the passage way. Tansen lifted a discarded lamp to light the way to Reatta's chamber. As she approached the entrance the heavy plush curtain began to move, palpitating like a gross furry insect. Tansen strode forward and thrust it aside.

The dim light barely probed the immensity of the darkness beyond. From rotting stems swayed the corpses of long pale leaves. Dying plants slumped in their pots. The slime of decomposing life squelched under her feet.

On a plinth a guttering candle, the wick flaring and spitting in a sea of blackened grease. An overturned pitcher, its contents leaking slowly through a crack. The symbolic fire and water. And a Drui wand thrown aside. As though Reatta had been in the midst of some propitiating ritual when news of Ecfrith's defeat had sent her scurrying into hiding.

"So you've come back?" It was a mere movement of the air.

Tansen turned. A face sprang out at her, glaring eyes, grimacing mouth, protruding tongue.

"And where are your gilded robes and sparkling jewels?" breathed the voice again.

The lamplight gleamed on shining swollen breasts, carved from wood and polished almost to blackness. Derisive pointed nipples jutted upward.

"Where then are your silken furs and fine silver cups?"

Tansen's whole being became centred on the gross Idol, on its immense pregnant abdomen, half-covered in a creeping greenish mould.

"Where are your courtiers, your admirers, your slaves?"

Heads of corn sprouted from its pubic hair. Tansen could not draw her eyes away.

"Where are your spell-crazy Druad and blood-mad Clan Mothers?"

The gross misshapen legs were spread apart. From between her thighs sprang the Royal Bull, his huge penis trailing, engorged with blood. Sweat broke out on Tansen's forehead as she struggled with her horror.

"Where now are your lovers? Gone back to the sea, to the mountains. Gone to the Island of Iona to atone for your deeds."

The primitive power of the Dark Idol surged towards Tansen, surrounding her, sucking at her body, tempting her senses.

"Where now is your brave son, spawned by a murderer, that son who will one day be King of the Pretani?"

On the edges of her mind, in darkness, Tansen felt Reatta hovering, head tilted, black eyes gloating, elfin mouth pursed in that dimpled smile. How had she known of the prophecy?

"And what kind of King will he make, begotten of two murderers?"

Tansen closed her eyes. At once a chasm opened inside her and her whole being fell into it and was swallowed up. She had no will to resist the persuasive power of the voice with the impish chuckle and the words that seared her heart.

"And yet, how I envy you." A sigh. "Me, I shall find another King, enjoy his wealth, practise my magic. And still I envy you. For you have killed! Killed in battle with your own hand!" The husky yearning voice suddenly became more intense. "What was it like, Tansen? What did you feel? Was it like a rushing wind or the slow creep of a snail?"

Tansen wanted to flee from the cold smothering judgemental wickedness of the room. Her mind willed her body to move. Her body was rigid, her legs like iron, her feet clamped to the floor.

In the silence Tansen heard Reatta's ragged breathing, could almost feel the hot breath on her cheeks.

"Tell me about the spurting blood. And how it lit a fire your groin!" There was both a quiver and a groan in the breathless voice.

Tansen sensed the jealousy of the woman who had used others to kill for her, who had never known the heat of battle.

"Did your mind reel and your body explode in delight?" A wild exultation in the voice.

"Fragments flying! Bone and gristle, sinew and brain!" Reatta's voice rose to a scream in the frenzied orgasm of her lust.

And she moaned in the aftermath and her voice died away into a purring gurgle of satisfaction. "Oh, tell me, was it good!"

Tansen's whole life began to flow past her mind's eye in images of death and destruction. Words began to spill from her mouth.

"I will tell you. It was when the Angle raped my sister." She heard her voice sounding far away and weird. "And I wanted him, his strong sweaty body." A mad pleasure took hold of her and her words came faster. "I worshipped his body even as I raised the stone. I loved each flying gobbet of brain. I bathed in his blood that rose like a fountain. I took his great purple organ in my hands and tore it apart with my teeth."

Her voice came out, shrill and screeching. And another voice beating inside her head, "No, no! This isn't me! This is only what Reatta wants to hear. Why am I saying this?"

"And Ecfrith?" went on the remorseless voice.

"I was the Avenging One. All-strong, All-powerful. I was ten men tall with the strength that was in me. My sword flew and bit and flew free again. It was easy! I laughed because it was so easy! I laced my fingers in his hair. I drew his head to my lips and kissed his grinning mouth. I was fulfilled, triumphant, all powerful!"

Someone was screaming like an old hag in a fake trance. And another voice faintly crying "No! It wasn't like that!"

Tansen found herself dancing in her excitement, the lamp swinging, her face screwed into a grimace.

The head of a wolf, fangs dripping, leered out of the darkness. It snapped at her face as it swung by. Terror gripped her and worried her in its jaws. "You see, I have you in my power." Reatta gave a short deep-throated laugh. And now Reatta's voice whispering through the air, whispering in her mind. "You must pay for your sins, you know. You must burn in the fire of your own making. You must repent." Reatta chuckled, imp-like, gleeful.

'Sin', 'repentance'. They were concepts that meant nothing to Tansen. They were empty words of the new man-made religion. The injustice of it all swept over her like a tide. She began to sob in an excess of self-pity.

"Why me? Why must I always suffer? Why was I chosen? Why am I tormented this way?" Dimly she remembered that she had cried out like this once before. But she could not remember what the tall man in the white robes had answered. She rounded on Reatta in the blackness.

"You've never suffered," she accused her. "Why was my husband murdered? Why was I given a tainted child? Why had I to suffer and starve and kill? And lose the love of those around me?"

She was weeping now, wallowing in the injustice of it all, resenting the tides of life and all that they had done to her.

"I did the best I could. I didn't ask to be raped or scorned. Or to be left sad and lonely. It wasn't my fault! I was trapped into it!" Her voice was coming from a long way off, shrill with resentment.

"Drink this. It is the wine of forgetfulness. Your Guardian Ones want you to drink. And sleep."

And Tansen wanted desperately to sleep and forget. And she knew she must obey. A goblet appeared before her. She bent her head in submission.

Yet in some corner of her mind dismay, disgust at herself, lumps of revulsion rising out of a black clinging mud. She was yielding, she who had never bowed in submission to anyone! This was all hideously wrong! Words kept forming in her mind and she tried to grasp at them but there was a slushing and a slithering that distorted them.

"Drink!" commanded a voice. It was Reatta's voice yet it was not. "Your Loved Ones have come for you. Don't keep them waiting." It was a sliding voice, that slunk from low to high and back again. Yes, she would drink and find oblivion.

She grasped the goblet in both hands. She tried to lift it to her lips. Why was it so heavy?

Clear and high came a thought. The chime of a bell, the tinkle of silver.

"Protect yourself!"

From what? Her mind stirred sluggishly. She wanted to finish with this world where folk accused and judged her. And none of it had been her fault. She who had been trapped in a spiral of events. She who had not been to blame.

"From the Force of Darkness!" came the thought, imperative and insistent "You did not ask us for protection! You came within the power of the Force with an opened mind. And with blood on your hands!"

Yes, she had done that. Did it matter? If only these thoughts would leave her alone like everyone else.

"But you are not alone."

Tears of self-pity still rained down her cheeks unheeded.

"The Force of Light is here, ready to fight for you. Only call to us and you will be saved."

"How?" she cried. It came out like the scream of an eagle thwarted of its prey.

Her throat and her mouth were dry. The desire to drink was overpowering.

"Only call to us! We cannot help you if you do not ask. The choice must be yours.""

She looked down into the deep red liquid and licked her lips..

"Think of the Light, think of the Flame within."

What flame? There was no flame but the searing fire of her thirst. Yet there was some strange invisible barrier between the cup and her lips. She felt a fierce need to struggle against it, There was a war going on inside her. One part of her mind screamed in fury. The other part sought for words that would release her.

And then they were there.

"I can do all things through the Power of Good that flames within me."

Grannie Bea had taught her that spell when she had nightmares as a child. She had said it was a powerful spell to banish the Darkness. She tried to speak the forgotten words knowing that they came shining and bright straight from Grannie Bea.

"I can do all things ... "

Deep in the cup a green slime began to form, pulsing, glowing. And she came to herself and hurled the poisoned cup from her with all her might. It slashed through the foul greenery. Terror gripped her. She recognised what she was facing and wanted to run and run, to escape into clean clear air. But she must defeat the Power once and for all.

"...through the Power of Good that flames within me." There was a quiver in her veins that was not fear but a flow of strength. Her own guilt had been the barrier that her Guiding Ones could not break through. Her terror had numbed her senses. If she had trusted them they could have come to her aid.

Now Tansen knew that her Guiding Ones had not deserted her. They had held back, testing her. Once before she had fled from Reatta's presence. And the Dark Force had won and worked through Reatta to bring misery to the land. Now she was being given the same choice. To run or to outface it. To learn to understand its fearsome powers. To combat her own terror and overcome it. Only by trusting wholly in that flame within, believing fully in that still small voice, could she vanquish it.

"I can do ALL things ..."

She knew what had to be done. And knew she could cope. Once before she had scorned Reatta for dabbling in Druad magic. Oh, how wrong she had been! For Reatta, powerless in herself, had opened her mind to a Dark Force that she could not control. It just needed a willing mind to attract entities from the Dark Spheres. Reatta was nothing in herself but a vessel that had been used to enslave the Pretani people and to spread lethargy and vileness throughout the land.

The ghostly wolf snapped viciously beside her head. Its foul breath fanned her cheek.

"Through the Power of GOOD that flames within and around me."

She sensed a blue light enfolding her, protecting her. The lamp glowed into the darkness beyond and glinted on a pair of burning unwinking eyes. She must stand before this Force now, strip it bare of all pretence and defeat it.

"Go from this woman!" she cried. "Go from this land! You are not welcome here."

She was speaking, not to Reatta, but to the entity that held her in its grasp.

"You misunderstand me," came the soft insinuating voice. "I come to teach those who open their hearts and minds to the Great One!"

Tansen felt herself growing tall. As her body grew strong and powerful, the lantern glowed brighter and brighter. She stretched out her arms and her voice rang out.

"I understand you, Oh Force of Darkness. Because my spirit was in turmoil my powers were weak. You crept into my mind, planting resentment and self-pity, doubt and guilt there. You enchanted me with false sermons. But now I am protected by the Powers of Light. You have no power over me!"

Again a silence and then a shriek of frustration and anger split the air and set the futile ghostly leaves quivering.

"Go!" cried Tansen. "You have no hope of destroying me now by poisoning either my cup or my mind."

The wolf growled in her ear.

"I banish you for ever from this land!"

And the growl rose to a howl, tearing at the heart with its loneliness and fading mournfully into the vast darkness on the edges of the room. The staring eyes flickered once and disappeared. A little human moan escaped into the air.

"I pity you, Reatta. But you chose the wrong pathway. Go forward now and seek for Peace and Love. And may you find Light breaking through your Darkness."

Tansen left. She did not know if she had released Reatta but she knew she had at last cleansed herself and her land from the Dark Force.

CHAPTER SIXTY FIVE

Bundles of kindling leant against the wooden sheds and palisades and gateways of Dalgynch. Tansen swept past the men lighting arrows from a torch.

Yet already she had heard the crackle of fire from Reatta's quarters. And the rattle of hoofbeats on cobbles. Reatta had gone, supremely confident that she would find another King, another Kingdom.

Tansen set her horse's head towards the west, taking at breakneck speed the path by the river where the Magnificent Ones had sent Eanfrith, riding golden out of the sun. Her breath came now in great dry sobs as she galloped across the moor to the plain called Balfargie that had been a sacred centre for thousands of years.

Reatta's words had stabbed her to the heart. What had she gained? Nothing! Except a name for murdering kings and abandoning bairns? And the battle she had fought with the Dark Force would never be made known, would never be placed in the balance.

"Oh, Grannie Bea," she cried in her distress. "The golden arrow you sent to cleanse the Citadel has destroyed it for ever!"

And a Presence nudged at the back of her neck. The barriers had melted away and her Guiding Ones were making themselves felt again.

"Every arrow that flies feels the pull of the Earth and veers in the sweep of the gale."

"But I've veered into death and destruction," she cried wildly. "I've done things I can't bear to think about! How can the Good Spirit help me now? Except to promise understanding and a sweet homecoming in the end."

Suddenly the horse slewed to one side and stopped, his flanks quivering. The glow of the fire on the cloud canopy reflected downwards onto the huge ditch that had once surrounded the Henge of Balfargie. Wider even, they said, than the great stone cathedral raised by her kin-folk in the south, the Bretani, as foreigners called them. These monumental Stones of the Henge still stood, aligned to the movements of the Celestial Light-givers. But the Balfargie cathedral had been built of wooden pillars which had rotted away in time. Only the stone portals at the entrance remained, grand and lonely in the oak-dotted plain.

She hobbled her horse and trod the worn pathway between the stones. Folk still came to sit here within the sacred Circle. And she asked the Circle to enfold and protect her while she opened her mind to the Wise Ones.

Slowly all the shattered pieces of herself came together. The dream of the child for the Queenship. The dream of the girl for love. The dream of the woman to create harmony between the Eternal Ones and Mankind, between the Mother and Mankind. Yet in the end all that had mattered had been the slaying of Ecfrith.

She was glad that her Guiding Ones were with her again. But she did not wish to speak with them. Their presence should bring peace and fulfilment. Yet inside she felt a yawning emptiness and that same old yearning that had never been appeased. For she was of the Earth and had to live out her time on Earth. And she yearned now for an earthly love that would last. But what man would love her now?

She led her horse among the cairns of the Ancestors who were now the Caring Ones, the Wise Ones. She saw the holes left by the parapet where their bones had been laid for the birds to pick them clean and fresh. And felt the patterns of their love like gentle hands touching her cheeks.

She came to another Circle of Stones and leaned against the leading stone. Slowly she raised her eyes from the ritual hearth in the centre to the fire that meant the end of Dalgynch.

She had set out to raise the status of the Clan Mothers. Instead she had become a warrior, killing with a savagery that she shared with the Scots and the Angles. Men who lusted and raped! Where in herself was the mercy and justice, the compassion and caring that a new generation of Clan Mothers would look to find in her?

And she thought about the bairn at Pitcarlie. A boy now he would be, running and talking and laughing with Verna and Nain.

"Don't let him become a King!" she pleaded. But the Wise Woman had foretold it with her dying breath.

"Then let me die before it happens," she whispered.

How strange it was! That Kings and Queens who were all related fought one another for power. How the Pretani elected foreign Kings and diluted the Royal Blood. It was an ancient Law that was going to work against her people. For one day a man would arise who would be elected King and who would fall heir to another Kingship. And he might be an Angle. Like Ean. And he might be a Scot. And she saw the independence of her people ended, not by war, but by their insistence on the ancient tradition.

The fire at Dalgynch blazed up suddenly in a cluster of blue flames.

Was that the last of the Dark Force? Or was it that the new Queen Tansen trailed clouds of fear and discord in her wake?

At first it was a shadow outlined by the glimmering air. Then it was a man walking towards her from the riverside. Dale, perhaps, to arrange the

Marriage that would place him securely in the Kingship. But she had forgotten. Dale had gone to Iona.

"I searched for you by the river," he said as he drew near. It was Wulf, a smell of smoke from his clothes and a smudge of ash on his cheek. He stood on the edge of the circle, the blazing sky at his back.

"Yes, I went there," she said. Ean was present in both their minds. Once he had stood between them. Now they shared him in a gentle sadness.

"I'm leaving tomorrow to rejoin the fleet," Wulf said. "We'll support Brudei as he sweeps the Lothians free of Angles and sets the Gododdin Kings back in their precarious Kingships."

Tears rose in her eyes. Her whole being cried out for his warm and comforting love. He came to her then, walking carefully round the outside of the circle and took her in his arms.

"Such a lot has happened since we parted," he whispered in her hair. "Once it was your duty that parted us. Now my duty calls."

She held him close, revelling in the warm male smell of him, needing to have someone who would keep her safe and care for her.

"What about your work with the Ancestor Stones?" she asked, wanting to keep him near.

"Some day, when I'm old and grey and salt-preserved I'll take it up again."

"There should be a Praise-stone for the Battle at the Pool of the Heron. A battle-scene."

"Showing the Danes with their nasty little nose-guards." Wulf laughed. "Yes, maybe I will."

He left her then and wandered round the circle, absently running his hands over the smoothed slabs, finding a small one with an ancient bowl-like hollow and a ring round it. Abruptly he turned back, as though he had made up his mind. "I have another Stone in mind," he said. "You see, at Eriboll when the days were short and bleak, some of the monks came from their cashels to share our bite and hearth. I talked with them. I want to raise a Praise-Stone in the shape of a Cross. For those who died."

Tansen's whole spirit rose in revolt. Every instinct told her this was wrong for her people.

"No!" she cried so violently that Wulf stared. "Remember Paulinus and the Cross of Gold! And Trumwine growing rich on tithes from the poor!"

"These were Roman priests, Tansen. The monks I know are different. You remember Coel at the inn? They're poor and humble like him."

"But deluded."

"Listen, Tansen. Small communities have grown up all along the coast.

Founded long ago by men called Ninian, Vigean, Colm and Fillan up in the Vale of Earn. Their leader is an Ab and he has twelve monks, like the twelve friends of their Man-God. I met them in their cashels, in Anster, PitnaWeem, Kilrymont, Deer, Aberdour, Isle of May. And if that's how their Man-God lived and taught, then that suits me."

"How can you turn aside from the ancient wisdom that you've believed in all your life?"

"Tansen, I believed in nothing. I feared the Arch-Drui and his knowledge. But these monks have manuscripts that hold great learning and some day I'll learn to read them."

"In Latin?"

"No, they're written in our own tongue, roll after roll, page after page."

He stopped pacing.

"I need a Man-God, Tansen. A Man of Peace, a Healer."

"You're fooling yourself, Wulf. The Eternal One is neither male nor female. Once folk start turning to a male God their whole way of thinking will change. This Man-God is the same One that the Scots and Angles bring in their train. Then Kings and Bishops will work hand-in-hand without regard for the ordinary folk. Sooner or later your Man-God will become a warrior with a sword blessed by Adomnan in Iona."

"You're wrong. These are Pretani monks, seeking peace. They're independent of Kings or authority from Rome."

She shook her head wanting to end this conversation, wanting to tell him how she needed his love.

"You forget that the Queen can make it illegal to incise the Cross-Symbol on our Ancestor Stones."

"Even the Queen can't stop me raising a stone on cashel land." He spoke sadly but firmly. "For you a battle scene. But on the front, a Cross."

Tansen felt drained. The long haul to defeat the Angles and then Reatta had sapped her strength and her courage. Where would she find the energy to face the Clan Mothers and Brothers and unite with them to build a new land for the young. She would have to leave it to another who came after to fight the three-cornered battle that would surely come, between the organised might of the Church of Rome, Wulf's humble Pretani Church and the Druad who held to the Natural Law, the Eternal Law that remained, no matter how many strange symbols and rules mankind chose to hedge it in with.

"It won't work," she cried. "You, son of Fael, should know that. How can you incise a battle-scene on a tall thin Cross-shape? Our slabs have always been broad, a natural shape to frame a picture and to display the symbols."

Thoughtfully Wulf let his hands flow over the rectangular shape of the largest stone in the circle.

"I believe you're right, Tansen. This is our shape. For Pretani folk alone. I think I know how to do it. Something completely new. A broad stone showing Brudei defeating the Angles. And plenty of room for the symbols of Nature. The Comet that lit the sky and foretold victory. And the Portals to the Places of Power crossed by the Lightning Stroke."

She could not contain her joy and folded him in her arms. Now she felt warm and secure. Their love would develop as they worked together.

"But on the front of the slab," said Wulf holding her off so that he looked earnestly into her face. "On the front a Cross, standing out in relief so that it has pride of place. The Cross used by Brendan the Navigator on his sails. His Cross with the Circle at its centre, drawing all the parts together."

Filled with dismay, Tansen listened.

"And the spaces that are left, above and below the cross-bar, I'll fill with symbols, revealed to me by my God. You want significance, Tansen? It'll be there, I promise. And then you'll understand."

Tansen turned her face away.

"Now I must leave you, Tansen, my love, my Queen."

Proudly she lifted her head to watch him stride away. And then she was alone. She stretched her arms up to the skies. And found to her surprise a sense of relief mingling with her sadness. Love was a sharing. For a time she and Wulf had shared, joys and sorrows, fear and success. Now they had grown apart and each had to take a different way.

She remembered another dream. She had set out to restore the Druad to their places of learning and their sacred groves. Where were the Druad now? Would they come from their hidden groves now that peace had been restored? Had the men Druad vanished into the cashels to meditate and to learn to write their wisdom into books, using new names for old meanings? The women Druad? Would they be found in every community, still gathering herbs, still healing, still chanting spells till the end of time?

"Hey, Caledonie!" Liath's voice came sounding over the heath.

Eagerly Tansen came back from her day-dreaming to greet him.

"Come with me to my mountains and we'll set fire to the kilt of Ferchar the Tall."

And he held out his plaid and enfolded her in the crook of his arm.

Peace, she thought thankfully, that's what she could have in the mountains. To be quiet within the circle of the sky and the land. To climb the ridges while the call of the cuckoo resounded round the peaks. To loiter in the dewy glens starred with meadowsweet and the scarlet berries of rowans. To glimpse sleek round-faced otters at play in pebbled brooks and dappled deer straying among the windflowers and water-cress. And Liath echoed her thought. But with only half of his heart.

"Peaceful the mountains are now. Not a Scot. Not an Angle. Benign mountains, you'll think, as you walk the long-backed ridge in your gown of blue. Then they'll turn on you, snarling, with a rousing of tides and a roaring of torrents. A wind strips you of warmth as it strips the crabbed trees. Your mantle is snow, your cloak is of hoarfrost, your robe a cold curtain of vapour. You stumble in snowdrifts where there was birdsong that morning. You lie on a sheet of silver ice, dank cloud is your blanket, feathers of snow are your fleece. Darkness hides the moon."

The picture he painted was cold and hard as iron, heavy as a sodden cloak. Always their days had been bright with the promise of a job to be done, a battle to be won. Now there was nothing that bonded them together. Though Liath's body warmed her, his heart was with Flam.

"Yet that's a battle that's worth fighting," Liath cried again. "To win at last to a pinnacle with the snow-clouds beneath you and the blue ecstacy of the sky above."

She could sense his mind already retreating to his mountains, longing to find refuge in their barrenness and kinship with their glowering mists. Where a tawny woman beckoned from the last surging glory of leaves dying on branches. Then he shook himself free of his dream and saluted her with regret.

"Tansen, of the blood-bright sword and the shield fiery-gold in the sun, I praise you, fit Queen for the warrior King, fit to win honour among people."

Suddenly the warm plaid was gone and she was alone and ice-cold. And he was striding off, head high. For he had no dream in common with the woman who had ground her fingers in the bloody hair of her enemy and who still wished in her heart that she had burned the Queen Viper in her nest.

And when Tansen looked down, her hands gleamed blood-red in the light from the fire. Crimson were the Pitcarlie thatches, crimson was the blood of the Angle. Crimson flames from the ships at York and crimson stumps that were Ean's arms. And a hearth-fire roared in her ears while Ecfrith hooked with his nails at the soft parts of her body. And a child crawled from between her thighs, grinning with Ecfrith's face, drooling mucus and spittle and blood. And the face growing until it was a great melting orb hanging above her, the fruit of her womb, rotting in the sky.

And she ran from the shine of it, blindly, her hand over her eyes. And fell, rolling over and over into blackness. And lay, screaming silently inside her head, sobbing inside her chest, her hands clawing at the Mother.

For she had failed, both herself and her people. She was desolate. There was nothing left, no one cared. No one understood. They had all deserted her.

A stone rattled. She twisted on her back. Feet and fists bunched to meet and survive this new unknown horror. The glaring orb had become a flame shining steadily, coming nearer.

A voice spoke. The words made no sense. But she was calm now. Waiting for the beauty of death, the end of grief and guilt, the journey through the tunnel, the awakening in the land of spirit.

"Tansen, is it you?" It was Brudei-Dale, that strange enigmatic man. What was he doing here? Then she knew. He had taken her body with him to Iona. To lie with the Pretani Kings and Queens of the past. To lie beside the murdering, lusting body of Ecfrith. To see for all eternity his ghastly leering face.

Brudei-Dale gouged a hole in the earth with his boot and stuck the great flaring torch in it.

"Be at rest, Tansen."

His leathers creaked as he sat on the edge of the ditch where she lay.

"It's past. It's all over." Dale spoke calmly as though they were having one of the chats they used to have while they waited for the great killing time to come. "I can scarcely believe it. Working and plotting and training for all these years. And now it's done."

A waft of acrid smoke from the torch cleared her brain.

"You are in Iona honouring Ecfrith," she whispered, still hardly able to believe her senses, that he was a man and not a wraith coming to taunt her.

"I turned back. It came to me that there was another who needed honouring more. A woman who, against all her instincts, struck the final blow to free this land of Angles. Who, at the cost of all her ideals, brought peace."

She turned her head away, laying her cheek on the moist grass. After all her self-loathing, it sounded brave and gallant when he put it that way.

"I didn't understand at first," he said wryly. "I was bemused by the honour of Kings. Yet now and again some mighty gesture is needed to warn other tyrants and to save lives in the end."

A little sob escaped her. How could he, how could anyone know the depths of the guilt she suffered now?

"You used to tell me that we come to this world to learn. To be human and to fail. To sacrifice and to suffer. So that we can rise again with a new understanding. And use that understanding."

Her head moved, her eyes questioned him.

"For example," he went on, "we could march south, take all these states, weakened by war, into our grasp, North Humberland, Dal Riata, Strathclyde."

And Tansen thought of the Kings who had done it in the past. Powerful Kings whose names lived in history.

"But we won't," she said simply.

She was aware that he was smiling although his face was in shadow.

"We've learned together, you and I. We've known what it's like to live in a land crushed under the boot of the conqueror. We'll never impose that on others. We'll leave folk to rebuild their communities in peace."

It sounded grand to be talking about helping folk, not just offering sympathy and understanding, but by knowing what was needed, because you had been there. Because you knew what it was like to despise yourself, to lose the will to pick yourself up and go on, to lose all hope. And it was grand to be talking to Dale about actions and ideas that mattered.

He held out his hand. After a moment she took it. His palm was rough and scaly, the hand of a swordsman. But warm and friendly and a lifeline back into the familiar world.

The air she breathed was clean now and scented. And the grass at her fingertips was fresh and damp with dew. And she was at peace with the great Circle of earth and sky

As she looked at the great Eternity of the sky she knew that however small and humble it might make her feel, she was a part, a tiny part, of the great Cosmos. And she had played her part in the small corner of the Universe where she had been sent to live and learn.

"Come, my steadfast graceful girl with the amber-coloured hair."

With Dale's help she climbed from the ditch. And stood within the circle of standing stones silvered in the moonlight.

"Come," Dale said again. "We'll build a new Capital in Strathearn. With a King-House fit for a Queen."

"No," she said. "All I want is a hearth and a home. And a man who will share it."

"And is it too much to ask," he said, placing his hands on her shoulders, "that the hearth and the home are in Strathearn. That the man who shares it is a King. That the woman is a Queen. That the bairns will be royal."

She waited for a moment while the future slotted itself into place. It felt right. In the knowing places of her body and mind it felt right.

"Only if there is love there," she said finally.

"There is love there," he said, simply. "A love that has always been there."

Again she waited, listening. The singing in her blood that she had felt with Ean was there. The feeling of safety she had felt with Wulf was there. In the leap of her veins she felt the wild surge of passion she had felt with Liath. But there was something more.

There was a challenge in him. A merging of mind and body that would continually spark off new ideas and actions.

And she felt the presence of those others who had played their part. Far, far in the past, they had lived and loved to make her what she was, to make her land, the land of the Pretani, what it was, now, in the present.

And as the Moon Maiden slipped from behind a cloud, he reached out a silver finger and tenderly touched her silvered cheek.

"My dear," he said softly. "Let the flame that is within you light the path for others to follow."

HISTORICAL NOTE

Although Pictish history is still shrouded in mystery, the Northumbrian Kings have been well documented by Bede. Therefore I ask readers to forgive me for telescoping some events so that they could happen within the life-span of my heroine.

Eanfrith was a hostage at the Pictish court and married a Pictish Princess. Their son, Talorcan, did become a King of the Picts later as the Old Woman of Lleyr foretold.

After Eanfrith, his brothers Oswald and Oswy reigned. In my story Ecfrith stands in place of all three Kings and was defeated at the Battle of Dunnichen or Nechtansmere as the Angles called it. I am indebted to Graeme Cruickshank for his research into this famous battle which laid the foundations for the later nation of Scotland.

Two Pictish Symbol Stones are described. The Hilton of Cadboll Stone, which I used as a praise-song to Caterin in the HONEY IN THE MEAD, and which was found and raised by Tansen and Wulf on the Black Isle will appear again in THE HARPS ARE HUSHED. The Stone with the farmer on his mule, described in my story as having been carved by Wulf is known as the Bullion Stone. Both stones can be seen in the Dark Age Sculpture Collection in Queen Street Museum, Edinburgh.

SOURCES

A History of the English Church	Bede
The Battle of Dunnichen	Graeme Cruikshank
The Picts	Isabel Henderson
The Symbol Stones of Scotland	Antony Jackson
The Archaeological Guide to Scotland	Euan W. Mackie
The Age of Arthur	John Morris
A Celtic Miscellany	Ed. Betty Radice
Picts	Anna Ritchie
The Pictish Nation : Its People and its Church	A.B.Scott
Celtic Scotland	W.F. Skene
The Problem of the Picts	Ed. F.T. Wainwright